THE BEST OF THE WEST

▼▼▼▼▼ THE ▼▼▼▼▼

MYSTERIOUS
WEST

Edited by

TONY HILLERMAN

HarperTorch
An Imprint of HarperCollins *Publishers*

HARPERTORCH
An Imprint of HarperCollins*Publishers*
10 East 53rd Street
New York, New York 10022-5299

Copyright © 1994 by Tony Hillerman and Martin Greenberg

"Forbidden Things" © 1994 by Marcia Muller; "New Moon and Rattlesnakes" © 1994 by Wendy Hornsby; "Coyote Peyote" © 1994 by Carole Nelson Douglas; "Nooses Give" © 1994 by Dana Stabenow; "Who Killed Cock Rogers?" © 1994 by Bill Crider; "Caring for Uncle Henry" © 1994 by Robert Campbell; "Death of a Snowbird" © 1994 by J.A. Jance; "With Flowers in Her Hair" © 1994 by M.D. Lake; "The Lost Boys" © 1994 by William J. Reynolds; "Tule Fog" © 1994 by Karen Kijewski; "The River Mouth" © 1994 by Lia Matera; "No Better Than Her Father" © 1994 by Linda Grant; "Dust Devil" © 1994 by Rex Burns; "A Woman's Place" © 1994 by D.R. Meredith; "Postage Due" © 1994 by Susan Dunlap; "The Beast in the Woods" © 1994 by Ed Gorman; "Blowout in Little Man Flats" © 1994 by Stuart M. Kaminsky; "Small Town Murder" © 1994 Harold Adams; "Bingo" © 1994 by John Lutz; "Engines" © 1994 by Bill Pronzini

Cover illustration by Peter Thorpe
ISBN: 0-06-109262-2

First HarperTorch paperback printing: September 2003
First HarperPaperbacks printing: November 1995
First HarperCollins hardcover printing: October 1994

HarperCollins®, HarperTorch™, and ♥™ are trademarks of HarperCollins Publishers Inc.

Printed in the United States of America

Visit HarperTorch on the World Wide Web at www.harpercollins.com

30 29 28 27 26 25 24

CONTENTS

▼▼▼▼▼ THE ▼▼▼▼▼
MYSTERIOUS
▲▲▲▲WEST▲▲▲▲

FORBIDDEN THINGS

MARCIA MULLER

Marcia Muller is finally getting her long-deserved recognition as the true creator of the modern female private detective.

In such memorable novels as There's Something in a Sunday *and* Wolf in the Shadows, *Muller shows us how serious—and truly entertaining—the modern mystery story can be.*

The following story, by turns melancholy, amusing, and suspenseful, tells of a southern California woman—one Ashley Heikkinen, no less—who tries to go home again.

FORBIDDEN THINGS

ALL THE YEARS that I was growing up in a poor suburb of Los Angeles, my mother would tell me stories of the days I couldn't remember when we lived with my father on the wild north coast. She'd tell of a gray, misty land suddenly made brilliant by quicksilver flashes off the sea; of white-sand beaches that would disappear in a storm, then emerge strewn with driftwood and treasures from foreign shores; of a deeply forested ridge of hills where, so the Pomo Indians claimed, spirits walked by night.

Our cabin nestled on that ridge, high above the little town of Camel Rock and the humpbacked offshore mass that inspired its name. The cabin, built to last by my handyman father, was of local redwood, its foundation sunk deep in bedrock. There was a woodstove and home-woven curtains. There were stained-glass windows and a sleeping loft; there was . . .

Although I had no recollection of the place we'd left when I was two, it somehow seemed more real to me than our shabby pink bungalow with the cracked side-walk out front and the packed-dirt yard out back. I'd lie in bed late at night feeling the heat from the woodstove, watching the light as it filtered through the stained-glass panels, listening to the wind buffet our secure aerie. I was sure I could smell my mother's baking bread, hear the deep rumble of my father's voice. But no matter how hard I tried, I could not call up the image of my father's face, even though a stiff and formal studio portrait of him sat on our coffee table.

When I asked my mother why she and I had left a place of quicksilver days and night-walking spirits, she'd grow quiet. When I asked where my father was now, she'd turn away. As I grew older I realized there were shadows over our departure—shadows in which forbidden things stood still and silent.

Is it any wonder that when my mother died—young, at forty-nine, but life hadn't been kind to her and heart trouble ran in the family—is it any wonder that I packed everything I cared about and went back to the place of my birth to confront those forbidden things?

I'd located Camel Rock on the map when I was nine, tracing the coast highway with my finger until it reached a jutting point of land north of Fort Bragg. Once this had been logging country—hardy men working the crosscut saw and jackscrew in the forests, bull teams dragging their heavy loads to the coast, fresh-cut logs thundering down the chutes to schooners that lay at anchor in the coves below. But by the time I was born, lumbering was an endangered industry. Today, I knew, the voice of the chain saw was stilled and few logging trucks rumbled along the highway. Legislation to protect the environment, coupled with a severe construction slump, had all but killed the old economy. Instead new enterprises had sprung up: wineries; mushroom, garlic, and herb farms; tourist shops and bed-and-breakfasts. These were only marginally profitable, however; the north coast was financially strapped.

I decided to go anyway.

It was a good time for me to leave southern California. Two failed attempts at college, a ruined love affair, a series of slipping-down jobs—all argued for radical change. I'd had no family except my mother; even my cat had died the previous October. As I gave notice at the coffee shop where I'd been waitressing, disposed of the contents of the bungalow, and turned the keys back to the landlord, I said no goodbyes. Yet I left with hope of a welcome. Maybe there would be a place for me in Camel Rock. Maybe someone would even remember my family and fill in the gaps in my early life.

I know now that I was really hoping for a reunion with my father.

◆ ◆ ◆

Mist blanketed the coast the afternoon I drove my old
Pinto over the bridge spanning the mouth of the Deer
River and into Camel Rock. Beyond sandstone cliffs the
sea lay flat and seemingly motionless. The town—a strip
of buildings on either side of the highway, with dirt
lanes straggling up toward the hills—looked deserted. A
few drifting columns of wood smoke, some lighted signs
in shop windows, a hunched and bundled figure walking along the shoulder—these were the only signs of life.
I drove slowly, taking it all in: a supermarket, some
bars, a little mall full of tourist shops. Post office, laun-
dromat, defunct real estate agency, old sagging hotel
that looked to be the only lodging place. When I'd gone
four blocks and passed the last gas station and the cable
TV company, I ran out of town; I U-turned, went back
to the hotel, and parked my car between two pickups
out front.

For a moment I sat behind the wheel, feeling flat. The
town didn't look like the magical place my mother had
described; if anything, it was seedier than the suburb I'd
left yesterday. I had to force myself to get out, and when
I did, I stood beside the Pinto, staring up at the hotel.
Pale green with once white trim, all of it blasted and
faded by the elements. An inscription above its front
door gave the date it was built—1879, the height of last
century's logging boom. Neon beer signs flashed in its
lower windows; gulls perched along the peak of its roof,
their droppings splashed over the steps and front porch. I
watched as one soared in for a landing, crying shrilly.
Sea breeze ruffled my short blond hair, and I smelled fish
and brine.

The smell of the sea had always delighted me. Now it
triggered a sense of connection to this place. I thought:
Home.

The thought lent me the impetus to take out my
overnight bag and carried me over the threshold of the
hotel. Inside was a dim lobby that smelled of dust and
cat. I peered through the gloom but saw no one. Loud

voices came from a room to the left, underscored by the clink of glasses and the thump and clatter of dice-rolling; I went over, looked in, and saw an old-fashioned tavern, peopled mainly by men in work clothes. The ship's clock that hung crooked behind the bar said four-twenty. Happy hour got under way early in Camel Rock.

There was a public phone on the other side of the lobby. I crossed to it and opened the thin county directory, aware that my fingers were trembling. No listing for my father. No listing for anyone with my last name. More disappointed than I had any right to be, I replaced the book and turned away.

Just then a woman came out of a door under the steep staircase. She was perhaps in her early sixties, tall and gaunt, with tightly permed gray curls and a faced lined by weariness. When she saw me, her pale eyes registered surprise. "May I help you?"

I hesitated, the impulse to flee the shabby hotel and drive away from Camel Rock nearly irresistible. Then I thought: Come on, give the place a chance. "Do you have a room available?"

"We've got nothing *but* available rooms." She smiled wryly and got a card for me to fill out. Lacking any other, I put down my old address and formed the letters of my signature—Ashley Heikkinen—carefully. I'd always hated my last name; it seemed graceless and misshapen beside my first. Now I was glad it was unusual; maybe someone here in town would recognize it. The woman glanced disinterestedly at the card, however, then turned away and studied a rack of keys.

"Front room or back room?"

"Which is more quiet?"

"Well, in front you've got the highway noise, but there's not much traffic at night. In the back you've got the boys"—she motioned at the door to the tavern— "scrapping in the parking lot at closing time."

Just what I wanted—a room above a bar frequented by quarrelsome drunks. "I guess I'll take the front."

The woman must have read my expression. "Oh,

honey, don't you worry about them. They're not so bad, but there's nobody as contentious as an out-of-work logger who's had one over his limit."

I smiled and offered my Visa card. She shook her head and pointed to a CASH ONLY sign. I dug in my wallet and came up with the amount she named. It wasn't much, but I didn't have much to begin with. There had been a small life insurance policy on my mother, but most of it had gone toward burying her. If I was to stay in Camel Rock, I'd need a job.

"Are a lot of people around here out of work?" I asked as the woman wrote up a receipt.

"Loggers, mostly. The type who won't bite the bullet and learn another trade. But the rest of us aren't in much better shape."

"Have you heard of any openings for a waitress or a bartender?"

"For yourself?"

"Yes. If I can find a job, I may settle here."

Her hand paused over the receipt book. "Honey, why on earth would you want to do that?"

"I was born here. Maybe you knew my parents— Melinda and John Heikkinen?"

She shook her head and tore the receipt from the book. "My husband and me, we just moved down here last year from Del Norte County—things're even worse up there, believe me. We bought this hotel because it was cheap and we thought we could make a go of it."

"Have you?"

"Not really. We don't have the wherewithal to fix it up, so we can't compete with the new motels or bed-and-breakfasts. And we made the mistake of giving bar credit to the locals."

"That's too bad," I said. "There must be some jobs available, though. I'm a good waitress, a fair bartender. And I . . . like people," I added lamely.

She smiled, the lines around her eyes crinkling kindly. I guessed she'd presented meager credentials a time or two herself. "Well, I suppose you could try over at the mall. I hear Barbie Cannon's been doing real good with her Beachcomber Shop, and the tourist season'll be here before we know it. Maybe she can use some help."

I thanked her and took the room key she offered, but as I picked up my bag I thought of something else. "Is there a newspaper in town?"

"As far as I know, there never has been. There's one of those little county shoppers, but it doesn't have ads for jobs, if that's what you're after."

"Actually, I'm trying to locate . . . a family member. I thought if there was a newspaper, I could look through their back issues. What about longtime residents of the town? Is there anybody who's an amateur historian, for instance?"

"Matter of fact, there is. Gus Galick. Lives on his fishing trawler, the *Irma*, down at the harbor. Comes in here regular."

"How long has he lived here?"

"All his life."

Just the person I wanted to talk with.

The woman added, "Gus is away this week, took a charter party down the coast. I think he said he'd be back next Thursday."

Another disappointment. I swallowed it, told myself the delay would give me time to settle in and get to know the place of my birth. And I'd start by visiting the Beachcomber Shop.

The shop offered exactly the kind of merchandise its name implied: seashells, driftwood, inexpert carvings of gulls, grebes, and sea lions. Postcards and calendars and T-shirts and paperback guidebooks. Shell jewelry, paperweights, ceramic whales, and dolphins. Nautical toys and candles and wind chimes. All of it was totally predictable, but the woman who popped up from behind the counter was anything but.

She was very tall, well over six feet, and her black hair stood up in long, stiff spikes. A gold ring pierced her left nostril, and several others hung from either earlobe. She wore a black leather tunic with metal studs, over lacy black tights and calf-high boots. In L.A. I wouldn't have given her a second glance, but this was Camel Rock. Such people weren't supposed to happen here.

The woman watched my reaction, then threw back her head, and laughed throatily. I felt a blush begin to creep over my face.

"Hey, don't worry about it," she told me. "You should see how I scare the little bastards who drag their parents in here, whining about how they absolutely *have* to have a blow-up Willie the Whale."

"Uh, isn't that bad for business?"

"Hell, no. Embarrasses the parents, and they buy twice as much as they would've."

"Oh."

"So—what can I do for you?"

"I'm looking for Barbie Cannon."

"You found her." She flopped onto a stool next to the counter, stretching out her long legs.

"My name's Ashley Heikkinen." I watched her face for some sign of recognition. There wasn't any, but that didn't surprise me; Barbie Cannon was only a few years older than I—perhaps thirty—and too young to remember a family that had left so long ago. Besides, she didn't look as if she'd been born and raised here.

"I'm looking for a job," I went on, "and the woman at the hotel said you might need some help in the shop."

She glanced around at the merchandise that was heaped haphazardly on the shelves and spilled over onto the floor here and there. "Well, Penny's right—I probably do." Then she looked back at me. "You're not local."

"I just came up from L.A."

"Me too, about a year ago. There're a fair number of us transplants, and the division between us and the locals is pretty clear-cut."

"How so?"

"A lot of the natives are down on their luck, resentful of the newcomers, especially ones like me, who're doing well. Oh, some of them're all right; they understand that

the only way for the area to survive is to restructure the
economy. But most of them are just sitting around the
bars mumbling about how the spotted owl ruined their
lives and hoping the timber industry'll make a comeback—and that ain't gonna happen. So why're *you*
here?"

"I was born in Camel Rock. And I'm sick of southern
California."

"So you decided to get back to your roots."

"In a way."

"You alone?"

I nodded.

"Got a place to stay?"

"The hotel, for now."

"Well, it's not so bad, and Penny'll extend credit if you
run short. As for a job . . ." She paused, looking around
again. "You know, I came up here thinking I'd work on
my photography. The next Ansel Adams and all that."
She grinned self-mockingly. "Trouble is, I got to be such
a successful businesswoman that I don't even have time to
load my camera. Tell you what—why don't we go over to
the hotel tavern, tilt a few, talk it over?"

"Why not?" I said.

Mist hugged the tops of the sequoias and curled in tendrils around their trunks. The mossy ground under my
feet was damp and slick. I hugged my hooded sweatshirt
against the chill and moved cautiously up the incline
from where I'd left the car on an overgrown logging
road. My soles began to slip, and I crouched, catching at
a stump for balance. The wet fronds of a fern brushed
my cheek.

I'd been tramping through the hills for over two hours,
searching every lane and dirt track for the burned-out
cabin that Barbie Cannon had photographed shortly after
her arrival in Camel Rock last year. Barbie had invited
me to her place for dinner the night before after we'd
agreed on the terms of my new part-time job, and in the
course of the evening she'd shown me her portfolio of

photographs. One, a grainy black-and-white image of a ruin, so strongly affected me that I'd barely been able to sleep. This morning I'd dropped by the shop and gotten Barbie to draw me a map of where she'd found it, but her recollection was so vague that I might as well have had no map at all.

I pushed back to my feet and continued climbing. The top of the rise was covered by a dense stand of sumac and bay laurel; the spicy scent of the laurel leaves mixed with stronger odors of redwood and eucalyptus. The mixed bouquet triggered the same sense of connection that I'd felt as I stood in front of the hotel the previous afternoon. I breathed deeply, then elbowed through the dense branches.

From the other side of the thicket I looked down on a sloping meadow splashed with the brilliant yellow-orange of California poppies. More sequoias crowned the ridge on its far side, and through their branches I caught a glimpse of the flat, leaden sea. A stronger feeling of familiarity stole over me. I remembered my mother saying, "In the spring, the meadow was full of poppies, and you could see the ocean from our front steps. . . ."

The mist was beginning to break up overhead. I watched a hawk circle against a patch of blue high above the meadow, then wheel and flap away toward the inland hills. He passed over my head, and I could feel the beating of his great wings. I turned, my gaze following his flight path—

And then I spotted the cabin, overgrown and wrapped in shadow, only yards away. Built into the downward slope of the hill, its moss-covered foundations were anchored in bedrock, as I'd been told. But the rest was only blackened and broken timbers, a collapsed roof on whose shakes vegetation had taken root, a rusted stove chimney about to topple, empty windows and doors.

I drew in my breath and held it for a long moment. Then I slowly moved forward.

Stone steps, four of them. I counted as I climbed. Yes, you could still see the Pacific from here, the meadow too.

And this opening was where the door had been. Beyond it, nothing but a concrete slab covered with debris. Plenty of evidence that picnickers had been here.

I stepped over the threshold.

One big empty room. Nothing left, not even the mammouth iron woodstove. Vines growing through the timbers, running across the floor. And at the far side, a collapsed heap of burned lumber—the sleeping loft?

Something crunched under my foot. I looked down, squatted, poked at it gingerly with my fingertip. Glass, green glass. It could have come from a picnicker's wine bottle. Or it could have come from a broken stained-glass window.

I stood, coldness upon my scalp and shoulder blades. Coldness that had nothing to do with the sea wind that bore the mist from the coast. I closed my eyes against the shadows and the ruin. Once again I could smell my mother's baking bread, hear my father's voice. Once again I thought: *Home*.

But when I opened my eyes, the warmth and light vanished. Now all I saw was the scene of a terrible tragedy.

"Barbie," I said, "what do you know about the North-coast Lumber Company?"

She looked up from the box of wind chimes she was unpacking. "Used to be the big employer around here."

"Where do they have their offices? I couldn't find a listing in the county phone book."

"I hear they went bust in the eighties."

"Then why would they still own land up in the hills?"

"Don't know. Why?"

I hesitated. Yesterday, the day after I'd found the cabin, I'd driven down to the county offices at Fort Bragg and spent the entire afternoon poring over the land plats for this area. The place where the ruin stood appeared to belong to the lumber company. There was no reason I shouldn't confide in Barbie about my search, but something held me back. After a moment I said, "Oh, I saw some acreage that I might be interested in buying."

She raised her eyebrows; the extravagant white eye shadow and bright-red lipstick that she wore today made her look like an astonished clown. "On what I'm paying you for part-time work, you're buying land?"

"I've got some savings from my mom's life insurance." That much was true, but the small amount wouldn't buy even a square foot of land.

"Huh." She went back to her unpacking. "Well, I don't know for a fact that Northcoast did go bust. Penny told me that the owner's widow is still alive. Used to live on a big estate near here, but a long time ago she moved down the coast to that fancy retirement community at Timber Point. Maybe she could tell you about this acreage."

"What's her name, do you know?"

"No, but you could ask Penny. She and Gene bought the hotel from her."

"Madeline Carmichael," Penny said. "Lady in her late fifties. She and her husband used to own a lot of property around here."

"You know her, then."

"Nope, never met her. Our dealings were through a realtor and her lawyer."

"She lives down at Timber Point?"

"Uh-huh. The realtor told us she's a recluse, never leaves her house and has everything she needs delivered."

"Why, do you suppose?"

"Why not? She can afford it. Oh, the realtor hinted that there's some tragedy in her past, but I don't put much stock in that. I'll tell you"—her tired eyes swept the dingy hotel lobby—"if I had a beautiful home and all that money, I'd never go out, either."

Madeline Carmichael's phone number and address were unlisted. When I drove down to Timber Point the next day, I found high grape-stake fences and a gatehouse; the guard told me that Mrs. Carmichael would see no one who wasn't on her visitors list. When I asked him to call her, he refused. "If she was expecting you," he said, "she'd have sent your name down."

Penny had given me the name of the realtor who handled the sale of the hotel. He put me in touch with Mrs. Carmichael's lawyer in Fort Bragg. The attorney told me he'd check about the ownership of the land and get back to me. When he did, his reply was terse: The land was part of the original Carmichael estate; title was held by the nearly defunct lumber company; it was not for sale.

So why had my parents built their cabin on the Carmichael estate? Were my strong feelings of connection to the burned-out ruin in the hills false?

Maybe, I told myself, it was time to stop chasing memories and start building a life for myself here in Camel Rock. Maybe it was best to leave the past alone.

The following weekend brought the kind of quicksilver days my mother had told me about, and in turn they lured tourists in record numbers. We couldn't restock the Beachcomber Shop's shelves fast enough. On the next Wednesday—Barbie's photography day—I was unpacking fresh merchandise and filling in where necessary while waiting for the woman Barbie bought her driftwood sculptures from to make a delivery. Business was slack in the late-afternoon hours; I moved slowly, my mind on what to wear to a dinner party being given that evening by some new acquaintances who ran an herb farm. When the bell over the door jangled, I started.

It was Mrs. Fleming, the driftwood lady. I recognized her by the big plastic wash basket of sculptures that she toted. A tiny white-haired woman, she seemed too frail for such a load. I moved to take it from her.

She resisted, surprisingly strong. Her eyes narrowed, and she asked, "Where's Barbie?"

"Wednesday's her day off."

"And who are you?"

"Ashley Heikkinen. I'm Barbie's part-time—"

"*What* did you say?"

"My name is Ashley Heikkinen. I just started here last week."

Mrs. Fleming set the basket on the counter and regarded me sternly, spots of red appearing on her cheeks. "Just what are you up to, young woman?"

"I don't understand."

"Why are you using that name?"

"Using . . . ? It's my name."

"It most certainly is not! This is a very cruel joke."

The woman had to be unbalanced. Patiently I said, "Look, my name really is Ashley Heikkinen. I was born in Camel Rock but moved away when I was two. I grew up outside Los Angeles, and when my mother died I decided to come back here."

Mrs. Fleming shook her head, her lips compressed, eyes glittering with anger.

"I can prove who I am," I added, reaching under the counter for my purse. "Here's my identification."

"Of course you'd have identification. Everyone knows how to obtain that under the circumstances."

"What circumstances?"

She turned and moved toward the door. "I can't imagine what you possibly expect to gain by this charade, young woman, but you can be sure I'll speak to Barbie about you."

"Please, wait!"

She pushed through the door, and the bell above it jangled harshly as it slammed shut. I hurried to the window and watched her cross the parking lot in a vigorous stride that belied her frail appearance. As she turned at the highway, I looked down and saw I had my wallet out, prepared to prove my identity.

Why, I wondered, did I feel compelled to justify my existence to this obviously deranged stranger?

The dinner party that evening was pleasant, and I returned to the hotel at a little after midnight with the fledgling sense of belonging that making friends in a strange place brings. The fog was in thick, drawn by hot inland temperatures. It put a gritty sheen on my face, and when I touched my tongue to my lips, I tasted the sea. I locked the Pinto and started across the rutted parking lot to the rear entrance. Heavy footsteps came up behind me.

Conditioned by my years in L.A., I already held my car key in my right hand, tip out as a weapon. I glanced back and saw a stocky, bearded man bearing down on me. When I sidestepped and turned, he stopped, and his gaze moved to the key. He'd been drinking—beer, and plenty of it.

From the tavern, I thought. Probably came out to the parking lot because the rest room's in use and he couldn't wait. "After you," I said, opening the door for him.

He stepped inside the narrow, dim hallway. I let him get a ways ahead, then followed. The door stuck, and I turned to give it a tug. The man reversed, came up swiftly, and grasped my shoulder.

"Hey!" I said.

He spun me around and slammed me against the wall. "Lady, what the hell're you after?"

"Let go of me!" I pushed at him.

He pushed back, grabbed my other shoulder, and pinned me there. I stopped struggling, took a deep breath, told myself to remain calm.

"Not going to hurt you, lady," he said. "I just want to know what your game is."

Two lunatics in one day. "What do you mean—game?"

"'My name is Ashley Heikkinen,'" he said in a falsetto, then dropped to his normal pitch. "Who're you trying to fool? And what's in it for you?"

"I don't—"

"Don't give me that! You might be able to stonewall an old lady like my mother—"

"Your mother?"

"Yeah, Janet Fleming. You expect her to believe you, for Christ's sake? What you did, you upset her plenty. She had to take one of the Valiums the doctor gave me for my bad back."

"I don't understand what your mother's problem is."

"Jesus, you're a cold bitch! Her own goddaughter, for Christ's sake, and you expect her to *believe* you?"

"Goddaughter?"

His face was close to mine now; hot beer breath touched my cheeks. "My ma's goddaughter was Ashley Heikkinen."

"That's impossible! I never had a godmother. I never met your mother until this afternoon."

The man shook his head. "I'll tell you what's impossible: Ashley Heikkinen appearing in Camel Rock after all these years. Ashley's dead. She died in a fire when she wasn't even two years old. My ma ought to know—she identified the body."

A chill washed over me from my scalp to my toes. The man stared, apparently recognizing my shock as genuine. After a moment I asked, "Where was the fire?"

He ignored the question, frowning. "Either you're a damned good actress or something weird's going on. Can't have been two people born with that name. Not in Camel Rock."

"Where was the fire?"

He shook his head again, this time as if to clear it. His mouth twisted, and I feared he was going to be sick. Then he let go of me and stumbled through the door to the parking lot. I released my breath in a long sigh and slumped against the wall. A car started outside. When its tires had spun on the gravel and its engine revved on the highway, I pushed myself upright and went along the hall to the empty lobby. A single bulb burned in the fixture above the reception desk, as it did every night. The usual sounds of laughter and conversation came from the tavern.

Everything seemed normal. Nothing was. I ran upstairs to the shelter of my room.

After I'd double-locked the door, I turned on the overhead and crossed to the bureau and leaned across it toward the streaky mirror. My face was drawn and unusually pale.

Ashley Heikkinen dead?

Dead in a fire when she wasn't quite two years old?

I closed my eyes, picturing the blackened ruin in the hills above town. Then I opened them and stared at my frightened face. It was the face of a stranger.

"If Ashley Heikkinen is dead," I said, "then who am *I?*"

Mrs. Fleming wouldn't talk to me. When I got to her cottage on one of the packed-dirt side streets at a little after nine the next morning, she refused to open the door and threatened to run me off with her dead husband's shotgun. "And don't think I'm not a good markswoman," she added.

She must have gone straight to the phone, because Barbie was hanging up when I walked into the Beachcomber Shop a few minutes later. She frowned at me and said, "I just had the most insane call from Janet Fleming."

"About me?"

"How'd you guess? She was giving me all this stuff about you not being who you say you are and the 'real Ashley Heikkinen' dying in a fire when she was a baby. Must be going around the bend."

I sat down on the stool next to the counter. "Actually, there might be something to what she says." And then I told her all of it: my mother's stories, the forbidden things that went unsaid, the burned-out cabin in the hills, my encounters with Janet Fleming and her son. "I tried to talk with Mrs. Fleming this morning," I finished, "but she threatened me with a shotgun."

"And she's been known to use that gun, too. You must've really upset her."

"Yes. From something she said yesterday afternoon, I gather she thinks I got hold of the other Ashley's birth certificate and created a set of fake ID around it."

"You sound like you believe there *was* another Ashley."

"I saw that burned-out cabin. Besides, why would Mrs. Fleming make something like that up?"

"But you recognized the cabin, both from my photograph and when you went there. You said it felt like home."

"I recognized it from my mother's stories, that's true. Barbie, I've lived those stories for most of my life. You know how kids sometimes get the notion that they're so special they can't really belong to their parents, that they're a prince or princess who was given to a servant couple to raise?"

"Oh sure, we all went through that stage. Only in my case, I was Mick Jagger's love child, and someday he was going to acknowledge me and give me all his money."

"Well, my mother's stories convinced me that I didn't really belong in a downscale tract in a crappy valley town. They made me special, somebody who came from a magical place. And I dreamed of it every night."

"So you're saying that you only recognized the cabin from the images your mother planted in your mind?"

"It's possible."

Barbie considered. "Okay, I'll buy that. And here's a scenario that might fit: After the fire, your parents moved away. That would explain why your mom didn't want to talk about why they left Camel Rock. And they had another child—you. They gave you Ashley's name and her history. It wasn't right, but grief does crazy things to otherwise sane people."

It worked—but only in part. "That still doesn't explain what happened to my father and why my mother would never talk about him."

"Maybe she was the one who went crazy with grief, and after a while he couldn't take it anymore, so he left."

She made it sound so logical and uncomplicated. But I'd known the quality of my mother's silences; there was more to them than Barbie's scenario encompassed.

I bit my lip in frustration. "You know, Mrs. Fleming could shed a lot of light on this, but she refuses to deal with me."

"Then find somebody who will."

"Who?" I asked. And then I thought of Gus Galick, the man Penny had told me about who had lived in Camel Rock all his life. "Barbie, do you know Gus Galick?"

"Sure. He's one of the few old-timers around here that I've really connected with. Gus builds ships in bottles; I sold some on consignment for him last year. He used to be a rumrunner during Prohibition, has some great stories about bringing in cases of Canadian booze to the coves along the coast."

"He must be older than God."

"Older than God and sharp as a tack. I bet he could tell you what you need to know."

"Penny said he was away on some charter trip."

"Was, but he's back now. I saw the *Irma* in her slip at the harbor when I drove by this morning."

Camel Rock's harbor was a sheltered cove with a bait shack and a few slips for fishing boats. Of them, Gus Galick's *Irma* was by far the most shipshape, and her captain was equally trim, with a shock of silvery-white hair and leathery tan skin. I didn't give him my name, just identified myself as a friend of Penny and Barbie. Galick seemed to take people at face value, though; he welcomed me on board, took me belowdecks, and poured me a cup of coffee in the cozy wood-paneled cabin. When we were seated on either side of the teak table, I asked my first question.

"Sure, I remember the fire on the old Carmichael estate," he said. "Summer of seventy-one. Both the father and the little girl died."

I gripped the coffee mug tighter. "The father died too?"

"Yeah. Heikkinen, his name was. Norwegian, maybe. I don't recall his first name, or the little girl's."

"John and Ashley."

"These people kin to you?"

"In a way. Mr. Galick, what happened to Melinda, the mother?"

He thought. "Left town, I guess. I never did see her after the double funeral."

"Where are John and Ashley buried?"

"Graveyard of the Catholic church." He motioned toward the hills, where I'd seen its spire protruding through the trees. "Carmichaels paid for everything, of course. Guilt, I guess."

"Why guilt?"

"The fire started on their land. Was the father's fault—John Heikkinen's, I mean—but still, they'd sacked him, and that was why he was drinking so heavy. Fell asleep with the doors to the woodstove open, and before he could wake up, the place was a furnace."

The free-flowing information was beginning to overwhelm me. "Let me get this straight: John Heikkinen worked for the Carmichaels?"

"Was their caretaker. His wife looked after their house."

"Where was she when the fire started?"

"At the main house, washing up the supper dishes. I heard she saw the flames, run down there, and tried to save her family. The Carmichaels held her back till the volunteer fire department could get there; they knew there wasn't any hope from the beginning."

I set the mug down, gripped the table's edge with icy fingers.

Galick leaned forward, eyes concerned. "Something wrong, miss? Have I upset you?"

I shook my head. "It's just . . . a shock, hearing about it after all these years." After a pause, I asked, "Did the Heikkinens have any other children?"

"Only the little girl who died."

I took out a photograph of my mother and passed it over to him. It wasn't a good picture, just a snap of her on the steps of our stucco bungalow down south. "Is this Melinda Heikkinen?"

He took a pair of glasses from a case on the table, put them on, and looked closely at it. Then he shrugged and handed it back to me. "There's some resemblance, but . . . She looks like she's had a hard life."

"She did." I replaced the photo in my wallet. "Can you think of anyone who could tell me more about the Heikkinens?"

"Well, there's Janet Fleming. She was Mrs. Heikkinen's aunt and the little girl's godmother. The mother was so broken up that Janet had to identify the bodies, so I guess she'd know everything there is to know about the fire."

"Anyone else?"

"Well, of course there's Madeline Carmichael. But she's living down at Timber Point now, and she never sees anybody."

"Why not?"

"I've got my ideas on that. It started after her husband died. Young man, only in his fifties. Heart attack." Galick grimaced. "Carmichael was one of these pillars of the community; never drank, smoked, or womanized. Keeled over at a church service in seventy-five. Me, I've lived a gaudy life, as they say. Even now I eat and drink all the wrong things, and I like a cigar after dinner. And I just go on and on. Tells you a lot about the randomness of it all."

I didn't want to think about that randomness; it was much too soon after losing my own mother to an untimely death for that. I asked, "About Mrs. Carmichael—it was her husband's death that turned her into a recluse?"

"No, miss." He shook his head firmly. "My idea is that his dying was just the last straw. The seeds were planted when their little girl disappeared three years before that."

"Disappeared?"

"It was in seventy-two, the year after the fire. The little girl was two years old, a change-of-life baby. Abigail, she was called. Abby, for short. Madeline Carmichael left her in her playpen on the veranda of their house, and she just plain vanished. At first they thought it was a kidnapping; the lumber company was failing, but the family still had plenty of money. But nobody ever made a ransom demand, and they never did find a trace of Abby or the person who took her."

The base of my spine began to tingle. As a child, I'd always been smaller than others of my age. Slower in school too. The way a child might be if she was a year younger than the age shown on her birth certificate.

Abigail Carmichael, I thought. Abby, for short.

The Catholic churchyard sat tucked back against a eucalyptus grove; the trees' leaves caught the sunlight in a subtle shimmer, and their aromatic buds were thick under my feet. An iron fence surrounded the graves, and unpaved paths meandered among the mostly crumbling headstones. I meandered too, shock gradually leaching away to depression. The foundations of my life were as tilted as the oldest grave marker, and I wasn't sure I had the strength to construct new ones.

But I'd come here with a purpose, so finally I got a grip on myself and began covering the cemetery in a grid pattern.

I found them in the last row, where the fence backed up against the eucalyptus. Two small headstones set side by side. John and Ashley. There was room to John's right for another grave, one that now would never be occupied.

I knelt and brushed a curl of bark from Ashley's stone. The carving was simple, only her name and the dates. She'd been born April 6, 1969, and had died February 1, 1971.

I knelt there for a long time. Then I said goodbye and went home.

The old Carmichael house sat at the end of a chained-off drive that I'd earlier taken for a logging road. It was a wonder I hadn't stumbled across it in my search for the cabin. Built of dark timber and stone, with a wide veranda running the length of the lower story, it once might have been imposing. But now its windows were boarded, birds roosted in its eaves, and all around it the forest encroached. I followed a cracked flagstone path through a lawn long gone to weeds and wildflowers, to the broad front steps. Stood at their foot, my hand on the cold wrought-iron railing.

Could a child of two retain memories? I'd believed so before, but mine had turned out to be false, spoon-fed to me by the woman who had taken me from this veranda twenty-four years earlier. All the same, something in this lonely place spoke to me; I felt a sense of peace and safety that I'd never before experienced.

I hadn't known real security; my mother's and my life together had been too uncertain, too difficult, too shadowed by the past. Those circumstances probably accounted for my long string of failures, my inability to make my way in the world. A life built on lies and forbidden things was bound to go nowhere.

And yet it hadn't had to be that way. All this could have been mine, had it not been for a woman unhinged by grief. I could have grown up in this once lovely home, surrounded by my real parents' love. Perhaps if I had, my father would not have died of an untimely heart attack, and my birth mother would not have become a recluse. A sickening wave of anger swept over me, followed by a deep sadness. Tears came to my eyes, and I wiped them away.

I couldn't afford to waste time crying. Too much time had been wasted already.

To prove my real identity, I needed the help of Madeline Carmichael's attorney, and he took a good deal of convincing. I had to provide documentation and witnesses to my years as Ashley Heikkinen before he would consent to check Abigail Carmichael's birth records. Most of the summer went by before he broached the subject to Mrs. Carmichael. But blood composition and the delicate whorls on feet and fingers don't lie; finally, on a bright September afternoon, I arrived at Timber Point—alone, at the invitation of my birth mother.

I was nervous and gripped the Pinto's wheel with

damp hands as I followed the guard's directions across a rolling seaside meadow to the Carmichael house. Like the others in this exclusive development, it was of modern design, with a silvery wood exterior that blended with the saw grass and Scotch broom. A glass wall faced the Pacific, reflecting sun glints on the water. Along the shoreline a flock of pelicans flew south in loose formation.

I'd worn my best dress—pink cotton, too light for the season, but it was all I had—and had spent a ridiculous amount of time on my hair and makeup. As I parked the shabby Pinto in the drive, I wished I could make it disappear. My approach to the door was awkward; I stumbled on the unlandscaped ground and almost turned my ankle. The uniformed maid who admitted me gave me the kind of glance that once, as a hostess at a coffee shop, I'd reserved for customers without shirt or shoes. She showed me to a living room facing the sea and went away.

I stood in the room's center on an Oriental carpet, unsure whether to sit or stand. Three framed photographs on a grand piano caught my attention; I went over there and looked at them. A man and a woman, middle-aged and handsome. A child, perhaps a year old, in a striped romper. The child had my eyes.

"Yes, that's Abigail." The throaty voice—smoker's voice—came from behind me. I turned to face the woman in the photograph. Older now, but still handsome, with upswept creamy white hair and pale porcelain skin, she wore a long caftan in some sort of soft champagne-colored fabric. No reason for Madeline Carmichael to get dressed; she never left the house.

She came over to me and peered at my face. For a moment her eyes were soft and questioning, then they hardened and looked away. "Please," she said, "sit down over here."

I followed her to two matching brocade settees positioned at right angles to the seaward window. We sat, one on each, with a coffee table between us. Mrs.

Carmichael took a cigarette from a silver box on the table and lit it with a matching lighter.

Exhaling and fanning the smoke away, she said, "I have a number of things to say to you that will explain my position in this matter. First, I believe the evidence you've presented. You are my daughter Abigail. Melinda Heikkinen was very bitter toward my husband and me: If we hadn't dismissed her husband, he wouldn't have been passed out from drinking when the fire started. If we hadn't kept her late at her duties that night, she would have been home and able to prevent it. If we hadn't stopped her from plunging into the conflagration, she might have saved her child. That, I suppose, served to justify her taking our child as a replacement."

She paused to smoke. I waited.

"The logic of what happened seems apparent at this remove," Mrs. Carmichael added, "but at the time we didn't think to mention Melinda as a potential suspect. She'd left Camel Rock the year before; even her aunt, Janet Fleming, had heard nothing from her. My husband and I had more or less put her out of our minds. And of course, neither of us was thinking logically at the time."

I was beginning to feel uneasy. She was speaking so analytically and dispassionately—not at all like a mother who had been reunited with her long-lost child.

She went on. "I must tell you about our family. California pioneers on both sides. The Carmichaels were lumber barons. My family were merchant princes engaging in the China trade. Abigail was the last of both lines, born to carry on our tradition. Surely you can understand why this matter is so . . . difficult."

She was speaking of Abigail as someone separate from me. "What matter?" I asked.

"That role in life, the one Abigail was born to, takes a certain type of individual. My Abby, the child I would have raised had it not been for Melinda Heikkinen, would not have turned out so—" She bit her lower lip, looked away at the sea.

"So what, Mrs. Carmichael?"

She shook her head, crushing out her cigarette.

A wave of humiliation swept over me. I glanced down at my cheap pink dress, at a chip in the polish on my thumbnail. When I raised my eyes, my birth mother was examining me with faint distaste.

I'd always had a temper; now it rose, and I gave in to it. "So *what*, Mrs. Carmichael?" I repeated. "So *common?*"

She winced but didn't reply.

I said, "I suppose you think it's your right to judge a person on her appearance or her financial situation. But you should remember that my life hasn't been easy—not like yours. Melinda Heikkinen could never make ends meet. We lived in a valley town east of L.A. She was sick a lot. I had to work from the time I was fourteen. There was trouble with gangs in our neighborhood."

Then I paused, hearing myself. No, I would not do this. I would not whine or beg.

"I wasn't brought up to complain," I continued, "and I'm not complaining now. In spite of working, I graduated high school with honors. I got a small scholarship, and Melinda persuaded me to go to college. She helped out financially when she could. I didn't finish, but that was my own fault. Whatever mistakes I've made are my own doing, not Melinda's. Maybe she told me lies about our life here on the coast, but they gave me something to hang on to. A lot of the time they were all I had, and now they've been taken from me. But I'm still not complaining."

Madeline Carmichael's dispassionate facade cracked. She closed her eyes, compressed her lips. After a moment she said, "How can you defend that woman?"

"For twenty-four years she was the only mother I knew."

Her eyes remained closed. She said, "Please, I will pay you any amount of money if you will go away and pretend this meeting never took place."

For a moment I couldn't speak. Then I exclaimed, "I don't want your money! This is not about money!"

"What, then?"

"What do I want? I thought I wanted my real mother."

"And now that you've met me, you're not sure you do." She opened her eyes, looked directly into mine. "Our feelings aren't really all that different, are they, Abigail?"

I shook my head in confusion.

Madeline Carmichael took a deep breath. "Abigail, you say you lived on Melinda's lies, that they were something to sustain you?"

I nodded.

"I've lived on lies too, and they sustained *me*. For twenty-three years I've put myself to sleep with dreams of our meeting. I woke to them. No matter what I was doing, they were only a fingertip's reach away. And now they've been taken from me, as yours have. My Abby, the daughter I pictured in those dreams, will never walk into this room and make everything all right. Just as the things you've dreamed of are never going to happen."

I looked around the room—at the grand piano, the Oriental carpets, the antiques, and exquisite art objects. Noticed for the first time how stylized and sterile it was, how the cold expanse of glass beside me made the sea blinding and bleak.

"You're right," I said, standing up. "Even if you were to take me in and offer me all this, it wouldn't be the life I wanted."

Mrs. Carmichael extended a staying hand toward me.

I stepped back. "No. And don't worry—I won't bother you again."

As I went out into the quicksilver afternoon and shut the door behind me, I thought that even though Melinda Heikkinen had given me a difficult life, she'd also offered me dreams to soften the hard times and love to ease my passage. My birth mother hadn't even offered me coffee or tea.

◆ ◆ ◆

On a cold, rainy December evening, Barbie Cannon and I sat at a table near the fireplace in the hotel's tavern, drinking red wine in celebration of my good fortune.

"I can't believe," she said for what must have been the dozenth time, "that old lady Carmichael up and gave you her house in the hills."

"Any more than you can believe I accepted it."

"Well, I thought you were too proud to take her money."

"Too proud to be bought off, but she offered the house with no strings attached. Besides, it's in such bad shape that I'll probably be fixing it up for the rest of my life."

"And she probably took a big tax write-off on it. No wonder rich people stay rich." Barbie snorted. "By the way, how come you're still calling yourself Ashley Heikkinen?"

I shrugged. "Why not? It's been my name for as long as I can remember. It's a good name."

"You're acting awfully laid back about this whole thing."

"You didn't see me when I got back from Timber Point. But I've worked it all through. In a way, I understand how Mrs. Carmichael feels. The house is nice, but anything else she could have given me isn't what I was looking for."

"So what *were* you looking for?"

I stared into the fire. Madeline Carmichael's porcelain face flashed against the background of the flames. Instead of anger I felt a tug of pity for her: a lonely woman waiting her life out, but really as dead and gone as the merchant princes, the lumber barons, the old days on this wild north coast. Then I banished the image and pictured instead the faces of the friends I'd made since coming to Camel Rock: Barbie, Penny, and Gene, the couple who ran the herb farm, Gus Galick, and—now—Janet Fleming and her son, Stu. Remembered all the good times: dinners and walks on the beach, Penny and Gene's fortieth wedding anniversary party, Barbie's first photographic exhibit, a fishing trip on Gus's trawler. And thought of all the good times to come.

"What was I looking for?" I said. "Something I found the day I got here."

NEW MOON AND RATTLESNAKES

WENDY HORNSBY

Wendy Hornsby is one of those miniaturists who can say, in a few simple lines imbued with great grace, what other writers never get to even in long and ponderous novels.

The story here, as Lise tries to make at least temporary sense of her embattled life, displays many of Hornsby's wonderful storytelling skills.

After you read this, you will no doubt seek out further Hornsby stories. Every single one of them is worth searching for.

LISE CAUGHT A RIDE at a truck stop near Riverside, in a big rig headed for Phoenix. The driver was a paunchy, lonely old geek whose come-on line was a fatherly routine. She helped him play his line because it got her inside the air-conditioned cab of his truck and headed east way ahead of her schedule.

"Sweet young thing like you shouldn't be thumbing rides," he said, helping Lise with her seat belt. "Desert can be awful damn dangerous in the summertime."

"I know the desert. Besides . . ." She put her hand over his hairy paw. "I'm not so young and there's nothing sweet about me."

He laughed, but he looked at her more closely. Looked at the heavy purse she carried with her, too. After that long look, he dropped the fatherly routine. She was glad, because she didn't have a lot of time to waste on preliminaries.

The tired old jokes he told her got steadily gamier as he drove east out Interstate 10. Cheap new housing tracts and pink stucco malls gave way to a landscape of razor-sharp yucca and shimmering heat, and all the way Lise laughed at his stupid jokes only to let him know she was hanging in with him.

Up the steep grade through Beaumont and Banning and Cabazon she laughed on cue, watching him go through his gears, deciding whether she could drive the truck without him. Or not. Twice, to speed things along, she told him jokes that made his bald head blush flame red.

Before the Palm Springs turnoff, he suggested they stop at an Indian bingo palace for cold drinks and a couple of games. Somehow, while she was distracted watching how the place operated, his hand kept finding its way into the back of her spandex tank top.

The feel of him so close, his suggestive leers, the smell of him, the smoky smell of the place, made her clammy all over. But she kept up a good front, didn't retch when her stomach churned. She had practice; for five years she had kept up a good front, and survived because of it. Come ten o'clock, she encouraged herself, there would be a whole new order of things.

After bingo, it was an hour of front-seat wrestling, straight down the highway to a Motel 6—all rooms $29.95, cable TV and a phone in every room. He told her what he wanted; she asked him to take a shower first.

In Riverside, he'd said his name was Jack. But the name on the Louisiana driver's license she found in his wallet said Henry LeBeau. He was in the shower, singing, when she made this discovery. Lise practiced writing the name a couple of times on motel stationery while she placed a call on the room phone. Mrs. Henry LeBeau, Lise LeBeau . . . she wrote it until the call was answered.

"I'm out," Lise said.

"You're lying."

"Not me," she said. "Penalty for lying's too high."

"I left my best man at the house with you. He would have called me."

"If he could. Maybe your best man isn't as good as you thought he was. Maybe I'm better."

Waiting for more response from the other end, she wrote LeBeau's name a few more times, wrote it until it felt natural to her hand.

Finally, she got more than heavy breathing from the phone. "Where are you, Lise?"

"I'm a long way into somewhere else. Don't bother to go looking, because this time you won't find me."

"Of course I will."

She hung up.

Jack/Henry turned off the shower. Before he was out of the bathroom, fresh and clean and looking for love,

Lise was out of the motel and down the road. With his wallet in her bag.

The heat outside was like a frontal assault after the cool, dim room; hundred and ten degrees, zero percent humidity, according to a sign. Afternoon sun slanted directly into Lise's eyes and the air smelled like truck fuel and hot pavement, but it was better than the two-day sweat that had filled the big-rig cab, had followed them into the motel. She needed a dozen hot breaths to get his stench out of her.

The motel wasn't in a place, nothing but a graded spot at the end of a freeway off-ramp halfway between L.A. and Phoenix: a couple of service stations and a minimart, a hundred miles of scrubby cactus and sharp rocks for neighbors. Shielding her eyes, Lise quick-walked toward the freeway, looking for possibilities even before she crossed the road to the Texaco station.

The meeting she needed to attend would be held in Palm Springs, and she had to find a way to get there. She knew for a dead certainty she didn't want to get into another truck, and she couldn't stay in the open.

Heat blazed down from the sky, bounced up off the pavement, and caught her both ways. Lise began to panic. Fifteen minutes, maybe twenty, under the sun and she knew she would be fried. But it wasn't the heat that made her run for the shelter of the covered service station. After being confined for so long, she was sometimes frightened by open space.

The Texaco and its minimart were busy with a transient olio show: cranky families in vans, chubby truckers, city smoothies in desert vacation togs and too much shiny jewelry, everyone in a hurry to fill up, scrape the bugs off the windshield, and get back on the road with the air-conditioning buffering them from the relentless heat.

As she walked past the pumps, waiting for opportunity to present itself, an old white-haired guy in a big new Cadillac slid past her, pulled up next to the minimart. He was a very clean-looking man, the sort, she thought, who doesn't like to get hot and mussed. Like her father. When he got out of his car to go into the minimart, the cream puff left his engine running and his air conditioner blowing to keep the car's interior cool.

Lise saw the man inside the store, spinning a rack of road maps, as she got into his car and drove away.

When she hit the on-ramp, backtracking west, she saw Mr. Henry LeBeau, half dressed and sweating like a comeback wrestler, standing out in front of the motel, looking upset, peering around like he'd lost something.

"Goodbye, Mr. LeBeau." Lise smiled at his tiny figure as it receded in her rearview mirror. "Thanks for the ride." Then she looked all around, half expecting to spot a tail, to find a fleet of long, shiny black cars deployed to find her, surround her, take her back home; escape couldn't be this easy. But the only shine she saw came from mirages, like silver puddles splashed across the freeway. She relaxed some, settled against the leather upholstery, aimed the air vents on her face and changed the Caddy's radio station from a hundred violins to Chopin.

Her transformation from truck-stop dolly to mall matron took less than five minutes. She wiped off the heavy makeup she had acquired in Riverside, covered the skimpy tank top with a blouse from her bag, rolled down the cuffs of her denim shorts to cover three more inches of her muscular thighs, traded the hand-tooled boots for graceful leather sandals, and tied her windblown hair into a neat ponytail at the back of her neck. When she checked her face in the mirror, she saw any lady in a checkout line looking back at her.

Lise took the Bob Hope Drive off-ramp, sighed happily as the scorched and barren virgin desert gave way to deep-green golf courses, piles of chi-chi condos, palm trees, fountains, and posh restaurants whose parking lots were garnished with Jags, Caddies, and Benzes.

She pulled into one of those lots and, with the motor running, took some time to really look over what she had to work with. American Express card signed H. G. LeBeau. MasterCard signed Henry LeBeau. Four hundred in cash. The wallet also had some gas company cards, two old condoms, a picture of an ugly wife, and a slip of paper with a four-digit number. Bless his heart, she thought, smiling; Henry had given her a PIN number, contributed to her range of possibilities.

Lise committed the four digits to memory, put the credit cards and cash into her pocket, then got out into the blasting heat to stuff the wallet into a trash can before she drove on to the Palm Desert Mall.

Like a good scout, Lise left the Caddy in the mall parking lot just as she had found it, motor running, doors unlocked, keys inside. Without a backward glance, she headed straight for I. Magnin. Wardrobe essentials and a beautiful leather-and-brocade suitcase to carry it consumed little more than an hour. She signed for purchases alternately as Mrs. Henry LeBeau or H. G. LeBeau as she alternated the credit cards. She felt safe doing it; in Magnin's, no one ever dared ask for ID.

Time was a problem, and so was cash enough to carry through the next few days, until she could safely use other resources.

As soon as Henry got himself pulled together, she knew he would report his cards lost. She also knew he wouldn't have the balls to confess the circumstances under which the cards got away from him, so she wasn't worried about the police. But once the cards were reported, they would be useless. How much longer would it take him? she wondered.

From a teller machine, she pulled the two-hundred-dollar cash advance limit off the MasterCard, then used the card a last time to place another call.

"You're worried," she said into the receiver. "You have that meeting tonight, and I have distracted you. You have a problem, because if I'm not around to sign the final papers, everything falls apart. Now you're caught in a bind: you can't stand up the congressman and you can't let me get away, and you sure as hell can't be in two places at once. What are you going to do?"

"This is insane." The old fury was in his voice this time. "Where are you?"

"Don't leave the house. Don't even think about it. I'll know if you do. I'll see the lie in your eyes. I'll smell it on every lying word that comes out of your mouth." It was easy; the words just came, like playing back an old, familiar tape. The words did sound funny to her, though, coming out of her own mouth. She wondered how he came up with such garbage and, more to the point, how he had persuaded her over the years that death could be any worse than living under his dirty thumb.

The true joy of talking to him over the telephone was having the power to turn him off. She hung up, took a deep breath, blew out the sound of him.

In the soft soil of a planter next to the phone bank, she dug a little grave for the credit card and covered it over.

After a late lunch, accompanied by half a bottle of very cold champagne, Lise had her hair done, darkened back to its original color and cut very short. The beauty parlor receptionist was accommodating, added a hundred dollars to the American Express bill and gave Lise the difference in cash.

Lise had been moderately surprised when the card flew through clearance, but risked using it one last time. From a gourmet boutique, she picked up some essentials of another kind: a few bottles of good wine, a basket of fruit, a variety of expensive little snacks. On her way out of the store, she jettisoned the American Express into a bin of green jelly beans.

Every transaction fed her confidence, assured her she had the courage to go through with the plan that would set her free forever. By the time she had finished her chores, her accumulation of bags was almost more than she could carry, and she was exhausted. But she felt better than she had for a very long time.

When she headed for the mall exit on the far side from where she had left Mr. Clean's Cadillac, Lise was not at all sure what would happen next. She still had presentiments of doom; she still looked over her shoulder and at reflections of the crowd in every window she passed. Logic said she was safe; conditioning kept her wary, kept her moving.

Hijacking a car with its motor running had worked so well once, she decided to try it again. She had any number of prospects to choose from. The mall's indoor ice-skating rink—bizarrely, the rink overlooked a giant cactus garden—and the movie theater complex next to it, meant parents waiting at the curb for kids. Among that row of cars, Lise counted three with motors running, air-conditioning purring, and no drivers in sight.

Lise considered her choices: a Volvo station wagon, a small Beemer, and a teal-blue Jag. She ran through "eeny, meeny," though she had targeted the Jag right off; the Jag was the first car in the row.

Bags in the backseat, Lise in the driver's seat and pulling away from the curb before she had the door all the way shut. After a stop on a side street to pack her new things into the suitcase, she drove straight to the Palm Springs airport. She left the Jag in a passenger loading zone and, bags in hand, rushed into the terminal like a tourist late for a flight.

She stopped at the first phone.

"You've checked, haven't you?" she said when he picked up. "You sent your goons to look in on me. You know I'm out. We're so close, I know everything you've done. I can hear your thoughts running through my head. You're thinking the deal is dead without me. And I'm in another time zone."

"You won't get away from me."

"I think you're angry. If I don't correct you when you have bad thoughts, you'll ruin everything."

"Stop it."

She looked at her nails, kept her voice flat. "You're everything to me. I'd kill you before I let you go."

"Please, Lise." His voice had a catch, almost like a sob, when she hung up.

She left the terminal by a different door, came out at the cab stand, where a single cab waited. The driver looked like a cousin of the Indians at the bingo palace, and because of the nature of the meeting scheduled that night, she hesitated. In the end, she handed the cabbie her suitcase and gave him the address of a hotel in downtown Palm Springs, an address she had memorized a long time ago.

"Pretty dead over there," the driver said, fingering the leather grips of her bag. "Hard to get around without a car when you're so far out. I can steer you to nicer places closer in. Good rates off season, too."

"No, thank you," she said.

He talked the entire way. He asked more questions than she answered, and made her feel uneasy. Why should a stranger need to know so much? Could the driver possibly be a plant sent to bring her back? Was the conversation normal chitchat? That last question bothered her: she had been cut off for so long, would she know normal if she met it head-on?

When the driver dropped her at a funky old place on the block behind the main street through Palm Springs, she was still wary. She waited until he was gone before she picked up her bag and walked inside.

Off season, the hotel felt empty. The manager was old enough to be her mother; a desert woman with skin like a lizard and tiny black eyes.

"I need a room for two nights," Lise told her.

The manager handed her a registration card. "Put it on a credit card or cash in advance?"

Lise paid cash for the two nights and gave the woman a fifty-dollar deposit for the use of the telephone.

"It's quiet here," the manager said, handing over a key. "Too hot this time of year for most people."

"Quiet is what I'm counting on," Lise said. "I'm not expecting any calls, but if someone asks for me, I'd appreciate it if you never heard of me."

When the manager smiled, her black eyes nearly disappeared among the folds of dry skin. "Man trouble, honey?"

"Is there another kind?"

"From my experience, it's always either a man or money. And from the look of you," the manager said, glancing at the suitcase and the gourmet shop's handled bag, "I'd put my nickel on the former. Don't worry, honey, I didn't get a good look at you, and I already forgot your name."

The name Lise wrote on the registration card was the name on a bottle of chardonnay in her bag: Rutherford Hill.

The hotel was built like an old adobe ranch house, with thick walls and rounded corners, Mexican tile on the floors, dark, open-beamed ceilings. Lise's room was a bit threadbare, but it was larger, cleaner, nicer than she had expected for the price. The air conditioner worked, and there was a kitchenette with a little, groaning refrigerator for her wine. For the first time in five years, she had her own key, and used it to lock the door from the inside.

From her tiny balcony Lise could see both the pool in the patio below and the rocky base of Mount San Jacinto a quarter mile away. Already the sun had slipped behind the crest of the mountain, leaving the hotel in blue shade. Finally, Lise was able to smell the real desert, dry sage and blooming oleander, air without exhaust fumes.

A gentle breeze blew in off the mountain. Lise left the window open and lay down on the bed to rest for just a moment. When she opened her eyes again, floating on the cusp between sleep and wakefulness, the room was washed in soft lavender light—hot, but fragrant with the flowers on the patio below. She could hear a fountain somewhere, now and then voices at a distance. For the first time in a long time, she didn't go straight to the door and listen for breathing on the other side.

Lise slipped into the new swimsuit. A little snug in the rear—she hadn't taken time to try it on before she bought it. She needed the ice pick she found on the sink to free the ice in the trays so she could fill the paper ice bucket. She liked the heavy feel of the tool. While she opened a bottle of wine and cut some fruit and cheese, she made a call.

"Sunset will be exactly eight thirty-two. No moon tonight. Rattlesnakes love a moonless night. You better stay indoors, or you might get bitten."

"What is your game?"

"Your game. I'm a quick learner. Remember when you said that? I think I have all your moves down. Let's see how they play."

"You're a rookie, Lise. You won't make it in the big leagues. And every game I play, baby, is the big one." He'd had some time to get over the initial surprise and anger, so he was back on the offensive. He scared her, but because he couldn't touch her, her resolve held firm as she listened to him. "You'll be back, Lise. You'll take a few hard ones to the head and realize how cold and cruel that world out there is. You'll beg me to take you in and watch over you again. You can be mad at me all you want, but it isn't my fault you're such a princess you can't find your way across the street alone. Blame your asshole father for spoiling you. If it wasn't for me—"

"If it wasn't for you, my father would be alive," she said, cutting off his windup. "I have the proof with me."

The moment of silence told her she had hit home. She hung up.

Lise swam in the small pool until she felt clean again, until the heat and the sweat and the layer of fine sand had all been washed away, until the warm, chlorinated water had bleached away the fevered touch of Henry LeBeau. Some of her new hair color was bleached away too; it left a shadow on the towel when she got out and dried off.

Lise poured a bathroom tumbler full of straw-colored wine and stretched out on a chaise beside the pool. There was still some blue in the sky when the manager came out to switch on the pool lights.

"Sure was a hot one." The manager nursed a drink of her own. "Course, till October they're pretty much all hot ones. Let me know when you're finished with the pool. Sun heats it up so much that every night I let out some of the water and replace it with cold. Otherwise I'll have parboiled guests on my hands."

"How many guests are in the hotel?" Lise asked.

"Just you, honey." The manager drained her glass. "One guest is one more than I had all last week."

Lise offered her the tray of cheese. "Can you sit down for a minute? Have a little happy hour with the registered guests."

"I don't mind." The manager pulled up a chaise next to Lise and let Lise fill her empty glass with chardonnay. "I have to say, off season it does get lonely now and then. We used to close up from Memorial Day to Labor Day—the whole town did. We're more year-round now. Hell, there's talk we'll have gambling soon and become the new Vegas."

"Vegas is noisy."

"Vegas is full of crooks." The manager nibbled some cheese. "I wouldn't mind having my rooms booked up again. But the high rollers would stay in the big new hotels and I'd get their hookers and pushers. Who needs that?"

Lise sipped from her glass and stayed quiet. The manager sighed as she looked up into the darkening sky. "Was a time when this place hopped with Hollywood people and their carryings-on. Liberace and a bunch of them had places just up the road here, you know. We used to get the overflow, and were they ever a wild crowd. I miss them. That set has moved on east, fancier places like Palm Desert. I still get an old-timer now and then, but most of my guests are Canadian snowbirds. They start showing up around Thanksgiving, spend the winter. Nice bunch, but awful tame." She winked at Lise. "Tame, but easier to deal with than Vegas hookers."

"I'm sure," Lise said.

With a thoughtful tilt to her head, the manager looked again, and more closely, at Lise. "I'm pretty far off the beaten track. How'd you ever find my place?"

"I passed the hotel when I was up here visiting. It seemed so . . ." Lise refilled their glasses. "It seemed peaceful."

Lise could feel the manager's shiny black eyes on her. "You okay, honey?"

Lise held up the empty bottle. "I'm getting there."

"That kind of medicine is only going to last so long. It's none of my business, but you want to talk about it?"

"I'm sure you've heard it all before. Long-suffering wife skips out on asshole husband."

"I've not only heard it, I've lived it. Twice." The manager put her weathered hand on Lise's bare knee and smiled sweetly. "You're going to be fine. Just give it some time."

The wine, fatigue, the sweet concern on the old woman's face all combining, Lise felt the cracks inside open up and let in some light. The last time anyone had shown her genuine concern had been five years ago, when her father was still alive. There was a five-year accumulation of moss on her father's marble headstone. Lise began to cry softly.

The manager pulled a packet of tissues out of her pocket. "Atta girl. Let the river flow."

Lise laughed then.

"Does he know where you are?"

Lise shook her head. "Not yet."

"Not yet?"

"Given time, he'll find me. He always does. No matter how far I run, he can find me. He's a powerful man with powerful friends."

"What are you going to do?"

Lise shrugged, though she knew very well. The answer was in the bag upstairs in the closet.

"Well, don't you worry, honey. No one knows about this old place. And I already told you, I don't remember what you look like and I don't recall your name." The manager picked up the empty bottle and looked at the Rutherford Hill label, sly humor folding the corners of her creased face. "Though come to think of it, the name does have a familiar ring."

The sun set at exactly 8:32. Lise showered and changed into long khakis and a pale-peach shirt, both in tones of the desert floor. She took her bag out of the closet and held it on her lap while she waited for the last reflected light of the day to fade.

The big story on the local TV news was what the manager had been talking about, the growing controversy over the proposal to build a Vegas-style casino on

Tahquitz Indian tribal land at the southern city limits of Palm Springs. A congressional delegation had come to town to investigate. As the videotaped congressmen, wearing sober gray and big smiles, paraded across the barren hillside site, Lise felt chilled; her husband, wearing his own big smile, was among the entourage. She knew why he was in town and who he would be meeting with. But she hadn't expected to see him before . . .

She pulled the bag closer against her and checked the clock beside the bed. If the clock was correct, he had nearly run out of time.

When Lise walked downstairs, she could see the flickering light of a television behind the front desk, could hear the manager moving around and further coverage of the big story spieling across the empty lobby. Quietly, Lise went out through the patio, the bag hanging heavily from her shoulder.

Maybe rattlesnakes do like a moonless night, she thought. But they hate people and slither away pretty fast. Lise walked along a sandy path that paralleled the road, feeling the stored heat in the earth soak through her sneakers. Palms rustled overhead like the rattle of a snake and set her on edge.

Lise slipped on a pair of surgical gloves and, being excruciatingly careful not to disturb the beautiful, five-year-old set of prints on the barrel, took the .380 out of her bag, pumped a round into the chamber in case of emergency, and walked on.

The house where the meeting would take place had belonged to her father. Before her marriage, she used to drive out on weekends and school vacations to visit him. After her marriage, after her father's funeral, her husband had taken the place over to use when he had deals to make in the desert. Now and then, when he couldn't make other arrangements for her, Lise had come along. It had been during a recent weekend, when she was banished to the bedroom during a business meeting, that Lise had figured out a way to get free of him. Forever.

The house sat in a shallow box canyon at the end of

the same street the hotel was on. Her father had built the house in the Spanish style, a long string of rooms that all opened onto a central patio. Like the hotel, it had thick walls to keep out the worst of the heat. And like the hotel, like a fort, it was very quiet.

All the lights were on. Lise knew that for a meeting this delicate, there would be no entourage. Inside the house, there would be only three people: the non-English-speaking housekeeper, Lise's husband, and the congressman. She knew the routine well; the congressman was as much a part of her husband's inheritance from her father as Lise and the house were.

Outside, there was a guard on the front door and one on the back patio, standing away from the windows so that his presence wouldn't offend the congressman. Both of the guards were big and ugly, snakes of another kind, and more intimidating than they were smart. By circling wide, Lise got past the man in front, made it to the edge of the patio before she was seen. It wasn't the hired muscle who spotted her first.

Luther, her father's old rottweiler guard dog, ambled across the patio to greet Lise. She pushed his head aside to keep him from muzzling her crotch, made him settle for a head scratch.

The guard, Rollmeyer, hand on his holstered gun butt, hit her with the beam of his flashlight, smiled when he recognized who she was. Part of his job was forestalling interruptions, so he walked over to her without calling out.

Lise hadn't been sure about what would happen when she got to this point, couldn't know who the guard would be or how he would react to her. How much he might know. She had gone over several possibilities and decided to let the guard lead the way into this wilderness.

"Didn't know you was here, ma'am." Rollmeyer kept his voice low, standing close beside her on the soft sand. "They're going to be a while yet. You want me to take you around front, let you in that way?"

"The house is so hot. I'll wait out here until they're finished." She had her hand inside her bag, trading the automatic for something more appropriate to the situation. "Been a long time, Rollmeyer. Talk to me. How've you been?"

"Can't complain."

Hand in the bag, she wrapped her fingers around the wooden handle of the hotel ice pick. "Don't you have a hug for an old friend?"

Rollmeyer, whose job was to follow orders, and whose inclination was to cop any feel he could, seemed confused for just a moment. Then he opened his big arms and took a step toward her. She used the forward thrust of his body to help drive the ice pick up into his chest. Holding on to the handle, she could feel his heart beating around the slender blade, pump, pump, pump, before he realized something had happened to him. By then it was too late. She stepped back, withdrawing the blade, met his dumb gaze for another three-count, watched the dark trickle spill from the tiny hole in his shirt, before he fell, face-down. His eyes were still open, sugared with grains of white sand, when she left him.

Luther stayed close to her, his bulk providing a shield while she lay on her belly beside the pool and rinsed away Rollmeyer's blood from her glove and from the ice pick. With the dog, she ducked back into the shelter of the oleander hedge to watch the meeting proceed inside.

Creatures of habit, her husband and the congressman were holding to schedule. By the time Lise arrived, they had eaten dinner in the elegant dining room and the housekeeper had cleared the table, leaving the two men alone with coffee and brandy. Genteel preliminaries over, Lise's husband went to the silver closet and brought out a large briefcase, which he set on the table. He opened the case and, smiling like Santa, turned it to show the contents to the congressman, showed them to Lise also in the reflection in the mirror over the antique sideboard: money in bank wrappers, three-quarters of a million dollars of it, the going price for a crucial vote on the federal level—the vote in question of course having to do with permits for Vegas-style casinos on tribal land.

There was a toast with brandy snifters, handshakes, then goodbyes. Once business had been taken care of, she knew her husband would leave immediately and the congressman would stay over for his special treat.

Lise dropped low behind the hedge when her husband, smiling still, crossed the patio and headed for the garage. She had the .380 in firing position in case he came looking for Rollmeyer. But he didn't. He went straight to the garage, started his Rolls.

As soon as he was out of sight, Lise moved quickly. Her husband would back down the drive to the road and signal the call girl who was waiting there in her own car, the call girl who always came as part of the congressman's package. Lise knew she had to be finished within the time it would take for the whore to drive into the vacant slot in the garage, freshen her makeup, spray on new perfume, plump her cleavage, and walk up to the house.

With Luther lumbering at her side, Lise crept into the dining room through the patio door just as her husband's lights cleared the corner of the house. The congressman had already closed his case of booty and set it on the floor, was just finishing his brandy when she stepped onto the deep carpet.

"Lise, dear," he said, surprised but not displeased to see her. He rose and held out his arms toward her. "I had not expected the pleasure of your company."

Lise said nothing as she walked up within a few feet of him. Her toe was touching the case full of money when she raised the .380, took aim the way her father had taught her, and fired a round into the congressman's chest, followed it, as her father had taught her, with a shot into the center of his forehead.

Luther, startled by the noise, began to bark. The housekeeper, in the kitchen, made "ah ah" noises and dropped something on the floor. Lise tucked the gun under the congressman's chest, picked up the case of money, and left.

Behind the hedge again, Lise waited for the call girl to

walk in and help the housekeeper make her discovery. The timing was good. Both women faced each other from their respective doorways, shocked pale, within seconds of the shooting.

Through the quiet, moonless night, Lise walked back to the hotel along the same sandy path. She stowed the case behind a planter near the pool and continued onward a block to place a call.

Rollmeyer would be a complication, but the police could explain him any way they wanted to. Lise dialed 911.

"There's been a shooting," she said. She gave the address, identified the congressman as the victim and her husband as the shooter. Then she went to another phone, further down the street, and made a similar call to the press and to the local TV station.

When she heard the first siren heading up the road to the house, she was mailing an unsigned note to the detective who had investigated her father's death five years ago, a note that explained exactly why her husband and the congressman were meeting in the desert in the middle of the summer and what her husband's motives might be for murder—for two murders. And why the bullets taken from the congressman should be compared with the two taken from her father. And where the assets were hidden. Chapter and verse, a fitting eulogy for a man who would never again see much open sky, whose every movement would be monitored in a place where punishment came swiftly, where he would never, ever have a key to his own door or the right to make the game plans. Trapped, for the rest of his life.

When the note was out of her hand, she finally took off the surgical gloves. Lise raised her face to catch a breeze that was full of sweet, clean desert air, looked up at the extravagance of stars in the moonless sky, and yawned. It was over: agenda efficiently covered, meeting adjourned.

On her way back to the hotel, Lise stopped at an all-night drugstore and bought an ice cream bar with some of Henry LeBeau's money. She ate it as she walked.

The manager was standing in front of the hotel, watching the police and the paramedics speed past, when Lise strolled up.

"Big fuss." Lise stood on the sidewalk with the manager and finished her ice cream. "You told me it was dead around here this time of year."

"It's dead, all right." The manager laughed her dry, lizard laugh. "Lot of old folks out here. Bet you one just keeled over."

Lise watched with her until the coroner's van passed them. Then she took the manager by the arm and walked inside with her.

Lise saw the light of excitement still dancing in the manager's dark eyes. Lise herself was too keyed up to think about sleep. So she said, "I have another bottle of wine in my room. Let's say we have a little nightcap. Talk about crooks and the good old days."

COYOTE PEYOTE

A MIDNIGHT LOUIE ADVENTURE

CAROLE NELSON DOUGLAS

Carole Nelson Douglas has written wonderful novels in several genres—mystery, science fiction, fantasy, and romance.

Here you'll meet her feline detective "Midnight Louie" and his own very special take on Las Vegas and environs.

The "Midnight Louie" adventures are now on their way to becoming bona fide best-sellers, and this tale of shadowy chicanery in the gambling capital will show you why.

▼▼▼▼▼

COYOTE PEYOTE

A LOT OF FOLKS don't realize that Las Vegas is the world's biggest Cubic Zirconia set in a vast bezel of sand and sagebrush. Glitz in the Gobi, so to speak.

Sure, most everybody knows that the old town twinkles, but that is all they see, the high-wattage Las Vegas Strip and Glitter Gulch downtown. Millions of annual visitors fly in and out of McCarran Airport on the big silver thunderbirds, commercial or chartered jets, like migratory flocks of junketing gooney birds equipped with cameras and cash.

They land at McCarran Airport, now as glittering a monument to the Vegas mystique as any Strip hotel, with shining rows of slot machines chiming in its metal-mirrored vastness.

Most stick to Las Vegas's advertised attractions and distractions: they soak up sun, stage shows, shady doings of a sexual nature, and the comparatively good clean fun in the casinos that pave the place. To them, Las Vegas is the holodeck of the good starship *Enterprise* in the twentieth century. You go there; it is like no place on earth; you leave and you're right back where you were, maybe poorer but at least dazzled for your dough.

Nobody thinks of Las Vegas as a huge, artificial oasis stuck smack wattle-and-daub in the middle of the Wild West wilderness like a diamond in the navel of a desert dancing girl. Nobody sees its gaudy glory as squatting on the onetime ghost-dancing grounds of the southern Paiute Indians. Hardly anyone ever harks back to the area's hairy mining-boom days, which are only evoked now by hokey casino names like The Golden Nugget.

Nobody ever figures that the sea of desert all around

the pleasure island of Las Vegas is good for anything but ignoring.

I must admit that I agree. I know Las Vegas from the bottom up, and some in this urban jukebox know me: Midnight Louie, dude-about-town and undercover expert. The only sand I like to feel between my toes is in a litter box, and I am not too fond of artificial indoor facilities at that. I prefer open air and good, clean dirt.

I prefer other amenities, such as the gilded carp that school in the decorative pond behind the Crystal Phoenix Hotel and Casino, the classiest hostelry on the Strip, hence carp so pricey that they are called koi. I call them dinner.

For a time I was unofficial house detective at the Crystal Phoenix, and the carp pond was my prime-time hangout. It is always handy to locate an office near a good diner. Location, location, location, say the real estate agents, and I am always open to an apt suggestion from an expert.

I hang out my shingle near the calla lilies that border the carp pond. I do not literally hang out a shingle, you understand. The word simply gets around where Midnight Louie is to be found, and the word on the street is clear on two subjects. One is that Midnight Louie will not look with favor upon any individual messing with his friends at the Crystal Phoenix, whether two- or four-footed. The other is that Midnight Louie is not averse to handling problems of a delicate nature now and again, provided payment is prompt and sufficient.

I am no lightweight, topping twenty pounds soaking wet, and I didn't weigh onto the scales just yesterday, either. Yet my hair is still a glossy raven black, my tourmaline-green eyes can see 20/20, and my ears know when to perk up and when to lie back and broadcast a warning. (Some claim my kind have no color sense, but they have never asked us straight out.) I keep my coat in impeccable sheen and my hidden shivs as sharp as the crease in Macho Mario Fontana's bodyguard's pants.

Despite my awesome physical presence, I am a modest

dude who gets along well with everyone—especially if every one of them is female—except for those of the canine persuasion.

This is a family failing. Something about the canine personality invariably raises the hair on the back of our necks, not to mention our spines, and makes our second-most-valuable members stand up and salute.

So you can understand how I feel one day when I am drowsing in my office, due both to a lack of cases and to a surfeit of something fishy for lunch, and I spot a suspicious shadow on the nearest sun-rinsed wall.

The hour is past 6:00 P.M., when Las Vegas hotel pools close faster than a shark's mouth, the better to hustle tourists into the casinos to gamble the night and their grubstakes away. Nobody much of any species is around. Even the carp are keeping low, for reasons that may have something to do with not-so-little me.

So my eyes are slit to half-mast, the sinking sun is sifting through the calla lilies, and life is not too tacky . . . and then, there it is, that unwelcome shadow.

Who could mistake the long, sharp snout, ajar enough to flaunt a nasty serrated edge of fangs, or the huge, long, sharp ears? No doubt about it, this angular silhouette has the avid, hungry outlines of that jackal-headed Egyptian god of the dead, Anubis. (I know something about Egyptian gods, seeing as how a forebear was one of them: Bast. Or Bastet, to be formal. You may have heard of this dude. Or dudette. And you may call me Louie anyway; I do not ride on family connections.)

Right then and there Midnight Louie has a bad-hair day, let me tell you, as I make like a croquet hoop and rise to my feet and the occasion. From the size of the shadow, this is not the largest canine I have ever seen, but it is one serious customer, and it does not take a house detective to figure that out.

"At ease!" the shadow jaws bark out, looking even more lethal. "I am just here on business."

I know better than to relax when I am told to, but I am not one to turn tail and run, either. So I wait.

"You this Midnight Louie?" my sun-shy visitor demands in the same sharp yet gruff voice.

"Who wishes to know?"

"Never mind."

So much for the direct route. I pretend to settle back onto my haunches, but my restless shivs slide silently in and out of my mitts. Unlike the average mutt, I know how to keep quiet.

Above me, a lazy bee buzzes the big yellow calla lily blossoms. I hiccup.

"You do not look like much," my rude visitor says after a bit.

"The opinion may be mutual," I growl back. "Step into the open and we will see."

He does, and I am sorry I asked.

There is no fooling myself. I eye narrow legs with long, curved nails like a mandarin's. I take in eyes as yellow and hard as a bladder stone. The head is even more predatory than I suspected. The body is lean, but hard. The terminal member is as scrawny as a foot-long hot dog and carried low, like a whip.

This dude is a dog, all right, but just barely—no mere domesticated dog but a dingo from the desert. I begin to appreciate how Little Red Riding Hood felt, and I do not even have a grandmother (that I know of) to worry about.

"What can I do for you?" I ask, hoping that the answer is not "Lunch." I do not do lunch with literal predators.

The dude sidles into the shade alongside me. My sniffer almost overdoses on the odor; this bozo has not taken a bath in at least a week, perhaps another reason I dislike the canine type.

He sits beside me under the calla leaves, his yellow eyes searching the vicinity for any sign of life.

"I need a favor," he says.

Well, knock me over with a wolverine. I am all too aware that the dude I am dealing with is normally a breed apart. He and his kind operate on the fringes of civilized

Las Vegas, out in the lawless open desert. Some call them cowardly; others, clever. Certainly they are hated, and hunted. Many are killed. All kill. Among other things.

"I do not do favors for those who practice certain unnatural acts."

"Such as?"

"I hear you and your kin will eat . . . . bugs."

"So will humans," the dude notes calmly.

"That is not all. I also hear that your kind will dine on"—I swallow and try not to let my whiskers quiver—"the dead." Why else was Anubis head jackal of the Underground in ancient Egypt? My visitor looks like a lineal descendant.

"We will, when there is nothing living to eat," he concedes with chilling calm. "In the city, such as we are called refuse managers."

I say nothing, unconvinced.

When sitting, this dude looks exactly like an Egyptian statue, and he gazes idly on the lush, landscaped surroundings, so different from his usual arid turf. I realize that it has taken some nerve and a good deal of courage for this popular pariah to venture into the very heart of Vegas. Just to see me. Well, Midnight Louie is a teensy bit flattered, come to think of it.

"When did you last," he asks, "partake of a bit of mislaid Big-o-Burger from down the street?"

"That is different," I begin.

"Dead meat," he intones relentlessly. "Someone else killed it, and you ate it." The yellow eyes slide my way. I detect a malicious twinkle. "What about the contents of the cans so feverishly hawked at your kind?"

I am not misled; this dude is about as twinkly as the mother-of-pearl handle on a derringer.

"I do my own fishing." I nod at the silent pond. "So what is your problem?"

"Murder." His answer sends a petite shudder through my considerable frame. I was hoping for something minor, like roadrunner attack.

"Who is the victim?"

"Victims."

"How many?"

"Six, so far."

"And the method?"

"Always the same."

"You are talking serial killer here, pal."

"Oh, are we friends?" Another shrewd golden glint. This dude has Bette Davis eyes, when she played the homicidal Baby Jane.

"Business associates," I said firmly. No dude in his right mind would turn down this character. "Who are the victims?"

"My brothers and sisters."

"Oh."

I do not know how to put it that one—or six—dead coyotes are hardly considered murder victims by the majority of the human population, and, face it, humans run this planet.

For now I know this dude, by type if not name: Don Coyote himself, one of an accursed species, with bounty hunters everywhere ready to clip their ears and tails for a few bucks or just the principle of the thing. It does not take a genius to figure out that any suspects for the so-called crime of killing coyotes are legion.

"If you are so smart," I note diplomatically, "you know that it would be easier to find those who *did* kill coyotes than otherwise."

"This case is different," he says sharply. "We are used to the hunters. We have outwitted them more often than not. We survive, if not thrive, and we spread, even while our cousin Gray Wolf clan has been driven to near extinction. We have evaded steel trap and strychnine poison. We are legendary for defying odds. What kills us now is new and insidious. Not just our green young succumb, but those who should know better. This is not the eternal war we wage with both prey and hunter; this is what I said . . . murder."

"That is no surprise, either. You are not exactly Mr. Popularity around here."

His lips peel back from spectacular sharp white teeth, much improved, no doubt, by grinding such roughage as beetle shells and bones. "That is why I seek an emissary."

"Why not try a police dog?"

"Frankly, your kind is more successful at undercover work. Even a domesticated dog"—his tone is more than condescending, it is majestically indifferent; on this subject we agree—"is handicapped. He is assumed to belong to some human, which attracts notice and sometimes misguided attempts at rescue. Your breed, on the other hand, although equally commonplace in human haunts, is known to walk alone by sly and secret ways and is more often ignored."

I shrug and adjust one of my sharp-looking black leather gloves. "Say I was to accept this commission of yours. What would I get?"

His long red tongue lolls out. I cannot tell if he is grinning or scanning the ground for a conga line of ants. Antipasto in his book, so to speak.

"I am head honcho around here," the coyote ruminates with a certain reluctance, like he is giving away the combination to the family safe. "I keep caches of hidden treasure here and there. If you successfully find—or simply stop—the coyote-killer, I will tell you the whereabouts of one. That would be your payoff."

"How much is it worth?" I demand.

The yellow eyes look right through me. "Beyond price."

"How do I know that?"

"I can only say that humans highly prize these objects."

Hmm. Coyotes are scavengers of the desert. I speculate on the array of inedible goodies they might run across in the wide Mojave, but silver comes first to mind, perhaps because Jersey Joe Jackson, the high roller who helped build and bilk Vegas in the forties, also hid huge caches of stolen silver dollars both in town and out on the sandy lonesome.

Then there are plain old silver nuggets left over from

mining days. I am not fussy. Or . . . maybe jewels. Stolen jewels. I do not doubt for a minute that this wily old dude knows secrets even the wind-singing sands do not whisper about.

I stand and stretch nonchalantly. "Where do I begin?" For a moment I am eye-to-eye with those ancient ocher orbs.

Then the dude also rises, and vanishes into the dark at the back of the calla lilies. "Follow me to the scene of the crimes."

It is night by the time we get there. I have forgotten that dudes of this type are always hot to trot and can keep it up for miles. After I showed him a quick exit from the city, we were off through the boonies.

Miles of surly sagebrush have passed under my tender tootsie pads when we finally stop for good. I huff and puff and could not blow down a mouse house at the moment, but I was loath to let this dancing dog outpace me.

Although I pride myself on my night vision, all I can spy are a skyful of stars the wizards of the Strip might do well to emulate for sparse good taste, towering Joshua trees with their thick limbs frozen into traffic-cop positions, and a lot of low scrub, much of it barbed like wire. Oh, yes, and the full moon floating overhead like a bowl of warm milk seen from a kitchen countertop, and, occasionally, the moonsheen in the coyote's sun-yellow eyes as he gives me mocking glances.

"I forget," he says, "that the city-bred are easily tired."

"Not in the slightest," I pant, hissing between my teeth. "But how can I study the crime scene in the dark?"

"I thought your breed could see despite the night."

"Not enough for a thorough investigation. Where are we anyway?"

"At an enclave of humans away from the city. My unfortunate brothers and sisters ventured near to snag the errant morsel and were cut down one by one."

"Listen, my kind are not noted for longevity, either, so I dig the problem. Still, what can I do about it?"

"Perhaps you can interview the survivors."

With that he steps back, braces his long legs, and lifts his head until his snout points at the moon. An unearthly howl punctuated by a series of yips emerges from between those awesome teeth.

So it is that in a few moments I am making house calls on a series of coyote families. While my guide has not stuck around for the painstaking interviews, soon an unsavory picture is emerging: the victims were indeed primo survivors, too savvy to be silently slain in the current manner.

I speak to Sings-with-Soul, the winsome widow of Yellow Foot-Feathers, the first to be found dead.

I no more advocate cross-species hanky-panky than I do bug-biting, but I must admit that Sings-with-Soul has particularly luminous amber eyes and a dainty turn of foreleg, from what I can tell in the dark.

After several interviews, I remain in the dark myself. Unfortunately, although they sometimes run in impressive packs, coyotes mostly hunt alone. The stories are depressingly similar.

Yellow Foot-Feathers did not return to the den after a night's prowl. When Sings-with-Soul left her kits with a friend to go searching, she followed his scent to find him dead, unmarked by any weapon, beside a stunted Joshua tree.

Sand Stalker was out rounding up a delicacy or two for his mate, Moonfinder, and their two helpless kits. In the morning, his body was found a three-minute trot toward the setting sun from Yellow Foot-Feathers'.

Windswift, a two-year-old female, died a four-minute trot away, two days later. The same distance farther on lay Weatherworn, an elder of the tribe and by far its wiliest member.

"We are used to the high death toll of our kind," Sings-with-Soul tells me with mournful anger, "but these deaths are systematic beyond the bounty hunters' traps and poison, or the so-called sportsmen with guns, or even the angry ranchers who accuse us of raiding their live-stock."

I nod. It is not a pretty picture, and I am used to the statistics of my own kind who share the supposed shelter of civilization. Four out of five cuddly kittens born die within a year, often within the environs of a death compound. Still, there is something demonic about these serial slayings. Even in the dark I sense a pattern.

By the wee hours I have settled beside a prickly poppy, counting on my choice of plant companion to keep away such night-roving characters as skunks, large furry spiders who are older than Whistler's mother, lizards, and snakes, although I would not mind meeting a passing mouse or two, for it has been some time since my last snack.

The coyotes have vanished back into the brush. From time to time they break into heartbroken howls that some might take for the usual coyote chorus but which I know express rage and sorrow at their helplessness to stop the slaughter.

I wait for daylight, eager to begin investigating for real. My curiosity has been roused, despite myself. As long as I am all the way out here in this desolate wilderness, I might as well earn my tempting coyote cache and maybe keep the young Foot-Feathers kits from the same fate as their father.

Despite the desert chill and the forbidding terrain, I manage to doze off. I awake to feel the sun pouring down on me like hot melted butter, softening my night-stiff bones.

I hear an odd tapping sound, as of someone gently rapping, rapping on a door to rouse me. Confused, I force my eyelids open, preparing for an onslaught of bright light.

In the sudden slit of my pupils I see a sight to curl the hair on a bronze cat—a whole city, a settlement, of buildings against the bright-blue morning sky. I sniff sawdust and stucco. I see pale pine skeletons rising into the sky.

I turn so fast I snag my rear member on a prickly poppy. Behind me extends the endless desert I imagined in the dark of last night when I interviewed the coyote crew. Did not their lost ones fall near where we stood, where I stand now?

I turn back to the hub of activity. A banshee saw whines, while men with bandannas around their foreheads and sleeveless T-shirts or bare muscled chests as tan as a Doberman move their blue-jeaned legs hither and yon, climbing, pounding, clamoring.

Stunned, I stick to basics. *A three-minute trot toward the setting sun.* I turn westward and start trotting, allowing for a difference in speed and stride. Indeed, I am soon sniffing a patch of sweet-smelling desert alyssum on which a stronger, sweeter, sicklier scent has settled recently.

The body is gone, no doubt removed by human pallbearers, but the land remembers. Sand Stalker's last stand.

I move on, tracing the path of death and finding the lingering scent where I expect. At no time does my route veer away from the huge clot of buildings under construction. The dead coyotes begin to form a ritual circle around the project, like guardian spirits slaughtered to protect the site.

The head coyote is right. Something stinks in this sequence of events, and it is not merely death.

I dust off my topcoat, quell my protesting empty stomach, and stalk casually toward the humans and their works.

Soon I am treading dusty asphalt, walking on roads, however primitive. Beyond the construction site I discover curving vistas of completed edifices—sprawling two-story buildings big enough to be strip shopping centers, sitting amid fresh-sodded grass. Sprinkler systems spray droplets on the turf like a holy-water blessing. After a while I realize that these erections are each single-family homes.

In an hour's stroll I have mastered the place. I am in

the midst of Henderson, Nevada, touring its vaunted housing boom. I have heard that this bedroom community just a hop, skip, and commute southeast of Las Vegas is jumping, but I've never had occasion to see for myself before.

No wonder the coyotes are goners. They were trespassing on some high-end new real estate of the first order. I sit under one of the paired yucca trees that mark the development's entrance to read the billboard, which features colors like trendy turquoise, orange, and lavender, bordered by a chorus line of alternating jalapeño peppers and howling coyotes.

PEYOTE SKIES: A JIMMY RAY RUGGLES PLANNED COMMUNITY, announces angular lettering meant to resemble the zigzags on a Native American blanket. Jimmy Ray's smiling photo discreetly anchors one corner of the sign. Although it is a well-kept secret that I can read, I am having no trouble in looking illiterate as I squint to decipher the tortured script. This is real detective work!

After much study, I know that Peyote Skies is an ecologically engineered environment that sets up no artificial barriers like fences between nature and the community. The words "Sante Fe-like serenity," "untrammeled nature," and "all the amenities" are invoked. No wonder. I have heard that refugees from the Quaker State of California are flocking to places north, south, and west of their unhappy home. Apparently, Henderson is providing a haven for escaping excesses.

I stroll the streets of Peyote Skies unquestioned, even unremarked, just as the coyote predicted. Perhaps my dramatic dark good looks seem right at home in the plethora of pastel colors painting every visible surface. Despite my empty stomach, I am soon ready to puke at the amount of dusty orange, lavender, and Peyote Skies turquoise I am forced to digest.

Earlier I remarked that I was not born yesterday. I am also pretty streetwise, so I know that "peyote" names a blue-green cactus whose flowers produce beads that dry into little buttons of mescal. Bite into one of these babies, and you are soon seeing visions as hallucinatory as the after-dinner-mint-colored development before me.

Mescaline's mind-tripping properties were, and are, used for Native American religious rites but are otherwise strictly illegal. I do not know if the Paiutes around here were, or are, into mescaline, but I do know that less native Americans definitely are.

As for myself, I take a little nip now and again but keep off the hard stuff in any form. Obviously, the designer of this mishmash was not so restrained.

The completed houses are occupied but mostly deserted, looking like pages from decorating magazines. Kids are at school, husbands and wives are at work or at play.

I find it macabre that while dead coyotes litter the back fringes of this theme-park development, the front doors and mailboxes bear the colorful image of the howling coyote made ad nauseam familiar of late on jewelry, coffee mugs, and fabrics.

Perhaps the surrounding color scheme accounts for the en masse howling, but, like the desert itself, these coyotes are silent, despite their posture. I do not blame them for complaining; my own kind's image has been appropriated for a panoply of merchandise we would not scrape kitty litter over. Humans are especially sentimental about creatures they kill.

Because of the lack of "artificial barriers," I can stroll around these palatial joints unimpeded, although I spot a ton of security service signs and even more discreet warning labels on windows.

The backyards are as manicured as the front, then end abruptly where the desert begins. I move to the verge between green and greige, my sand-blasted pads relishing the cushy emerald carpet of grass. Then a door cracks behind me. I turn to stare.

Something small, blond, and fluffy is flouncing toward me over the grass, barking. I glance to the house across sixty yards of crew-cut Bermuda. It is so distant that Fideaux's high, affected yips are beyond earshot, but I believe I hear a frantic human voice fruitlessly urging the little escapee homeward.

So I show my teeth and hold my place until Fideaux is within pouncing distance. It stops to tilt a head as adorably curly-topped as Shirley Temple's. It sits on its little hind end. It drops its tiny jaw. The big, bad, black pussycat is supposed to be scrambling up a tree or over a fence, but there are only Joshua trees here and they sting like hell, and there is no fence, just desert and the Great Sandy Beyond.

Fideaux's irritating yaps become a whimper.

"You," I tell it savagely, "are coyote meat."

Then I turn and stroll onto the sand—ouch! Still, it is a dramatic exit. I glance back to see Blondie barreling back to the rambling deck, whimpering for Mommy.

Then I ramble myself, out front to civilization, where I finally hitch a ride on a landscaping truck back to Vegas proper. (Or improper.)

I cannot decide which I am happier to escape: the sere, sharp-fanged desert of cactus and coyote, or the rotted-fruit shades of the faux-Southwest landscape at Peyote Skies.

After taking a dip in the carp pool, I avoid the vicinity and any new visits by strange dudes with odd-colored eyes by heading for a secret retreat of mine. Now that I have scouted the situation, I am ready to do some deep thinking.

Luckily, I know just the place: the ghost suite at the Crystal Phoenix. This is room 713, which used to be a permanent residence for Jersey Joe Jackson back in the forties, when the Crystal Phoenix was called the Joshua Tree Hotel. Jersey Joe didn't die until the seventies, by which time he was reputed to be a broke and broken man—and, worse, completely forgotten.

The empty suite stands furnished as when he died, partly because the current management recognized it as a snapshot of an earlier era that should not be destroyed, partly because certain parties claim to have seen a thin, silver-haired dude dancing through the crack in the door now and again.

I have spent many unmolested hours here in recent years. While I may have glimpsed an odd slash of light through the wooden blinds, I cannot say yea or nay to the notion of a ghost. No one bothers me here, but I have never found the door locked to my velvet touch.

I settle on my favorite seat, a chartreuse-green satin chair that happens to make a stunning backdrop for one of my coloring. I do my best thinking when I look particularly impressive, although I am often accused of simply sleeping at such times.

The silence is as potent as Napoleonic brandy (not that I have ever sampled such a delicacy, but I do have imagination). While I lap it, with my eyes closed and my claws kneading the chartreuse satin, certain surly facts darken my mind.

First, how. The lack of marks upon the bodies suggests poison. The victims' wary familiarity with strychnine, the poison of choice for coyote hunters, suggests another toxin. I do not rule out snakebite. It is possible that the hustle and bustle of Peyote Skies has disturbed nests of venomous critters and driven them to the boundaries of the development, which would explain the neat alignment of the bodies.

Snakebite, however, usually results in swollen limbs, and the survivors detected nothing of the sort.

All right. Say the perpetrator is the usual snake of the human sort. Say some other poison was used, which would take in the wiliest coyote.

Why? What is the motive? It cannot be for pelts, because the animals were left where they fell. It cannot be the ancient antipathy of sheep ranchers toward the ignoble coyote, because you can bet that the surrounding land, however vacant at the moment, is all owned by developers like the creators of Peyote Skies. Developments multiply around each other like fire ant mounds, gulping up huge tracts of land.

Round and round I go, mentally retracing the semi-circular path of the coyote corpses, my eyes always upon the grotesque hub of housing hubris and hullabaloo whose boundaries are marked with death.

My contact coyote, who was oddly shy about giving his name, no doubt due to a criminal past, said that nearby families have been warned to avoid the area. However, no number of nightly howls will warn off passersby, given the wide range of the average desert dog.

More coyotes could die, not that anybody much would notice, any more than anyone has much noted the current crop of dead coyotes. But I have no personal grudge against Don Coyote, and I do have a deep desire to get a piece of a coyote cache.

Odious as the notion is, I must return to the crime scene—and Peyote Skies—and set up a stakeout. Maybe I can talk Sings-with-Soul into leaving her kits with a sitter and keeping me some feminine company. An ace detective can always use a leggy secretary for dramatic effect.

It is no dice on the dame, but I do get the loan of Happy Hocks, a half-grown pup with time on his tail. The head coyote himself is nowhere to be seen. I hope he does not pull this vanishing act when it is time to reward Midnight Louie for successfully concluding the investigation. After being forced to hop a ride on a gravel truck to get to the site, I am not in a good mood.

"Keep down and out of sight when I say so," I instruct the gangly youngster.

"Yes, sir, Mr. Midnight. I want to be a famous crime solver like you when I grow up. I will be as quiet as a cactus."

I doubt it. There is too much vinegaroon in this punk.

We work our way closer to the settlement, Happy Hocks bounding hither and thither among the brush and occasionally running out whimpering to rub his snout in the sand.

"Catclaw," I diagnose as I survey the particular cactus patch he has just learned to leave alone. "Did not some elder tell you about those spines?"

"Naw, we have to learn some things on our own, Mr. Midnight." Happy sneezes and then grins idiotically.

"Well, stay out of the flora and stick close to me. You might learn something really useful."

He bounds over and keeps me pretty tight company, close enough so I can see him lower his nosy snout to the sand again, snuffle, and come up smacking an unidentified insect. It is a good thing I skipped breakfast, or I might have lost it right there. I am far from squeamish about the unadorned facts of life, since I have eaten a lot of meals raw in my time, but I draw the line at insects.

I can see that it will be a long day, yet as we creep on our bellies toward the completed houses, plain awe quashes a lot of Happy Hocks's more annoying qualities.

"What are these painted canyons, Mr. Midnight?" he asks.

I appreciate a suitably humble tone of address. "Houses, Happy. Modernistic mansions for idle humans with tons of money and a *soup's-on* of social conscience." (I like to expose the young to a little French.)

"Dens, Mr. Midnight?"

"Right. Dens . . . and exercise rooms and wet bars and state-of-the-art kitchens."

Happy frowns at my laundry list of amenities, being a country boy, but grins again. "Dens. Are there kits inside?"

"Sure. Little kits and big kits."

He frowns again. "Is that green that surrounds the dens some fancy water, for safety?"

"No, my lad. That is a moat of the finest Bermuda grass, imported to cushion the humans' bare feet and clipped to permit a few practice golf balls."

"It grows, and they cut it?"

"Strange behavior, I know."

"Can I walk on it?"

I eye the house before us, which is not the one that hosts the obnoxious Fideaux. "I guess it is okay, kid. Just here at the edge, though."

So he trots along the sharp demarcation line between desert and cushy carpet of grass, his long legs pumping on the Bermuda.

"It is cool and soft," he says with another grin.

"But not for you." I gesture him back on the sand with me. If anyone is going to patrol on the emerald plush, it will be the senior member of this team.

Happy Hocks gives a yip only slightly less annoying than Fideaux's and forgets himself enough to bound over to a clump of beaver-tail cactus.

"Watch those spines!" I warn again, beginning to sound like a nanny.

"Look, Mr. Midnight, bonanza!"

I trot over, hoping for a clue. Is it possible the amiable idiot could have stumbled across something important?

I see a bright patch of tissue paper on the ground. Orange. Then my less lengthy nose finally catches a whiff of what roped Happy's attention. The paper is a Big-o-Burger wrapper. Nestled at its center is a nice bit of bun, burger, and exclusive Big-o-Burger Better Barbe-Q Sauce, which I have been known to sample myself.

Happy steps politely back from his find. "You can have it, Mr. Midnight."

Do I detect a glint of hero worship in those bright yellow eyes? Certainly it is unheard of for a coyote to share with a dude of another species, and usually even with his own.

My nose tells me that the Better Barbe-Q Sauce is permeating a thick slab of meat, which is cooked but is also indubitably dead. I am about to partake, when I recall my conversation with the head coyote about superior species spurning dead meat. I cannot go back on my avowed position, at least not within witnessing distance by any of the coyote clan, so I shake a mitt and mince back from the find.

"Go ahead, kid. I prefer sushi."

"Fish!" he says in disgust, wrinkling his long nose. Happy Hocks nails the remaining Big-o-Burger with one bite.

We continue our rounds, observing the activity. Happy Hocks is full of wonder at the ways of humans. I know their ways and am watching for any that are out of the ordinary.

Not much happens here. Any kids too young to be in school are kept in from the heat and nearby construction dangers. I see faces of my kind peering out from windows, never looking as downcast as I would expect at their imprisoned lot.

Except for the escaping Fideaux, I do not spy any dogs, no loss to me personally, except that this breed must go out, whether free or on lines, to do their disgusting duty.

Imagine, leaving such unwanted items in plain view for someone else to pick up and bury! Such vile habits explain why the canine family occupies a lower rung of the evolutionary ladder than the feline.

I express my disdain to Happy, who frowns again.

"But, Mr. Midnight, if we of coyote clan were to bury our water and dung, we would not know where we had been, or who had been there first. We would have no way to mark territory."

"Who would want such tainted territory?" I mutter.

But I get to thinking. Maybe this whole case *is* a matter of marking territory.

In a couple of hours I have toured as much of Peyote Skies as I can stand. I have also had enough of Happy Hocks's prattle. I send the kid home, watching his yellow coat blend instantly with the dung-shaded desert. Our discussion of bathroom habits has definitely colored my outlook.

With relief, I take up a lone outpost under a newly planted oleander bush—no seedlings for these Peyote Skies folks, only expensive full-grown plantings.

Three houses down, workmen hammer, saw, and shout. Here all is peaceful. Too peaceful. Although I welcome a world without dogs, I am uneasy at the absence of these popular house pets in this development. The entire outdoors is dogless, except for the undomesticated coyotes, and any of those that came within howling distance of here are dead.

Is Peyote Skies too pristine for dogs? I know some housing developments rule against many things.

Human voices disturb my reverie. I cringe deeper into the oleander shade. A woman exits the house, wearing slacks and sweater in the same putrid shades that saturate the development. Sure enough, a turquoise coyote is howling on her chest.

The man wears a suit, but the color is pale and the jacket is open. "Which sprinkler isn't working, Mrs. Ebert?"

"More than one, a whole line, down by the oleanders."

"Oh, at the edge of the lot."

He walks my way, but he does not see me, because I am dark as dirt and I shut my eyes to thin green slits. His foot kicks at the small silver spikes poking up like lethal flowers through the expensive grass.

"Looks like a line's out, Mrs. Ebert." He bends down to fiddle with a sprinkler, but his eyes are skipping over the edge of the desert so close you can smell the sweet alyssum on the hot, dry breeze. At least coyotes use room deodorizers.

He is big, overweight like a middle-aged busy man will get, with a fleshy face too tan for an officebound dude. He has thinning brown hair and dirt-brown eyes, sneaky brown eyes. The short hairs on my shoulder blades begin to rise. He acts like he knows someone is watching, but he never notices me, and I am even gladder of that fact now.

His back still to the woman, he reaches into his pocket to pull out something, maybe a handkerchief. Sweat beads on the hairless patches atop his head. His mouth quirks into what would be a grin if he were happy. He looks nervous, intent.

He throws the handkerchief past the oleanders, out toward the desert, as he stands. A good hard throw. Even I know that cloth is too flimsy to carry for a distance like that.

"Just a bum line, Mrs. Ebert. The company will replace it free of charge."

"That's great, Mr. Phelps." The woman expected this, but she makes gratified noises anyway.

"Peyote Skies wants its residents happy with everything." Mr. Phelps is donning a genial face and moving over the thick grass toward the woman. "Jimmy Ray Ruggles didn't develop this concept from the ground up to let a broken water line turn a band of your Bermuda brown."

"Plus, a broken line could be wasting water," she reminds him.

"Right." I hear his smirk, though his broad polyester-blend back is turned to me. "No water wasted here," he says, standing on an ocean of emerald-green grass. "Peyote Skies is a Jimmy Ray Ruggles baby, down to the last leaf of landscaping. It's gotta be perfect."

They smile at each other and amble toward the pale-yellow house together. I do not wait to see them enter. I have turned and streaked into the desert.

Not far away I find the orange handkerchief. A stone the size of a catnip mouse lies near it, but it is not really a handkerchief. I take one look and go bounding into the deeper desert at a coyote pace, thinking furiously. I do not like the idea of a new victim dying while I am on the job.

It is easiest to find Sings-with-Soul's den, next to the big stand of coyote cactus, whose gourds are catnip to coyotes. With the kits yipping serially in the background, I tell her my problem. Her yellow eyes show their whites.

"I can call, but then what?" she asks me.

"Just get him here. I will think of something."

She assumes a position that uncannily mimics the image on the home owner's sweater, lifts her head until her yellow throat aims at high noon, and lets loose an ungodly series of yowls.

Sings-with-Soul has Janis Joplin beat by a Clark County mile. My own ears flatten as much as hers, in self-defense. Even the kits quit yipping and join in with falsetto minihowls. Ouch!

Daylight howls seem out of place, but I figure they will attract attention. Sure enough, soon coyotes spring out of the drab desert floor as if they were made of animated dust. Frankly, they all look alike to me, so I do not recognize any I met the night before.

One comes slowly. My gut tightens as I recognize my quarry, Happy Hocks. The old dude who commissioned me is nowhere to be seen, and I am not unhappy. I do not have good news.

Once I am the center of a circle of quizzical coyotes (it is a good thing I am not the nervous type), I explain.

"I have discovered who is killing your kin—and how. Unfortunately, Happy Hocks ate some poisoned food."

Heads snap toward Happy, whose own head is hanging a trifle low. His big ears are not as erect as before, and I notice his eye whites are turning yellow.

"I was feeling . . . tired, Mr. Midnight," he whimpers. "What can I do?"

"Is there anything you do *not* eat around here?" I ask the others.

"There is little coyote clan will not eat, if they have to," a gray-muzzle answers.

"There must be something that you wouldn't touch on a bet—some cactus, some plant, that makes you sick."

Sings-with-Soul's head lifts. "Of course. We were too shocked to think. An antidote."

"No sure bet," I warn, eyeing the listless Happy Hocks. "I have already thought of oleander, but that is so poisonous the cure could kill as well. Whatever this unknown poison is, if we act quickly enough—"

"Alyssum leaves," says the unnamed grizzle-muzzle, "taste hot and harsh."

"Prince's plume," another coyote offers. "Worse taste!"

"Desert tobacco," the oldster suggests again. "Paiutes smoked it. Such stinkweed should make this youngster plenty sick."

"I know!" Sings-with-Soul edges away from the big-eyed, big-eared kits watching our powwow. "Brushtail was sick only a week ago after I nipped her home from that plant there."

We turn as one to regard a modest, foot-high growth covered with tiny dull-green leaves. Small leafless stalks are crowned with seed beads.

Happy Hocks is nosed over to the plant and watched until he bites off several tiny pods. Meanwhile, grizzle-muzzle trots off, returning with a fragrant bouquet of desert alyssum.

Happy Hocks's muzzle develops a perpetual wrinkle as he downs these desert delights, but his eye whites gleam with fear.

"Sharp," he comments with a short bark. "Hot. Burning."

I say nothing. The hot burning, I fear, could be the poison working. I have no love for vegetables, but in the interests of science, I nibble a pod. I am not an expert, either, but I have nicked the occasional burger fragment and I recognize this plant's terrible taste. Ironically, Happy Hocks is having lots of fresh mustard on his death-o-Burger.

We watch the poor pup gum down these tough little taste bombs. Finally, his skinny sides begin to heave. I am surprised to see the gathered coyotes politely turn their heads from this unpleasant sight.

When it is over, the dirty work is left to Midnight Louie.

I amble over to examine the remains. In a pile of regurgitated greens lies the fatal lump of meat. It looks fairly undigested. With one sharp nail I paw the meat. After a few prods it falls open along the fault line. Inside lies a metallic powder.

"Bury it," I growl at the assembled coyote clan.

Happy Hocks's hangdog look lifts. "I think I feel better, Mr. Midnight."

"Keep it that way and, ah, drink lots of liquids and get plenty of rest." What can it hurt?

Amid a chorus of coyote thanks, I flatten my ears and head back to the dangerous turf of Peyote Skies.

I now know the means (if not the brand of poison), and I know the motive. I even know the perpetrator. What I don't know is how to stop him.

So I shadow him.

This is no big deal. For one thing, my coloration makes me a born shadow, and I have always been good at tailing. For another, Mr. Phelps is all over this development.

Apparently, he is a troubleshooter for this Jimmy Ray Ruggles. Mr. Phelps inspects deck planking that gapes too much for an owner's aesthetic sense. He orders shriveling bushes replaced. He keeps everybody happy.

And he obligingly confesses to the crime. So to speak.

"My kids are real upset about having to keep Rocky inside," a harried householder in a thousand-dollar suit complains when he buttonholes a passing Mr. Phelps in his aggregate driveway. "We never thought about coyotes running off with our pets. What about stockade fences?"

"Jimmy Ray wants the development open to the desert; that's the whole point. We're working on the coyote problem. Maybe electric fences."

"What about those dead coyotes on the perimeter? That's not healthy, dead animals so close to the houses."

"We clean up the area as soon as they're found."

"What's killing them? They're not rabid?"

"No, no," Mr. Phelps says quickly. You can see the word "rabid" conjuring visions of damage suits and buyer panic. "Just varmints. Pests. Coyotes die all the time. Old age. Gunshot wounds. Don't worry, sir. As soon as the coyotes catch on that this area is populated now, they'll keep their distance."

The busy man in the suit hops into a red BMW convertible and takes off, looking unconvinced.

Mr. Phelps heads on to the biggest house in the completed section, a white stucco job with a high red-tile roof the size of a circus tent.

I follow, the only free-roaming critter in the complex. The feeling is spooky. At the back of the big house is a circular sun room with floor-to-ceiling windows surrounded by a bleached redwood deck.

Mr. Jimmy Ray Ruggles soon comes out with a woman carrying a kid. These Peyote Skies people sure like their backyards and their desert view.

I stay low in the landscaping and edge close enough to hear every word.

"It's going great, Jimmy Ray." Mr. Phelps's hearty, adman voice gives "phony" a gold plating.

"What about the pet-killing problem?" the top man asks.

"We'll be rid of all coyotes, dead or alive, any day now. We're trying low-profile electric fences."

The boss man's face darkens. "That'll ruin the view."

Mr. Jimmy Ray Ruggles is as nice-looking as his picture. Though he is only in his mid thirties, he even smells rich, thanks to some Frenchy men's cologne. Mrs. Jimmy Ray Ruggles, a slender woman with sun-streaked blond hair, wears Chanel No. 5 with her tennis whites.

She puts down the little girl, whose dark hair suggests that Mama's been in the bleach bottle. The kid is a little doll of maybe four, in a pink dress. She grabs onto her mother's shorts and hides behind her.

Mr. Phelps looks nervous again. He glances down the green expanse of lawn to the broad brown swath of desert. Between here and there stands the bright Tinkertoy construction of a kiddie play set that sports enough swings, slides, and monkey bars to outfit a whole playground.

"We're putting the wires real low," Mr. Phelps says.

"The coyotes'll jump 'em if they want to come in bad enough."

"Maybe not," Mr. Phelps adds lamely.

I can smell what he's thinking: not if enough of them die. So the boss does not know about this guy's one-man pest-control plan.

Mr. Phelps suddenly bends down and smiles at the little

girl. "How are you, Caitlyn? Want Uncle Phil to take you for a swingsy?"

Caitlyn doesn't look too good. In fact, she looks as down in the mouth as Happy Hocks did not long ago. Her dark eyes are as round as two moons in eclipse, and her precious opposable thumb is stuck in her mouth like a lollipop, where it can do no good whatsoever. What I would give for one of those! Preferably two; I am a balanced kind of dude.

"What do you say, Caitlyn?" her mother prods. "Uncle Phil was awful nice to get you that recreation set." Mrs. Jimmy Ray looks apologetically at Mr. Phelps. "She's so shy for her age."

"That's okay." Mr. Phelps is really turning on the hard sell now. "She knows her Uncle Phil is her best friend. Come on, Caitie, upsy-daisy."

He swoops the little girl up on one arm, and I can see the fear in her eyes. I myself do not care to be swooped up. As for being forced to swish to and fro at a height in the name of fun . . . please!

The fond parents smile as Uncle Phil leads little Caitie to the swing set.

I slink under the oleanders until I am level with the gaudy swing set, most unhappy. I will not overhear anything good way down here, but I must follow Mr. Phelps until I get something on him that will stick. At least I now know that his dirty deeds are a solo act.

Mr. Phelps lifts the little girl onto the swing seat. Her clinging mitts turn white-knuckled on the chains. He shoves off. She goes sailing to and fro above his head, down to the ground and up again forward and then down and back.

I shut my eyes. This is worse than watching Happy Hocks lose his Big-o-Burger.

Mr. Phelps looks up as Caitlyn swings over him, her skirt lifting in the wind. Her eyes flash by, terrified.

Then he slows the swing.

"Phil!" Mrs. Jimmy Ray Ruggles is calling from the deck.

Mr. Phelps bends down to whisper something to the little girl. Her fingers do not uncurl from the swing chains.

Mr. Phelps goes up the green lawn to the deck. I turn to follow, but something makes me look back at Caitlyn.

The swing is still. She has bent to pick up something from the grass and is setting it in her lap, gazing at it unhappily. Then, as if taking a pill that will make a bad headache go away, she lifts a hand to her mouth.

I scope the entire scenario in a nanosecond. My mind flashes back to Mr. Coyote-killer Phelps, his hands up, pushing the swing. Again I see his open suit-coat swinging back, side pockets tilted at an angle. I can imagine something falling out and down to the grass, unnoticed.

The little girl, a shy, unhappy kid who is afraid of almost everything. A familiar package, bright orange, with a tasty piece of Big-o-Burger still in it. Maybe she thinks you can swallow fear, push it back down. Maybe some kids will eat anything, just like coyotes.

I am over in a slingshot.

I leap up to paw the too-familiar orange paper, then to push her hand away from her mouth. She is chewing. Now her eyes grow enormous, and her fear erupts in a scream.

"Mommy, Mommy!"

She is still chewing.

I leap onto her lap (claws in), to rap her cheek.

Some half-chewed food falls to the orange wrapper covering her short pink skirt like a napkin.

She is still chewing in dazed reflex.

I pat her cheek until she coughs out something more.

But I have seen her swallow.

Then they come for me, three running figures.

"Caitlyn!" they shriek.

"Shoo!" they shout. "Get away!"

I leap down with the Big-o-Burger wrapper in my mouth, dragging it from the yard.

"Mommy, Mommy!" Caitlyn cries as she is swept into

her mother's arms, as the two men in their big shoes come after me.

I could outrun them in the snap of a maître d's fingers, but I dare not leave behind the poisoned Big-o-Burger. It is evidence. Uncle Phil knows now that he has to destroy it.

I drag it into the last oleanders between me and the desert, working myself deep into the shrubbery and shadows.

"Jimmy Ray!" Caitlyn's mother sounds annoyed. "I think she ate some of the food that filthy alley cat dragged into the yard. What was it?"

The men's feet stop pounding beside me. "I saw the wrapper," Jimmy Ray Ruggles shouts back. "A Big-o-Burger."

"Can you imagine how long that was sitting around?" she demands. "Oh, Caitie—"

She turns to retreat to the house, carrying the kid.

I see her husband's feet swiveling to follow her.

I see Mr. Phelps's feet moving closer along the oleanders.

I do not need to see his face to know that he looks even more nervous than ever, and angrier. At this moment, Midnight Louie is one should-be-dead coyote.

"Phil!" The boss is calling. "Forget the cat. We better get Caitlyn calmed down for a nap. Come up to the house, and we'll talk later."

The feet before me do not move, and I know why. I am a hunter myself. Uncle Phil wants to destroy— evidence and me. I do not move. If I must, I will desert my hard-won prize, but not without a fight. This time my shivs are out and my teeth are bared.

Finally, the feet turn and thump away.

I withdraw, but not far. I know what I wait for.

The moon is out again, full as a tick.

I watch the dark house.

At what must be my namesake midnight hour, a light blinks on upstairs. I edge forward to watch lights turn on through the house, down to the kitchen.

In five minutes, I can hear sirens. The wash of revolving red lights splash the sides of the big white house like gouts of blood. Soon the sirens wail away, fading, but the house stays brightly lit. Out on the dark, unseen desert, coyotes keep the siren heartfelt company.

Dawn is no surprise. I wait.

Around noon, Mr. Jimmy Ray Ruggles comes out onto the deck. He looks even younger in jeans and a rumpled T-shirt. He walks down the lawn, Mr. Phelps a deferential step behind. Mr. Jimmy Ray Ruggles' face is more rumpled than his shirt. I glimpse in his eyes the same fear that filled his daughter's less than a day ago. I know the swing that Mr. Jimmy Ray Ruggles has been riding for the past twelve hours. I want to know what has happened to Caitlyn.

"It was near here," Mr. Jimmy Ray Ruggles says in a weary, angry voice.

"That cat is long gone, with his booty," Mr. Phelps says. Hopes.

"I've got to look. I've got to know what it was, Phil."

Mr. Jimmy Ray Ruggles gets down on his hands and knees to peer under the oleanders.

I am waiting, where I always was.

"By God, the damn cat's still here!" he hisses. "I can see the wrapper too!"

"There won't be anything left."

"Damn it, Phil! They can analyze even little bits, molecules, maybe. I've got to know what—" His voice breaks. "That's all right, kitty. I just want the paper."

He sticks his hand under the bush. I see his pale face. I see Mr. Phelps peering over his shoulder, twice as worried.

"Jimmy Ray, that's a big cat. He could have rabies. He could scratch or bite you—"

"I don't care! It's for Caitie." His hand reaches the crumpled orange paper in front of me, with the two lumps of mashed food on it.

I sit very still and let him take it. He slowly draws it away, seeping fear. I am sorry that I am such a scary dude.

Then he is gone and Mr. Phelps is staring at me through the spiky oleander leaves with as much hatred as I have ever seen.

"Black devil!" he says like a curse.

I am not sorry that I am such a scary dude after all.

I wait again. I want to know.

But the house is empty and the hours pass. I am hungry, but I wait. When I am thirsty, I slink out to lap up some sprinkler water. Then I return to my post.

The odds are that I will never know, just as they are one hundred percent that I will never tell. But I wait.

I am rewarded at dusk, when the desert sky bleeds a Southwest palette of lavender and peach . . . and orange . . . that developers can only dream of.

Two men on the lawn. Lights in the house.

"Tell me," Mr. Jimmy Ray Ruggles is saying, and I think the iron tone in his voice could force even me to talk.

"Tell you what?" A nervous laugh.

"The dead coyotes. You said you were handling it. How? Phil, how!"

"Jim—"

"It was with poisoned food, wasn't it? And somehow Caitie got into it. Listen, you can tell me now. Caitie will be fine, thank God. She's still unconscious, but the doctors say she didn't get enough poison to cause permanent damage. They hope not anyway. Listen, I won't blame you. I know you're devoted to Peyote Skies, like I am. Maybe too much. Tell me."

"All right." Mr. Phelps sounds empty. The men walk toward the oleanders, toward me. "I never dreamed, Jimmy Ray—I just wanted to discourage the damn coyotes, and it was working. We haven't found any dead ones since a week ago. I salted the Big-o-Burgers. Somehow, one of the . . . traps fell out of my pocket yesterday and I never knew. Caitie swooped it up, and I never saw—"

"Don't you remember? She's always loved Big-o-Burgers," Mr. Jimmy Ray Ruggles says softly.

Mr. Phelps's voice is breaking now, but this theatrical touch does not break Midnight's Louie's heart. "I was going to stop soon."

"But . . . thallium, Phil, an outlawed poison! With no taste, no smell, a poison that never degrades even though it's been illegal for decades. Didn't you realize it could kill more than coyotes—pets, children? Where on earth did you get it?"

"I own some old houses in town. The carpenters back then used it as rat poison, inside the walls. It was still there. I figured it would fool the coyotes; they're too smart for anything else. I swear to God, Jimmy Ray, if I had known it would hurt Caitie I would have cut off my right arm—"

"I know. I know."

Mr. Jimmy Ray Ruggles has stopped directly in front of me. "I suppose that big ole black cat is dead from it by now, but thank God he fought Caitie for it. Thank God we found him and a sample of the poison so they could treat her."

His shoes turn, then go. Mr. Phelps's do not.

"Black devil," he whispers to the twilight air.

I accept my plaudits with silent good grace and finally depart.

It takes me a full day to recover my strength and placate my defrauded appetite. I am satisfied that no more coyotes will be sacrificed on the altar of Peyote Skies and that the developer's daughter will be well, but I do wish that Mr. Phelps would find the fate he deserves. I fear that the scandal would hurt Peyote Skies too much for even a fond father to pursue the matter.

Then I begin to worry about my payoff. I am, after all, not doing charity work. I dash out to the desert on the nearest gravel truck, to find that Happy Hocks is as peppy as ever (alas!) and that these coyote clan types have never heard of the strange old dude who commissioned me.

So I am soon languishing beside the carp pond at the

Crystal Phoenix again, feeling that I have been taken in a shell game, when I spot a familiar profile on the sun-rinsed wall.

"I thought you had headed for the hills."

"Foolish feline," the big-eared coyote silhouette answers. "I always keep my bargains. I merely had to ensure that you had done as agreed."

"And then some. Where is my reward?"

I watch the shadow jaws move and hear the harsh desert voice describe a site that, to my delight, is on the Crystal Phoenix grounds.

"Once all of Las Vegas was desert," the coyote says, "and my ancestors had many secret places. You will find my cache behind the third palm on the east side of the pool."

"Where?"

"In the ground. You will have to dig for it. You can dig?"

"I do so daily," I retort.

"Deep."

"What I can do shallow, I can do deep."

"Good. Goodbye."

With that terse farewell, me and the coyote call it quits.

I spring for the pool area. I dodge stinking tourists basting on lounges, dripping coconut oil between the plastic strips.

I count off palms. I retire discreetly behind one and dig. And dig. And dig.

About a half-foot down, I hit pay dirt. Coyote pay dirt. Excavating further, I uncover my treasure. Then I sit back to study it.

I regard a deposit of small brown nubs. Of pods, so to speak. Of coyote dung intermixed with a foreign sub-stance: the button of the mescal cactus, called peyote by the Indians. I have been paid off, all right. In Coyote pey-ote, both forms. Apparently this big-eared dude thinks that his leavings are caramel. The worst part is feeling that it serves me right for trusting a coyote.

By nightfall I have retreated to the ghost suite of the Crystal Phoenix to salve my wounded psyche. It does not soothe my savage soul to have been taken to the cleaners by a dirty dog. A yellow dog. By Don Coyote. Maybe the mescaline is worth something, but not in my circles. I do not do drugs, and my only vice, catnip, is a legally available substance. As for coyote dung, it does not even have a souvenir value.

As I muse in the antique air of suite 713, I recall that there is coyote, and then there is Coyote. Coyote of Native American legend is also called the Old Man, the Trickster, the Dirty Old Man who is at times advised by his own droppings. It is said that Coyote takes many forms and that to deal with him is always dicey, for he embodies the worst and the best of humankind.

I contemplate that though I have saved coyote clan from an underhanded attack, I have also saved humankind from the ricochet of that attack upon itself; that I have suffered hunger and thorns in my feet, not to mention threats to body and soul, and I have nothing to show for it but coyote peyote.

My self-esteem is so low that I could win a limbo contest dancing under it.

And then I notice that a console across the room has flipped its lid. I have seen that ash-blond oblong of furniture for many years and never knew that it had a lid to flip.

By the way the light dances inside the lid, like an aurora borealis, the lid interior is mirrored, and in that mirror is reflected an oval image.

The image flickers eerily, then resolves. Sound issues from the bowels of the cabinet. I sit mesmerized, even when I realize that I am watching a late-forties-vintage TV set display a perfectly ordinary contemporary television show I do not normally deign to watch—that exercise in tabloid journalism known as *The Daily Scoop* but which I call the Daily Pooper Scooper in my septic moments. Or do I mean skeptic?

Whatever, what to my wandering eyes should appear but a camera pan across the entry sign to Peyote Skies. An offscreen voice begins saying what a tony development this is and discusses the rash of coyote poisonings, culminating in the tragic poisoning of the developer's daughter. Caitlyn's image flashes across the screen, smiling and happy.

Next I see an image of Mr. Phelps being led away in handcuffs by grim-looking men. Hallelujah!

Then Miss Ashley Ames, a most attractive anorexic bottle blonde with bony kneecaps, comes on-screen with a breathless narrative.

It seems that little Caitlyn Ruggles's poisoning was considered a tragic mistake stemming from a misguided attempt by a Peyote Skies employee to rid the development of pet-napping coyotes . . . until the child victim regained consciousness and began speaking of the unspeakable. "Uncle Phil" had been sexually abusing her.

Caitlin's shocked parents called the police. An investigation revealed that P. W. Phelps, a vice president in the Peyote Skies company, had been molesting the child, who was beginning to talk of telling.

"It is alleged," Miss Ashley Ames says in a tone that is most delightfully dubious about the "alleged" part, "that he poisoned the half-dozen coyotes to create a pattern in which the 'accidental' death of young Caitlyn Ruggles would be seen as a tragic side effect.

"Had it not been," she goes on, and I can hardly believe my ears, even though they are standing at full attention, "for the lucky chance that a starving stray black cat fought the child for the poisoned piece of a major fast-food-chain hamburger, this nefarious scheme would never have been discovered."

I am more than somewhat taken aback by my description as "starving."

The next shot distracts me: Caitlyn and her parents at the Las Vegas Humane Society, adopting a small black kitten, all smiles. Even the kitten is smiling.

I am smiling. Hell, I suspect that somewhere Coyote is smiling.

In fact, as the ancient television's image and sound fade, I believe I glimpse a silver-haired human dude with mighty big ears vanishing through a crack in the door.

I recall that Jersey Joe Jackson hid a few caches around Las Vegas in his time. And that Coyote never changes, and always does. And that he performs tricks, maybe even with vintage television sets.

The best and the worst of both beast and man himself.

Indeed.

NOOSES GIVE

DANA STABENOW

*In swift succession, Dana Stabenow's
novels about modern-day Alaska have
won her a new genre (she began as a science fiction writer), an Edgar, and thousands of new fans.*

*Stabenow's Alaska tales are filled with two
primary elements—her almost journalistic
take on the sociology of the place (native
and non-native alike) and her sardonic
take on her frequently troubled cast of
characters. Note the ease with which she
paints Bernie Koslowski—the mark of a
fine and artful writer.*

▼▼▼▼▼

THE BODIES HAD FALLEN around the table like three cards from a spent deck. Jeremy Mike, the jack of spades. Sally Jorgenson, queen of hearts. Ted Muktoyuk, the king of diamonds. The King of the Key, they called him from the bleachers, at five feet ten the tallest center Bernie Koslowski had ever had the privilege of coaching.

Bernie's mouth was set in a grim line. "What happened?"

Billy Mike had a mobile moon face, usually beaming with good nature and content. This morning it was grim and tired. The jack of spades had been a nephew, his youngest sister's only child. She didn't know yet, and he didn't know how he was going to tell her. He told Bernie instead. "They were drunk. It's Jeremy's pistol."

"How do you know?"

Billy's face twisted. "I gave it to him for Christmas." Bernie waited, patient, and Billy got himself under control. "He must have brought it from home. Sally's parents are in Ahtna for a corporation conference, so they came here to drink."

"And play Russian roulette."

Billy nodded. "Looks like Ted lost. He was left-handed—remember that hook shot?"

"Remember it? I taught it to him."

"Sally was on his right. She couldn't have shot him in the left side of his head from where she sat." He pointed at the pistol, lying on the table a few inches from Sally's hand. "You know Ted and Sally were going together?"

Bernie grunted. "You figure Sally blamed Jeremy? For bringing the gun?"

"Or the bottle, or both." The tribal chief's nod was

weary. "Probably grabbed the gun and shot Jeremy, then herself." He stooped and picked up a plastic liquor bottle from the floor.

He held it out, and Bernie examined the label. "Windsor Canadian. The bootlegger's friend. Retail price in Anchorage, seven-fifty a bottle. Retail price in a dry village, a hundred bucks easy."

"Yeah." The bottle dropped to the table, next to the gun.

"You talk to him?"

"I tried. He shot out the headlights on my snow machine."

"Uh-huh."

"Town's tense. You know the DampAct passed by only five votes. There's plenty who think he's just doing business, that he's got every right to make a living, same as the rest of us."

"No," Bernie said, "Not the same as the rest of us."

"No," Billy agreed. "Bernie. The trooper's chasing after some nut who shot up a bank in Valdez, and the tribal police . . . well, hell, the tribal policemen are okay at checking planes for booze and getting the drunks home safe from the Roadhouse. Like I said, the town's tense. Anything could happen." A pause. "We're not going to be able to handle this on our own."

"No." Bernie's eyes met Billy's. "But we know someone who can."

The tribal chief hesitated. "I don't know, Bernie. There's some history there."

Bernie gave the bodies a last look, a gaze equal parts sorrow and rage. "All the better."

The next morning Bernie bundled himself into a parka, gauntlets, and boots, kissed his wife and children good-bye, and got on his snow machine. There had been a record amount of snow that winter, drifting twenty feet deep in places. Moose were unable to get at the tree bark that was their primary food source and were starving to death all over the Park, but the snow machining had never been better. An hour and thirty-five miles later, his cheeks frostbitten and his hands and feet numb, he burst into a small clearing. He cut the engine and slid to a stop six feet from the log cabin.

It sat at the center of a half circle of small buildings, including a garage, a greenhouse, a cache, and an outhouse. Snow was piled high beneath the eaves of the cabin, and neat paths had been cut through it from door to door and to the woodpile between cabin and outhouse. Beyond the buildings were more trees and a creek. Beyond the creek the ground fell away into a long, broad valley that glittered hard and cold and white in what there was of the Arctic noon sun, a valley that rose again into the Teglliq foothills and the Quilak mountain range, a mighty upward thrust of earth's crust that gouged the sky with 18,000-foot spurs until it bled ice-blue glaze down their sharp flanks.

It was a sight to steal the heart. Bernie Koslowski would never have seen any of it if he hadn't dodged the draft all the way into British Columbia in 1970. From there it was but a step over the border into Alaska and some fine, rip-roaring years on the TransAlaska Pipeline. By the time the line was finished, he had enough of a stake to buy the Roadhouse, the only establishment legally licensed to sell liquor in the twenty-million-acre Park, and he settled down to marry a local girl and make babies and boilermakers for the rest of his life.

He sold liquor to make a living. He coached basketball for fun. He had so much fun at it that Niniltna High School's Kanuyaq Kings were headed for the Class C State Championship. Or they had been until Ted Muktoyuk's resignation from the team. Bernie's eyes dropped from the mountains to the clearing.

She hadn't been off the homestead in the last four feet of snow; he'd had to break trail with the machine a quarter of a mile through the woods. The thermometer mounted next to the door read six below. He knocked. No answer. Smoke was coming from both chimneys. He knocked again, harder.

This time the door opened. She stood five feet tall and small of frame, dwarfed by the wolf-husky hybrid standing at her side. The wolf's eyes were yellow, the woman's hazel, both wary and hostile. The woman said, "What?"

"What 'what'?" Bernie said. "What am I doing here? What do I want? Whatever happened to this thing called love?" He gave a hopeful smile. There was no response. "Come on, Kate. How about a chance to get in out of the cold?"

For a minute he thought she was going to shut the door in his face. Instead she stepped to one side. "In."

The dog curled a lip at him, and he took this as tacit permission to enter. The cabin was a twenty-five-foot square with a sleeping loft. Built-in bookshelves, built-in couch, table and chairs, and two stoves, one oil, one wood, took up the first floor. Gas lamps hissed gently from brackets in all four corners. She took his parka and hung it next to hers on the caribou rack mounted next to the door. "Sit."

He sat. She poured out two mugs of coffee and gave him one. He gulped gratefully and felt the hot liquid creep all the way down his legs and out into his fingertips, and as if she had only been waiting for that, she said, "Talk."

Her voice was a hoarse, croaking whisper, and irresistibly his eyes were drawn to the red, angry scar bisecting the smooth brown skin of her throat, literally from ear to ear. None of the Park rats knew the whole story, and none of them had had the guts to ask for it, but the scar marked her throat the way it had marked the end of her career seven months before as an investigator on the staff of the Anchorage district attorney's office. She had returned to her father's homestead sometime last summer. The first anyone knew about it was when her mail started being delivered to the Niniltna post office. Old Abel Int-Hout picked it up and presumably brought it out to her homestead, and the only time anyone else saw her was when she came into Niniltna for supplies in October, the big silver wolf-husky hybrid walking close by her side, warning off any and all advances with a hard yellow stare.

Her plaid shirt was open at the throat, her long black hair pulled back into a loose braid. She wasn't trying to hide the scar. Maybe it needed air to heal. Or maybe she was proud of it. Or maybe it was only that she wasn't ashamed of it, which wasn't quite the same thing. He looked up from the scar and met eyes beneath an epicanthic fold that gave her face an exotic, Eastern flavor. She was an Aleut icon stepped out of a gilt frame, dark and hard and stern. "I've got a problem," he said.

"So?"

"So I'm hoping you'll make it your problem, too." He drank more coffee, preparing for a tough sell. "You know about the DampAct?" She shook her head. "In November the village voted to go dry. You can bring in booze for your own consumption but not in amounts to sell." He added, "I'm okay because the Roadhouse is outside tribal boundaries." She didn't look as if she'd been worrying about him or his business. "Well, Kate, it ain't working out too good."

There was a brief pause. "Bootlegger," she said.

"Yeah."

She doubled her verbal output. "Tell me." He told her. It must have been hard to hear. She was shirttail cousin to all three of the teenagers. Hell, there weren't very many people in the village of Niniltna or the entire Park for that matter she couldn't call cousin, including himself, through his wife. It was the reason he was here. One of them.

"You know who?" she said.

He snorted into his coffee and put the mug down with a thump. "Of course I know who. Everybody knows who. He's been flying booze into remote villages, wet or dry, for thirty years. Wherever there isn't a bar—shit, wherever there is a bar and somebody'd rather buy their bottle out of the back of a plane anyway—there's Pete with his hand out. God knows it's better than working for a living."

Her face didn't change, but he had the sudden feeling that he had all her attention, and remembered Billy Mike's comment about history. "Pete Liverakos," she said. He gave a gloomy nod. "Stop him. The local option law says the state can seize any equipment used to make, transport, sell, or store liquor. Start confiscating."

This time a gloomy shake. "We don't know where to start."

A corner of her wide mouth turned down. "Gee, maybe you could try his plane. You can pack a lot of cases of booze into the back of a 180, especially if you pull all the seats except the pilot's."

"He's not using it," Bernie said. "Since the DampAct passed, the tribal council has been searching every plane that lands at gunpoint. Pete's been in and out in his Cessna all winter, Billy Mike says clean as a whistle every time."

"How often?"

"Once a week, sometimes twice." He added, "He's not even bringing in anything for personal use, which all by itself makes me suspicious, because Pete and Laura Anne are a couple what likes a little caribou with their cabernet."

"Get the trooper."

"Kate, you know and I know the trooper's based in Tok, and his jurisdiction is spread pretty thin even before he gets within flying distance of Niniltna. Besides, he's already in pursuit of some yo-yo who shot up a bank in Valdez and took off up Thompson Pass, on foot, no less. So much for state law. The DampAct—" He shrugged. "The DampAct is a local ordinance. Even if they catch him at it, all the council can do is fine him a thousand bucks. Like a speeding ticket. In any given year Pete spends more than that on olives for martinis."

"He got somebody flying it in from Anchorage?"

Bernie gave a bark of laughter. "Sure. MarkAir." At her look, he said, "Shit, Kate, MarkAir runs specials with the Brown Jug in town. Guy endorses his permanent dividend fund check over at the local MarkAir office,

MarkAir carries it to Anchorage and expedites it to the Brown Jug warehouse, Brown Jug fills the order, MarkAir picks it up and takes it out to the airport and flies it to the village."

"Competition for you," she said.

He met her eyes levelly. "That isn't what this is about, and you know it. I serve drinks, not drunks, and I don't sell bottles."

She looked away. "Sorry."

He gave a curt nod.

There was a brief silence. She broke it. "What do you want me to do?"

He drained his mug and set it on the table with a decisive snap. "I got a state championship coming up. I need sober players who come to practice instead of out earning their next bottle running booze for that asshole. Preferably players who have not previously blown their brains out with their best friend's gun. I want you to find out how Pete's getting the booze in, and stop him."

The next morning she fired up the Polaris and followed Bernie's tracks up the trail to the road that connected Niniltna with Ahtna and the Richardson Highway. The Polaris was old and slow, and the twenty-five miles between her homestead and the village took the better part of an hour, including the ten-minute break to investigate the tracks she spotted four miles outside the village. A pack of five wolves, healthy, hungry, and hunting. The 30.06 was always with her, and there was always a round in the chamber, but she stopped and checked anyway. One wolf was an appetite with attitude. Five of them looked like patrons of a diner, with her as the blue-plate special.

The tracks were crusted hard, a day old at least. Mutt's sniff was interested but unalarmed, and Kate replaced the rifle and continued up the road. It wasn't a road, really; it was the remains of the gravel roadbed of the Kanuyaq and Northwestern Railroad, built in 1910 to carry copper from the mine outside Niniltna to freighters docked in Cordova. In 1936 the copper played out, the railroad shut down, and locals began ripping up rails to get to the ties. It was an easy load of firewood, a lot easier than logging out the same load by hand.

The rails and ties were all gone now, although in summertime you could still pick up the odd spike in your truck tires. Twice a year, once after breakup, again just before the termination dust started creeping down the mountains, the state ran a grader over the rough surface to smooth over the potholes and the washouts. For the rest of the time they left itself to itself, and to the hundreds of Park rats who used it as a secondary means of transportation and commerce.

In the Alaskan bush, the primary means was ever and always air, and it was to the village airstrip Kate went first, a 4,800-foot stretch of hard-packed snow, much better maintained than the road. A dozen planes were tied down next to a hangar. Across the strip was a large log cabin with the U.S. flag flying outside, which backed up the wind sock at the end of the runway. Both hung limp this morning, and smoke rose straight up into the Arctic air from a cluster of rooftops glimpsed over the tops of the trees.

Kate stopped the snow machine next to the hangar, killed the engine, and stripped off her fur gauntlets. The round white thermometer fixed to the wall read twelve below. Colder than yesterday. She worked her fingers. It felt like it. Mutt jumped down and went trotting inside. A moment later there was a yell. "God*damn*!" Kate followed the sound.

A tall man in a gray coverall leaned up against the side of a Cessna 206 that looked as if it had enough hours on the Hobbs to put it into lunar orbit. The cowling was peeled back from the engine, and there were parts laid out on a canvas tarp. Both man and parts were covered with black grease. He scowled at her. "The next time that goddamn dog sticks her nose in my crotch from behind, I'm going to pinch her head off!"

"Hi, George."

Mutt nudged his hand with her head. He muttered something, pulled a rag out of a hip pocket, wiped his hands, and crouched down to give her ears a thorough scratching. She stood stock-still with an expression of bliss on her face, her plume of a tail waving gently. She'd been in love with George Perry since she was a puppy, and George had flown Milk-Bones into the setnet site Kate fished during her summer vacations. Kate had been in love with George since he'd flown Nestlé's Semi-Sweet Morsels into that same site.

The bush pilot gave Mutt a last affectionate cuff and stood to look at Kate. "I heard you were back."

She nodded in answer to his question, without offering an explanation. He didn't ask for one. "Coffee?"

She nodded again, and he led the way into his office, a small rectangular corner walled off from the rest of the building, furnished with a desk, a chair, and a Naugahyde couch heavily patched with black electrician's tape. The walls were covered with yellowing, tattered maps mended with Scotch tape. George went into a tiny bathroom and came out with a coffeepot held together with three-inch duct tape. He started the coffee and sat down at the desk. "So—how the hell are you, Shugak? Long time no see." His eyes dropped briefly to the open collar of her shirt. "*Long* time. You okay?" She nodded. "Good. Glad you're back anyway. Missed you."

"Me too."

"And the monster." He rummaged through a drawer for Oreo cookies and tossed one to Mutt. The coffeemaker sucked up the last of the water, and he poured out. Handing her a mug, he said, "What brings you into town?"

She nodded at the wall. "Wanted to take a look at your maps."

His eyebrows rose. "Be my guest." Mug in hand, she rose to her feet and began examining the maps beneath his speculative gaze, until she found the right one. Pete Liverakos's homestead was on Beaver Creek, about a mile downstream from the village. She traced a forefinger

down the Kanuyaq River until she found it. The map
indicated the homestead had its own airstrip, but then
what self-respecting Alaskan homestead didn't?

George's voice sounded over her shoulder. "What are
you looking for?"

She dropped her hand. "Just wanted to check something, and my maps are all about fifty years out of date."

"So are mine." He paused. "Dan O'Brien's bunch just
did a new survey of the Kanuyaq. Source to delta, Copper
Glacier to Kolinhenik Bar. They did the whole thing this
summer. I thought those fucking—excuse me, Mutt—
those frigging choppers never would leave."

"Have they got the new maps yet?" Though her voice
was still harsh and broken, and according to the doctors
always would be, the more she talked, the less it hurt.
The realization brought her no joy.

He shook his head. "They're printing 'em this winter.
They'll be selling 'em in the spring." He paused. "Dan's
probably got the originals at Park Headquarters."

She drained her mug and set it on the desk. "Can I
bum a ride up to the Step?"

He set his mug next to hers. "Sure. The Cub's prepped
and ready to fly."

George took off hot, as straight up as he could with only
150 horsepower under the hood. The sky was clear and
the air was still and it was CAVU all the way from the
Quilak Mountains to the Gulf of Alaska. He climbed to
2,000 feet and stayed there, the throttle all the way out, a
typical taxi driver whose sole interest was in there and
back again. All rubbernecking did was burn gas. Twenty
minutes later they landed on a small plateau in almost the
exact geographical center of the Park. The north end of
the airstrip began at the base of a Quilak mountain; the
south end fell off the tip of a Teglliq foothill into the long
river valley below. The airstrip on the Step was approxi-
mately 3,800 feet shorter than the one in Niniltna, and
George stood on the pedals the instant the Super Cub
touched down. They roared to a halt ten feet from the

front door of the largest building in the group of prefabri-
cated buildings huddled together at the side of the runway. They climbed out, and Mutt vanished into the trees.
"I won't be long," Kate said.

George nodded. "I'll go down to the mess hall and
scare up a free meal."

Dan O'Brien had dodged alligators in the Everglades
and a'a in Kilauea with enough success to be transferred
to the Park on December 3, 1980, the day after Jimmy
Carter signed the d-2 lands bill, which added over a hundred million acres to already existing park lands in
Alaska. Dan was fiercely protective of the region under
his jurisdiction, and at the same time respectful of the
rights of the people around whose homesteads and fish
camps and mines and villages the Park had been created,
which was why he was the only national park ranger in
the history of the state never to get shot at, at least not
while on park duties. Ranger by day, he was a notorious
rounder by night. He'd known Kate since she was in college, and he'd been trying to lay her for at least that
long.

The news of her return hadn't reached the Step, and he
started around the desk with a big grin and open arms,
only to skid to a halt as she unzipped her parka and he
saw the scar. "Jesus Christ, Shugak," he said in a shaken
voice, "what the hell did you do to your neck?"

She shrugged open the parka but kept it on. "George
Perry tells me your boys have been making some new
maps of the Kanuyaq."

Her harsh voice grated on his ears. He remembered the
guitar, and thought of all the long winter evenings spent
singing sea chanteys, and he turned his back on the subject and walked away. It might be the only thing he could
do for an old friend, but he would by God do it and do it
right. He did ask one question. "Mutt okay?"

"She's fine. She's chasing lunch down outside. About
those maps."

"Maps?" he said brightly. "You bet we got maps. We
got a map that shows every hump and bump from Eagle

to Anchorage. We got a census map that shows the location of every moose bull, cow, and calf from here to the Kanuyaq River delta. We got maps that show where every miner with a pickax sunk a hole more than a foot deep anywhere within two hundred miles. We got maps that show the spread of spruce beetles north of Ikaluq. We got—"

"I need a map that shows me any airstrips there might be around Beaver Creek."

"Pete Liverakos' place? Sure, he's got a strip. About twelve hundred feet, I think. Plenty long enough for his Cessna, but he lands her at Niniltna." His brow puckered. "Been curious about that myself. Why walk a mile downriver in winter when you can land on your own front doorstep?"

She nodded, although she wasn't curious; she knew why. "Is there another airstrip further up the creek, say halfway between his homestead and Ahtna?"

He thought. "Yeah, I think there's an old mine up there somewheres. Let's take a look." He led the way into a map room, a place of large tables and cabinets with long, wide, shallow drawers. He consulted a key, went to a drawer, and produced a map three feet square, laying it out on a table with a double-jointed lamp bolted to the side. He switched on the light, and they leaned over the map. A stubby forefinger found Niniltna and traced the river from the village to Beaver Creek, and from there up the creek to the homestead. He tapped once. "Here's Pete's place. A twelve-hundred-foot strip just sitting there going to waste. And Ahtna's up this way, to the northwest, about a hundred miles from Niniltna," adding apologetically, "The scale's too large to show it on this map." He marked the spot with an eraser and produced a yardstick, laying it on the map, one end pointing at Beaver Creek, the other at the eraser. With his hand he traced the length of the yardstick. "And presto chango, there it is. Like I thought, it's an airstrip next to a gold mine. Two thousand footer. Probably needed the extra to land heavy equipment. Abandoned in . . . oh, hell, 'long about '78? Probably about the time Carter declared most of the state an antiquity." He patted her on the ass and leered when her head snapped up. "Just think what you'd be missing if he hadn't."

"Just think," she agreed, moving the target out of range. "Is the strip maintained?"

He made a face. "I doubt it. Never was much gold there to begin with, and too fine to get out in commercial quantities anyway. Myself, I think the mine was just an excuse to come in and poach moose."

Her finger came back down the yardstick. "Beaver Creek runs right up to it."

"Uh-huh." Showing off, he produced another map, with a flourish worthy of Mandrake the Magician. "This shows the estimated animal population in the same area." They studied it. "Neat, huh? A couple moose moved in five years ago, been real good about dropping a calf or two every spring. There's half a dozen pairs of eagles. Beaver, mostly, on the creek." He snapped his fingers. "Sure. I remember one time I was at the Roadhouse and Pete brought in a beaver hide. Said he was running a trapline up the creek." His lip lifted in a sneer. "Said he'd cured it himself. Shape it was in, nobody doubted it for a minute."

He looked up from the map. The hazel eyes had an edge sharp enough to cut. He remembered a time when those eyes could laugh. "Hell of a trapper and hunter," he said, "that Pete. That is, if you don't count him joining in that wolf hunt the state had last year." He grinned. "Nobody else does."

"Why not?"

"He shot three inches off the prop of his plane, leaning out to draw a bead on a running female."

"He wreck the plane?" Dan shook his head. "Too bad. Okay, Dan. Thanks."

He followed her out of the room. "'Okay'? 'Thanks'? Is that it? Is that all I get? Of all the ungrateful—"

The front door shut on the rest of it.

George flew back to Niniltna by way of a stop at

Ahtna to pick up the mail, fresh off the daily MarkAir flight from Anchorage. Kate waited by the Cub, watching cargo unload from the 737 Ahtna, at the junction of the Park road with the Richardson Highway, was a wet town, with a population of a thousand and three flourishing bars. An entire pallet of Olympia beer was marked for the Polar Bar, a case of Jose Cuervo gold and another of assorted liqueurs for the Midnight Sun Lounge. The 737 took off, and a Northern Air Cargo DC-6 landed in its place, off-loading an igloo of building supplies from Spenard Lumber and a pallet of Rainier beer, this one marked for the Riverside Inn.

No Windsor Canadian in either cargo, but then she didn't see Pete or his 50 Papa around anywhere, either. Once a week, Bernie had said. This wasn't the day.

Ahtna, like Niniltna, was on the Kanuyaq. Downriver was Niniltna. Farther downriver was Prince William Sound. Upriver was a state highway maintenance camp. Last year during a spring storm a corner of the yard had crumbled into the river, taking a barrel of methanol with it. The barrel had floated downriver, to wash ashore outside Ahtna. Four high school kids, two sixteen, one fifteen, one fourteen, already drunk, had literally stumbled across it and instead of falling in the river and drowning tapped the barrel and died of poisoning.

George returned with the bag as the pallet of Rainier was loaded onto the back of a flatbed. He read her silence correctly and said, "They're a common carrier, Kate, just like me. We fly anything, anywhere, anytime, for cash money. That's how we make a living."

"You don't fly booze."

He shrugged. "Not up to me. The town voted to go dry."

"And if it hadn't?"

He shrugged again. A half hour later they were back in Niniltna.

The land, low and flat near the river, began to rise soon after she left it. Blueberry bushes, cottonwoods, and scrub spruce were left behind for currants, birches, and hemlocks. The snow was so deep and was packed down so well beneath its own weight that the Polaris skimmed over it, doing better than forty miles an hour. In spite of the wide swing to avoid the homestead, she reached the abandoned gold mine at four-thirty, with more than an hour of twilight left.

She ran the machine into some birches, the nose pointing downhill, and cut branches for camouflage and to sweep the snow free of tracks. Strapping on the snowshoes that were part of the standard winter survival kit she kept beneath the Polaris's seat, she shouldered her pack, slung the 30.06, and hiked the quarter of a mile to the mine entrance that gaped blackly from halfway up the hill next to the creek. It was dark inside until she got out the flashlight. The snow in the entrance was solidly packed down, as if something heavy had been stacked there.

Kate explored and found a branching tunnel, where she pitched the tent and unrolled the sleeping bag. Taking the ax and a collapsible bucket, she went down to the creek and chopped a hole in the ice beneath an overhanging bush. She filled the bucket with ice and water. Back at the tent, she lit the Sterno stove. The exertion and the cold had left her hungry, and she ate two packages of Top Ramen noodles sitting at the entrance to the mine, surveying the terrain in the fading light.

The airstrip ran parallel to the creek, which ran southeast-northwest around the hill of the mine. A narrow footpath led from the mine to one end of the airstrip. She squinted. A second, wider trail started at the other end of the strip, going in the opposite direction. Birches and scrub spruce clustered thickly at the edges of the strip and both trails. The creek was lined with cottonwoods and diamond willow. Mutt visited them all, sniffing, marking territory.

Kate went back for a Chunky and sat again at the mine entrance, gnawing at the cold, hard chocolate as she waited for the moon to come up. An hour later it did, full and bright. By Agudar's light she walked down the footpath. Mutt trotted out of the woods and met her on the strip. It was as hard and smooth as the strip at Niniltna. The second, wider trail was a snow machine track. It followed the creek southeast, dodging back and forth, taking the easiest way through the trees and undergrowth without coming too close to the bank.

The creek itself was frozen over. No snares. No holes cut into the ice in any of the likelier places Kate spotted for snares.

She went back up to the mine and crawled into her sleeping bag, Mutt next to her. Mutt didn't dream. Kate did, the same dream as always, children in pain. In the night she moved, restless, half waking, moaning a little. In the night Mutt moved closer to her, the animal's 140-pound weight warm and solid. Kate slept again.

The next morning the sun was up by nine, and Kate and Mutt were on the creek trail as the first rays hit and slid off the hard surface of the frozen landscape. Kate kept to the trail to minimize the track she left behind. She moved slowly, ears cocked for the sound of an airplane engine, eyes on the creek side of the trail. Again there were no holes, and no snares for holes. There was nothing more to see. Old habits are hard to break, especially the habit of verification instinctive in every good investigator. It had compelled her to give Pete the benefit of the doubt. Now there was none. She went back to the mine.

They waited, camping in the tunnel, carrying water from the creek, Mutt grazing the local rabbit population, for three days. Every morning she broke down the camp and packed it down the hill to the Polaris, and every evening she packed it back up again.

She'd had worse stakeouts. The first morning a pair of eagles cruised by overhead, flying low and slow, eyes alert for any movement on the ground. A gaunt and edgy moose cow and her two calves passed through the area on the second day, moving like they had a purpose. That night they heard the long-drawn-out howl of a wolf. Purpose enough. Down by the creek, a gnawed stand of diamond willow confirmed the presence of Dan's beavers,

although the winter's heavy snowfall kept Kate from
spotting the dam until the second day. The third afternoon a fat black raven croaked at them contemptuously
on his way to make mischief elsewhere. That evening
Kate ran out of Top Ramen and had to fall back on
reconstituted freeze-dried spaghetti. Some prices are
almost too high to pay.

Late on the afternoon of the fourth day, as she was
thinking about fetching her camp up again from the
Polaris, Mutt's ears went forward and she got to her feet
and pointed her muzzle west. Kate faded back into the
mine, one hand knotted in Mutt's ruff, the other gripping
the handle of her ax, as the Cessna 180 with the tail numbers marking 50 PAPA came into view over the trees. It
touched down and used up all of the strip on the runout,
bright shiny new in its fresh-off-the-assembly-line coat of
red and white. Only bootleggers could afford new planes
in the Alaskan bush.

The pilot was tall and rangy and well-muscled, and the
unloading was easy and practiced. All the seats save the
pilot's had been removed and the remaining space filled
up with case after case of Windsor Canadian whiskey, in
the plastic bottles. Glass bottles weighed more and took
more gas to get into the air. Glass bottles cut into the
profit margin.

When he had all the boxes out on the ground, he
tucked one box beneath each arm and started up the path
toward the mine. Kate and Mutt retreated farther into the
darkness.

He made the trip up and back six times, twelve cases
in all, stacking them inside the mouth of the mine where
the snow was packed down all nice and hard, where he'd
stacked different cases many times before. He whistled
while he worked, and when he was done he paused in the
mine entrance to remove his cap and wipe his forehead
on his sleeve. In the thin sun of an Arctic afternoon, his
fifty-year-old face was handsome, although his nose and
chin were a little too sharp, like his smile.

He replaced his cap and started down the hill,

whistling again. He wasn't halfway to the plane before he heard it, and the sound spun him around on his heels.

Kate stood in front of the stack of boxes, swinging from the hips. The blade of the ax bit deep. A dark-brown liquid spurted out when she pulled it free. The smell of alcohol cut through the air like a knife.

"Hey!" he yelled. "What the hell!" He started back up the slope.

Without a break in her swing, Kate said one word. "Mutt."

A gray blur streaked out of the mine to intercept him, and he skidded to a halt and almost fell. "Shit!"

The blade bit into another case. More whiskey gushed out.

"Goddamn it! Kate!"

"Hello, Pete," she said, and swung.

"Kate, for chrissake cut that out—that stuff's worth a hundred bucks a bottle to me!"

The ax struck again. He made as if to move, but Mutt stood between them, lips drawn back from her teeth, head held low, body quivering with the eagerness to attack.

"You fly to Ahtna and pick up your shipment," Kate said, torn voice harsh in the still afternoon air. The ax bit into the sixth case. "You drop it here and store it in the mine entrance. You fly back to Niniltna, landing at the village strip so the tribal policemen can see how squeaky clean you are. You hike back down to your homestead and spend the next week running your trapline. You were catching beavers, you told everybody at the Roadhouse one night. You even showed them a pelt."

Cardboard and plastic crunched. "Only you don't have a trapline. There isn't a hole in the ice between here and your homestead, or a single snare to drop down a hole. You're not trapping beaver—you're using your snow machine to bring the booze down a case at a time."

He shifted from one foot to the other and tried a disarming smile. "Well, shit, Kate. Guy's got to make a living. Listen, can we talk about this? Don't!" he shouted when she swung again. "Goddamn it, I'll just buy more!"

"No, you won't."

"You can't stop me!"

"No?" She swung. The ax chunked.

It took fifteen minutes in all. Kate had always been very good with an ax. He cursed her through every second of it, unable to walk away. When she was finished, she struck a wooden match on the thigh of her jeans and tossed it into the pile of broken boxes. There was a whoosh of air and a burst of flame. She shouldered the ax and walked down the hill. Mutt followed, keeping between Kate and Pete, hard, bright gaze watching him carefully.

When she approached the Cessna, Pete's voice rose to a scream. "You fucking bitch, you lay a hand on that plane and I'll—"

Mutt snarled. He shut up. Kate raised the ax and swung with all her strength. The blade bit deep into the airframe just above the gear where the controls were located. She pulled the blade free, raised the ax for another swing, and several things happened at once.

A bottle she'd missed exploded in the mine entrance and everybody jumped. Mutt barked, a single, sharp sound, and kept barking. There was a scrabble of feet behind Kate. The ax twisted out of her hands and thudded into the snow six feet away, and she whirled to face a blade that gleamed in the reflection of the whiskey fire. She halted in a half crouch, arms curved at her sides.

Where was Mutt? A bark answered the question somewhere off to her right. She couldn't look away from the blade to see what Mutt had found more important than guarding her back. They would discuss the matter, in detail. Later.

The bootlegger's grin taunted her, and he wasn't looking so handsome anymore. "Sorry, Kate." He gestured at her scar with the knife. "Guess I get to finish what one of your baby-rapers started. No offense," he added. "I'm just making me too much money to let you walk away from this one."

"No offense," she agreed, and as he took a step forward dropped to her hands, kicked out with her right foot, hooked his ankle, and yanked his feet out from under him. He landed hard on his back, hard enough to jolt the knife out of his grip. She snagged it out of the air and in one continuing smooth motion had the point under his chin. The grin froze in place.

She pressed up with the blade. Very slowly and very carefully he got to his feet. She kept pressing, and he went all the way up on tiptoe. "What is this," she said, "a six-inch blade?" A bead of bright-red blood appeared, and he gave an inarticulate grunt. "I personally think your brain is too small for the blade to reach if I stick it in from under your chin." She pressed harder. "What do you think?"

His voice broke on a sob. "Jesus, Kate, don't, please don't."

Disgusted, she relaxed enough for him to come down off his toes. The point of the knife shifted, and he jerked back out of range. Blood dripped from his chin. He wiped at it and gave his hand an incredulous look. "You cut me! You bitch, you cut me!" He backed away from her as if he could back away from the blood, too. His heel caught on something, and he lost his balance and fell over the bank of the creek. It was short but steep, and momentum threw him into a heavy, awkward backward somersault. He landed on a fallen log. Kate heard the unmistakable crack of breaking bone from where she stood. The whiskey fire was high enough to show the white gleam of bone thrusting up through the fabric covering his left thigh.

Becoming aware of a low rumble of sound, she turned. Mutt stood in the middle of the airstrip, legs stiff, hackles raised, all her teeth showing as she stared into the trees. A steady, menacing growl rumbled up out of her throat. Kate followed her gaze. Five pairs of cold, speculative eyes met her own. Five muzzles sniffed the air, filled with the scents of burning whiskey, leaking hydraulic fluid, broken flesh, the rust-red smell of fresh blood.

Behind them Pete clawed his way up the creekbank and saw. "Kate." His voice sweated fear.

She turned her head to look at the man lying on the

frozen creekbank, and she did not see him. She saw instead eight kids in Alakanuk, drunk and then dead drunk. She saw a baby drowned in Birch Creek, left on a sandbar by parents too drunk to remember to load him into the skiff with the case of beer they had just bought, and just opened.

She saw her mother, cold and still by the side of the road, halfway to a home to which she never returned and a husband and a daughter she never saw again.

Kate picked up the ax and took a step back. Five pairs of eyes shifted from the prone man to follow her progress. "Mutt," she said, her torn voice low.

The steady rumble of Mutt's growl never ceased as she, too, began to retreat, one careful step at a time.

"Kate," Pete said. "That thing with your mother, that was business. A guy has a right to make a living, you know?"

Her camp was already packed and stowed. The ax went in with it. The brush concealing the Polaris was easily cleared, and she'd left the machine pointed downhill for an easy start. She straddled the seat.

"Kate!" His voice rose. "Your mother would fuck for a bottle! Shit, after a while she'd fuck for a drink! Goddamn you, Kate, you can't leave me here! Kate!"

The roar of the engine drowned out his scream.

Gathering clouds hid the setting sun. It would snow before morning. It was sixty miles across country to her homestead. Time to go. Mutt jumped up on the seat behind her, and Kate put the machine in gear.

WHO KILLED COCK ROGERS?

BILL CRIDER

Bill Crider is one of today's most under-
appreciated writers. Equally at home in
several genres, he's never more enjoyable
than in his folktales of one Sheriff Rhodes of
Clearview, Texas.

But as with all storytellers of the first rank,
when you look just below the surface, you'll
find some serious observation going on—sort
of like Andy Griffith's Mayberry skewing a
bit to the dark side.

All of Crider's considerable literary virtues
are on display in this wry little gem.

MRS. JANELLE TABOR, an attractive widow in her early forties, was spattered with cow manure. It was green, mostly, and it didn't go well with her yellow blouse. It didn't smell good, either.

"And it's all your fault, Sheriff Rhodes!" she said, wagging a finger in his face.

Rhodes had to agree, at least partially. If he hadn't defeated Ralph Claymore in the most recent county elections, Claymore wouldn't have gone back to cattle ranching in a big way, throwing all his energy into it. And if Claymore weren't ranching, along with hauling cattle for ranchers in six or seven adjoining counties, the big double-decked cattle trucks, each one of them carrying as many as eighty cows, wouldn't be driving right down the main street of Clearview on their way to the weekly auction sale. And if the cattle trucks hadn't been driving down the main street, Mrs. Tabor wouldn't be standing in the Sheriff's Office, waving her finger around and smelling like a feedlot on a rainy day.

But there she was, and she was blaming it all on Rhodes.

"I thought folks knew better than to try crossin' the street behind one of them cattle trucks," Hack Jensen said. Jensen, who was even older than he looked, was the Blacklin County dispatcher, and he didn't have much use for people who blamed their own troubles on someone else.

"I wasn't trying to cross the street," Mrs. Tabor said. "I was standing on the curb, waiting for the light to change. And when the truck started up—"

"You got splashed," Rhodes finished for her.

It was becoming a familiar story. The cattle, because

of their diet and the stress of being loaded up and hauled off the ranches, relieved themselves in the trucks. A lot of the waste went out a drain in the floor and splattered on the street, which was another problem. However, a lot of the waste sloshed out the front of the truck if the driver made a sudden stop at a light, and another wave of it sometimes swirled out the back when the driver started forward after the same stop. It was hard for some people to believe how much of the foul green liquid could accumulate in the truck in just the few miles from Claymore's ranch into town. Or at least it was hard for them to believe until they experienced it. After that, they believed it, all right.

"I think it's shameful," Mrs. Tabor said, pushing a strand of hair back from her forehead. "And I think you should put a stop to it."

Rhodes noticed that there were flecks of green in her hair too, but he decided it would be better not to mention them. "We've ticketed some of the drivers," he said.

"And what good did that do?" Mrs. Tabor asked. "It didn't help little Billy Sandlin when he slipped down in that mess and broke his arm. It didn't help Mrs. Yarborough when she was trying to get change out of her purse for her granddaughter to buy some candy with."

Rhodes remembered Mrs. Yarborough. She had told her story with a horrified look on her face, and then she'd shown Rhodes the contents of her purse. He didn't have to be told that Mrs. Yarborough didn't ever want to put her hand in there again.

"Folks ought to know better than to get close to that street on Thursdays," Hack said. "That's sale day."

Mrs. Tabor looked at him. "I guess you'd like to tell the merchants of Clearview just to close down on Thursdays, wouldn't you, Mr. Jensen? I wonder how they'd like *that* idea?"

They wouldn't like it at all, and everyone in the office knew it.

"A lot of people are avoiding downtown on Thursdays already," Mrs. Tabor went on. "What there is left of it. Most everybody goes out to Wal-Mart now anyway, and this is going to drive the rest of them out there. Pretty soon there won't *be* a downtown anymore."

She had a point, but Rhodes couldn't really do anything about it. He couldn't stop Claymore from sending his trucks through town, which just happened to be on the state highway that led to the auction sale in another county. He could keep giving the drivers tickets, but that was about all.

He explained all that to Mrs. Tabor, but she wasn't satisfied. "I thought that's what you'd say. But something has to be done. And if I can't get any satisfaction from the law, well, I'll just go to Red Rogers!"

She turned and went out the door. There were spots of manure on the back of her blouse.

"Smells better in here now that she's gone," Hack said when the door shut behind her. "Bet it don't smell too good out in the street, though."

"The smell doesn't last long," Rhodes said. "Not if there's any kind of a breeze. Besides, there's nothing we can do about it. The state Supreme Court ruled on that case out in Erath County this year and decided that the smell of cow manure isn't an air contaminant."

"Maybe so," Hack said, "but that won't matter much to Red Rogers."

Rhodes nodded. Hack was right about that. Rogers, whose real name was Larry Redden, was the closest thing Clearview had to a local radio personality. He did just about everything at KVUE ("Radio K-Vue," as Rogers called it). He was the news director and the music director. He was also the only reporter, and he did news broadcasts at 7:00 A.M., 12:00 noon, and 5:00 P.M.

Those things didn't bother Rhodes. What bothered him was Rogers' new show.

Rogers had concluded that since talk radio was the hot new format, Clearview needed talk radio, and he had managed to convince the station's owner. But because the station couldn't afford any of the syndicated shows, Rogers decided to do his own. He called it *The Cock Pit* and hosted it himself.

The show aired for an hour every afternoon and dealt with both national and local issues. Rogers took on all comers. In a blatant attempt to get listeners, he called Rush Limbaugh a "draft-dodging wimp" who was afraid to confront anyone who disagreed with his views. Rogers then declared that he would put anyone on the air, whether that person agreed with him or not. He seemed to aspire to become something like the Geraldo Rivera of talk radio. Rhodes wasn't certain that was a worthy aspiration.

"Sure do a lot of people listen to that *Cock Pit,*" Hack said. "Nearly ever'body in town, I bet. I listen to it myself, sometimes. 'Providin' a clear view for Clearview,' that's what Rogers says. 'KVUE stands for a clear view.'"

Rogers brought a clear view to his show, all right. Rhodes had to agree with that. The trouble was that Rogers's idea of providing a clear view was to talk about anything that was controversial. Rhodes was surprised that Rogers hadn't talked about the cattle truck problem before now.

"Maybe Mrs. Tabor won't really bring Red Rogers into this," Rhodes told Hack. But he had a horrible feeling that she would.

"So you deny that your trucks are causing the problem? You deny that they're spreading cow manure from one end of Clearview to another? What about the danger of disease? What about the danger of food contamination? What about economic ruin for the downtown merchants?"

The Cock Pit had been going on for about thirty minutes, and Red Rogers was getting into high gear.

"Turn that radio down, Hack," Rhodes said. "I think I've heard enough."

Indeed, Mrs. Tabor had gone to Red Rogers, who had jumped at the chance to participate in a growing local controversy. He had gotten Ralph Claymore and Randall Persons, one of Claymore's drivers, to go on the air with him, along with Mrs. Tabor and Mrs. Yarborough, who presented their side of the argument. Not to mention Billy Sandlin.

Hack turned the radio down, but Rhodes could still hear it.

"I'm not trying to hurt the downtown merchants," Claymore said. He had a deep voice that sounded very good on the radio. Rhodes envied him the voice but not his current situation.

"What about these people here?" Rogers asked. "The ones who've had their purses filled with cattle scour, the ones who've had their clothing ruined, the ones who've spent hundreds of dollars trying to get the smell out of their cars?"

"If you'll just give me a chance," Claymore said, "I'll try to explain."

But Red Rogers didn't give him a chance to explain. Rogers started up again about economic ruin, slime in the streets, filth in the air, and cattle scour spotting formerly pristine clothing of the children of Clearview.

Up until that point, Randall Persons hadn't had much to say. Now he spoke directly to Rogers. "You little turd."

In the background there was a horrified gasp. Probably Mrs. Tabor, Rhodes thought.

On a national show, there would have been a delay of several seconds between the utterance of the words and their broadcast, allowing for the bleeping of offensive terms. Not in Clearview. Everyone in town heard Persons call Red Rogers a turd. And no one was particularly surprised. Persons was big, hot-tempered, and mean. Rhodes suspected that Rogers had invited him on the show in hopes that he would say exactly what he had said.

"If you were half the man you think you are," Persons went on, "you'd follow me outside and get your skinny little ass whipped."

There was another horrified gasp, the sound of a chair falling over, and then everyone was talking at once. Rhodes thought he heard Ralph Claymore say something like, "Everyone calm down," but he wasn't sure.

"Turn the radio back up," Rhodes told Hack.

"I thought you didn't want to be bothered by this

stuff," Hack said. "I thought you didn't want to hear it. I thought you didn't—"

"Hack," Rhodes said.

Hack turned the radio up.

The scuffling sounds were louder, and there were several grunts and some muffled noises that might have been blows being struck. Someone was screaming.

And then Radio K-Vue went off the air.

When it came back on, after a lapse of only a few seconds, a record was playing, something by Dwight Yoakam, country music being the only thing on KVUE's playlist.

"You goin' out there?" Hack asked, looking over at Rhodes. Rhodes sighed and stood up. "I guess I'd better," he said.

The radio station was a flat-roofed white stucco building with the call letters painted on the side. It was located just outside Clearview, on the same highway that the trucks took to the auction sale. A chinaberry tree grew on one side, and the transmitter tower was in back. There were several cars in the parking lot, including Ralph Claymore's Lincoln and Randall Persons' new Dodge pickup.

Not far from the chinaberry tree, Persons was whipping Red Rogers' skinny little ass, or at least giving it a good try. He was hampered by Claymore, who had a pretty good grip on one of Persons' arms, and by Mrs. Tabor, who was more or less hanging from Persons' back, her arms wrapped around his size-eighteen neck.

Mrs. Yarborough and Billy Sandlin were watching. Mrs. Yarborough looked as if she might do something if she only knew what. Billy Sandlin seemed to be the only one who was enjoying himself, even if his arm was in a sling.

Rhodes walked over and stepped between Persons and Red Rogers. Mrs. Tabor released her hold and dropped to the ground.

"That's enough fighting," Rhodes said. "I think it's time everyone here cooled off and went home."

"I'm not cooling off, Sheriff," Rogers said. He was panting a little from hopping around and staying out of Persons' reach. "I'm filing charges against this maniac."

"Who're you callin' a maniac, you little turd?" Persons said, edging forward. "If it wasn't for a woman hangin' on my neck, I'd have beat you to a pulp."

"Anytime," Rogers said, putting up his fists and dancing backward. "Anytime you're ready."

Rhodes kept his place between them. "You think you can get Randall home all right?" he asked Claymore.

"Sure," Claymore said. He was wearing double-knit jeans, highly polished boots, and a silver belt buckle not much smaller than one of the Lincoln's hubcaps. "Come on, Randall. You've caused enough trouble here."

"You let me catch you in town, you're a dead man," Persons said to Rogers as Claymore led him away.

"Not if I see you first," Rogers said.

Persons tried to break away, but Claymore had a good grip on his arm and got him turned back toward his truck. Everyone watched until he got inside and drove away.

"Lord have mercy," Mrs. Tabor said as Claymore got into his own car. "I never thought things would turn out like this. I wish I'd just taken a hot bath and forgotten about getting covered with cow mess. And then those terrible things that Mr. Rogers was saying about Ralph—" She blushed. "Mr. Claymore, I mean—well, it was just all too much."

"You had every right to get your story on the radio," Mrs. Yarborough said. "Every time I think about what happened to my purse, I shudder."

She shuddered.

"That's right, Mrs. Tabor," Rogers said. "We still have freedom of speech in this country, no matter how many people try to censor us and shut us up. The U.S. Constitution guarantees you your right to have your say, and don't let Randall Persons or any of those others tell you that you don't. I want you to come back on my show as soon as possible."

"Wait a minute," Rhodes said. He turned to Mrs. Tabor. "What 'others' is he talking about?"

"I don't know," Mrs. Tabor said. "There were some phone calls . . ."

"We got some at the station too," Rogers said. "Bomb threats."

Rhodes looked at him. "And you didn't report them?"

Rogers stared back defiantly. "I wanted to. Mr. Griggs said they were just crank calls."

Griggs was the station manager. Rhodes would talk to him later.

"I didn't get any bomb threats," Mrs. Tabor said. "But someone sure enough threatened me. They said I'd better not go on *The Cock Pit* if I knew what was good for me."

"Did you recognize the voice?" Rhodes asked.

"No. It was a funny kind of voice, real husky. And whoever it was didn't really sound sincere, if you know what I mean. It was more like some teenager pulling a prank."

"Did you notice anything else? Anything that would help you identify the voice?"

Mrs. Tabor screwed up her face in thought. "There was something. . . ." She gave up. "I just can't put my finger on it."

Rhodes hoped she would think of it later. "And why didn't you call my office?"

"I didn't really see any reason to. It was just somebody on the phone. People get calls like that all the time. I didn't think it was serious."

"You should have reported it," Rhodes said. "You never can tell who's serious and who's not. Those calls could have been made by someone dangerous."

Rogers and Mrs. Tabor didn't agree, but it turned out that Rhodes was right. The radio station didn't get bombed, but two weeks later Red Rogers was killed.

Ralph Claymore called it in. Rhodes drove out and met him at one of his feedlots. The cattle were rounded up and held there before being loaded for the auction. Rhodes wasn't sure what they were fed in the lot, but he knew the feed had something to do with the problem Mrs. Tabor had complained about.

There was an old water well near the feedlot, but it wasn't being used any longer. The top had collapsed inward, and a tall tickle-tongue tree beside it stretched out sticker-covered limbs. Bramble vines surrounded the well so that no one could have gotten close enough to the well to draw any water, which was fine with Rhodes. He wouldn't want to drink any water from a well that close to a feedlot.

The lot had a sturdy wooden fence around it, and a cattle chute at one end. There were no cattle in the lot, but the dried scour stuck to the sides of the chute smelled a lot like Mrs. Tabor had in Rhodes's office. The smell wasn't really unpleasant, Rhodes thought, not when you were out in the country.

Red Rogers was just outside the feedlot, lying near the chute. Rhodes walked over to the body, being careful where he stepped. There were cow patties scattered all around, and not all of them had dried out.

Rogers had been shot twice in the chest, and one of the bullets must have hit his heart. He hadn't bled much.

"Anybody hear anything?" Rhodes asked Claymore.

Claymore looked over beyond Rhodes at the green pasture that stretched out toward a low hill. It was planted in Coastal Bermuda, but there were no cows grazing it.

"There's no one around to hear," Claymore said.

He was right about that. A county road ran near the feedlot, but the nearest house was at least half a mile away.

"How long do you think he's been here?" Claymore asked.

Rhodes felt the body. It was cold and appeared to have passed through rigor mortis. The clothing was damp with dew.

"I'm no expert," Rhodes said. "We'll have to wait for an autopsy. But I'd say since last night sometime. Can you think of any reason for Rogers to be out here?"

Claymore took off his Stetson and ran a hand through his black, wavy hair. Rhodes was envious.

"Not unless he was spying on me for some reason," Claymore said. He settled the hat back on his head. "You think this had anything to do with that radio program?"

"Maybe," Rhodes said. "What were you doing out here so early?"

Claymore pretended to be surprised by the question. "You don't suspect me of this, do you? I ran for sheriff!"

"That doesn't make you a saint," Rhodes said.

"Maybe not. Anyway, I came to check on some cattle. I was going to drive down in the bottom, but I saw Rogers lying there when I opened the gate. So I gave you a call."

Rhodes looked at him quizzically.

"Car phone," Claymore said, pointing to his truck, a red and white Ford Ranger.

"Oh." Rhodes didn't have a car phone, but he had a radio, and he used it to call Hack. He told the dispatcher to send for the justice of the peace and an ambulance.

"Have you seen Randall Persons today?" he asked Claymore after talking to Hack.

"What do you mean by that, Sheriff?"

"Never mind. I'll talk to him myself. Can you account for your whereabouts last night?"

"Of course."

"Good," Rhodes said. "Why don't you tell me where you were from about dark yesterday until you found Rogers this morning."

After hearing Claymore's story, Rhodes took some Polaroids of the body and the area around it. Then he made a thorough investigation of the scene. He didn't find anything unusual—no shell casings, no strange footprints, no matchbooks with addresses written inside the covers.

The JP arrived and declared Rogers dead, and the ambulance came and took the body away. Rhodes sent Claymore home, then climbed the feedlot fence and sat on the top board while he looked out across the pasture.

It was a cool day, but the sun was shining and there wasn't much of a breeze. Rhodes enjoyed sitting there and looking out over the green Coastal, but he wished the circumstances were different. It seemed like the only time he ever got out in the country these days was when somebody broke the law.

Claymore's story was that he had spent the previous night reading a book in his bedroom while his wife watched television in the den. Then he'd gone to sleep.

"You can ask my wife," he said. "She was there all the time too."

Rhodes didn't doubt it. He'd met Dora Claymore, and she seemed to spend most of her time watching game and talk shows on television. She hardly ever left the house.

The trouble was that she paid so much attention to her TV set that she often wasn't aware of what her husband was up to. There had been at least one time in the past, a time that Rhodes was well aware of, that her husband had been paying visits to a young woman, a woman who later wound up dead. Dora Claymore hadn't known about her husband's activities, though Rhodes had eventually found out. Maybe her husband had sneaked out again. Rhodes would have to talk to her, see what she knew.

Then there was Randall Persons. He'd threatened Rogers at the station, tried to beat him up, and after that he'd more or less promised to kill him if he caught him in town.

Rhodes heard a mockingbird call down in the bottom. This wasn't exactly in town, but that probably wouldn't matter to Persons.

The threatening phone calls were another thing. Rhodes didn't know where they fit in. Jobe Griggs, the station manager, said they'd gotten two. Both from some husky-voiced anonymous caller, both saying there was a bomb in the station.

Griggs hadn't been bothered. "There wasn't any bomb, though," he told Rhodes. "There's no way anyone could get in the station past our secretary, and when she's not there the place is locked up tighter than Dick's hat-band. I checked the doors. The locks were just fine. Believe me, it was a prank. When you do controversial shows, you get threats like that."

Maybe it had been just a prank, Rhodes thought, but now Red Rogers was dead. That wasn't a prank. It was murder.

Randall Persons lived in a one-story frame house about a mile out of Clearview. The house needed paint, and its appearance wasn't improved any by the eighteen-wheeler parked in the front yard. The big Peterbilt tractor wasn't the problem. It was pitch black, and the paint and chrome shone more brilliantly than a marine's combat boots.

The problem was the trailer. It was one of the double-deckers, dried manure stuck on all the slats, and it smelled considerably worse than the feedlot. Rhodes wondered when Persons had last hosed it out. Probably never.

Persons was sitting on the porch, smoking a cigarette and watching Rhodes. He was wearing a bulging white T-shirt and jeans. A black cat that must have weighed close to twenty pounds was lying in the sun by the steps. It was watching Rhodes too, but with less suspicion in its gaze than Persons.

"Good morning," Rhodes said as he approached the porch.

Persons nodded. "Mornin'."

The cat got up, stretched, and jumped off the porch. It came to Rhodes and started rubbing against his leg.

"Not making a run today?" Rhodes asked Persons.

"Not a sale day. I don't drive 'cept on sale day." Persons dropped his cigarette butt on the step and crushed it. "Listen, Sheriff, about that fight I had. I didn't really mean to hurt that damn Rogers. He just got me mad, talkin' that way. He don't know a thing about workin' for a livin', just sits in that big chair with a microphone in front of him and runs his mouth. If it was up to him, he'd put me out of a job."

"I don't think he'll be doing that," Rhodes said. "Have you seen him today?"

Persons laughed. "You gotta be jokin', Sheriff. It ain't even nine o'clock yet. He's prob'ly down at that station, runnin' his mouth on the news or something."

The black cat moved away from Rhodes and walked back to the porch. It sat down beside Persons and started grooming itself.

"He's not at the station," Rhodes said.

"What's he up to, then? You here to warn me that he's comin' after me with a shotgun? 'Cause that's what it'd take for him to get the best of me."

As far as Rhodes could tell, Persons was sincere in his remarks. He seemed really to believe that Red Rogers was alive and well and still upset by what had happened at the radio station.

"What did you do yesterday?" Rhodes asked. "After you got home, I mean."

Persons rubbed the head of the black cat. "Watched a little TV. Then I went out to the Palm Club. Why?"

"And after that?"

"What's goin' on here, Sheriff? Why're you askin' me all these questions?"

Rhodes didn't see any harm in telling the truth. "Because somebody killed Red Rogers last night."

Persons didn't seem upset by the information. "Can't say I'm sorry, and it don't surprise me much. He had an awful big mouth on him."

"Not anymore," Rhodes pointed out.

"Yeah. Well, he might not've got killed if he'd kept it shut." Persons shoved the cat aside and stood up. "But I didn't kill him. There was plenty of people saw me at the Palm Club last night. And after that I took somebody home. I was there till just about an hour ago."

"Who did you take home?" Rhodes asked.

"That's my business," Persons said. "There's some things a man don't talk about."

"You might have to."

Persons shrugged. "Maybe. Maybe not. You gonna arrest me?"

Rhodes said that he wasn't.

"Then I ain't talkin'."

Rhodes didn't really blame him.

Dora Claymore was small and frail, and she looked older than her husband. She was alone in her den, watching *The Price Is Right*, where Bob Barker was urging a contestant to spin a giant wheel with numbers on it.

"She needs to hit sixty cents," Dora explained. "Otherwise she won't get to try for the Showcase."

She watched the contestant spin and was plainly disappointed when the woman got a seventy. The TV audience groaned, while Barker commiserated with the woman. Then a commercial came on and Dora was able to concentrate on Rhodes.

"What were you asking?" she said.

"About your husband. Where is he?"

"Oh, yes. He had to go talk to some ranchers over in the next county about hauling their calves to the auction next week. He'll be back this afternoon."

He didn't seem to be showing much grief about Red Rogers, Rhodes thought.

"It was terrible about that radio host," Dora said, as if reading Rhodes's mind. "I listened to his show every day."

"Did you like it?"

"Oh, no. I hated it. I thought he was terrible, always tearing things down and never building them up. I'm surprised that nobody had shot him before now."

Rhodes didn't ask why she listened to the show if she disliked it so much. He said, "Ralph's been doing very well for himself lately."

Dora brightened. "You know, he really has. I was so worried after he lost the election." She gave Rhodes a dark look. "But it was the best thing that ever happened. Until then he'd been just resting on his laurels. He never got out of the house or showed much interest in anything. But now he's as busy as he can be, and he really seems to be enjoying himself. I'm very proud of him."

That was probably true, Rhodes thought. Dora had no

real life of her own. She lived through the TV shows she watched and through her husband.

"What about the complaints?" Rhodes asked. "Didn't they bother him?"

"Well, of course they did. He's a public-spirited man, as you know. He's widely respected. He ran for sheriff, and he's in the Lions Club. And he's worried about the downtown merchants. But it's not his fault that the cattle sometimes make a mess."

"What about Red Rogers? Was Ralph worried about the radio program?"

Dora reddened. "All that Rogers did was stir up trouble! The nerve of that man! The way he talked to Ralph was a disgrace! And he had the gall to call here yesterday afternoon and talk to Ralph about going on the air again. He said he wasn't finished with him!"

Claymore hadn't mentioned that. Rhodes wondered why.

"Did Ralph go out after that call?" he asked. "Or any-time last night?"

Dora seemed flustered. "Well, no. He was here all the time. I'm sure of that."

"Did he watch television with you?"

"No. He . . . he doesn't like TV very much. But he was here. He was . . . working on his accounts."

That wasn't exactly what Claymore had said. Rhodes was going to have another talk with him soon. If he could find him.

"Did Ralph say which ranchers he was going to talk to?" he asked.

Dora couldn't remember. "But they were in another county. I'm sure about that."

Rhodes thanked her, and as he left she turned to the TV set.

"Oh, no!" she cried.

Rhodes turned around. "What's the matter?"

Dora was practically in tears. "I missed the Showcase," she said. "It's the best part of the whole show."

◆ ◆ ◆

Claymore had evidently gone to visit the ranchers in his pickup. His Lincoln was parked in the drive beside the house. Rhodes walked past it on his way back to his own car. The Lincoln was swanky, but it could have used a wash job. Rhodes glanced into the car. There was a .38 revolver lying on the back seat.

Although the pistol was a prohibited weapon according to Texas law, there was nothing wrong with its being in plain sight in the car—as long as the car was on Claymore's property. If the Lincoln had been parked in the street, that would have been a different matter. In that case, the law required that the pistol be locked in the trunk or the glove compartment. Rhodes could simply have taken it from the car without a warrant and taken it to the jail. But because the car was in the driveway, Rhodes needed a warrant to take the gun.

That was all right. He knew a judge.

Dora Claymore was watching *The People's Court* when Rhodes returned. She was much more interested in whether a man's cat was responsible for damaging a flower bed than in what Rhodes might find in the Lincoln. She hardly glanced at the warrant before telling him to do whatever it was he needed to do.

Rhodes hadn't asked her for a key to the car, but hardly anyone in Blacklin County locked a car parked in his own driveway. Rhodes tried the back door of the Lincoln. It opened easily, and Rhodes went to his own car for an evidence bag.

After the pistol was safely stowed, Rhodes examined the Lincoln's tires to see if there was any cow manure in the treads. There was, but considering the places where Claymore drove, Rhodes would have been more surprised if the tires had been clean.

There were no doubt scientific ways to prove whether the car had been driven near the feedlot where Rogers had died, so Rhodes got another evidence bag from his own car and scraped some of the manure into the bag. If the car had been at the feedlot, Claymore had a ready-made excuse. He owned the land, after all. Still, it was worth knowing. Now all Rhodes had to do was get someone to do an analysis of the manure in the bag and do the same for some samples from the area of the feedlot. He wondered if the crime lab had ever had such a request before.

Probably not, but there was always a first time for everything.

Rhodes went by the jail to put the weapon and the cow manure in the evidence locker.

"Nobody's goin' to steal that manure," Hack observed. "You don't have to lock it up."

"Chain of evidence," Rhodes said.

Hack snorted. He didn't have any patience with all the niceties of the law. "Pretty stupid of someone to leave that pistol in the back seat of a car right in plain sight," he said.

Rhodes had been thinking the same thing. "What do you know about Mrs. Tabor?" he asked. Hack kept up with Clearview gossip far better than Rhodes did.

"How do you mean?"

"Is she going out with anybody?"

Hack thought for a second. "Been five years since Glenn Tabor died, just about. Janelle's a churchgoin' woman. Best place in Clearview to meet a woman is a church."

"That's not exactly what I was asking," Rhodes pointed out. "I wanted to know whether she was seeing anybody in particular."

Hack sighed. "I was gettin' to that. She goes to the First Baptist." He paused.

Rhodes waited patiently. He wasn't about to interrupt again. Hack would eventually tell the story his own way.

When he saw that he couldn't bait Rhodes again, Hack said, "Sometimes you meet the wrong man, even at church."

Rhodes couldn't resist asking. "What wrong man?"

"The one she got in trouble on the radio."

"Ralph Claymore? You're saying that Janelle Tabor is dating Ralph Claymore?"

"I didn't say anything about datin'. I said they met, is all. If they stepped out, I don't know it. But they've been talked about."

Rhodes remembered the way Mrs. Tabor had blushed when she said "Ralph" at the radio station.

"That Dora," Hack said. "I feel sorry for her."

So did Rhodes.

Rhodes had a lot of things to mull over, but first he had to talk to Deputy Ruth Grady. He asked her to finger-print the .38 and then go out to Claymore's and finger-print the Lincoln. Because the car hadn't been locked, there was always a chance that someone had planted the pistol there in order to implicate Claymore.

Rhodes also asked Deputy Grady to get some samples of the manure around Claymore's feedlot. Especially from any cow patties that looked as if they'd been run over by a car. To Ruth's credit, she didn't ask why. Then she could send the pistol off for ballistics tests and send the manure for analysis.

After Ruth left, Rhodes went over to the county court-house, where he had a private office. No one ever looked for him there, and he used it for a hideout when he needed to get away and think things over. The old red-stone building was a typical example of a lot of Texas courthouse architecture, and its onion-shaped dome had always reminded Rhodes just a little of pictures he'd seen of the Kremlin. He didn't think you could get bottled Dr Pepper in machines at the Kremlin, however.

He sat tipped back in his swivel chair, his feet up on the desk, eating peanut butter and cheese crackers from a vending machine and drinking a Dr Pepper. It was better than no lunch at all, and while he ate he could think over what he knew and try to figure out what might have happened to Red Rogers.

Randall Persons, who had at first seemed the most likely suspect, had faded into the background as far as

Rhodes was concerned. If Rhodes was any judge, and he liked to think that he was, Persons had been genuinely surprised to hear about Rogers' death.

But what about Mrs. Tabor and Ralph Claymore? Rhodes suspected that they met at church after Mrs. Tabor had been splattered. She probably told him about it and about going to Red Rogers. They began talking, and one thing led to another. It could have happened that way, and of course they would have kept the relationship secret, or tried to. If Hack knew, however, a lot of other people in town did.

Was that secret enough to cause one of them, or both of them, to kill Rogers? Maybe if Rogers was going to use it against either of them on the air . . . But why would Claymore have called Rhodes about the body? Why not just drag it to the bottom and dump it in the creek? And why would Claymore leave the pistol right there in his car? What if someone *had* planted it there?

Besides, Claymore had an alibi. He'd said that he was at home all night. His wife had backed him up, not that that meant anything, since their stories didn't quite match.

What if Claymore *hadn't* been at home? As Rhodes was well aware, it wouldn't have been the first time. And what if he had been with Janelle Tabor?

The swivel chair squealed as Rhodes put his feet on the floor. He brushed cracker crumbs off his shirt and took a last sip from the Dr Pepper bottle. It was time to see what Janelle Tabor had to say.

As it turned out, she didn't want to say much at all. She was in her kitchen, mixing up some tuna salad in a Pyrex bowl, and she was wearing an apron. Rhodes hadn't seen an apron in years.

"Who I see is my business," she told him, putting a dollop of mayonnaise in the bowl and mixing it with the tuna. "I don't see what it has to do with anything."

Rhodes told her that it might have to do with murder.

"*Murder?* That's going a little too far, isn't it, Sheriff? This is just about some cow manure and a bad smell."

"No," Rhodes said. "It's not." Then he told her about Rogers.

Mrs. Tabor put the bowl down on the cabinet and sat at her kitchen table. "Who did it?" she asked.

"I was hoping you might be able to help me with that. Did Ralph Claymore say anything about Rogers? About Rogers asking him to be on the radio again?"

"Surely you don't think Ralph had anything to do with killing anyone! He wouldn't hurt a fly."

Rhodes doubted that, but he said, "Maybe not. But someone did. My job is to find out who it was."

"What about the threatening phone calls? Maybe there was something to them after all."

Rhodes hadn't thought about the calls. "That's a possibility. Do you remember anything else about them? Anything that might help?"

"I was thinking about that just yesterday," Mrs. Tabor said. "I still can't put my finger on it."

"Try," Rhodes said. "Was it something about the voice that you recognized?"

Mrs. Tabor didn't respond. Rhodes added, "Or was it something else?"

"It had to be something else. I'm sure the caller was trying to disguise the voice."

"What else could it have been?" Rhodes asked. "Was there any background noise?"

Mrs. Tabor brightened. "That's it. There was some other noise on the line. I could hear someone else talking."

"Who?" Rhodes asked.

The smile faded on Mrs. Tabor's face. "It's not a who. It's a what. And now that I remember what it was, I don't think it'll help you any."

"Try me," Rhodes said.

"It was just some TV show."

"What TV show?"

"I'm not sure," Mrs. Tabor said. She thought for a few seconds. "I guess it sounded a little like *The Price Is Right.*"

◆ ◆ ◆

Dora Claymore came to the door. Rhodes could hear Alex Trebek reading a *Jeopardy* question in the room where the TV set was.

"Hello, Sheriff," Dora said. "Ralph's still not at home. Do you know who Thomas Jefferson's vice president was?"

"I'm afraid not," Rhodes said. "When's the last time you saw Ralph?"

"Oh, it was early. Probably six o'clock. He always gets off early when he has things to do."

"And he hasn't been back here since?"

"No, but I'm sure he'll be back sometime this afternoon, if you want to talk to him."

"No," Rhodes said. "I think you're the one I have to talk to."

"I should have thought of that this morning," Rhodes told Hack later. "She knew about Rogers being shot, but Claymore hadn't been back home to tell her, and it hadn't been on the radio yet. Rogers is the reporter, and he was dead. She knew because she was the one who shot him. Besides, who else could have made those threatening calls *before* Claymore went on the air? Hardly anyone knew about it."

"How come she left the pistol in the car?" Hack asked.

"Just indifference. Ralph wouldn't have been that careless, but she didn't really give it any thought. Just pitched the gun in the back seat and left it there."

"How'd she get Rogers out to that feedlot?"

"She told him that she had some information for him. Something about mistreatment of animals. Rogers didn't have any reason to think she was just luring him out of town to shoot him where no one would hear."

"Okay," Hack said. "I guess she shot him, then. But I can't figger out why."

"Because he was upsetting her life. Claymore had a little verve for the first time in years, and Dora liked him that way. His business kept him busy and out of her way, the way the campaign had. She didn't want things to change. If Ralph was happy, she was happy. She could watch TV all day, and no one bothered her. And she loved her respectability. Red Rogers was trying to destroy that, as far as she was concerned."

"Speakin' of respectability, did she know about Janelle Tabor?"

"I don't think so. And I didn't tell her."

Hack nodded. "Just as well she didn't know. She might've shot her too. What does Claymore think about all this?"

"He doesn't believe it. The worst part of it to him is that he found out that Dora took him for granted just the way he did her. He used her as his alibi, and he never dreamed that it worked both ways. They had separate bedrooms, and he knew Dora never checked on him, but he never checked on her, either. She found it just as easy to slip away as he did."

"Was he really at home last night?"

"No. He admitted that much. He was with Janelle Tabor. For part of the time anyway."

"Well, he can be with her all he wants to from now on."

Rhodes didn't think so. "She doesn't want anything to do with him now. She feels sorry for Dora."

"Too bad for ever'body," Hack said. "Hard to believe all this was caused just by a truckful of cows."

"It wasn't the cows," Rhodes said. "It was the manure."

Hack chuckled. "Ain't it always?" he said.

CARING FOR UNCLE HENRY

ROBERT CAMPBELL

Robert Campbell has written in a number of different crime subgenres, and always with distinction.

His years as a screenwriter endowed him with the ability to tell a complex story in the simplest and most powerful terms possible.

In the following story of human extinction, Campbell reminds us that at its best, crime fiction offers its practitioners an ideal vehicle for both social commentary and personal poetry.

▼▼▼▼▼

YOU'VE NO DOUBT seen it on a bumper sticker or heard somebody say it: "Old age ain't for sissies."

Henry Ridder was seventy-seven, alone and getting stiff, but still able to take care of himself. Ellie, his wife of fifty-two years, had worn him to the bone the last two years of her life; caring for somebody with Alzheimer's wasn't for sissies, either. Henry'd shouldered that burden all alone and without complaint because there were no living brothers or sisters, sons or daughters, to lend a hand, and he viewed help and respite offered by church groups and the Visiting Nurse Service as charity, which he would not accept.

There was a nephew, son of his only sister, long since dead and her husband dead as well, but he lived off somewhere in the east, far from the small town in Iowa where Henry'd lived all his life.

He'd been not quite a farmer and not quite a day laborer and not quite a carpenter and not quite a plumber since he'd been a boy; but he'd been all those things and more. Hard work was all he'd ever known; made him tough as rawhide. His wife used to say of him that all his bones were on the outside; he rang like a clapper when struck.

But the Alzheimer's that changed Ellie so and finally killed her had been almost more than he could stand up to; it had shaved him thin. And now he was beginning to be plagued by a similar failure of the mind.

"What's the difficulty, Henry?" Dr. David Cushing, nearly as old as Henry, had asked when he'd gone to him for consultation.

"I get distracted easy. I forget simple things."

"Headaches?"

"Nothing to mention."

"Auras? Distortions of your vision?"

"Nothing to complain about."

Nor would you complain, even if your head was clamped in a vise or your vision shrunk down to a tunnel the diameter of a dime, Cushing thought. Henry knew far too much about mental disorders and the causes thereof, having informed himself during the long rigors of Ellie's disease, to give anything away. He'd avoid giving any clues to Alzheimer's or such maladies as tumors if he could; the commonplace trickery patients played upon their doctors; a natural avoidance of unpleasant truths.

"What are you doing these days, Henry?"

"Doing, Dave? Doing nothing but putting one foot in front of the other. I've been retired for ten years, you know that."

"Well, I didn't mean what sort of job were you working at. I just meant how are you keeping yourself occupied?"

"After Ellie passed away, you mean? I'm still resting up from that. It was hellish."

"I know."

"Well, no, you don't. You know *about* it, but you don't *know* what it's like. Nobody can know what it's like who never actually went through it. She used to think the closet was the toilet and do her business there. She used to wander out into the winter cold in nothing but her nightgown. I had to change all the locks in the house and keep the doors and windows double bolted all day and all night."

"What's your address, Henry?" Dr. Cushing asked, interrupting the flow of old complaints, which obviously, even at this late date, caused Henry such distress.

"Is this one of them trick questions, Dave?"

"Just checking the record, Henry."

"Not likely. I haven't changed my address. It's the same old house I was born in. The one my mother left me after she died. It's still 153 Elm, just there at the crossing of Whitely."

"That's right," Cushing said, making a mark on the page. "That a two-bathroom house you got there?"

Henry made a rushing sound with his lips, his patience frayed.

"I just wondered, Henry. No need to get upset."

"I'm not upset. I'd just like to know what the number of bathrooms in my house has got to do with my health? You want to know how many chances you got to take a leak in case you have to make a house call?"

Dr. Cushing laughed as though he thought Henry was making a joke, but Henry wasn't making a joke. He was getting annoyed beyond reason, but he wasn't making any jokes.

"Will you tell me the names of your children and their birth dates?" Dr. Cushing asked.

Henry looked at his hands and then down at his feet, as if the answers to those questions would be printed on his fingers or found strewed on the carpet.

"What the hell's wrong with me?" Dr. Cushing finally said after a long, watchful pause. "I know you've never had any children."

"That's right," Henry said quickly. "Maybe it's about time for you to retire, Dave, if your memory's going like that."

"You've got brothers and sisters, though, haven't you?"

Henry sat up straighter in his chair; he seemed energized, as though a switch had been thrown; twenty years younger, impatient and alert, wanting this session with the doctor over so he could get on about his business.

"You're playing goddamn games again," Henry said, smiling knowingly. "Testing me. That's okay. You've got to do your job and earn your fee. You know perfectly well that I only had one sister, and she's long sinced passed away. Her husband, my only brother-in-law, he's gone too, which leaves their son, my nephew, my only living relative."

"You keep in touch?"

"Never hear from him."

"You got a location on him?"

"He lives back in New Jersey somewheres. I've got an address, but I don't write. The last time was to tell him that his aunt had passed away."

"He didn't come out for her funeral, did he?"

"I didn't expect him to. He sent a condolence card, and even that came as a surprise."

"You don't happen to have his address on you?"

"I got it writ down in my book in my desk drawer."

"You suppose you could copy it out for me?"

"Don't you even think it, Dave. I don't want you calling Earl and telling him his old uncle needs anything."

Dr. Cushing looked solemn. "Something's happening, Henry. I don't yet know what."

"What Ellie had?"

"I don't know for sure. We'll pay attention and see."

And Dr. Cushing did pay attention, in the careful, caring way that only small-town doctors can manage nowadays.

He sent his nurse, Margaret Burney, to visit Henry on some pretext or other, and she thought there was nothing wrong in going upstairs, supposedly to use the toilet, and looking for the nephew's address in Henry's desk, just in case it was wanted and needed.

Bumping into Henry on the street, Dr. Cushing asked apparently innocent questions, like, "What'd you have for breakfast today, Henry?" and "What do the headlines say, Henry?" until Henry's replies, along with local gossip about his growing oddities and eccentricities, convinced the doctor that Henry's mind was going fast.

For a while there, he thought it was Alzheimer's visiting his old friend and patient, just as it had visited Henry's wife, but after he'd managed to trick Henry into two examinations, three months apart, he diagnosed the condition as Pick's disease, the symptoms of which are so similar to Alzheimer's as to make little practical difference.

Characteristically, there were periods of minutes, even of hours, when Henry was perfectly lucid and competent.

Dr. Cushing sat Henry down in the living room during one such window of opportunity and told him the hard truth, unadorned, straight and simple.

"Why fool around splitting hairs about what to call it, Henry? Alzheimer's or Pick's or whatever. What you've got is just as bad as what Ellie had, and there are times when you know it. Your condition will run a steady and relentlessly progressive course. There's no known method of medical or surgical management. In other words, therapy is of no avail, and the prognosis is hopeless. You're going to need constant care."

"You're not going to send me anyplace where they'll strap me into one of them chairs and leave me sitting there in my own shit, drooling on my bib," Henry said. "I'd run off before I'd let you do that to me."

"I want to avoid that as much as you do, Henry. I'd rather you got the kind of care you gave Ellie. I'd rather you could stay in your house and not have to sell it off and give it to some nursing home until you're impoverished enough to qualify for public assistance."

Henry made a face composed of self-pity and rage and denial and pleading, so graphic and powerful that Dr. Cushing involuntary reared back as though fearful that Henry's head would literally explode.

"But to do that, you've got to make some compromises," he went on.

"Like what?"

"Like asking your nephew for help."

"The boy lives in New Jersey, for God's sake, Dave. He's no doubt got a job, maybe a wife and children, I don't know. He's surely got a house or a flat of his own. Why should he pull up stakes and come out here to a town in the middle of nowhere just to take care of an old man he hardly knows?"

"Because he'd want to, maybe. Because he's not a boy, he's a forty-five-year-old man who hasn't got a wife. A live-in girlfriend but not a wife. And no kids. And no job worth talking about. Because you could make an agreement and pay him something besides free rent and board.

You could make it in your will that the house would be his when you were gone."

"No!" Henry said sharply.

"What do you mean, no? You've got nobody else to leave it to," Dr. Cushing said, afraid that the window of lucidity and reason was closing.

"I got friends I might want to remember," Henry insisted.

"You've outlived just about all your friends except for me and Maggie, Henry, and neither one of us needs or wants your house or anything else you might have. Everything's going to go to pay for institutional care one way or to reward your nephew the other. Might as well keep what there is of it in the family."

"How do you know all this about Earl anyway?" Henry demanded.

"Because I got his address and then I got his number and called him. He's waiting for you to call and ask. At least do that, Henry. Call him and see if you can make an arrangement."

"God almighty," Henry said.

"You can consult Him in your prayers, if you want to, but do this one thing for yourself before other people have to make your decisions for you."

Henry's eyes narrowed and his mouth hardened. He stared at Dr. Cushing until his old friend looked away.

"I'm sorry, Henry, but I'll have to move to have you declared incompetent pretty soon. The court'll appoint a guardian. You'll probably end up in that institution, strapped in that chair you're so worried about. Call your nephew. Make an arrangement. He sounded like a nice enough fella to me."

"You're nice enough when you want to be, Earl, but you're a clown," Clara said. "You think I'm going to let you drag me halfway across the country to some godforsaken hole in the wall, living with your gaga old relative, wiping his ass and changing his pissy sheets until he finally dies?"

"I wouldn't expect you to do that. I'd take care of him."

"For how long?"

"As long as it takes."

"Well, I'm not stupid. I read up on this disease he's got. It could take years before he dies."

"He's seventy-seven, for God's sake."

"Those old farm types can live to be a hundred."

"I don't think so."

"What did you say?"

"I said I don't think so. I'd be willing to lay a bet with you right here, right now, that old Uncle Henry isn't going to live more than seven, eight months on the outside."

She peered at him through the smoke from the cigarette clamped in her red-lipsticked mouth, touched her frizzed blond hair—a caricature of a vamp, still in feathered mules and flowered dressing gown past noon, her breasts billowing from the gaping front of the negligee, looking like she'd stepped out of a movie from the twenties.

"How much you want to bet?" she asked, her voice grown husky.

"I figure the house and land could be worth maybe eighty thousand dollars, and I don't know how much more he's got saved up. So all right, I'll bet you a hundred thousand dollars. I can't say it plainer than that."

Dr. Cushing couldn't be there when Earl and Clara, billing themselves as Mr. and Mrs. Carteret, arrived in a taxi at Henry's front door, but Margaret Burney, as shrewd a lady at reading a sly or calculating eye as anybody for miles around, was there.

"Oh, Uncle Henry," Clara Carteret gushed, throwing her arms wide, running up the four steps to the porch, flooding her powder and perfume over a passive Henry (who was having one of his placid gaga days) like a cloud, crushing his balding head between her ample breasts.

Earl brought up the rear, a suitcase under each arm and another in each hand, playing bashful at meeting the old relative he hadn't seen in thirty-five years or talked to in maybe twenty.

"Uncle Henry," he said, putting down the suitcase and sticking out his hand. "We come to take care of you."

At the touch of their fingers, Margaret Burney saw a flicker behind Ridder's eyes, and she knew that Henry had awakened inside his head.

Well, here's a pair, Henry thought. *Here's a couple of sharks ready to take a bite out of this old piece of moldy bait. But ain't she got a set of tits on her. If I was only seventy again, I'd give that mewly nephew of mine a little competition. Not even married. She could be looking for offers.*

He patted her roughly in the vicinity of her ass.

"Why, I do believe he recognizes us, Earl, darlin'," Clara squealed.

"How could he recognize you, darlin'? He ain't never seen you," Earl said, talking the way he thought down-home, genuine farm folk talked.

"Well, recognizes *you,* then."

"And he ain't seen me since I was knee-high to a pup. Besides, I don't think he remembers much." He looked at Margaret Burney for confirmation.

"Sometimes he remembers quite a lot," Margaret said. "Other times he won't know somebody he's said hello to every day for fifty years and met that very morning. Do you remember your uncle, Mr. Carteret?"

"Oh, yes, oh, yes. My uncle and this old house and that grove of trees beyond the meadow. I remember him and all with great fondness. Uncle Henry and Aunt Ellie. I sure do remember."

Rattles on, don't he? Henry thought. *The way a man with nothing to say rattles on. Pushing buttons, hoping to find one that'll open the way to useful affection. He'll kiss my ass in front of witnesses if he thinks it'll be worth his while, but I'll have to watch him like a hawk when we're alone.*

The thought caused a door to close in his mind. Margaret Burney was watching him, and she saw the light go out. Henry looked at her, thoroughly confused, even a little afraid, waiting for her to tell him what was expected of him.

"Might as well get settled inside, if you'd be pleased to show us the room we're going to be calling home," Earl said, smiling at one and all.

"Top of the stairs and turn right," Margaret Burney said. "Mr. Ridder's room is to the left at the end of the hall. Only one bathroom in the house—you'll have to share—but there's a toilet off the mudroom downstairs."

Clara, empty-handed, was walking up the stairs beyond the tiny entry; Earl, with two of the bags, followed close behind. Margaret Burney picked up a suitcase and went in after them. At the foot of the stairs she paused and looked back. Henry was standing there, helpless and resigned, a stranger on his own front porch.

"They're not nice people," Margaret Burney declared in the soft way she sometimes had that brooked no argument.

"You don't know that for sure, Maggie," Dr. Cushing said.

"I know it, and Henry knows it. You don't know it because you haven't laid eyes on them yet, but when you do, you'll know it too."

"Do you think we should've made some other arrangement instead of calling the Carterets?"

There was a certain challenge in the question. He was really asking what else they might have done. It was an institution or home nursing care in the hands of strangers, which would impoverish him soon enough, or these relatives that Margaret and Henry had taken a dislike to without actual evidence that they'd do no good and might do harm.

"I suppose we've done the best by Henry that we can," Margaret Burney finally said, without much conviction.

"All right, then. I'm counting on you to make the Carterets feel at home. Invite them to church or something. Now will you please go out there and send in the next patient?"

"What the hell does he do in the bathroom?" Clara asked

in that special voice she'd developed when complaining about Henry. "He can't be taking a pee this long, because half the time he does it in his pants."

Wouldn't she just like to know what he was doing, Henry thought. *Wouldn't she just love to know that he was listening in on them, confirming what he'd known the first second he laid eyes on them: that they didn't like him any better than he liked them.*

"He's trying to take care of himself," Earl said. "Give him credit for that much at least. At least you don't have to go in there and wipe his ass."

I'd let you do that, sweetie. You come in here and see me with my pants down, and I'd let you do that.

"Not likely. Not goddamn likely. It comes to that, you'll be doing all the wiping, Earl, and you'll be doing it on your own."

Well, all right for you, you want to be that way.

"Don't start on me, Clara. What the hell you want me to do?"

"I want you to do what you said you were going to do."

There it was again. What he'd said he was going to do. You didn't have to be a lawyer to figure that one out. What he'd promised he was going to do, in order to get her away from the city in the East to a house in farm country, was fleece his old uncle of every dime he had and then take a powder. Well, when he'd had all his faculties, he'd taken care of that. He and Dr. Cushing and Margaret Burney and John Turk, his lawyer. They'd tied up his house and what money he had in such a tangle of trusts and guardianships that there was no way for anybody to get any of his assets except maintenance money before he died. After that—after he was dead—who gave a damn what happened to what was left behind?

"Keep it down. The bathroom's right on the other side of the wall, and walls have ears," Earl warned Clara.

"All right, then, but just think about getting started on it at least."

"We got to give it a little time. It's only been three months."

"All right, I said. Right now, for right this minute, I'd appreciate it greatly if you'd go knock on the bathroom door and ask your crazy old uncle if he fell in. I want to take a hot bath before I go to bed. I want to melt some of the goddamn boredom out of my bones."

Henry waited. Seven shuffling footsteps (Earl in his slippers, coming along the carpeted hallway), and then there was a knock on the bathroom door.

"You almost done in there, Unc? Unlock the door, Henry—it's only me."

Henry unlatched the door, and Earl walked in.

"Who are you?" Henry asked, glancing away from the mirror in which he was shaving his face and glaring at Earl.

"It's your nephew, Uncle Henry. It's only Earl. What have you been doing in here so long?"

"Shaving."

"Well," Earl said with an air of amusement and patience, taking the safety razor from Henry's hand, "you've got to have a blade in the razor if you want to shave."

"Oh? Well, who stole my blade?"

Henry stood still as Earl wiped the lather from his stubbled cheeks and chin with a cold, wet washrag.

"You want a shave, you ask me, Unc. I'll give you a shave."

Henry looked into the mirror. The dark curtain fell.

"Who the hell is that?" he asked, startled by his own reflection.

"Somebody you used to know before you went away, Henry. Just somebody you used to know."

Earl got into the habit of dressing up at least once a week and going into town to see John Turk, trying to coax or trick another fifty or a hundred dollars out of him.

He'd leave Clara to watch over Henry so he wouldn't get into any mischief, lighting the gas stove and forgetting he had a dry pot on it . . . burning the house down . . . anything like that.

She teased the old man to amuse herself, sitting opposite him in nothing but her negligee, smoking cigarettes and drinking pink gins in the mornings and early afternoons.

Henry was in deepest Gagaland. She could tell by the look of his eyes, the dark mirrors with nothing but murk behind them. She wondered if he knew she was a female, let alone who she was, as he sat in his moldy platform rocking chair, staring into the shadows behind the old piano in the corner of the parlor.

She put one leg up on the arm of the chair in which she sat, moving the negligee aside to bare her leg, sticking one finger in her pink gin and tracing a long, wet line, like the track of a snail, from her knee, up the length of her pale thigh, almost to the edge of the crisp, dark pubic hair, watching him like a hawk all the while.

He sat there unmoving, though his eyes twitched, glanced down, and fixed on the luminous line of wet.

"Don't you wish that you'd made that with your tongue, you old bastard?" she said, smiling as though she were saying the nicest things in the nicest way. She drew the skirt furthur aside, graphically proving that she was not a natural blonde. "You want a taste, Henry? You want a little lick?"

He sat there.

"You're off your nut, ain't you, Henry? Off your bird. Nothing in the pantry, nothing in the cage."

The window of his mind opened. He kept the lenses of his eyes from revealing that he was in his head again. He'd learned to do that. He thought it strange that when he was away he had no idea where his mind had gone, where it waited to return, as return it did every now and then. But it was peaceful wherever it was. It was only coming back to his senses that hurt, that made him afraid. Yet if he'd had the choice of one or the other, he'd choose to be aware, no matter how painful the fear and anguish. He supposed that practically everyone in the world made that choice on waking in the morning. To be mad and safe or sane and afraid.

There was a time, if you showed me your treasure like you're doing, I'd have had you on the rug with your knees bent back, riding you to glory, you whore, you fucking, tormenting whore.

"God, Henry, you are such a caution," Clara said, covering herself, bored by the game.

Down in John Turk's office, the lawyer, tiring of the litany of detailed complaint, drew up a check for a hundred dollars and handed it to Earl Carteret.

"How's your uncle doing?"

"He's doing okay, so long as either my wife or me keep an eye on him every second. It's like having a six-month-old baby, just learning to crawl, getting into everything that ain't nailed down. I got to lock him in his bedroom nights because he wanders outside and I'm afraid he'll kill himself. So when I do that, he wakes up and has to take a pee. Hammers on the door until I get up or he pisses in his shoe. It ain't easy, I got to tell you. Just the other day I happened to catch him trying to climb out his bedroom window and down the old apple tree. He thought I was his pa. Later on, when he had a couple of sane minutes, I told him what he tried to do and who he thought I was, and he laughed and told me how he used to shinny down that old tree and go fishing early on a Saturday morning when he was a boy. I told him he could have fell and busted his ass. Then he faded out like he does when I say something he doesn't want to hear, and that was all I could get out of him. I'm telling you, it's harder than I thought it was going to be."

"You're being compensated, aren't you, Mr. Carteret?" Turk said.

"I'm getting free rent and what to eat. I'm not getting much by way of extras. I'm not getting anything put away in the bank."

"Well, you'll be getting everything that Henry has when the time comes."

"Don't get me wrong. I'm happy to do what I can for the old man. He's my only living blood relative, you know, and that counts for a lot with me."

"We're grateful you feel that way, Mr. Carteret, all of us who know and like Henry. So thank you."

"Okay," Carteret said, getting to his feet. "Look here, don't think I like coming to you every week or so asking for more money. It makes me feel like a beggar, and I shouldn't be made to feel that way."

"Maybe the beginning of the month we'll take another look at the budget, bump it up here and there."

"That'd be good."

"It's no good, Earl," Clara said. "I'm going to be as crazy as that old man if I don't get out of here. It's been almost six months."

"I said seven or eight months," Earl replied.

"On the outside. You said seven or eight months on the outside, and the old man would be gone. All I'm asking for you to do is to move it up a month."

"You've got to cut me a little slack, Clara. It's got to look right."

"You don't fool me, Earl. You were hoping he'd die all on his own. You said it wouldn't be more than seven or eight months on the outside—you'd see to that—just to get me to come here with you. Well, Henry may be gaga, but he's as strong as a horse. He could end up outliving both of us. I caught him crawling along that little roof along the side of the house that runs outside his bedroom window. He told me some trash about going fishing, but I think he was crawling along so he could peek in the bedroom window while I was getting dressed or the bathroom window while I was on the toilet or in the tub."

"I'll do something about nailing up the window."

"I wouldn't. I'd put the story around about the things he does, and then I'd say he fell off that roof."

"What makes you think that'd kill him, if I pushed him off the roof, that tough old man? All it'd maybe do is break a couple of his bones and put him into bed, where it'd be twice as hard taking care of him."

"You're not listening to me, Earl. I'm not talking about caring for him. I'm talking about getting rid of him so it looks like it was an accident he brought on himself. You come up with a better idea—I don't care what—but you got to do something, Earl, and you got to do it soon, else you'll come home from town one day and I won't be here."

There was a long silence.

Why have they stopped talking? Henry asked himself as he crouched by the wall between bathroom and bedroom, his ear pressed against the tile. *Why are they so quiet all of a sudden? They're setting it up, the accident that's supposed to kill me.*

Panic washed over him in waves. He felt his mind slipping away behind the familiar dark curtain. He tried as hard as he could to stay in the light of reason. Because if he didn't, he'd be helpless and they'd kill him, maybe tonight, and if not tonight very soon. And he wouldn't be able to do a thing to stop them; he wouldn't even know it when they took his life. He wouldn't even know.

Sheriff Acuff came down the narrow stairs and into the parlor, where Dr. Cushing and Margaret Burney waited. A call had been made to John Turk, but he'd not yet arrived.

Acuff looked at Henry sitting in the platform rocking chair by the window, where he remembered Ellie Ridder sitting hour after hour the last couple of years of her life. Henry was still in his flannel nightshirt and a gray flannel robe. There were worn and faded carpet slippers on his feet. The skin on his ankles and shanks was so white it was almost blue, and there were bruises caused by age as big as quarters.

He was staring out the window, oblivious to all.

"What do you think, Sheriff?" Dr. Cushing asked.

Acuff jerked his head in Henry's direction.

Margaret Burney looked at Henry. "It's all right; he's out of it. He won't understand."

"You say this Earl Carteret, the nephew, was in the habit of locking Henry in his room at night?" Acuff said.

"That's what he told us," Dr. Cushing replied. "Did it for Henry's safety. That would have been the logical thing to do. Henry wandered off and could have hurt himself."

"If he was in the habit of locking the door, how come he didn't nail up the window? You tell me Henry's confused enough to maybe think a window was a door."

"All the windows are double-bolted, difficult to manage if you haven't got your wits about you, and if he had his wits about him, there'd be no reason for Henry to open them thinking they were something else," Margaret Burney said. "Does it signify anything?"

"Probably not. I just wondered. The way it looks to me is the Carterets had a quarrel that turned into a fight," Acuff said. "The woman took a pair of scissors and stabbed the man several times. He could've been laying down, his back to her, trying to ignore her, maybe, when she struck the first couple of times. Then he tried to get away from her, tried to fend her off—there's defensive wounds on his arms and hands—but she kept at him until he got the gun out of the nightstand and shot her. Killed her on the spot. But it was too late for him. I reckon he died of his wounds soon after he got to his uncle's room, looking for help. Tried to unlock the door. There's the mark of his bloody hand all over it, but I don't know if he ever turned the key."

"He didn't," Margaret Burney said. "It was locked when I got there."

One of the morgue team looked into the parlor.

"You can bag them up," Acuff said. He turned back to Margaret Burney. "What made you come over this hour of the night?"

She hesitated half a beat. Dr. Cushing caught it, but Acuff didn't know her quite well enough to do the same. In that split second she decided not to tell the sheriff about how the telephone rang and there was nothing but breathing for half a minute, until the party on the other end hung up. And how that got her to thinking it might be Henry.

"I got a busy signal when I called to invite Mrs. Carteret to the church social on Thursday," she said.

"You were friendly?"

"No, but I was trying to be neighborly. They were from the East, from a big city, and you could tell they weren't used to being in a small town like this. It was so hard being tied down to this house, taking care of an old man who was mental most of the time, so I thought I'd give the Carterets a little respite. Get someone in to look after Henry for the night and let them get to meet some of the folks around here."

"This was what time?"

"Eight o'clock, near as not. I called again at nine, and it was still busy. So I called every ten minutes for maybe an hour. Then I called the operator and found out the line was open but not being used."

"So you came over?"

"I'm a nurse. It's what I do when I can't rouse a patient on the phone, so that's what I did when I couldn't get the Carterets."

"And you found them like I saw them?"

"Exactly like that."

"And you didn't touch them to make sure they were dead?"

"I didn't have to do that. I could tell at a glance."

"Henry was locked in his room, you say?"

"He was. I was careful to disturb things as little as possible—the key in the lock, I mean—getting him out of his room, but I had to get him out of there, evidence or no evidence. He was shouting and moaning and weeping. He was terrified, and I had no idea what he might do: even throw himself out the window."

"The window was closed, was it?"

"Closed and double-bolted, yes."

Acuff stared at Henry for a long minute, then shook his head, dismissing any random notions he might have had.

"I guess that about does it, then. Double homicide." Acuff looked at Henry again. "What're you planning to do with him?"

"I'll take him home with me for tonight," Dr. Cushing said. "Tomorrow I suppose we'll have to look into a rest home that can take him in. If not that, the public institution will have to do."

"Well, at least he's alive," Margaret Burney said. "It could have been him laying dead, all that anger and hate flying around between them two because of him."

"What makes you say that?"

"Why else would they have cause to quarrel so bitterly? You can just bet it had to do with him."

Henry looked up and fixed his gaze on Margaret Burney's face.

She saw Henry there inside his head and knew he'd let her see him. He was smiling behind his eyes. He wasn't altogether helpless, the smile said. When the chips were down, he'd been the one to take care of Uncle Henry.

DEATH OF A SNOWBIRD

J. A. JANCE

J. A. Jance's mystery novels combine nonstop storytelling with a good number of wise perceptions about our times and ourselves.

The following story is about several things, not least about dreams that go awry and new dreams that spring from old ones.

Agnes and Oscar may just be Jance's two greatest creations. They're full of noisy life and secret sorrows.

As we already knew from her novels, J. A. Jance just keeps on getting better.

▼▼▼▼▼

AGNES BARKLEY DID THE DISHES. She always did the dishes. After breakfast. After lunch. After dinner. For forty-six years she had done them. Maybe "always" was a slight exaggeration. Certainly there must have been a time or two when she had goofed off, when she had just rinsed them and stacked them in the sink to await the next meal; but mostly she kept the sink clear and the dishes dried and put away where they belonged. It was her job. Part of her job.

Back home in Westmont, Illinois, the single kitchen window was so high overhead that Agnes couldn't see out at all. Here, in Oscar's RV, the sink was situated directly in front of an eye-level window. Agnes could stand there with her hands plunged deep in warm, sudsy dishwater and enjoy the view. While doing her chores she occasionally caught sight of hawks circling in a limitless blue sky. In the evening she reveled in the flaming sunsets, with their spectacular orange glows that seemed to set the whole world on fire.

Even after years of coming back time and again, she wasn't quite used to it. Every time Agnes looked out a January window, she couldn't help being amazed. There before her, instead of Chicago's gray, leaden cloud cover and bone-chilling cold, she found another world—the wide-open, brown desert landscape, topped by a vast expanse of sunny blue sky.

Agnes couldn't get over the clean, clear air. She delighted in the crisp, hard-edged shadows left on the ground by the desert sun, and she loved the colors. When some of her neighbors back home had wondered how she could stand to live in such a barren, ugly place three months out of the year, Agnes had tried in vain to explain the lovely contrast of newly leafed mesquite against a red, rockbound earth. Her friends had looked at her sympathetically, smiled, shaken their heads, and said she was crazy.

And in truth she was—crazy about the desert. Agnes loved the stark wild plants that persisted in growing despite a perpetual lack of moisture—the spiny, leggy ocotillos and the sturdy, low-growing mesquite; the majestic saguaro; the cholla with its glowing halo of dangerous thorns. She loved catching glimpses of desert wildlife—coyotes and jackrabbits and kangaroo rats. She even loved the desert floor itself—the smooth sands and rocky shales, the expanses of rugged reds and soothing, round-rocked grays, all of which, over the great visible distances, would fade to uniform blue.

At first she had been dreadfully homesick for Westmont, but now all that had changed. Agnes Barkley's love affair with the desert was such that, had she been in charge, their snowbird routine would have been completely reversed. They would have spent nine to ten months out of the year in Arizona and only two or so back home in Illinois.

No one could have been more surprised by this turn of events than Agnes Barkley herself. When Oscar had first talked about retiring from the post office and becoming a snowbird—about buying an RV and wintering in Arizona—Agnes had been dead set against it. She had thought she would hate the godforsaken place, and she had done her best to change Oscar's mind. As if anyone could do that.

In the end, she had given in gracefully. As she had in every other aspect of her married existence, Agnes put the best face on it she could muster and went along for the ride, just as Oscar must have known she would. After forty-six years of marriage, there weren't that many surprises left.

In the past she would have grudgingly tolerated whatever it was Oscar wanted and more or less pretended to like it. But when it came to Arizona, no pretense was necessary. Agnes adored the place—once they got out of Mesa, that is.

Oscar couldn't stand Mesa, either. He said there were too many old people there.

"What do you think you are?" Agnes had been tempted to ask him, although she never did, because the truth of the matter was, Agnes agreed with him—and for much the same reason. It bothered her to see all those senior citizens more or less locked up in the same place, year after year.

The park itself was nice enough, with a pool and all the appropriate amenities. Still, it made Agnes feel claustrophobic somehow, especially when, for two years running, their motor home was parked next to that of a divorced codger who snored so loudly that the racket came right through the walls into the Barkleys' own bedroom—even with the RV's air conditioner cranked up and running full blast.

So they set out to find someplace else to park their RV, someplace a little off the beaten track, as Oscar said. That's how they had ended up in Tombstone—The Town Too Tough to Die. Outside the Town Too Tough to Die was more like it.

The trailer park—that's what they called it: the O.K. Trailer Park, Overnighters Welcome—was several miles out of town. The individual lots had been carved out of the desert by terracing up the northern flank of a steep hillside. Whoever had designed the place had done a good job of it. Each site was far enough below its neighbor that every RV or trailer had its own unobstructed view of the hillside on the opposite side of a rocky draw. The western horizon boasted the Huachuca Mountains. To the east were the Whetstones and beyond those the Chiricahuas.

The views of those distant purple mountain majesties were what Agnes Barkley liked most about the O.K. Trailer Park. The views and the distances and the clear, clean air. And the idea that she didn't have to go to sleep listening to anyone snoring—anyone other than Oscar, that is. She was used to him.

"Yoo-hoo, Aggie. Anybody home?" Gretchen Dixon tapped on the doorframe. She didn't bother to wait for Agnes to answer before shoving open the door and popping her head inside. "Ready for a little company?"

Agnes took one last careful swipe at the countertop before wringing out the dishrag and putting it away under the sink. "What are you up to, Gretchen?"

At seventy-nine, Gretchen Dixon was given to chartreuse tank tops and Day-Glo Bermuda shorts—a color combination that showed off her tanned hide to best advantage. She wore her hair in a lank pageboy that hadn't changed—other than color—for forty years. It was one of fate's great injustices that someone like Gretchen, who had spent years soaking ultraviolet rays into her leathery skin, should be walking around bareheaded and apparently healthy, while Dr. Forsythe, Aggie's physician back home in Westmont, after burning off a spot of skin cancer, had forbidden Aggie to venture outside at all without wearing sunblock and a hat.

Agnes Barkley and Gretchen Dixon were friends, but there were several things about Gretchen that annoyed hell out of Agnes. The main one at this moment was the fact that despite the midday sun, Gretchen was bareheaded. Agnes loathed hats.

Gretchen lounged against the cupboard door and shook a cigarette out of a pack she always kept handy in some pocket or other. "So where's that worthless husband of yours?" she asked.

Not that Gretchen was really all that interested in knowing Oscar's whereabouts. She didn't like Oscar much, and the feeling was mutual. Rather than being worried about their mutual antipathy, Agnes found it oddly comforting. In fact, it was probably a very good idea to have friends your husband didn't exactly approve of. Years earlier, there had been one or two of Aggie's friends that Oscar had been crazy about. Too much so, in fact—with almost disastrous results for all concerned.

"Tramping around looking for arrowheads as per usual," Aggie said. "Out along the San Pedro, I think. He and Jim Rathbone went off together right after lunch. They'll be back in time for supper."

"That figures," Gretchen said disdainfully, rolling her eyes and blowing a plume of smoke high in the air as she slipped into the bench by the table.

"Aggie," she said, "do you realize you're the only woman around here who still cooks three square meals a day—breakfast, lunch, and dinner?"

"Why not?" Agnes objected. "I like to cook."

Gretchen shook her head. "You don't understand, Aggie. It gives all the rest of us a bad name. You maybe ought to let Oscar know that he's not the only one who's retired. It wouldn't kill the man to take you into town once in a while. He could buy you a nice dinner at the Wagon Wheel or at one of those newer places over on Allen Street."

"Oscar doesn't like to eat anybody else's cooking but mine," Aggie said.

Gretchen was not impressed. "He likes your cooking because he's cheap. Oscar's so tight his farts squeak."

Agnes Barkley laughed out loud. Gretchen Dixon was the most outrageous friend she had ever had. Agnes liked to listen to Gretchen just to hear what words would pop out of her mouth next. Even so, Agnes couldn't let Gretchen's attack on Oscar go unchallenged. After all, he was her husband.

"You shouldn't be so hard on him," she chided. "You'd like him if you ever spent any time with him."

"How can I spend time with the man?" Gretchen returned sarcastically. "Whenever I'm around him, all he does is grouse about how it isn't ladylike for women to smoke."

"Oscar was raised a Southern Baptist," Agnes countered.

"Oscar Barkley was raised under a rock."

Agnes changed the subject. "Would you like some lemonade? A cup of coffee?"

"Aggie Barkley, I'm not your husband. I didn't come over here to have you wait on me hand and foot the way you do him. I came to ask you a question. The senior citizens in town have chartered a bus to go up to Phoenix to the Heard Museum day after tomorrow. Me and Dolly Ann Parker and Lola Carlson are going to go. We were wondering if you'd like to come along."

"You mean Oscar and me?"

"No, I mean you, silly. Aggie Barkley by her own little lonesome. It's an overnight. We'll be staying someplace inexpensive, especially if we all four bunk in a single room. So you see, there wouldn't be any place for Oscar to sleep. Besides, it'll be fun. Just us girls. Think about it. It'll be like an old-fashioned slumber party. Remember those?"

Agnes was already shaking her head. "Oscar would never let me go. Never in a million years."

"Let?" Gretchen yelped, as though the very word wounded her. "Do you mean to tell me that at your age you have to ask that man for permission to be away from home overnight?"

"Not really. It's just that . . ."

"Say you'll go, then. The bus is filling up fast, and Dolly Ann needs to call in our reservation by five this afternoon."

"Where did you say it's going?"

Gretchen grinned triumphantly and ground out her cigarette in the ashtray Agnes had unobtrusively slipped in front of her. "The Heard Museum. In Phoenix. It's supposed to be full of all kinds of Indian stuff. Artifacts and baskets and all like that. I'm not that wild about Indians myself—I can take them or leave them—but the trip should be fun."

Agnes thought about it for a minute. She didn't want Gretchen to think she was a complete stick-in-the-mud. "If it's only overnight, I suppose I could go."

"That's my girl," Gretchen said. "I'll go right home and call Dolly Ann." She stood up and started briskly toward the door, then paused and turned back to Agnes. "By the way, have you ever played strip poker?"

"Me?" Agnes Barkley croaked. "Strip poker? Never!"

"Hold your breath, honey, because you're going to learn. The trick is to start out wearing plenty of clothes to begin with, so if you lose some it doesn't matter."

With that Gretchen Dixon was out the door, her flip-flops slapping noisily on the loose gravel as she headed down the hill toward her own mobile, parked two doors away. Agnes sat at the table, stunned. They would be playing strip poker? What on earth had she let herself in for?

Agnes wasn't so sure she had said yes outright, but she certainly had implied that she would go. She could have jumped up right then, swung the door open, and called out to Gretchen that she'd changed her mind, but she didn't. Instead she just sat there like a lump until she heard Gretchen's screen door slam shut behind her.

In the silence that followed, Agnes wondered what Oscar would say. It wasn't as though she had never left him alone. For years, she had spent one weekend in May—three whole days—at a Women's Bible Study retreat held each year at the YMCA camp at Lake Zurich, north of Buffalo Grove. And always, before she left, she had cooked and frozen and labeled enough food to last two weeks rather than three days. All Oscar and the girls ever had to do was thaw it out and heat it up.

Well, a Bible study retreat at a YMCA camp and four old ladies sitting around playing strip poker in a cheap hotel room weren't exactly the same thing, but Oscar didn't need to know about the poker part of it. Actually, the idea of Agnes going off someplace with Gretchen Dixon and her pals might be enough to set Oscar off all by itself.

And what if it did? Agnes Barkley asked herself, with a sudden jolt of self-determination. Sauce for the goose and sauce for the gander, right? After all, she never balked at the idea of him going off and spending hours on end wandering all over the desert with Jimmy Rathbone, that windy old crony of his, did she? So if Oscar Barkley didn't like the idea of her going to Phoenix with Gretchen, he could just as well lump it.

That was what Agnes thought at two o'clock in the afternoon, but by evening she had softened up some. Not that she'd changed her mind. She was still determined to go, but she'd figured out a way to ease it past Oscar.

As always, her first line of attack was food. She made his favorite dinner—Italian meat loaf with baked potatoes and frozen French-cut green beans; a tossed salad with her own homemade Thousand Island dressing; and a lemon meringue pie for dessert. Agnes never failed to be amazed by the amount of food she could coax out of that little galley-sized kitchen with its tiny oven and stove. All it took was a little talent for both cooking and timing.

Dinner was ready at six, but Oscar wasn't home. He still wasn't there at six-thirty or seven o'clock, either. Finally, at seven-fifteen, with the meat loaf tough and dry in the cooling oven and with the baked potatoes shriveled to death in their wrinkled, crusty skins, Agnes heard Oscar's Honda crunch to a stop outside the RV. By then, Agnes had pushed the plates and silverware aside and was playing a game of solitaire on the kitchen-nook table.

When Oscar stepped in through the door, Agnes didn't even glance up at him. "Sorry I'm so late, Aggie," he said, pausing long enough to hang his jacket and John Deere cap in the closet. "I guess we just got a little carried away with what we were doing."

"I just guess you did," she returned coolly.

With an apprehensive glance in her direction, Oscar hurried to the kitchen sink, rolled up his sleeves, and began washing his hands. "It smells good," he said.

"It probably was once," she replied. "I expect it'll be a little past its prime by the time I get it on the table."

"Sorry," he muttered again.

Deliberately, one line of cards at a time, she folded the solitaire hand away and then moved the dishes and silverware back to their respective places.

"Sit down and get out of the way," she ordered. "There isn't enough room for both of us to be milling around between the stove and the table while I'm trying to put food on the table."

Obediently, Oscar sank into the bench. While Agnes shifted the lukewarm food from the stove to the table, he struggled his way out of the nylon fanny pack he customarily wore on his walking jaunts. Agnes wasn't paying that much attention to what he was doing, but when she finished putting the last serving bowl on the table and went to sit down, she found a small earthen pot sitting next to her plate.

Agnes had seen Mexican *ollas* for sale at various curio shops on their travels through the Southwest. This one was shaped the same way most *ollas* were, with a rounded base and a small, narrow-necked lip. But most of those commercial pots were generally unmarked and made of a smooth reddish-brown clay. This was much smaller than any of the ones she had ever seen for sale. It was gray—almost black—with a few faintly etched white markings dimly visible.

"What's that?" she asked, sitting down at her place and leaning over so she could get a better view of the pot.

"Aggie, honey," Oscar said, "I believe you are looking at a winning lottery ticket."

Agnes Barkley sat up and stared across the tiny tabletop at her husband. It wasn't like Oscar to make jokes. Working in the post office all those years had pretty well wrung all the humor out of the man. But when she saw his face, Agnes was startled. Oscar was actually beaming. He reminded her of the grinning young man who had been waiting beside the altar for her forty-six years earlier.

"It doesn't look like any lottery ticket I've ever seen," Agnes answered, with a disdainful sniff. "Have some meat loaf and pass it before it gets any colder."

"Agnes," he said, not moving a finger toward the platter, "you don't understand. I think this is very important. Very valuable. I found it today. Down along the San Pedro just south of Saint David. There's a place where one of last winter's floods must have caused a cave-in.

This pot was just lying there in the sand, sticking up in the air and waiting for someone like me to come along and pick it up."

Agnes regarded the pot with a little more respect. "You think it's old, then?"

"Very."

"And it could be worth a lot of money?"

"Tons of money. Well, maybe not tons." Oscar Barkley never allowed himself to indulge in unnecessary exaggeration. "But enough to make our lives a whole lot easier."

"It's just a little chunk of clay. Why would it be worth money?"

"Because it's all in one piece, dummy," he replied with certainty. Agnes was so inured to Oscar's customary arrogance that she didn't even notice it, much less let it bother her.

"If you read *Archaeology,* or *Discovery,* or *National Geographic,* once in a while," he continued, "or if you even bothered to look at the pictures, you'd see that stuff like this is usually found smashed into a million pieces. People have to spend months and years fitting them all back together."

Agnes reached out to pick up the pot. She had planned on examining it more closely, but as soon as she touched it, she inexplicably changed her mind and pushed it aside.

"It still doesn't look like all that much to me," she said. "Now, if you're not going to bother with the meat loaf, would you please go ahead and pass it?"

The grin disappeared from Oscar's face. He passed the platter without another word. Agnes saw at once that she had hurt his feelings. Usually, just a glimpse of that wounded look on his face would have been enough to melt her heart and cause her to make up with him, but tonight, for some reason, she still felt too hurt herself. Agnes was in no mood for making apologies.

"By the way," she said, a few minutes later, as she slathered margarine on a stone-cold potato, "Gretchen and Dolly Ann invited me to come up to Phoenix with

them on a senior citizen bus tour the day after tomorrow.
I told them I'd go."

"Oh? For how long?" Oscar asked.

"Just overnight. Why, do you have a problem with
that?"

"No. No problem at all."

He said it so easily—it slipped out so smoothly—that
for a moment Agnes almost missed it. "You mean you
don't mind if I go, then?"

Oscar focused on her vaguely, as though his mind was
preoccupied with something far away. "Oh, no," he said.
"Not at all. You go right ahead and have a good time.
Just one thing, though."

Agnes gave him a sharp look. "What's that?"

"Don't mention a word about this pot to anyone. Not
Gretchen, not Dolly Ann."

"This is yours and Jimmy's little secret, I suppose?"
Agnes asked.

Oscar shook his head. "Jimmy was a good half mile
down the river when I found it," he said. "I brushed it off
and put it straight in my pack. He doesn't even know I
found it, and I'm not going to tell him, either. After all,
I'm the one who found it. If it turns out to be worth
something, there's no sense in splitting it with someone
who wasn't any help at all in finding it, do you think?"

Agnes thought about that for a moment. "No," she
said finally. "I don't suppose there is."

The meat loaf tasted like old shoe leather. The potatoes were worse. When chewed, the green beans snapped
tastelessly against their teeth like so many boiled rubber
bands. Oscar and Agnes picked at their food with little
interest, no appetite, and even less conversation. Finally,
Agnes stood up and began clearing away the dishes.

"How about some lemon pie," she offered, concilia-
tory at last. "At least that's *supposed* to be served cold."

They went to bed right after the ten o'clock news
ended on TV. Oscar fell asleep instantly, planted firmly in
the middle of the bed and snoring up a storm, while
Agnes clung to her side of the mattress and held a pillow

over her ear to help shut out some of the noise. Eventually she fell asleep as well. It was close to morning when the dream awakened her.

Agnes was standing on a small knoll, watching a young child play in the dirt. The child—apparently a little girl—wasn't one of Agnes Barkley's own children. Both of her girls were fair-skinned blondes. This child was brown-skinned, with a mane of thick black hair and white, shiny teeth. The child was bathed in warm sunlight, laughing and smiling. She spun around and around, kicking up dirt from around her, looking for all the world like a child-sized dust devil dancing across the desert floor.

Suddenly, for no clear reason, the scene darkened as though a huge cloud had passed in front of the sun. Somehow sensing danger, Agnes called out to the child: "Come here. Quick."

The little girl looked up at her and frowned, but she didn't seem to understand the warning Agnes was trying to give, and she didn't move. Agnes heard the sound then, heard the incredible roar and rush of water and knew that a flash flood was bearing down on them from somewhere upstream.

"Come here!" she cried again, more urgently this time. "Now!"

The child looked up at Agnes once more, and then she glanced off to her side. Her eyes widened in terror at the sight of a solid wall of murky brown water, twelve to fourteen feet high, churning toward her. The little girl scrambled to her feet and started away, darting toward Agnes and safety. But then, when she was almost out of harm's way, she stopped, turned, and went back. She was bending over to retrieve something from the dirt—something small and round and black—when the water hit. Agnes watched in helpless horror while the water crashed over her. Within seconds, the child was swept from view.

Agnes awakened drenched in sweat, just as she had years before when she was going through the change of life. Long after her heart quit pounding, the vivid, all-too-real dream stayed with her. Was that where the pot had come from? she wondered. Had the pot's owner, some small Indian child—no one in Westmont ever used the term Native American—been swept to her death before her mother's horrified eyes? And if it was true, if what Agnes had seen in the dream had really happened, it must have been a long time ago. How was it possible that it could be passed on to her—to a rock-solid Lutheran lady from Illinois, one not given to visions or wild flights of imagination?

Agnes crawled out of bed without disturbing the sleeping Oscar. She fumbled on her glasses, then slipped into her robe and went to the bathroom. When she emerged she stopped by the kitchen table, where the pot, sitting by itself, was bathed in a shaft of silver moonlight. It seemed to glow and shimmer in that strange, pearlescent light, but rather than being frightened of it, Agnes found herself drawn to it.

Without thinking, she sat down at the table, pulled the pot toward her, and let her fingers explore its smooth, cool surface. How did you go about forming such a pot? Agnes wondered. Where did you find the clay? How was it fired? What was it used for? There were no answers to those questions, but Agnes felt oddly comforted simply by asking them. A few minutes later she slipped back into bed and slept soundly until well after her usual time to get up and make coffee.

Two nights later, at the hotel in Phoenix, Agnes Barkley was down to nothing but her bra and panties when Gretchen Dixon's irritated voice brought her back to herself. "Well?" Gretchen demanded. "Do you want a card or not, Aggie? Either get in the game or get out."

Agnes put down her cards. "I'm out," she said. "I'm not very good at this. I can't concentrate."

"We should have played hearts instead," Lola offered.

"Strip hearts isn't all the same thing as strip poker," Gretchen snapped. "How many cards?"

"Two," Lola answered.

Agnes got up and pulled on her nightgown and robe. She had followed Gretchen's advice and started the game wearing as many clothes as she could manage. It hadn't helped. Although she was usually a quick study at games, she was hopeless when it came to the intricacies of poker. And now, with the room aswirl in a thick cloud of cigarette smoke, she was happy to be out of the game.

Agnes opened the sliding door and slipped out onto the tiny balcony. Although the temperature hovered in the low forties, it wasn't that cold—not compared to Chicago in January. In fact, it seemed downright balmy. She looked out at the sparse traffic waiting for the light on Grand Avenue and heard the low, constant rumble of trucks on the Black Canyon Freeway behind her. The roar reminded her once more of the noise the water had made as it crashed down around the little girl and overwhelmed her.

Although she wasn't cold, Agnes shivered and went back inside. She propped three pillows behind her, then sat on the bed with a book positioned in front of her face. The other women may have thought she was reading, but she wasn't.

Agnes Barkley was thinking about flash floods—remembering the real one she and Oscar had seen last winter. January had been one of the wettest ones on record. The fill-in manager at the trailer park commuted from Benson. He had told them one afternoon that a flood crest was expected over by Saint David shortly and that if they hurried, it would probably be worth seeing. They had been standing just off the bridge at Saint David when the wall of water came rumbling toward them, pushing ahead of it a jumbled collection of tires and rusty car fenders and even an old refrigerator, which bobbed along in the torrent as effortlessly as if it were nothing more than a bottle cork floating in a bathtub.

Agnes Barkley's dream from the other night—that still too vivid dream—might very well have been nothing more than a holdover from that. But she was now convinced it was more than that, especially after what she'd learned that day at the Heard Museum. Just as Gretchen Dixon had told her, the museum had been loaded with what Agnes now knew enough to call Native American artifacts—baskets, pottery, beadwork.

Their group had been led through the tour by a fast-talking docent who had little time or patience for dawdlers or questions. Afterward, while the others milled in the gift shop or lined up for refreshments, Agnes made her way back to one display in particular, where she had seen a single pot that very closely resembled the one she had last seen sitting on the kitchen table of the RV.

The display was a mixture of *Tohono O'othham* artifacts. Some of the basketry was little more than fragments. And just as Oscar had mentioned, the pots all showed signs of having been broken and subsequently glued back together. What drew Agnes to this display was not only the pot but also the typed legend on a nearby wall, which explained how, upon the death of the potmaker, her pots were always destroyed lest her spirit remain trapped forever in that which she had made.

Oscar's pot was whole, but surely the person who had crafted it was long since dead. Could the potmaker's spirit somehow still be captured inside that little lump of blackened clay? Had the mother made that tiny pot as some kind of plaything for her child? Was that what had made it so precious to the little girl? Did that explain why she had bolted back into the path of certain death in a vain attempt to save it? And had the mother's restless spirit somehow managed to create a vision in order to convey the horror of that terrible event to Agnes?

As she stood staring at the lit display in the museum, that's how Agnes came to see what had happened to her. She hadn't dreamed a dream so much as she had seen a vision. And now, two days later, with the book positioned in front of her face and with the three-handed poker game continuing across the room, Agnes tried to sort out what it all meant and what she was supposed to do about it.

The poker game ended acrimoniously when Lola and

Dolly Ann, both with next to nothing on, accused the fully dressed Gretchen of cheating. The other three women were still arguing about that when they came to bed. Not wanting to be drawn into the quarrel, Agnes closed her eyes and feigned sleep.

Long after the others were finally quiet, Agnes lay awake, puzzling about her responsibility to a woman she had never seen but through whose eyes she had witnessed that ancient and yet all too recent drowning. The child swept away in the roiling brown water was not Agnes Barkley's own child, yet the Indian child's death grieved Agnes as much as if she had been one of her own. It was growing light by the time Agnes reached a decision and was finally able to fall asleep.

The tour bus seemed to take forever to get them back to Tombstone. Oscar came to town to meet the bus and pick Agnes up. He greeted her with an exultant grin on his face and with an armload of library books sliding this way and that in the back seat of the Honda.

"I took a quick trip up to Tucson while you were gone," he explained. "They made an exception and let me borrow these books from the university library. Wait until I show you."

"I don't want to see," Agnes replied.

"You don't? Why not? I pored over them half the night and again this morning, until my eyes were about to fall out of my head. That pot of ours really is worth a fortune."

"You're going to have to take it back," Agnes said quietly.

"Take it back?" Oscar echoed in dismay. "What's the matter with you? Have you gone nuts or something? All we have to do is sell the pot, and we'll be on easy street from here on out."

"That pot is not for sale," Agnes asserted. "You're going to have to take it right back where you found it and break it."

Shaking his head, Oscar clamped his jaw shut, slammed the car in gear, and didn't say another word until they were home at the trailer park and had dragged both the books and Agnes Barkley's luggage inside.

"What in the hell has gotten into you?" Oscar demanded at last, his voice tight with barely suppressed anger.

Agnes realized she owed the man some kind of explanation. "There's a woman's spirit caught inside that pot," she began. "We have to let her out. The only way to do that is to break the pot. Otherwise she stays trapped in there forever."

"That the craziest bunch of hocus-pocus nonsense I ever heard. Where'd you come up with something like that? It sounds like something that fruitcake Gretchen Dixon would come up with. You didn't tell her about this, did you?"

"No. I read about it. In a display at the museum, but I think I already knew it, even before I saw it there."

"You already *knew* it?" Oscar sneered. "What's that supposed to mean? Are you trying to tell me that the spirit who's supposedly trapped in my pot is telling you I have to break it?"

"That's right. And put it back where you found it."

"Like hell I will!" Oscar growled.

He stomped outside and stayed there, making some pretense of checking fluids under the hood of the Honda. Oscar may have temporarily abandoned the field of battle, but Agnes knew the fight was far from over. She sat down and waited. It was two o'clock in the afternoon— time to start some arrangements about dinner—but she didn't make a move toward either the stove or the refrigerator.

For forty-six years, things had been fine between them. Every time a compromise had been required, Agnes had made it cheerfully and without complaint. That was the way it had always been, and it was the way Oscar expected it to be now. But this time—this one time— Agnes Barkley was prepared to stand firm. This one time, she wasn't going to bend.

Oscar came back inside half an hour later. "Look," he

said, his manner amiable and apologetic. "I'm sorry I
flew off the handle. You didn't know the whole story,
because I didn't have a chance to tell you. While I was up
in Tucson, I made some preliminary inquiries about the
pot. Anonymously, of course. Hypothetically. I ended up
talking to a guy who runs a trading post up near Oracle.
He's a dealer, and he says he could get us a ton of money.
You'll never guess how much."

"How much?"

"One hundred thou. Free and clear. That's what
comes to us after the dealer's cut. And that's at a bare
minimum. He says that if the collectors all end up in a
bidding war, the price could go a whole lot higher than
that. Do you have any idea what we could do with that
kind of money?"

"I don't care how much money it is," Agnes replied
stubbornly. "It isn't worth it. We've got to let her out,
Oscar. She's been trapped in there for hundreds of
years."

"Trapped?" Oscar demanded. "I'll tell you about
trapped. Trapped is having to go to work every day for
thirty years, rain or shine, hoping some goddamned dog
doesn't take a chunk out of your leg. Trapped is hoping
like hell you won't slip and fall on someone's icy porch
and break your damned neck. Trapped is always working
and scrimping and hoping to put enough money together
so that someday we won't have to worry about outliving
our money. And now, just when it's almost within my
grasp, you—"

He broke off in midsentence. They were sitting across
from each other in the tiny kitchen nook. Agnes met and
held Oscar's eyes, her gaze serene and unwavering. He
could see that nothing he said was having the slightest
effect.

Suddenly it was all too much. How could Agnes betray
him like that? Oscar lunged to his feet, his face contorted
with outraged fury. "So help me, Aggie . . ."

He raised his hand as if to strike her. For one fearful
moment, Agnes waited for the blow to fall. It didn't.

Instead Oscar's eyes bulged. The unfinished threat died in his throat. The only sound that escaped his distorted lips was a strangled sob.

Slowly, like a giant old-growth tree falling victim to a logger's saw, Oscar Barkley began to tip over. Stiff and still, like a cigar store Indian, he tottered toward the wall and then bounced against the cupboard. Only then did the sudden terrible rigidity desert his body. His bones seemed to turn to jelly. Disjointed and limp, he slid down the face of the cupboard like a lifeless Raggedy Andy doll.

Only when he landed on the floor was there any sound at all, and that was nothing but a muted thump—like someone dropping a waist-high bag of flour.

Agnes watched him fall and did nothing. Later, when the investigators asked her about the ten-minute interval between the time Oscar's broken watch stopped and the time the 911 call came in to the emergency communications center, she was unable to explain them. Not that ten minutes one way or another would have made that much difference. Oscar Barkley's one and only coronary episode was instantly fatal.

Oh, he had been warned to cut down on fat, to lower his cholesterol, but Oscar had never been one to take a doctor's advice very seriously.

The day after the memorial service, Gretchen Dixon popped her head in the door of the RV just as Agnes, clad in jeans, a flannel shirt, and a straw hat, was tying the strings on her tennis shoes.

"How are you doing?" Gretchen asked.

"I'm fine," Agnes answered mechanically. "Really I am."

"You look like you're going someplace."

Agnes nodded toward the metal box of ashes the mortician had given her. "I'm going out to scatter the ashes," she said. "Oscar always said he wanted to be left along the banks of the San Pedro."

"Would you like me to go along?" Gretchen asked.

"No, thank you. I'll be fine."

"Is someone else going with you, then? The girls, maybe?"

"They caught a plane back home early this morning."

"Don't tell me that rascal Jimmy Rathbone is already making a move on you."

"I'm going by myself," Agnes answered firmly. "I don't want any company."

"Oh," Gretchen said. "Sorry."

When Agnes Barkley drove the Honda away from the RV a few minutes later, it looked as though she was all alone in the car, but strangely enough, she didn't feel alone. And although Oscar hadn't told Agnes exactly where along the riverbank he had found the pot, it was easy for Agnes to find her way there—almost as though someone were guiding each and every footstep.

As soon as she reached the crumbled wall of riverbank, Agnes Barkley fell to her knees. It was quiet there, with what was left of the river barely trickling along in its sandy bed some thirty paces behind her. The only sound was the faint drone of a Davis-Monthan Air Force Base jet flying far overhead. Part of Agnes heard the sound and recognized it for what it was—an airplane. Another part of her jumped like a startled hare when what she thought was a bee turned out to be something totally beyond her understanding and comprehension.

When Agnes had arrived home with Oscar's ashes, she had immediately placed the pot inside the metal container. Now, with fumbling fingers, she drew it out. For one long moment, she held it lovingly to her breast. Then, with tears coursing down her face, she smashed the pot to pieces. Smashed it to smithereens on the metal container that held Oscar Barkley's barely cooled ashes.

Now Agnes snatched up the container. Holding it in front of her, she let the contents cascade out as she spun around and around, imitating someone else who once had danced exactly the same way in this very place sometime long, long ago.

At last, losing her balance, Agnes Barkley fell to the ground, gasping and out of breath. Minutes later she realized, as if for the first time, that Oscar was gone. Really gone. And there, amid his scattered ashes and the broken potsherds, she wept real tears. Not only because Oscar was dead but also because she had done nothing to help him. Because she had sat there helplessly and watched him die, as surely as that mysterious other woman had watched the surging water overwhelm her child.

At last Agnes seemed to come to herself. When she stopped crying, she was surprised to find that she felt much better. Relieved somehow. Maybe it was just as well Oscar was dead, she thought. He would not have liked being married to both of them—to Agnes and to the ghost of that other woman, to the mother of that poor drowned child.

This is the only way it could possibly work, Agnes said to herself. She picked up a tiny piece of black pottery, held it between her fingers, and let it catch the full blazing light of the warm afternoon sun.

This was the only way all three of them could be free.

WITH FLOWERS IN HER HAIR

M. D. LAKE

M. D. Lake's novels put a new spin on the traditional mystery, lending it a midwestern flavor, for one thing, and also giving it the ensemble charm of an old radio series—lots of endearing nutcases walking on and off stage.

Lake writes deftly about people and places, and does so with an eye that is observant and yet unforgiving.

This is a story about spiritual time travel—going back to a place you used to live, to take another look at a person you used to be.

▼▼▼▼▼

WHAT SHE REMEMBERED most about Minnesota was Denise, who'd taught her to sail, smoked marijuana, and dreamed of going to San Francisco with flowers in her hair. She also remembered her cousins, Ellen and Peter, and wondered how the years had treated them. Ellen must have done well for herself, of course, since she was a senator's wife now. Kate hadn't liked her, but Peter had been nice.

Sara, her daughter, and Sara's husband, Rob, met her at the airport. Sara asked about Hank and said it was too bad he couldn't have come too. Kate replied that he didn't have enough vacation time. What she meant was, her husband didn't have enough vacation time to waste a week of it in Minnesota, cooped up with relatives of Kate's she hadn't seen in almost thirty years and wasn't sure she wanted to see now.

When they'd got her bags, they walked out into the Minnesota winter, and the cold struck her like a blow. "My God! How can you stand it?" she exclaimed. "The last time I was here, the temperature must have been ninety degrees above zero. What's it now, ninety below?"

Sara laughed. "Not even close, Mom. It's ten above. Almost balmy."

Kate smiled to herself. Her daughter was proud of the midwestern hardiness she'd acquired since coming to Minnesota, and she'd fallen in love with Minnesota's seasons too. Southern California didn't have seasons.

"You'll be fine, Mrs. Austin," Rob assured her, "once we get you into a proper down jacket. The attic at the island's full of clothes for every season, if you don't mind wearing castoffs."

"I don't. Why don't you call me Kate, Rob, if you can handle calling a woman in her forties by her first name."

"I can handle it," he said. "Thanks."

He had a nice grin. Kate had seen that in the photographs Sara had sent her. He looked the way she remembered Peter, his father, had looked at that age.

Rob guided the big car, a British Range Rover, onto the freeway heading north. After a while, Sara asked her mother if the scenery looked familiar.

"After twenty-seven years? I'm afraid not. Besides, it was summer, and everything was so green—almost tropical, at least in my imagination. Minnesota seems even flatter than I remember it, probably because everything's so white now."

"Snow's a big field crop here," Rob said.

The scenery began to change, become hillier, with birch and pine forest breaking the monotony of the snow-covered farmland. At Duluth they drove along the shore of Lake Superior, then Rob turned inland on a road that wound through forest. It was getting dark, although it was only a little after five.

"This looks familiar," Kate said. "Except that I remember the road being narrower and bumpier. Maybe it was a different road."

"Same road," Rob said, "but it's been improved a lot, with the growth of the tourist industry up here the past fifteen, twenty years."

The last time she'd been on this road, Kate had been going the other way, back to the airport in Minneapolis. Her uncle, Jim Bishop—Big Jim, she remembered the locals called him—had been driving, and his wife was sitting next to him in the front seat, where Sara was sitting now. Kate hadn't paid much attention to the scenery then: She'd been too concerned about what she'd find when she got back to Los Angeles.

She'd been fourteen and had spent August on Heron Lake with her father's family, while her parents worked out the details of their divorce and her mother had a nervous breakdown.

She glanced at her daughter and son-in-law in the front seat of the big warm car and thought about the sequence of events that had brought her back to Minnesota now.

Her parents had met as students at Carleton, a rich-kids' college south of Minneapolis. Instead of returning to Heron Lake and taking over the family resort, her father had gone to medical school and then moved to California. After divorcing Kate's mother, he and his new young wife had moved to Arizona, and Kate rarely saw him again. He'd died in the crash of his private plane a few years later.

Kate's mother got a good settlement in the divorce and an even better one when her ex-husband's will was read. She'd used some of that money to send her grand-daughter, Sara, to Minnesota—back to Carleton College. While there, Sara had looked up her grandfather's family, met Rob, her second cousin, and they'd fallen in love and eloped to avoid a wedding that would have involved too many divorced relatives.

Maybe Sara would get it right the first time, Kate thought. At least she'd waited until she graduated from college to marry. Kate had married Sara's father at eighteen and divorced him at twenty.

And now she was returning to the island on Heron Lake, to spend the week after Christmas with her daughter and son-in-law, and to see again the family she hadn't seen since her parents' divorce.

"There's the lake," Sara said, when they reached the top of a hill and Rob turned the car onto a private road.

Kate saw it as a white clearing in the snow-covered trees. As the road wound down the hill, she remembered that it ended on the shore, next to the boathouse with the dock in front of it. The dock wasn't there now, and instead of stopping at the boathouse, Rob kept going— right out onto the lake.

Kate gasped.

"It takes a little getting used to," Sara said, turning to

grin at her mother. Kate suspected Sara had been waiting for her reaction and that she hadn't disappointed her.

"God didn't intend us to walk on water," she said. "Or drive on it, either."

"The ice is about eighteen inches thick," Rob said, "thick enough to support a semi."

The road—a ribbon of dark-blue ice that had been cleared of snow—went straight across the lake to the island. Dotting the surface of the lake were little shacks. Sara had described in letters how Minnesota fishermen put them on frozen lakes and sat in them and fished through holes in the ice. Kate shuddered at the thought. Somehow it didn't seem fair to the fish.

Rob pointed ahead to a shack sitting about a hundred feet off the island shore. "That's your uncle Jim's fish house, Kate. He spends most of his time fishing now, summer and winter. I hope you like fish—we eat a lot of it."

"I think it's strange she was here the week Gunnar drowned and Denise hanged herself," Peter said, watching the lights of the Range Rover as it nosed down the hill onto the ice. He went to the drinks cart, poured Scotch into a glass, swallowed some of it.

"It wouldn't seem strange at all," Steve said, "if she'd never come back to the island." He was standing in front of the fireplace, filling his pipe from a soft leather pouch.

"It's not the least bit strange," Ellen said flatly. "Once Sara married Rob, it was inevitable we'd see cousin Kate again." She turned her attention back to her crocheting.

"She and Denise were thick as thieves that summer," Peter said.

Ellen's crochet hook paused over the shawl in her lap. "How ominous!" she said, smiling up at her brother.

"It was your fault, damn it!" he flared. "If you'd spent more time with her, she'd never have known of Denise's existence. You had nothing better to do! You and Steve—" He broke off, glancing over at his brother-in-law.

"I know, I know," Ellen admitted with a mock sigh. "I'm just not a very nice person, am I?"

"What if Denise said something to her?"

"It's been twenty-seven years, Peter," Steve reminded him, striking a match and sucking flame into his pipe. "Kate was only fourteen. It's not very likely she even remembers Denise. What can you remember from twenty-seven years ago?"

"Ask him what he can remember from yesterday," Ellen said.

"She'll only be here a week," Steve said. "Let's make it pleasant for her."

"But not so pleasant she wants to come back anytime soon," Ellen said.

Kate remembered the long flight of stone steps up from the lake, and the cabin, two-storied, with the big picture window in the living room. She remembered the fireplace too, because she'd never seen one like it before, built into a wall of huge stones. It hadn't been used that summer, but a fire was burning in it now.

She looked at Ellen and Peter. She recognized them only because Sara had sent photographs.

"Hello, Kate," Ellen said. She was sitting on a couch, crocheting something that looked like a white shawl, a basket of yarn on the floor at her small feet. "It's been a long time." She looked Kate up and down critically. "I'm afraid I wouldn't recognize you again." She made it sound as though that were something Kate should work on changing.

"It's nice to see you again, Ellen," Kate said pleasantly.

Whenever she'd thought of her cousin, Kate remembered her as twenty-two going on thirty-five. Now she looked every one of her forty-nine years, although she still had curly blond hair that bobbed when she moved her head, the same big china-blue eyes, and a wide mouth that did a sneer more convincingly than a smile. Something between a princess and a frog, Kate thought.

She went over to Peter, at the window. "Hi, cousin,"

she said with a big smile. He quickly put down his glass, and they embraced warmly. "I'm not surprised my new son-in-law's such a nice young man, considering how nice his father was to me that summer."

"Ouch!" Ellen said quietly.

Peter turned pink and looked flustered. "Oh, well," he stammered, "I suppose Rob's mother had something to do with it too." Peter's ex-wife lived somewhere on the mainland.

He had the same head of unruly brown hair Kate remembered, but it was flecked with gray now, and she noted with sadness that his face seemed to have aged without maturing. A faint network of red threads under the soft flesh of his cheeks told her he drank too much.

Kate turned to the man standing in front of the fireplace and held out her hand. "And you're Steve," she said. She'd seen the Republican senator from Minnesota on television a few times and once on a magazine cover, holding up a string of fish he'd caught in Heron Lake.

He looked like an advertising agency's idea of a lumberjack, a big florid man of about fifty, with broad shoulders, a muscular neck sticking out of a red flannel shirt, and thick iron-gray hair. He smoked a pipe and tended it with slow, deliberate movements of his large hands.

Kate had often wondered why voters seemed to find men like him attractive. The Minnesota voters had just returned Steve to the Senate for a second term.

After Peter had made Kate a drink and they'd sat and talked awhile, he announced that dinner would be ready at seven.

"Show your mother to her room, Sara," he added, "so she can dress down for the occasion. I'm sure we've got wool shirts and jeans in the attic that'll fit her."

"Check them for spiders, though," Ellen said with a grin. "I remember how you hated our spiders." She turned to Rob. "Go fetch Dad from the fish house. And make sure he washes the propane and bait stink off his hands and face before he comes to the table."

As they went upstairs, Kate turned to her daughter. "I'm afraid age hasn't mellowed Ellen any."

"You just have to know how to take her," Sara said.

"I'll take her the way I did when I was fourteen—I'll try to avoid her, like the spiders." Then she squeezed her daughter's arm and said, "Don't worry, kiddo, they're not my family anymore, they're yours. I'll behave myself. It's only for a week, after all."

"I want you to have a good time, Mom," Sara said.

"I will, darling. Who cooks dinner? I'd be surprised if Ellen knew where the stove was."

"Peter. He's a good cook, too. He moved back here after he and Rob's mom split up. He takes care of the house and his father as well as runs the business. Someday, of course, everything's going to be Peter's—the resort and the island, I mean—since Ellen and Steve don't want it. When Steve's not being a senator, he's a partner in a big law firm in Minneapolis. Besides, he'll probably run for President someday."

Most Minnesotans do, Kate thought. "And maybe, someday, all this'll be yours and Rob's," she said.

"Maybe. I really do love it here. It's so beautiful, and so peaceful."

She had the same room she'd had when she was fourteen. Even the chest of drawers was the same, and some of the pictures on the walls, pencil drawings of the lake that were dark and old even then. Suddenly she remembered something else. A few days after she'd arrived at the lake, homesick and worried about her parents and told to scram once too often by Ellen, she'd scratched "I hate Ellen's guts" on the inside of the closet with a pair of scissors. It was still there. Kneeling in front of it now brought back the moment as if it had just happened, and her eyes filled, inexplicably, with tears.

Rob was right: Dinner was fish that her uncle Jim had caught that afternoon. Sara was right too: Peter was a good cook.

"I suppose there've been a lot of changes since you were here last, Kate," Rob said.

"Not really. The place looks almost unchanged, as if time's stood still. The big difference is me, I suppose. I'd never spent any time in the woods before, much less on an island. I'd never heard thunder right overhead, or seen spiders so big. I dreamed about the spiders for months after I got back home—"

"Why?" Uncle Jim asked, glancing up at her from his plate of fish bones and skin. Kate had been shocked at how old and feeble he looked. She remembered him as a tall, vigorous man of about fifty, with a bristling mustache, thick hair, and a long, purposeful stride. Now, in his late seventies, he reminded her of an unwrapped mummy she'd seen once in a case in a museum—shriveled, bald, age-burned. Only his small eyes still glittered with an angry intelligence.

Kate laughed, embarrassed, glanced at Ellen, and then down at her plate.

"I suppose because I once dropped a wolf spider down her back," Ellen said. "Sorry, Kate—I was a bitch in those days, wasn't I? I hope there's a statute of limitations on tormenting cousins."

Kate assured her that there was.

"Where's that shiny little camera you were so proud of?" Peter asked. "You were always sneaking around taking pictures of people when they weren't looking. Remember?"

"I didn't think you'd seen me," Kate said. "That camera's gone, but I brought some of the pictures I took that summer with me."

"Oh, God!" Ellen said. "I make a point of never looking at pictures of myself—especially pictures from the Stone Age."

"You're a newspaper photographer, aren't you?" Peter said. "That sounds interesting."

"It sometimes is," Kate told him. "I work for a small-town newspaper chain. Most of the time I take pictures of ribbon cuttings and PTA picnics, local politicians and liquor store openings—all the things that are important to small towns. Sometimes a fire or a fatal car accident, once a convicted murderer."

"How exciting," Ellen murmured.

"Oh, I'm sure it's not as exciting as being a U.S. senator's wife," Kate replied, giving her cousin a sweet smile, and enjoyed watching Ellen's face flush with anger.

"You don't look anything like my brother," Uncle Jim said. "He was a good-looking fella."

The others laughed, and Peter said, "I don't think Dad meant that quite the way it sounded."

"And you're divorced too, aren't you?" Jim went on.

"And remarried," she said.

He shook his head. "I don't know what's wrong with the world. One marriage was enough for people in my day. Edna and me was married almost fifty years before she passed on, and Ellen and Steve've been married going on thirty. I didn't like your mother," he added.

"She didn't think very highly of you, either, Uncle Jim," Kate replied easily, "so I guess that makes you even."

He blinked at that, but with something almost like respect in his eyes.

"I'd forgotten you owned a ski resort," she went on, changing the subject because she'd promised Sara she'd try to be good. "I just remembered the café and the lodge and the boat rentals."

"You didn't remember the ski resort because it wasn't there back then," he retorted.

"Uncle Jim built it after he bought Gunnar's Hill, Mom," Sara told her. "That's the name of the best downhill run in the whole area. We'll take you up there tomorrow."

"Uncle Jim started the winter sports industry here," Rob said, giving his great-uncle an admiring look, "before downhill skiing became as popular as it is now. He saw it coming. He was a real visionary."

"You make it sound like I'm dead," Jim growled, but he looked pleased.

"Gunnar's Hill," Kate repeated. "That must've been the man who drowned while I was here. I even saw him once."

"It probably wasn't the same Gunnar," Rob said. "The area's crawling with people with Scandinavian names."

"It was the Gunnar who owned a hill Uncle Jim wanted to buy," Kate said.

Ellen looked up at her with a faint smile. "You remember that, do you?"

"Yes, I remember it quite well. He drowned shortly before I left, and I was glad I wouldn't have to swim in the lake again—I thought the water would taste of death."

"Of Norwegian, more likely," Ellen said.

After dinner, they returned to the living room. Steve threw logs on the fire, Peter passed drinks around, Ellen crocheted. Sara and Rob worked a jigsaw puzzle, their foreheads touching over the table.

Kate could hear Uncle Jim interrogating his son about the holiday business at the lodge, in his peevish old man's voice. Peter's answers sounded defensive. Every now and then, Kate caught him looking at her, and he'd give her an uncertain smile.

Steve contributed little to the conversation. He was idly jotting down notes for a speech he was going to give when the Senate reconvened in January. Kate didn't want to talk politics with him, so instead she asked him how he and Ellen had met.

"We knew each other in high school," he replied, "and we met again at the University in Minneapolis, after I returned from Vietnam."

"We bumped into each other on the Mall," Ellen added. "Steve offered to carry my books, but of course what he really wanted was my body. Right, Steve?"

He looked at her without smiling. "If you say so, Ellen." He picked up his pipe and lit it.

"We were meant for each other," she continued. "It was love at first sight." And with a little sneer trembling on her mouth, she dug the crochet hook into the shawl on her lap.

Kate remembered that Peter had played the trumpet, even played in a local band. She asked him if he still did.

He shook his head. "No. When I took over the operation of the resort, I had to put childish things behind me." He got up and went over to the drinks cart.

"What's your strongest memory of the lake, Kate?" Rob asked her.

"Oh, I've got lots of memories. But I guess the strongest is of a young woman named Denise. She worked as a waitress in the café that summer."

There was a crash, as Peter's glass shattered on the tile floor.

"Sorry," he mumbled. He went out to the kitchen and returned with a broom and dustpan.

"I spent quite a lot of time with her," Kate went on. "She wanted to go to San Francisco and become a hippie. I wonder what she's doing now."

Nobody said anything.

"She went to high school with you, I think, Ellen. Do you know what happened to her?"

Peter started to say something, but Ellen cut him off. "She died," she said.

Kate hadn't expected that. "What of?"

"She committed suicide."

"Why?"

"I'm afraid she didn't confide in me," Ellen replied evenly. "Do you play bridge?"

Kate didn't. She went ice-skating instead with Sara and Rob, grateful to be out in the cold, clean air on the frozen lake.

Jim, Ellen, Peter, and Steve were sitting around the bridge table in the living room.

"Why'd you tell her Denise died?" Peter demanded.

"Because she asked about her, Peter," Ellen replied. "We could hardly pretend we didn't remember—which is what you were going to do."

"You didn't have to tell her she killed herself."

"Of course she did," his father snapped, sorting his cards with his trembling fingers.

"She remembered Gunnar drowning too," Peter went on.

Ellen laughed softly. "Sounds like the makings of a story, doesn't it? Nemesis in the guise of little cousin Kate."

"It's not funny, Ellen! She might try to find out why Denise killed herself—and when!"

"So what?" Steve asked.

"Don't you see? You—Denise died the last day Kate was here! She might know Denise wasn't suicidal."

"How can anybody know that, Peter?" Ellen asked. "And even if she didn't think Denise was the suicide type—what could she do about it?"

"Well, let's hope Kate's curiosity or her journalistic instincts aren't aroused," Steve said. "It'll make it easier on all of us."

"'Journalistic instincts,'" Jim said with a hoarse laugh. "'Journalistic instincts.' The girl's a small-town newspaper photographer—and it happened so long ago."

"Right, Dad," Peter said, his voice rising. "It happened so long ago!" He threw down his cards, got up, and stared down at the others. "When all the kids wanted to go to San Francisco and be hippies. Denise—"

"Shut up!" Steve said.

Kate couldn't sleep, thinking about Denise. It had been hard to sleep back then too, because she wasn't used to the heat and the humidity. She remembered the restless breeze in the trees outside her open window, and the noise of insects thudding against the screen when she had the light on so she could read.

She got up and went to her window. The night was clear and bright, and she could see the fish houses on the lake, like little boats frozen in time. She and Denise had sailed out there a lot that summer.

She'd arrived in Minneapolis in a heat wave, and it hadn't taken her long to realize she was a nuisance to everybody—especially her cousin Ellen.

Peter had taken her waterskiing a few times and shown her around the island—she remembered that he'd taught her the names of some of the flowers and pointed out poison ivy to her—and he'd taken her to movies in town once or twice too. But he didn't have much free time; he had to work for his father at the resort on the mainland, and he played trumpet in a band at night.

Ellen didn't do much of anything except sit around and read fashion magazines and work on her tan. She often took one of the cars and drove to Minneapolis, where she spent long weekends with friends. She'd just graduated from the university there. She never offered to take Kate with her, and Kate remembered that she usually came back to the island grouchy and it was best to avoid her.

Kate had her camera, a Leica M3 that her father had given her the day she left for Minnesota. It was the most expensive small camera you could get back then. "Take lots of pictures," he'd told her, "so you can show me how the old place has changed since I was there last." She'd never had the chance to show those pictures to him.

She spent a lot of that month exploring the island and taking pictures. She didn't ask any of the family to pose for her—even as a child she hadn't liked posed pictures—but she sometimes snuck up on them and took their pictures without their knowing. She had an especially good one of Ellen scratching her butt. She almost wished she'd brought it with her.

After she'd been there a week, she persuaded her aunt to let her use an old rowboat that nobody else used. At first she just rowed around the island, sticking close to the shore, but after a while she grew bolder and rowed across the lake to the Bishops' resort on the mainland. It had a café, with a dock in front where they kept rental canoes and sailboats.

She met Denise for the first time one afternoon during a thunderstorm. She remembered how the humidity had increased and the sky—the air itself—turned green as she rowed across the lake. By the time she reached the mainland, the thunder and lightning were coming simultaneously right above her head, and the wind-driven rain was whipping the lake into an angry sea that almost capsized her boat. She thought an angry god was out to get a miserable fourteen-year-old girl for some reason, or at least scare one to death—and she'd been chosen.

Drenched to the skin, she bought a Coke at the café and took it out on the screened porch to watch the progress of the storm. A young woman dashed onto the porch through the rain and flopped down in a chair. Kate had seen her before; she was a waitress at the café. She said, "You can be number twelve and I'll be thirty-five." When Kate looked blank, she continued: "You know, Bob Dylan, 'Rainy Day Women #12 & 35.'" When she sang a snatch of it, Kate remembered she'd heard it.

"There aren't any women in the song, or any mention of rain," Denise went on, giving Kate a meaningful look. "It's probably some kind of code for drugs, like 'Lucy in the Sky with Diamonds' means LSD. You're the kid from the Bishops' island, aren't you?"

Kate said she was.

"From L.A., right?"

"Uh-huh."

"You go to San Francisco much?"

"Once," Kate said, "when I was a little kid." She remembered the Golden Gate Bridge, the zoo, Chinatown. Not much else.

Denise shrugged. "It's probably changed a lot since then."

She was tall and thin, willowy, with long, straight dark hair, a beaded headband, large dark eyes behind granny glasses, and a dreamy smile. Except when she was waitressing, she always wore a dark ankle-length dress that she'd bought at the Goodwill. She'd embroidered the flowers on the hem herself, she told Kate.

She asked Kate how she liked living with the Bishops, and Kate said it was okay.

"Must be lonely, though, you being the only kid on the island. I don't guess Icy Ellen and Peter Rabbit spend a lot of their precious time with you, do they?"

"Peter Rabbit?" Kate had no trouble with "Icy Ellen."

"That's what they used to call him in high school, because he was such a wimp—always doing what Ellen told him to do. Ellen's a first-class bitch." Remembering where she was and who she was talking to, she lowered her voice and looked around. "Forget I said that, okay? I don't wanna get fired just yet. You like to sail?"

Kate said she'd never sailed. Peter had promised to take her, but he'd been too busy.

"And Icy Ellen wouldn't take you even if she liked sailing, which she doesn't. She likes things that go fast—including men, I bet." Denise giggled. "You wanna go sailing with me? The lodge lets us slaves sail all we want when we're not on duty. That's so's they don't have to pay us a living wage."

Denise taught her to sail—to work the rudder and the sheet, to tack, jibe without capsizing, and be sure to always call out "Hard alee!" when coming about. She could sometimes still hear Denise's patient voice instructing her, when she and Hank sailed their catamaran off the California coast.

Denise would wait until they were in the middle of the lake, and then she'd turn the boat over to Kate. She'd crawl to the front, sprawl with her back against the mast, her long brown legs poking out under her dress, and light up a marijuana cigarette, sucking the smoke in deeply, holding it as long as she could, letting as little as possible leak back out.

"I get grass from some guys I know in town," she told Kate, gazing up at the big clouds in the pale summer sky. "Promise you won't tell anybody about it. If you do, the pigs'll put me in jail for a long, long time."

Kate knew a little about marijuana. At first it made her nervous to be alone in the middle of the lake with Denise when she was smoking it, but after a while she got used to it, when she saw that all it did was make Denise talky. It was fun sharing the secret, and it was a way of revenging herself on the Bishops for their almost total neglect of her. To Denise's credit, she never offered to let Kate try marijuana. "You're too young," she explained, apologetically.

◆ ◆ ◆

The next day, Sara and Rob took Kate downhill skiing. The little café on the dock where she'd met Denise had given way to a three-story lodge that looked vaguely European, with chalet-like cabins on the hill behind it. Higher up, to the right and left, she could glimpse ski runs through the pines, and chairlifts carrying skiers to the top of the hill. People in expensive-looking ski outfits were everywhere.

Kate wasn't an expert skier, but after one run she knew that what passed for black diamond slopes here would be only intermediate in the southern California mountains where she and Hank skied sometimes. Rob explained that Minnesota didn't have any real mountains, just the sides of valleys that had been carved by glaciers out of the flat midwestern plains.

As Sara had told her the night before, the longest and most challenging run was Gunnar's Hill. Kate laughed. "He'd turn over in his grave," she said.

Her daughter looked at her curiously. "Why, Mom?"

"Denise—my friend that summer, the girl we were talking about at dinner who committed suicide—told me Gunnar didn't want to sell his hill to Uncle Jim. He thought the Bishops were ruining the area by increasing the tourist trade. I'm surprised the hill's named after him."

Rob told her the locals had given it the name after Uncle Jim bought it from Gunnar's widow. "They did it to annoy him," he added with a laugh. "But when he heard about it, Uncle Jim made signs that said 'Gunnar's Hill'—his way of telling people he didn't care what they thought of him—and the name stuck."

After a couple of runs, Kate left Sara and Rob on the slopes and strolled over to the restaurant in the lodge. She found a table by a window where she could drink coffee and look out over the frozen lake with the Bishops' island in the distance.

She and Denise had sailed together two or three times a week. Kate rowed over to the mainland and waited on the porch for Denise to show up. Denise always wore the same long, dark dress with the flower-embroidered hem, and Kate was pretty sure that if the boat ever capsized, she'd sink and never come up.

She told Kate a lot about San Francisco as they sailed around the lake. You could get really good grass there, she'd assured her. The grass they got in Minnesota—at least up here in the boonies—was mostly ground-up fish-line and catnip. She'd heard you were supposed to get a really good high with banana skins and spearmint chewing gum—you dried them together in the oven, then crumbled them up and smoked the powder. She'd tried it once; it was horrible, and she didn't think she'd got high, just a headache.

She talked about Haight-Ashbury—"the Haight," she'd called it—where everybody lived in harmony together and owned everything in common, even each other. "I don't know that I'd like that!" she said, and glanced at Kate to see how she was taking all this hippie lore. "You live in California, but you don't know anything, do you? Well, you're just a kid. Maybe when you're older, you'll run away to San Francisco. You're a Bishop, so your mom's got plenty of money—she don't need you to support her like mine does." She laughed, inhaled smoke. She seemed to think the summer of love would last forever, would be waiting for her when she finally got to San Francisco.

In addition to waitressing at the café at night, she worked as a cashier in a grocery store in town several days a week. On those days Kate didn't see her.

One afternoon, Denise directed Kate to the east end of the lake, where there was another island, much smaller than the Bishops'. As Kate ran the sailboat up onto the sandy beach, Denise jumped overboard with a splash and pulled it up onto the shore. "Follow me," she said.

She led the way across the little island, through a woods of birch and pine, until they came to a one-room cabin in a clearing. The paint was peeling off the walls, the windows were boarded up, and there was a padlock on the door. The walls, roof, and door were riddled with small holes.

"A guy from Minneapolis—a doctor or something—built it years ago," Denise said. "The next year, some locals shot it up. They was drunk, and mad they didn't get their deer—or something," she added, giving Kate a sly look that implied she knew more about what had happened than she was telling. "The doctor fixed it up again—and it got shot up again the next year. He took the hint and hasn't ever been back. If I show you something, you promise not to tell anybody?"

Kate promised. Denise went up to a window, pulled on one of the boards covering it, and all the boards swung away in one piece.

"Hinges," she explained. "My boyfriend made it so he could get in without breaking the lock on the door." She jumped onto a tree stump, threw one of her long legs over the sill, and crawled through the window into the cabin. By the time Kate had followed her inside, Denise was across the room, climbing the wall, using pieces of wood nailed between the studs for steps. She disappeared through a hole in the ceiling.

Thin shafts of sunlight crisscrossed the dusky room from the holes in the walls and glittered on broken glass on the floor as Kate crossed to the wall, climbed it, and pulled herself through the hole in the ceiling into the loft. It was hot and close up there, and she began to sweat as she crawled to where Denise was waiting for her by the window at the far end.

She was sitting on a mattress covered with a cheap spread with an Indian print. On the ceiling and walls were posters of popular rock singers and groups: the Mamas and the Papas, the Doors, the Beatles, the Stones. In a corner sat a little transistor radio in a battered leather case and next to it a brass incense burner and a cracked black plastic ashtray full of gray ash. The faint smell of marijuana and incense hung in the loft.

Denise switched the radio on, and a song that was just becoming popular, "Ode to Billy Joe," came softly into the room. Denise turned the dial until the static disappeared. Kate had a radio just like it at home.

"I come here when I want to be by myself," Denise told Kate. "Usually I come early in the morning, because I like to watch the sun come up over the hill behind Gunnar's house." She nodded out the window, across the lake to the shore.

From the window, Kate could see the mainland, about a hundred yards away, with the forested hill behind it. There was a boathouse on the shore, and a dock sticking out into the lake next to it. A man was climbing into an outboard motorboat at the dock.

"That's Gunnar," Denise said, "Gunnar Johanson. He owns a lot of the land around here. He hates your family, you know—he thinks they're ruining the lake, getting more and more outsiders to come up here. And Big Jim Bishop hates him too, 'cause he thinks Gunnar's holding up progress. What he really means," she added knowledgeably, "is Gunnar's keeping Big Jim from getting richer than he already is. Big Jim wants to start some kind of ski resort like they have in Colorado and Europe and places like that, but Gunnar won't sell him that hill behind his place, even though Big Jim got the county to raise the taxes on it."

Denise worked her legs laboriously into the lotus position and put her hands, palms up, on her knees, then stared out the window. Kate thought she looked pretty hilarious. The radio was playing the Beatles' "All You Need Is Love."

"It wouldn't be the same," Denise said dreamily, "watching the sun come up over a hill full of rich outsiders on skis."

"Do you come up here with your boyfriend?" Kate asked. She felt the same sense of participating in something wicked and dangerous as when she'd first sailed the boat while Denise smoked marijuana.

"We used to," Denise said. "Then he went to Vietnam—he was a Green Beret. You know the song about the Green Berets?"

Kate did. She hated it because the hero dies in the end, and because the guy singing the song, whose name she couldn't remember, looked crazy. She asked Denise if her boyfriend had been killed in Vietnam.

"Wounded. He was in the VA hospital in Minneapolis, but now he's going to the university—he thinks he wants to be a lawyer. To tell you the truth, he isn't my boyfriend anymore. Now that he's a hero," she added with heavy sarcasm, "he's too good for me.

"A friend of mine's going to Minneapolis in a couple weeks," she went on. "There's a hippie commune down there that's getting ready to head west as soon as they get enough money to buy a van. She wants me to go with her, but I can't—not right now anyway. My mom's had a lot of medical problems and she can't work, so I gotta stay here and help pay the bills. You could go, though, Kate," she added, giving her a big grin.

"No, thanks!" Then she asked Denise if she could take pictures of the cabin.

"Uh-uh. Somebody might ask you why you'd bothered taking pictures of this old place, and I'll bet you're a lousy liar. Only you, me, and my boyfriend know about it, and I promised him I wouldn't tell anybody. It's bad karma to break a promise."

Whenever Kate thought about Denise after that summer, she imagined her still living somewhere in the area, married and with children, or still working as a waitress someplace, or both. But it wouldn't have surprised her, either, to learn that she'd actually gone to San Francisco and, like so many other kids in the sixties, vanished off the face of the earth.

She couldn't have imagined suicide. She wondered what terrible thing had happened to make Denise kill herself.

At dinner that night, she asked Ellen and Peter Denise's last name.

"Foley," Ellen told her. "Why?"

"I guess I feel I have some unfinished business with her. I'd like to know what happened."

"I told you what happened," Ellen said, putting a

forkful of fish into her mouth and chewing as she gazed steadily at her cousin. "She committed suicide."

"How?"

"Hanged herself, I think."

"When?"

"I don't remember."

Kate looked at Peter, who shook his head. "Sorry," he mumbled.

"Is her mother still alive?"

"Damn it!" Jim struck the table with a fist, making his water glass jump. "The girl worked at the café—a waitress. Lots of kids have worked for us over the years—cooks, dishwashers, waitresses. We don't keep up with 'em after they leave us."

"Take it easy, Dad," Ellen said.

"What about you, Peter?" Kate asked, ignoring the outburst. "You worked at the resort that summer—you must have known Denise a little."

"I—I never knew anything about her background," he stammered, unable to meet her eyes.

"She couldn't have been very important to you, Kate, could she?" Steve asked.

Their indifference suddenly made her angry. "No," she answered, looking around at all of them. "She wasn't at all important in the great scheme of my life. But she paid attention to me—something Ellen had no interest in doing and Peter had no time to do—and she taught me to sail. She talked to me. Damn it, she was my friend!"

Tears sprang suddenly into her eyes, as they had when she'd seen the words "I hate Ellen's guts" that she'd scratched into the closet nearly thirty years ago. "I never got to tell her goodbye," she continued, more quietly. "I know it sounds corny, but I'd like to do that—to tell her goodbye. And I'd like to know why she killed herself." She looked around the table. "Does anybody mind if I try to find out?"

"Fine with me," Ellen said with a shrug.

Nobody else said anything, although Sara looked a little embarrassed, as daughters will when their mothers act out.

Sara and Rob went on an all-day cross-country skiing trip with friends the next morning. They invited Kate, but she'd never done much cross-country skiing and she knew she would just slow down the others. Besides, she wanted to see what she could find out about Denise.

There weren't any Foleys in the phone book, so she called the Office of Records at the county courthouse. A clerk looked up the death certificate and told Kate they didn't know the exact date of Denise's death, but her body had been found on September 29, 1967. She'd hanged herself.

September 29—that was less than a month after Kate had returned to California!

"Why so pensive, dear cousin?" Ellen asked, coming up behind her, making her jump.

"She must have killed herself soon after I left here," Kate exclaimed.

"Who?"

"Denise, of course!" Kate replied, glaring at her cousin. "Can I borrow one of the cars after lunch?"

"Certainly. Why?"

She told Ellen she wanted to drive into town and look up Denise's death in the old newspapers at the library.

Ellen rolled her eyes, but after lunch she gave Kate the keys to one of the cars and told her how to get to town.

Peter watched the car disappear up the road on the other side of the lake. Then he turned to Steve: "You didn't have to kill her! We could've just given her the money she needed to get to San Francisco."

"She wanted more than that, Peter," Ellen said, looking up from her crocheting. "She had a sick mother, remember? We were supposed to support her, while Denise was sharing her monkey bread, her body, and her pills with all the gentle, unwashed people. It was the summer of love," she added dreamily.

"Besides," Steve said, "she would have blabbed to her hippie friends sooner or later—drugs always made Denise blab."

Ellen looked up at her husband, gave him an icy smile, said, "Who'd know that better than you?"

He shrugged. "Good thing somebody knew Denise, wasn't it? Otherwise you might have ended up with a tribe of hippies living on the island—or you might have had to turn the resort into a spiritual retreat for some Indian sect!"

Ellen laughed. "More likely, Denise would just have come back home, sadder but wiser. And do you think she would've been satisfied growing old as a waitress, knowing her employer had murdered a man?"

"I didn't murder Gunnar," her father whined. He was slumped in his chair in front of the fireplace. "I hit him, but I didn't mean to kill him."

"You stood on the dock and watched him drown," his son-in-law said.

"It was an accident—but who would've believed me? Not even you believe me."

"It's all right, Daddy," Ellen said soothingly. "And you were right to let us deal with Denise."

"She's going to find out!" Peter whispered, and pressed his forehead to the cold glass of the window. "I know it."

"I don't see how she can," Ellen said, and got up and went over and put her arm around her brother. "She's just our little cousin Kate—hardly an avenging angel."

"But if she does find out," her father said, "Steve'll have to kill her too."

When Kate returned late that afternoon, Ellen looked up from her crocheting and asked, "Any luck, cousin?" Then she took a closer look at Kate and asked, "What's the matter?"

"I must have been one of the last people to see Denise alive," Kate answered, going to the fireplace to warm up. "According to the newspaper, her mother saw her for the last time on the morning of Friday, September first—that was the day I left here to return to California!"

"How can you remember that?" Steve asked.

"Because it was the start of the Labor Day weekend. I flew back to California in time to get ready to begin school on Tuesday."

"Maybe the world lost all meaning for Denise the day you left," Ellen suggested.

"For God's sake, Ellen!" Peter cried.

"Just kidding, Peter." For once, Ellen almost looked contrite.

"I saw her that day," Kate said. "September first."

"Where?" Steve asked.

"On the little island, where they found her body. They didn't find her for almost a month, when somebody exploring the island looked into the cabin through one of the bullet holes in the wall and saw her. She was hanging from a rafter."

Steve closed the magazine he'd been reading when she came in and regarded Kate with interest, waiting for her to continue.

"We usually sailed in the afternoon," she told them, "before Denise had to go to work, but we couldn't on Friday afternoon because I had to leave for Minneapolis. So we agreed we'd meet in the morning. But when I rowed over to the café, she wasn't there. After about forty-five minutes, I decided I couldn't wait any longer, I'd go sailing by myself. I'd never gone out in the sailboat alone, but I didn't care—it was my last day, what could anybody do about it?"

After she'd been out a while, she sailed close to the little island and remembered that Denise had told her she often went there in the mornings to watch the sunrise. She wondered if Denise was there now.

She sailed ashore through the reeds, pulled the boat up onto the beach, and crossed the island to the cabin. As she approached, she heard music, knew it was coming from Denise's portable radio. Something told her Denise didn't want to be disturbed now—but she went on anyway, walking as stealthily as she could through the dense underbrush.

As she came to the clearing in front of the cabin, she

stopped when she saw a man's bare legs through the birch trees. She crouched down and crawled closer, until she could see into the clearing.

He was wearing cutoffs and lying in the grass, his head propped against a tree, and Denise was standing in front of him, dancing to the music. The front of her dark dress had slipped from her shoulders, and her small white breasts moved slowly with the rhythm of her body. She had flowers in her hair that matched the embroidered flowers on the hem of her dress, she was barefoot, and she was smiling.

Almost without thinking, Kate moved her camera to her eye. As she did, the man sat up, holding out his arms. Kate snapped the picture as Denise came to him, her bare arms outstretched. Kate backed away quickly, returned to the boat, sailed back to the mainland, and that was the last she'd seen of Denise.

It wasn't until she looked at the photographs a few weeks later that she saw the scars on the man's naked back: As though the flesh had turned liquid, like lava, then hardened again.

Peter, his head in his hands, was sitting on the arm of the couch, next to his sister. Steve hadn't taken his eyes off Kate since she'd started speaking. Jim, small and ancient, sat slumped in his chair before the fire, his hooded eyes staring into the flames. Except for the faint wheeze of his breathing, he might have been dead. Ellen was contemplating her crochet hook, as if wondering what it was for.

"She looked so happy, you see," Kate went on. "The guy she was with must have been her old boyfriend—the one I sort of thought she'd made up—the Vietnam vet who'd been wounded."

"Not necess—" Peter began, looking up.

Steve cut him off, asking Kate how she'd got the pictures developed. "I didn't think drugstores developed pictures like that in those days—especially for a kid."

"I developed them myself," Kate answered. "I've had my own darkroom since I was twelve."

"Where's that picture now?" he asked. He brought out his tobacco pouch, began filling his pipe. "You said you'd brought some pictures to show us. I'd certainly like to see that one—I'm sure we all would—if you still have it."

"I didn't bring it, but I still have it, although I haven't looked at it in years. I was too young to know what to do with it back then—I just knew I'd better not show it to any adult, especially my mother. I didn't want to show it to my friends, either—that would have been a betrayal of the moment, I thought, and of my friend Denise.

"But I couldn't bring myself to throw it away. It was just a lucky shot, of course, but I had a good enough eye to know it was a wonderful picture. Later, as I learned more about the sixties, it seemed even more wonderful to me: a young hippie girl—that's what Denise looked like in the picture at least—dancing in front of a scarred Vietnam vet, each reaching out to the other. It looked like a scene of total reconciliation."

Regarding her husband with bleak eyes, Ellen said, "You should have tried to sell it, Kate. It would have looked good on an album cover—Denise's little naked breasts, her flowers, his scars. It would have sold a lot of records."

"It's probably not that good a picture," Kate said.

"What are you going to do now, Kate?" Peter asked her finally.

"Call Hank when he gets home from work tonight. He knows where I keep my file of old photographs. He can fax it to me at the lodge tomorrow."

"To what purpose?" Steve asked.

"Don't you think it's strange that the man who was with her never came forward?"

"Not at all," he replied. "This is a small community. He might have been married—or simply didn't want to get involved. Most people don't want to get involved in things like that, you know."

"Would *you* want to get involved, Kate?" Peter asked her.

"I'd like to try to find him, ask him what happened. Maybe one of you'll recognize him. Or I can ask somebody in the local VFW chapter. Denise implied that he was a local hero."

"Kate—!" That was Peter.

"It's all right, Peter," Ellen said, giving him a warning glance.

Kate knew it wouldn't do any good to call Hank until at least nine, since it was two hours earlier in California and he seldom got home before seven.

She went over to the window and stood next to Peter, put an arm around him, looked out at the dark lake.

She was a little worried about Sara and Rob, since it was supposed to start snowing soon.

"They said they might be late," Ellen told her. "They know their way around these hills."

"Do you know if that old cabin on the little island is still standing?"

"No. Why?"

"I'd like to go over there—to say goodbye to Denise." She laughed, a little embarrassed—a little defiant too, since she knew what Ellen would think about that. "I thought of going to the cemetery when I was in town, but that didn't seem like the right place."

"No, you're right," Ellen said, surprising her.

"I'll try to get back by dinnertime." They usually ate dinner at seven.

When Kate had left, Ellen said to her husband, in a voice of ice: "I hired you to kill the girl—you didn't have to fuck her first."

"You didn't hire me," Steve said. "I did it because you asked me to."

"You did it because you wanted me—and the Bishop family money."

He shrugged, lit his pipe. "We all got what we wanted out of it," he said.

"If you'd just killed her, if you hadn't—"

"If I'd just killed her, Ellen, Kate would have stumbled on us in the cabin and I'd have had to kill her too!"

"You're going to have to kill her now anyway, aren't you?"

"No!" Peter cried.

"Not alone, this time," Steve said. "One of you is going to have to help me."

"There's got to be some other way," Peter begged. "We can talk to her—she's family, for God's sake. Think of Sara!"

"She's going to show that photograph to members of the local VFW chapter, Peter," Ellen said, as if speaking to a child. "In the unlikely event one of them doesn't recognize Steve's face, they'll recognize his back. How many votes has that back got you over the years, Senator?"

Steve ignored the sarcasm. "It's got to be done before she calls her husband, of course, and before Rob and Sara get home. They've both seen my back too, and they've seen pictures of me when I was young."

"What are you waiting for?" Ellen asked, and bent her head to her crocheting.

As she skied down the lake, Kate remembered how warm it had been that day, and how cool the breeze had felt out on the water. She remembered the dragonflies hovering around the sailboat and wondered where they went in the winter. There wasn't any wind now, just a few snowflakes, and the temperature was in the mid twenties. The snow was a ghostly blue in the light from the overcast sky.

She skied ashore, remembered the shushing sound the boat had made as she'd nosed it through the reeds. She half skied, half walked across the island, stumbling on tree roots and dead underbrush buried in the powdery snow. She was almost to the other side when she came to the cabin. Birch and aspen grew in the clearing around it where she'd seen Denise dancing for her boyfriend, and a large birch tree that hadn't been there twenty-seven years ago had fallen or been blown against the cabin. The door was missing, and the boards were gone from the windows too, and there were more holes in the walls than she remembered.

She took off her skis and leaned them against a tree,

then stepped into the cabin, wishing she'd thought to bring a flashlight. Her foot hit a tin can, sending it noisily across the floor. In the dim light, she could see rifle and shotgun shells, empty cans, broken bottles, and paper. The wind had blown snow into the cabin through the windows and the door; it was gathered in corners and against the walls.

Denise had been found hanging from one of the ceiling beams. As Kate's eyes wandered around the room, getting used to the darkness, she tried to visualize it: According to the newspaper account, she'd been wearing her long, dark dress with the flowered hem, and she'd had flowers in her hair.

She crossed the room, tested the boards that Denise's boyfriend had nailed on the wall as steps, then climbed into the loft. It wasn't as easy as it had been the first time, she reflected with a grim smile: she wasn't as young, as agile, or as thin.

Feeling a little foolish, she crawled over to the window at the back of the loft, trying to avoid the animal droppings and the spiderwebs. The rotting remains of the mattress were still there, under the window, mixed with snow. The yellowed corners of the posters Denise had stapled to the walls and ceiling were there too, the staples rusted, but where the faces of the rock stars had been was just rough wood now.

As she pushed the mattress away from the window, something black fell out of it: half a plastic ashtray. The last time she'd seen it, it had been full of marijuana ash.

She made herself comfortable in front of the window and tried to recall her last days at the lake and anything that might explain Denise's suicide.

The big event had been Gunnar Johanson's drowning. At the library that day, after she'd finished reading about Denise's death, Kate had paged back through the volume of old local newspapers until she found the account of it.

Gunnar had drowned on Wednesday, August 30. His wife saw him alive for the last time early that morning, when he'd left the house to go fishing. She'd found his body later that day under the dock in front of his boathouse. There was a deep cut on his temple, and blood on the post at the end of the dock that explained it. The coroner had called his death an accidental drowning.

Kate and Denise hadn't gone sailing that day or the next, Thursday, either. She remembered that because she'd wanted to talk to Denise about the drowning—she didn't have anybody else to talk to about it—and she was looking forward to Friday morning, when they were going to sail for the last time. And when Denise hadn't shown up, she'd wondered if it might be because of Gunnar's drowning—maybe Denise didn't want to sail on the lake, just as Kate hadn't wanted to swim in it.

As far as Kate knew, nothing else out of the ordinary had happened that last week—except, of course, that Denise's boyfriend had unexpectedly shown up.

Kate's thoughts were interrupted by a noise outside the cabin, a twig breaking: an animal of some kind, probably, or just a clump of snow falling from a tree.

Denise's boyfriend's visit must have been a surprise, because if Denise had been expecting him, she would have mentioned it to Kate. Denise wasn't good at keeping secrets.

Kate shook her head angrily. No matter what had happened between Denise and her boyfriend that day or any day, she wouldn't have killed herself on account of it! Kate was as certain of that as if Denise were there in the loft with her, telling her so. In fact, Denise wouldn't have killed herself at all—she had a sick mother to support! If she wouldn't abandon her mother to go to San Francisco, she wouldn't abandon her by killing herself.

That left only one alternative—murder. But that didn't make sense, either. Denise wasn't involved in anything that would cause anybody to murder her. Was she?

Across the lake, through the falling snow, Kate saw light in the windows of a house on the hill. That had been Gunnar's house. The boathouse was still on the shore

where she'd first seen it, but the dock had been taken in
for the winter. She remembered how she'd seen Gunnar
sitting in his outboard motorboat, untying it from the
dock post—the one he'd hit his head on a week or so
later.

Goose bumps began to crawl on Kate's skin as the
thought grew in her: Denise could have been sitting here
that morning—in her awkward lotus position—watching
the sun rise above Gunnar's hill. She could have seen him
stumble, hit his head, and fall into the lake.

But what if Gunnar hadn't tripped and fallen? What if
he'd been murdered and Denise had seen that? Suddenly
Kate didn't want to be alone in the loft any longer. She
began to crawl back to the hole in the ceiling.

A can clattered across the floor below.

Her heart skipped a beat. "Who's there?" she called out.

"It's me, Kate—Peter. Sorry if I scared you. I didn't
know where you were."

"What do you want, Peter?"

"We—we were worried about you. It's starting to
snow more heavily now. Ellen and Steve—they asked me
to come and bring you home."

It wasn't really snowing that hard. Ellen and Steve
weren't the worrying kind.

They'd all behaved oddly whenever she'd wanted to
talk about Denise. They'd tried not to let her know when
she'd died, or where. Jim Bishop had hated Gunnar
because he wouldn't sell him the hill. As far as Kate
knew, the Bishops were the only people who'd profited
from Gunnar's death.

"Did you come alone, Peter?"

"Yes." He tried to laugh. "How many Bishops does it
take to bring you home for dinner, Kate?"

Kate, you're nuts, she thought. She'd wait for the photograph, see if she could find anybody who could identify the
man with Denise. She began lowering herself through the
hole.

And smelled Steve's tobacco. And heaved herself up
into the loft again.

"What's wrong, Kate?"

Steve had gone to the university at the same time Ellen had. They'd met there, and they'd known each other in high school before that—which meant he must have known Denise too. During the time Kate was at the lake, Ellen spent weekends in Minneapolis. Steve had been in Vietnam, and he'd been studying law, like Denise's boyfriend.

"I guess I'm not ready to go back yet, Peter," she said. She was looking frantically around for something to use as a weapon. There was only the broken ashtray.

"Kate—please!"

"Go away, Peter."

She heard somebody at the wall, and then Steve's head came through the hole in the floor. He started to pull himself up into the loft, but Kate smashed at his face with the ashtray. He ducked, lost his footing, fell.

"All right, Kate," he called up from below, his voice still calm. "You seem to have caught on to us. That's too bad, but it's not going to change anything. We only wanted to make it easier for you, but we'll burn you alive if we have to. Shout all you want—nobody'll be able to hear you on the mainland."

"People will know it wasn't an accident," she said.

"Of course they will. But even in unspoiled places like this, it's not wise for women to go out alone at night. These days there are maniacs everywhere. Peter, holler if she tries to come down."

She crawled to the hole and peered down at Peter. "What's he got, Peter? Kerosene?"

"Kate, I'm sorry. It shouldn't have happened this way. If only you'd never come back!"

She could hear Steve walking around outside, the sound of liquid sloshing against the cabin.

"If only our children hadn't met and fallen in love," she said. "Peter, I'm coming down."

She began lowering herself through the hole, groping for the step with her foot. As she clung to the wall, she turned and looked at Peter and said, "Look, Peter—

Denise! Hanging there from the rafter in her Goodwill dress. And she's got flowers in her hair!"

He looked up at her, his face contorted in agony, then turned away. She threw herself on him, striking at his head with the ashtray as he stumbled and fell. She landed on top of him, tried to get up to run, then ducked as, out of the corner of her eye, she saw the red blur of the kerosene can Steve was swinging at her head. It struck her painfully on the shoulder, and she screamed and rolled off Peter and tried to scramble away. Steve came after her, swinging the can again, stepping over Peter. Peter, blood running into his eyes, grabbed Steve's leg and twisted.

Smoke was filling the cabin, flame crawling over the windowsill and probing through the bullet holes in the walls.

On the floor, Steve dug into his jacket, pulled out a pistol, and pointed it at Kate.

Peter lunged for the gun, missed, but knocked Steve's arm aside as Kate, gripping the ashtray in both hands, swung it as hard as she could into the side of Steve's head.

Ellen stood in the window, watching as two figures skied slowly down the lake toward the house. They seemed to be holding each other up, but they were too far away for her to recognize through the falling snow. Behind them, the glow of a fire on the far side of the little island was just visible. After a few minutes, headlights came over the hill at the other end of the lake, and then the Range Rover nosed down the road and onto the ice.

She turned back to the approaching figures, held her breath as the headlights of the car caught them.

"Who's that with Peter?" her father demanded, coming up to stand beside her.

"An avenging angel," Ellen replied, and she dug her fingers into her long white shawl and pulled it up over her hair.

THE LOST BOYS

WILLIAM J. REYNOLDS

*William J. Reynolds has given us several sly
novels that are and always will be "medium-
hard boiled" and, at least in places, "comic
or parodic" (his own words).*

*Reynolds is one of those people who seem to
get better every time out: more
certain of plot, more certain of phrase,
and increasingly certain of his colorful
characters.*

*His books also show us a Midwest seldom
seen in the literature of crime—in a Reynolds
novel, the Midwest is a lively and frequently
dangerous place to live and not at all the
bucolic pastureland that some would
have it be.*

▼▼▼▼▼

THE LOST BOYS

SNOW TRAILED IN ghostly fingers across the highway. The sky, the fields, and the road were all the same color—gray, unbroken, and unsympathetic gray—and the raw January wind had its own idea of where the little car should go. The wind's idea and mine were not always the same.

I was not quite smack in the middle of South Dakota—just a bit beyond it, actually, some little distance north and west of the capital, Pierre. In French, *pierre* means "rock," and it was obvious that the Mount Rushmore State's capital city had been aptly named even if the locals pronounced it *peer:* There was a lot of rock around the countryside, great scabrous outcroppings of pinkish and reddish granite that jutted out above the hard-crusted snow as if trying to break away from the earth's stubborn grasp. This was a harsh and unforgiving land, here on the edge of the Badlands, hard and rugged, a land far removed in both distance and aesthetics from the gently rolling prairie farmland of the eastern portion of the state.

To continue westward, I knew, would take me up and into those craggy mountains modestly dubbed the Black Hills, up and into Deadwood, Lead, Custer, and other towns whose names promise the Wild West but whose main streets deliver glossy tourist traps. But my destination was nearer in than that—fortunately, given the look of the sky, the increasing persistence of the wind, and the hypnotic tendrils of gritty snow that drifted across the two-lane highway. Although I hadn't even heard of the place until two days earlier, I was now glad that my destination was a town called Monument, thirty-five miles up the highway, and not some more exotic and distant locale. The weather shaping up as it was, I would be glad to make it to Monument. At least, that's what I told myself at the time.

There was a reason for the journey, a reason beyond road testing the new Civic sedan I had bought a few weeks earlier, after my faithful old Impala had gone to that big used-car lot in the sky. I was on my way to this tiny community of Monument—population 2,900, according to my American Express road atlas—in search of two boys. Ryan Lund was sixteen; his brother, Matthew, was fourteen. They had disappeared from their mother's suburban Omaha home two days earlier. The mother, Tricia Russell, had remembered my name from a World-Herald article, an account of how I'd had a certain amount of luck tracing adolescent runaways and reuniting them with their folks. I no longer did as much bloodhounding as I had done in those days, but bills still needed paying and I always was a sucker for what we used to call a damsel in distress, even when the damsel was closer to middle-aged. As was Tricia Russell.

"Never," Ms. Russell had replied when I asked, pro forma, whether either or both of her sons had ever run away before. "They're such good boys, no trouble at all. But they . . ."

I had waited. She finished filling my coffee cup, topped off her own, then sat opposite me in the comfortable deep-pile living room of her two-car, three-bedroom, finished-basement ranch house. Tricia Russell was several years younger than me, thirty or thirty-five, say, with short auburn hair betraying only a dusting of silver-gray. She wore expensive "casual" clothes, turquoise jewelry on her fingers and wrists, pink gloss on her lips and fingernails, and the sort of tan an Omahan usually wears in January only if she bought it in a store. She was an attractive woman, but the glare of the winter sun through the picture window revealed to me what she would look like in old age: thin and hard and somehow incomplete.

"You don't have children," she said at last; it wasn't a question, but I shook my head anyway. "Then of course you can't know what it's like for children, for young children, when their parents separate and divorce. Gordon and I divorced almost three years ago, and I moved back here to Omaha with the boys. To be nearer to my parents and my sister. The boys took that hard, and in retrospect, perhaps it wasn't such a good idea. Ryan and Matthew had friends back in Monument, they were doing well in school, they were involved in sports. And of course, moving here took them far away from their father—which was *not* my intention, honestly. But I knew that *I* needed to be away from Gordon, and I also knew that it would be impossible in Monument."

"I suppose so, in a small town. . . ."

"It's not just that," Ms. Russell said, and her thin little pink-painted lips were turned down. "If Gordon Lund worked at the corner gas station back in Monument, South Dakota, that would be one thing. But my ex-husband is the president, CEO, and major shareholder of Mid-Continent Quarriers. Mid-Continent is one of the largest quarrying and stonecutting operations in the upper Midwest; it is far and away the largest employer in and around Monument, and has been for a century. Which makes my former husband a pretty powerful individual. Influential. Important. And that sort of thing means something to young boys Ryan and Matthew's ages. In Monument, everyone knew who they were: their father was an important man; that made them important kids. In Omaha, nobody knows them. Their mother is not an important woman; they are not important kids."

"So you think they've gone back to their father, back to that lifestyle?"

She nodded. "They miss him terribly—as they should—and even frequent visits aren't the same. And they miss the life they had."

"I always hate to talk myself out of a job," I said after she had leaned across the coffee table and refilled my cup, "but have you tried just telephoning your former husband and asking if the boys are with him?"

Ms. Russell pursed her lips. "Gordon and I did not part on good terms—part of the reason I wanted to leave Monument. We communicate through intermediaries. Lawyers. His secretary. My answering machine. The boys." She paused, as if considering something. I had the feeling it was something from the distant past. Finally, she returned to the moment: "I honestly couldn't tell you the last time we *talked,* directly, about anything. I have left several messages with Gordon, at his home and at his office, but none has been returned. Which only further makes me certain the boys are with him."

It made sense—in the wacky-doodle context of feuding ex-spouses, where "sense" has a meaning only remotely related to the more traditional definition. I said, "Have you talked to the police?"

She shook her head. "I read somewhere that someone has to be missing for twenty-four hours before the police will look for them, and the boys have only *just* been gone that long." That rule doesn't apply to missing minors; but I said nothing, since I felt that wasn't the true reason she hadn't made a report. "Besides," she said after a moment, confirming my suspicion, "no one's done anything *wrong*—it isn't as if Gordon kidnapped the boys. I don't want to make trouble. I don't want to do anything that would make things between Gordon and me any more difficult than they already are. For my boys' sake. I just want to make sure that Ryan and Matthew are all right."

Which did not make sense, even in the context of divorce. Even assuming that Tricia Russell's guess was correct, that her sons had fled the Big O to reunite with their father, there's still a lot of nasty that can happen to a couple of kids in transit. And if her guess *wasn't* correct . . .

"All right," I said, although it wasn't. "Have you tried calling someone else in Monument—a friend, a former neighbor, one of the boys' teachers—to see if they've seen the kids around?"

Ms. Russell was shaking her head even before I'd finished the question. "There's no one I could call," she said quietly, "no one I could talk to in that town without word getting back to Gordon. Virtually everyone there directly or indirectly owes their livelihood to him, to the quarry. At the risk of sounding melodramatic, my ex-husband *is* the town of Monument. It's important you understand that."

"I understand less the more we talk. You're afraid of irking your former husband. All right, fine—I don't know the man and you do, and you're the one who'll have to have some sort of relationship with him, because of your sons, when this is all over, so you need to do what you need to do. But surely he would understand your being concerned that the boys have turned up missing! And what if he doesn't have them?"

"He has them."

I suppressed a sigh of exasperation. "All right. You call OPD and tell them what you've told me—I can give you the names of a couple of sympathetic officers. They call the police or the sheriff or whoever in Monument, and someone there drops in on your ex. That's a whole lot more discreet than sending in a private investigator, and it'll take maybe an hour or two. . . ."

The auburn head was going again, side to side, resolutely. "You don't know Gordon," she said. "You don't know what he can be like if he gets his back up. And I trust you to be far more discreet than the Monument city police—all eight of them—could ever hope to be." She looked at me—for the first time, I think, since I had entered the house, she really looked at me. Her eyes were dry and had been all along, but they were infinitely, if indefinitely, sad. "Will you help me?" she asked simply, and of course I said I would try.

The Honda, after all, could use a good shakedown trip.

There was a single motel in Monument, the Sleep Inn, an eighteen-unit barracks-like building on the edge of town, where the highway tapered down into Monument's main drag. The town's little low-roofed police station was situated right across from the motel—coincidentally enough, right where the speed limit dropped from fifty-five to twenty miles an hour.

Ordinarily the first order of business upon coming to a strange town is to pay a courtesy call on the local law, let them know who I am and what I'm about, see if they have any insights that might be helpful to me, and like that. Cops, and not just small-town cops, are notoriously jealous of their turf, and the hat-in-hand visitation spares hurt feelings later on.

But this trip I was skipping the courtesy call. At my client's insistence, I was traveling incognito; more correctly, I was traveling under false colors, using my own name but pretending to be in Monument as a freelance writer preparing an article on midwestern quarries for *Modern Stone,* a trade magazine. It was easy to gin up the cover story. I'd done more than a little freelance writing over the years, so my credentials would bear any amount of checking. And *Modern Stone*'s editor, an acquaintance of another editor for whom I'd written a few times, was prepared to vouch for me. Prepared, hell—she was *eager,* and I imagined she was just hoping someone would check up on me so she could use the little fiction we had concocted yesterday. People somehow have the impression that this is a glamorous profession and believe that by doing their little bit to help out, some of the glamour might rub off onto them. Who am I to tell them otherwise?

Glamorously, as always, I entered the Sleep Inn's minuscule office. The manager, an old, colorless fellow roughly the size and shape of a drinking straw, greeted me like a long-lost friend—which he should have done, since there were only two other cars in the miniature parking lot out front—and got me fixed up with a room. The walls were painted cinder block, the floors were industrial carpet, and the furniture was eligible for Social Security, but it would do. It would have to do.

I settled in, to the extent I ever settle into a rented room, then ventured back out into the raw January wind.

The snow had picked up just in the few minutes since I'd checked in, and was beginning to gather in drifts wherever the wind would give it a moment's peace. It was just four-thirty in the afternoon, but already the sky was the color of old ashes, and the cars that crept along Monument's main street—cleverly named Main Avenue—were preceded by the beams of their headlights.

Against my better judgment, given the weather, I drove back out of town, following the directions Tricia Russell had given me. Gordon Lund's place was four miles beyond the city limits, just off the county highway. It was a big house but not overwhelming, nice but nowhere near opulent, distinguished primarily by the vaulted ceiling at the entrance and the granite facade that fanned out from the front door.

The place was dark, had that indistinct "empty" look to it.

I stopped at an Amoco station along the highway and called the Lund residence. After four rings, an answering machine kicked in. A man's voice; the usual sort of greeting. I didn't leave a message.

Enamored as I am of the direct approach, I toyed with going back to the house, ringing the doorbell, and seeing if Matthew or Ryan Lund answered. But Tricia Russell had insisted on discretion, and it was her dime. That's the problem with this racket: a person has at least a small obligation to observe his client's wishes, even when they seem not in the client's own interests.

Besides, if Lund was hiding his kids, he had undoubtedly instructed them not to answer the phone, not to answer the door, not to turn on any lights that could be seen from the road.

The place was distinctly unsuited to a stakeout: The terrain was flat, or nearly so, in all directions; there were no mature trees or other natural screens; and because the road was a highway, there was no legitimate, unobtrusive place to park and keep watch from the car.

It didn't break my heart. A one-man stakeout is possible—and I've done them, when there's no alternative—

but it's damn difficult for one pair of eyes to watch all of a given building's entrances and exits, round the clock.

I went back to town.

The Monument Coffee Cup was indistinguishable from any number of small-town cafés and coffee shops I'd been in: fluorescent lights, cracked linoleum, vinyl upholstery, Formica table- and countertops. Country music bleated from a cheap radio in the kitchen. Two customers, in clothing that suggested they were dairy workers, sat together in one of the booths along the north wall. A thin, ageless man in a T-shirt puttered in the kitchen as a heavy, squarish woman in an aquamarine waitress's uniform laboriously chalked the next day's menu on a small blackboard she had laid on the counter.

I sat on a stool and watched her. She worked carefully, neatly, spelling most of the words correctly. "What'll it be, honey?" she asked without seeming to have taken note of me.

"Just coffee."

She finished up her chore and fetched me a thick-walled beige mug. The coffee had a slightly burned flavor, but it was plenty hot. I slurped some, then warmed my hands on the cup.

"Pretty wicked out there," the waitress said. The plastic pin on her breast said her name was Vi. Like the region in which she lived, her voice was hard and flat. "S'posed to get six inches tonight." She smiled, displaying three chins and grayish teeth. "Hope you don't mind hanging around town a day or two until we get dug out."

"I'd planned to stay a day or so," I answered truthfully. "I'm doing a magazine article about Mid-Continent Quarriers."

"No kidding. Well, there's plenty to write about there. They do all kinds of stuff—stuff you'd expect, like tombstones, mausoleums, and that, but also building stone, decorative rock, and like that. My brother-in-law works up there, and he says the next big thing is countertops." Vi lovingly stroked the worn plastic countertop with her chubby little fingers. "Can you imagine? People want *granite* counters in their kitchens and bathrooms."

"That'll go good in the article," I said. "I'm going to be interviewing Gordon Lund in the morning, and I'll be sure to ask him about that." I slurped some more coffee. "Do you know Gordon Lund?"

She laughed. "This is a small town, honey. I imagine I know ninety-nine out of a hundred people in a hundred-mile radius."

I laughed along with her. "What's he like?"

Vi shrugged, and the aquamarine uniform whispered. "He's like anybody," she said. "He has lunch here a couple times a week—the office is just around the corner, in the old bank—and he's always friendly enough. Good tipper."

"A man like that must have a lot of pull in a town like this."

She looked at me. "A town like what?"

"A town this size. From the research I've done, I know Mid-Continent is the largest employer around, by a considerable margin. That would make the boss an important man."

Her gaze hadn't wavered. "I s'pose so," Vi said evenly. "But he has to go make wee-wee just like everyone else in the world, doesn't he?" She cut me off as I started to say something. "Here's some free advice, honey. I don't know what sort of article you plan to write, but if your idea is to do some kind of hatchet job, well, I think you'll find out real fast that that sort of thing doesn't go down real smooth. In a town like this."

"Hey, I didn't mean anything. I was just trying to get some idea what sort of fellow Gordon Lund is."

"Well, you'll have to find out from him, I guess." Vi smiled. "Warm that up for you?"

Gordon Lund was a tall fellow, the sort who in his youth must have been gangly. He had broad, open Scandinavian features, thin pale hair, and the corner office in a building that dated from a time when banks were meant to look solid and formidable. He also had the only granite desk I have ever seen, a glossy dark-pink number that must have weighed almost, literally, a ton. "Prairie Rose," Lund told me, patting the desktop. "Our premium granite. My dad had this desk built back when he ran the business. The floor underneath this office is shored up with oak timbers, ten inches in diameter, to hold the weight. Needless to say, I don't rearrange the furniture very often."

Sitting in on the interview was Mid-Continent's sales manager, a dark, calm-looking woman named Fiona Hermanson. She said little as I conducted my "interview" with the boss. She seldom took her deep-set eyes from Gordon Lund's face, and I noticed him sending frequent glances in her direction. But in the gender-integrated workplace of the nineties, such glances could be nothing more than glances, nonverbal communication between company president and company sales manager. And if I had wheels, I could be a wagon.

The morning wore on. I pitched the usual trite questions about the business, caught the usual trite answers. Found out more about granite than I had ever hoped to know—enough to get me thinking about going ahead and writing the fictitious article for *Modern Stone*. I found out that quarries hardly ever blast anymore: it wastes too much stone. Most of the granite Mid-Continent quarried was used in building: only a small percentage was used for tombstones, which in the business were called "memorials." The company had begun branching out into "home applications"—the kitchen and bath countertops that Vi had mentioned, coffee table tops, other things. None of the granite was wasted: anything that was of inferior quality, or contained unsightly variegations, or otherwise didn't pass muster, was crushed and sold as "decorative stone."

"Use everything but the squeal," I said, referring to the old gag about meatpackers using virtually every part of the hog.

Lund laughed. "That's about the size of it," he said.

Fiona Hermanson made one of her few contributions to the conversation. "This is a surprisingly competitive business," she said. "If you don't stay right on top of everything, well, pretty soon you have to find another business to be in."

Eventually I steered the "interview" around to the key people. There were four: the quarry foreman, the plant foreman, the sales manager, and of course the president. Fiona Hermanson readily confessed to her age, background, education, and family status. Gordon Lund did all right with the first three of those, but then, for the first time since I'd entered his office, he became equivocal. "I don't mean to tell you how to do your job, but I just don't see where that sort of thing has anything to do with the business—and after all, it's the business you're writing about, right?"

"Sure, but a business is nothing more than the people who run it. People like to read about people. Little details like these humanize a business."

"Well, I like to keep my private life private. You understand." The tone of his voice was apologetic, but there was a hardness beneath the surface. Someone with less self-restraint than I might be tempted to make references to a granitelike hardness. Either way, Lund had clammed up.

Fiona Hermanson bought me lunch—not at the Monument Coffee Cup, but at the considerably more upscale Elks Club just outside town. We talked about the business in particular, the industry in general, all the usual trade magazine blather. I tried, delicately, to draw her out on the subject of Gordon Lund, but she was just as elusive as her boss had been. "It's like Gordon said," she told me. "He's an incredibly private man. I've worked with him for five years, and I know almost nothing about him—you know, outside of business."

"Well, you must know *something* about his personal life," I said, mindful of the frequent glances between her and Lund as I spoke with them that morning. "Just something I can put in the article: Is he married? Does he have any hobbies? Does he have kids? How many and what kind? Of kids, I mean."

Ms. Hermanson did not look at me for a little while, preferring instead to trace the floral pattern on the edge of her plate with a tine of her fork. When she did turn her dark eyes toward me, it was to give me a kind of resolute, penetrating gaze that I imagine the Mid-Continent sales force experienced when quarterly orders were below the target level. "I understand your wanting to learn as much as you can for your article. But you have to understand what a private individual Gordon is. He's made his feelings clear on this subject, and it would be disloyal of me to go against his wishes. Please don't ask again."

I didn't. We stuck to noncontroversial subjects, some related to the business, some not. I wasn't paying much attention, frankly. I was trying to put myself in the position of someone who had two kids and an ex-wife, wanted to keep the two kids with him, and didn't want the ex-wife to know for sure that he had them. Although I was having a little difficulty with the scenario, I imagined I would do pretty much what Gordon Lund seemed to be doing: stonewalling. No pun intended.

After lunch, Fiona Hermanson took me for a drive out into the country. The wind had dropped, and the snowplows had been out to break open the highways, but the road was by no means clear. To the north and south of the highways, the land stretched out to meet the distant blue horizon. The snow cover gave the illusion of flatness, but I knew that beneath the soft blanket, the landscape was coarse and cragged. I seemed to encounter that all the time in this life I had made for myself—the illusory covering. Frequently it was up to me to peel back the covering. Frequently I wished I hadn't.

Mid-Continent's plant occupied a sprawling metal-sided building three miles outside town. Here, Fiona explained, was where the "rough-sawn" granite that came from the quarry—which was just down the road a few more miles—was cut, carved, polished, assembled, whatever a particular job required; from here the finished pieces were shipped out via truck or, less often, rail.

The plant was pretty much like any other plant in any other industry: big, noisy, dusty, loud, cold. Gargantuan block-and-tackle rigs hauled immense slabs to and fro throughout the operation. Diamond-tipped circular saw blades taller than a man sliced the slabs into smaller sections; wire saws further cut the slabs down to size. Rugged machines handled carving, polishing, edging. I watched a man assemble a crypt, a special order that was destined for Louisiana. I watched a row of small granite plaques roll down a rubber conveyor belt. I watched uncarved tombstones—"dies" was the somewhat ironic term in the trade—being crated for shipping. I talked to the plant foreman. I talked to the shipping chief. I talked to some of the people on the plant floor. We only talked business; Fiona Hermanson stayed at my elbow the whole time.

I got back to the Sleep Inn shortly after three, and the red light on the telephone in my room was blinking. The manager gave me the name and number of the editor of *Modern Stone*. I called her from the pay phone of a gas station down the street—having learned long ago never to trust motel switchboards—and she rather breathlessly told me that "some woman" from Mid-Continent Quarriers had called that afternoon to "check up" on me. That did and yet did not surprise me.

After thanking the editor for lying on my behalf, I fed the Honda and swung round to the Coffee Cup for something warm. The place was about as busy as it had been the previous day, but my friend Vi was all business, nowhere near as chatty as she had been yesterday. I didn't think much of it, though: my head was elsewhere too. For not the first time in what I laughingly refer to as my career, I was dealing with a client whose instructions were in conflict with her own best interests, as I saw them. My orders were to ascertain that Tricia Russell's sons were with their father. No overwhelming obstacle there. But I was to do so "discreetly," even clandestinely, striving to make sure Gordon Lund didn't tumble to the real nature of my mission. Which amounted to making sure no one *else* knew the real nature of my mission. Which made it pretty tricky to complete my mission, since it eliminated all of the straightforward, tried-and-true methods I would ordinarily apply: talking to law enforcement agents, school officials, Lund's neighbors, and so on.

It made me think of a friend of mine in the ad-agency business, who once complained to me about clients who know they *should* advertise but yet have misgivings. "They want you to come up with an ad campaign that won't call attention to them," she groused. Now I knew how she must have felt. Tricia Russell wanted me to do a job but didn't want me to use any of the tools of my trade. It must have been an interesting marriage, hers and Lund's: three years after the divorce, he was still controlling her by long distance, refusing to return her phone calls, sitting in his granite fortress and letting her stew about their sons. It made me want to adopt a distinctly *un*discreet approach, one that would involve taking Gordon Lund by the scruff of the neck and shaking him until something rattled loose. But still, I felt obliged to observe my client's request. At least to a point.

By the time I left the Monument Coffee Cup, I had decided to play out my cover story and see what turned up. If the answer, as I expected, proved to be "nothing," I would make appropriate recommendations to my client. The rest would be up to her.

Although it was barely four in the afternoon, the sky was already dark and close. A faint and tentative snow hung in the air. Monument was an old town, dominated by beautiful oaks and maples that loomed above even the two-story houses and that now, in the gloom, looked like the ghosts of long-dead sentinels, still at their posts, shrouded in white.

My car was parked diagonally just down the wide boulevard from the café, near Kjellsen's Sportsman's

Barber Shop, where the dark figures of two men loitered. They were big men, made bigger by the heavy coats, boots, and gloves they wore. "When in doubt, go for the obvious," I muttered under my breath. I sighed inwardly and approached them. Despite their gear, they were both visibly shivering.

"Too cold a night for this kind of monkey business," I said helpfully.

"Could heat up," said one of them, the one nearest the car.

Now I sighed audibly. "No one talks like that," I said. "You watch too much TV." I started to move past them, and the one who had spoken moved too, to block my path.

I looked at him, then looked at his friend. They were cut from the same cloth: husky guys, broad-faced, narrow-eyed. Ike and Mike, they look alike. I took them to be of German or Scandinavian heritage, farm boys who didn't like the farm and went to work at the quarry. They weren't toughs; they were just a couple of big guys. Someone had made a mistake in sending them. They were out of their element, and we all three knew it.

"This isn't as good an idea as whoever sent you thought it was," I said, trying to sound reasonable. "Someone could get hurt. So let's save time: You're bigger than me, you're stronger than me, and there are twice as many of you as me. Okay? I'm impressed already. So now you can tool along and tell your boss that you tried your damnedest to scare me off but I wouldn't scare. It's too blasted cold for this dime-novel malarkey."

With that I moved again toward the Honda, and Ike, the man nearest me, moved again too, toward me. I was watching for it. I ducked under his right arm and came up behind him, my two hands clamped around his right wrist. I shoved him up against the side of a Dodge pickup parked next to my car, and levered his arm up behind his back until I felt the resistance; then I levered it another quarter inch. He grunted.

"I have a thirty-eight-caliber revolver in my coat

pocket," I lied, loosening the grip of my right hand and shoving it into the pocket in question. "I don't much care which of you gets plugged first."

My taking down Ike had temporarily paralyzed Mike. Then, half a heartbeat ago, he had started to move in. Now he froze again.

I let go of Ike and quickly backstepped out of reach. With my fist in my empty coat pocket, I felt like Alan Ladd. Except Alan Ladd would have had his fist wrapped around a gun, not pocket lint.

The big man edged away from the pickup. "Take it easy, mister," he said. The waver in his voice may or may not have been caused by the cold night air. "We don't want nobody gettin' hurt."

I was pretty sure that "nobody" didn't include me. I angled my chin at them. "Go home."

They went.

I took the scenic route back to the motel, making sure the dark held no other little surprises. When the coast seemed clear, I parked the Civic, collected my .38 from the glove box—better late than never, but I dislike guns—pocketed it, and went to my room.

Or tried to, at least. The key didn't seem to fit the lock anymore.

I went down to the office. The manager seemed surprised to see me.

"Key doesn't work."

He licked his colorless lips, looked around, perhaps for cue cards, then ultimately focused his eyes somewhere just south of my chin. "Little problem," he said feebly. He cleared his throat and tried again: "There's a little problem. My fault. Had the room already booked before you called. I'd forgotten, and, well, this other party *did* book first."

"Uh-huh. I don't mind moving to another room."

"Well, sorry, we're just full up."

I looked out the rime-caked window at the parking lot. There were two cars in it, and one of them was mine.

"Full up?"

"Sorry."

I sighed. "I don't suppose there's another motel in town?"

The old man shook his head.

"Well, can I at least get my things?"

He reached behind the phony-wood counter and dragged out my garment bag and briefcase. "I got everything," he said. "I double-checked."

"How thoughtful of you," I mumbled, taking my gear and heading toward the door.

"Sorry for the inconvenience," the old man said, and I had a fleeting impression that he *was* sorry.

"Forget about it," I said, and went out to the Honda, and pointed it in the direction of Omaha.

It stayed pointed in that direction for twenty minutes or so. I had figured to head back down to I-90 and find a motel there, out of Gordon Lund's sphere of influence. But as the wind rose on that lonely highway, so did my ire. If Gordon Lund wanted to play control games with Tricia Russell, that was one thing. If Tricia Russell was so intimidated by her ex-husband, even from three hundred miles' distance, that she didn't want me to annoy or upset him, that was one thing. But when their asinine games put me and others at risk, then it was something else again. True, my little showdown with Ike and Mike had been a whole lot of nothing, and it had been obvious from twenty paces that they were just a couple of big old boys, not roughnecks or leg-breakers. But I might just as easily have had the .38 in my pocket as in my car, and Ike and Mike might have been more gung-ho, more foolhardy than they were, and something terrible might have happened.

And then there was the little matter of two lost boys.

Somehow, about eighteen miles outside town, the little sedan got itself U-turned around on the highway and aimed back toward Monument.

◆ ◆ ◆

By then it was after five, but I drove straight to the Mid-Continent offices anyhow. The receptionist and a few others were still finishing up the day's work—there's that unbeatable midwestern work ethic you hear so much about. Lund's office was black, and the receptionist told me I had just missed him. "But he and Ms. Hermanson had to stop out to the quarry first, he told me, and see the foreman. You might be able to catch him out there."

I knew where to go, since Fiona Hermanson had told me that the quarry was just beyond the plant I had visited that afternoon. The sky was dark now, but big pinkish sodium-vapor lamps illuminated the snow-packed parking area just off the highway. There was only another car in the lot, a Buick, and a well-used Ranger pickup. At the far end of the lot, on a short rise, I saw a metal-sided building inset with small, grimy windows that glowed yellow. I parked the Honda and headed for the building, the hard snow squeaking beneath my boots.

The building's entrance was on the east, away from the lot. There were sodium-vapor lamps around that side too, mounted on high poles, providing a strange imitation of daylight. Just beyond the metal building, below the rise on which it sat, was the quarry. It was about what you'd expect a quarry to be—namely, a big hole in the ground. It was a squarish hole, as deep as a ten-story building is tall, cut down into the hard and uncooperative earth. The wound was pinkish, the deep pink of Mid-Continent Quarriers' signature Prairie Rose granite. A chest-high metal railing enclosed it. All around, in the quarry and above it, machinery stood in silent watch: cranes, loaders, open-car elevators, lifts, compressors, trucks. It all waited there, in that strange light, for the workers to return in the morning. Everything was silent except for the unceasing rustle and hum of the wind. It was like being on the set of some science fiction movie.

The metal building's door opened, and Fiona Hermanson emerged. Right behind her were Gordon

Lund and a man I didn't know, a short, square man who looked like he may have been cut from the very stone that was being ripped from the ground here: hard and rough and ruddy. They were surprised to see me: Lund not as surprised as I might have expected.

"I thought we were going to meet out here in the morning," Fiona Hermanson stammered. "As you can see, there's nothing going on here toni—"

"No, there's plenty going on," I said tightly. "Too much, in fact."

"What on earth are you talking about?" Lund said.

"Many things. At the moment, I'm talking about a couple of men who could have gotten badly hurt tonight, thanks to their boss being a megalomaniac. There's more, but I think it'd be best if we talked in private. My client did so want me to be discreet."

"Client," Lund said flatly.

Ms. Hermanson's calm demeanor evaporated. "Damn it, Gordon, I *told* you—"

"Fiona," Lund said peremptorily. He turned to the rough-hewn fellow behind them. "There's no need to tie you up here, Bob. See you later."

The man looked doubtful. "I can hang around awhile, if you need me."

"Go on home, get some supper." Bob moved off, around the side of the building. A moment or two later, above the wind, we heard his pickup start. Only then did Lund speak again.

"All right, let's quit playing games. I know who you are, I know what you are. So the only question is, what the hell are you doing here? What is it you want from me?"

Two questions, but why quibble. "The truth would be nice. You've checked up on me—I already know that. No doubt you've guessed that I'm here on behalf of Tricia Russell—"

"Shit! I knew that crazy woman was behind it all," Fiona Hermanson said bitterly. "Didn't I tell you so? She's never going to leave you alone! She's never going to forgive you—"

Again, Lund cut her off, this time with a raised hand. He looked at me, had been looking at me the whole time.

"Tricia sent you," he said quietly, as quietly as he could and still be heard above the wind. "I should have guessed. But you said something about two men. . . ."

I looked past him, over his left shoulder, and into Fiona Hermanson's face. It was, I thought at first, distorted with rage; but when I made contact with her dark eyes I could see that the emotion was pain, pain and a little fear.

After a moment she nodded. "It was me."

Lund looked at her.

"Now it makes sense," I said. "Lund's supposed to be a private guy, publicity shy. Siccing a couple of would-be toughs on a fellow, and then getting him bounced out of his motel room, is not a quiet thing to do. Quiet guys usually know that silence is a greater obstacle than muscle."

Lund was still staring at Fiona. She had a hard time meeting his gaze. "I'm sorry, Gordy, but I had to do *something*. I know you said we should just play along, assume he really was here for the magazine story. Your instinct was right, and I should have listened. But when we found out he was a private detective . . . I don't know. I just wanted him *gone*. We have so much to lose."

Gordon Lund turned back toward me. "Tricia always suspected that Fiona and I were involved with each other before the divorce. That is absolutely false. Anyhow, what possible difference could it make to her now? Hauling me into court is only going to make the lawyers richer, and it isn't going to change anything. After all we've been through—all of us—why can't she just go on and lead her own life and stay the hell out of mine?"

"Don't tell me, tell her," I said. "Pick up the damn phone, call your ex-wife, and let her know the boys are all right. That's all she—"

Lund was tall; he covered the three or four feet between us in one quick stride and nailed me squarely on the chin. I went down. The night sky was thick with clouds, but I saw stars nevertheless. As if from a distance, I heard voices: Lund's and Fiona Hermanson's, I suppose, since no one else was around and I wasn't feeling too chatty at the moment.

After resting for a minute or two, I got slowly to my feet. Fiona was helping me. My head was fuzzy and my jaw throbbed, but I was wide awake. "He always this much fun?" I said, and regretted it as pain shot through the lower half of my face.

"He was upset," Fiona said.

"Yes, I think so too."

She helped me into the metal building. It was a combination office and break room, dusty—everything out here was covered with a layer of fine pink powder—and cold, but at least it was out of the wind. She got me seated in the foreman's desk chair and filled a paper cup with water from a dispenser. I wasn't thirsty, but I accepted it anyway.

"Where's your boyfriend now?" I asked—gingerly— after taking a few sips.

"I convinced him to wait in the car. I thought that would be best." She pulled a steel-and-plastic chair from a round table in the far corner and sat beside the desk. "Tell me why Tricia Russell sent you up here."

I gave it a little thought, decided there were few confidences left to be violated, and gave her a Cliff Notes version of the story: "Ryan and Matthew Lund disappeared from their mother's home three days ago. She is certain they came here, to be with their father. She wanted me to verify that, but quietly—she didn't want Lund to know why I'm here. I'm not expecting a big bonus on this gig." I rubbed my aching jaw. "Look, Fiona, obviously you and Lund are close. Why is he playing this asinine game? For crying out loud, the woman only wants to make sure her sons are all right."

Fiona had been studying her gloved hands in her lap. Now she looked at me and said quietly, "Her sons aren't all right. That's the problem."

I felt a chill that had nothing to do with the Dakota

winter wind. "Damn it, I knew I should have called the cops myself, no matter what Tricia Russell wanted. They've been gone for days now, while we've been farting around. They could be anywhere."

"No, I know where they are."

The wind died off a bit, then came back hard, rattling the filthy panes in the little building. "Just a little bit east of here," she said. "Emmaus Cemetery. The boys are beneath two very fine monuments made of top-grade Prairie Rose granite." Her eyes welled up and spilled over.

I felt numb. Even my jaw didn't ache so much.

"It's been just over three years," Fiona said quietly. "A bad winter, not much different from this one. The boys and Gordon had been up north, ice fishing. On the way back, they hit a patch of black ice on the highway. The wind was gusting to fifty miles an hour. The van flipped and rolled and rolled and rolled. . . ." When she recovered, she told me that Ryan Lund had been killed instantly, Matthew Lund had lived for two days without regaining consciousness, and Gordon Lund almost perished too, emerging with a broken back and two broken legs.

The crash ended the Lunds' already fragile marriage. Ended too, apparently, Tricia Russell's already fragile hold on reality.

"She's been in and out of therapy ever since the accident," Fiona told me. "One day she's absolutely paralyzed with grief; the next day she refuses to even acknowledge there ever *was* an accident; the next—well, there's no telling. Last year she called our chief of police and insisted that Gordon had kidnapped the boys from her home and was hiding them." That explained Tricia Russell's demanding that I leave the cops out of the drama. It explained a lot. I felt I now understood my client's strange, somehow ambiguous demeanor.

Fiona sadly shook her dark head. "We—I mean, Gordon hasn't heard from her for several months. He'd hoped that she was finally dealing with the situation, finally getting on with her life. I guess she isn't. . . ."

I didn't say anything. Maybe there was nothing to say. Maybe I just wasn't bright enough to know what it was.

Fiona must have mistaken my silence for disbelief. "I can show you," she said. "You know. Where the boys are. I can show you, if you want."

That wasn't necessary, and I said so. "I need to be getting back to Omaha. I have to report to my client." I stood, less wobbly than a few minutes earlier.

"What will you tell her?"

I had no answer for her; I had no answer for myself. Beyond the filthy little windows, the relentless wind rushed across the dark and rugged landscape, unceasing, uncaring. I envied it.

TULE FOG

KAREN KIJEWSKI

Sacramento's Kat Colorado has all the
attributes the modern female private eye is
supposed to have, which is why she is one
of today's more popular gumshoes.

Karen Kijewski, her creator, won the Best
First Private Eye Novel award for Katwalk
and has gone on to write several other
agreeable entries in the series.

Here we see Kat in familiar circumstances,
doing everything the modern female private eye usually does, notably trying to
balance a somewhat difficult
personal life with her very demanding
professional one.

WE ARE NOT FIGHTING, not exactly, although our voices are raised.

"Why don't you just believe me?" Nell cries. "Alma does."

"Alma believes soap operas," I remind her.

Alma is my eighty-one-year-old grandmother and the reason I am here. Nell's mother and Alma were childhood friends, and Alma believes as strongly in friends as she does in soap operas. More strongly.

I try again, try to make my voice patient. "Here's the deal, Nell. When there is a crime, you have a victim, a perpetrator, a reason for the crime, a crime scene, perhaps a weapon, and—if you're lucky—a bunch of halfway reliable and halfway sober witnesses and various assorted clues."

"I know, yeah, but—" Nell sounds frustrated, even cross.

I ignore it. "The more of these elements that are missing, the tougher it is to figure out what's going on."

"Well, sure, but Kat, Alma said *you* could."

I bite my tongue—it is the only reason I don't say something impatient.

"What do we have here?" I ask politely. "No apparent crime, no victim, no perpetrator. No crime scene, no weapon, witnesses, or clues. Shoot, this is the kind of setup that makes soap operas look factual and logical." Uh-oh. Politeness is giving way to sarcasm.

"Alma said you were a hotshot detective."

"Yes. I am. Want to know what the hotshot-detective terms for a case like this are?"

She looks at me sideways. "Not really."

Tough. I tell her anyway. "*Next to impossible. A waste of time. Hopeless.* It's like that, Nell."

The silence between us stretches out endlessly like the freeway under my singing tires, flowing into the horizon in front of us and behind us as seen in the rearview mirror. Road signs tell me what I already know: that Los Angeles is hundreds of miles to the south, that the speed limit is 65 mph, that it is illegal to litter. I am neither speeding nor littering. An eighteen-wheeler ignores the speed limit and climbs up my bumper. I pull the Bronco into the fast lane. We are on I-5 south of Stockton and Sacramento.

Now that I am speeding, I do not stop.

"Kat, it bothers me. It's making me crazy."

I push the eighteen-wheelers and the signs and the black bug with iridescent wings that is caught and struggling on the windshield wiper out of my mind.

"It must have been a crime, it had to have been, else why would I remember?"

I think of all the nightmares I have had and remember in vivid detail, though there was no crime, and I do not answer her. I want to point out that I am an investigator, not a therapist. I don't do that, either. The needle on the speedometer hovers around eighty, and I slow down.

"Tell me what you remember about the crime," I say instead.

"Blood. Something bright and shiny and flashing. Loud voices and noise."

That's it, that's what she remembers. Good, huh? Right here is where Sam Spade, Lew Archer, and Travis McGee would have walked, where I would have too, except for Alma and the ties of friendship and family.

"Tell me about your family," I say, trying for the get-the-background angle.

The bug is dead, the iridescence fading.

"My father was a farmer. A grower," she amends. "Our ranch was just over two thousand acres, small for the Valley. He loved the land, loved it maybe more than us, more than his family. He gave to it more than he gave to us, that's God's truth. He used to tell me stories of the Valley he remembered, or of the Valley he couldn't remember but had heard tell of, of things he had seen in old pictures and books. He had newspapers from way back, and *Life* magazines, and he'd turn the cracked and yellowed pages carefully to show me."

The bug corpse flips in the wind rush, then lifts off in dead flight back to the desert of its beginning.

"He talked about people some, but mostly it was the land, the way it was then and the way it used to be. He loved the land."

We both stare out the bug-smeared windshield and think about a California we never knew and never will, a California that is gone now. The freeway pulls us south. Interstate 5 cuts through California's Great Central Valley like a silver ribbon laid down with hardly a ripple in it. The Central Valley stretches north to south for over 430 miles and is five million acres, a vast flat patchwork of fields, orchards, and desert dotted with towns and cities, slashed by occasional highways and the blue ribbon of the California Aqueduct. Sacramento is my hometown, is a Valley city. We are driving from there south to Bakersfield, another Valley city.

There is desert on either side of us here, sagebrush and tumbleweed and hardy desert grasses. It is May, and already everything is turning to varying shades of brown. The sky runs a short gamut from a rich deep blue to a medium hue hanging docilely over the horizon, and there are long white clouds that trail like puffy unshapen masses of feather-light biscuit dough.

Later, in the summer, the sky will bleach from blue to almost white, and the heat will bend and dance and shimmer in thermal waves and crash down on land and people alike in relentless merciless blows. Then mirages twist in the air and in the mind. In the winter the tule fog—white, damp, and cold—envelops everything like a shroud.

We pass a small flattened carcass. Roadkill. Impossible to tell what it was. Unwise to ask.

"I wish I'd seen it then, but God, Kat, I love the Valley, just like my pa did."

Yes. Me too. Its pulse is our own.

"My father, he was a good hardworking man. There

was dirt in the cracks of his hands and under his fingernails that didn't come out, no matter how hard he scrubbed. He claimed he knew every inch, every clod of dirt on our place, not from sitting in the air-conditioned cab of a tractor but from working it with his hands and a shovel."

"Over two thousand acres and you didn't have a tractor?" I ask, disbelief and amazement rivals in my voice.

"Yeah, we did. Sure." She smiles. "We had tractors and harvesters, a disk plow and"—her face darkens—"all sorts of equipment. I just mean—" She shrugs and holds out a hand, moving her fingers as though she is crumbling dirt clods.

I nod. I know what she means. We are the kind of Californians who work hard and get dirty, who drink beer and shoot pool and play softball, who stare long into a cloudless sky. We are the ones who curl our lips at people who sneer and say the Valley is hot and flat and boring, and speed through it in an air-conditioned rush in their BMWs and Italian shoes and snooty attitudes to get to San Francisco in search of the perfect little restaurant, the perfect bed-and-breakfast, and the perfect chardonnay.

Okay, I wouldn't turn down the perfect chardonnay, either, but you know what I mean. The radio is tuned to a country-western station, and Garth Brooks is singing that he's got friends in low places. Don't we all?

"Want a Coke?" I ask as a freeway sign flashes past.

FOOD GAS NEXT EXIT
NEXT GAS 41 MILES

The desert is unforgiving.

"Sure."

We get Cokes and vanilla-chocolate-swirl soft ice cream cones and get back in the car. We are in a hurry. I don't know why, exactly—as the crime that might not be a crime happened years ago—but I am infected by Nell's sense of urgency. Bakersfield is five and a half hours from Sacramento, and we are halfway there. And speeding, putting miles on the Bronco. At 75 mph, the odometer clicks over rapidly. I eat my ice cream quickly; it is melting in the warm spring air and the breeze. There's a song Dwight Yoakam sings about Bakersfield, and I try to remember what it is, but I can't.

A news break cuts in on the radio, and the announcer tells us that a carload of kids crashed drag racing, that a small plane has slammed into the ground east of Fresno. He says this in a bored voice, like I would say, *These cornflakes are stale.* No, maybe not; I really hate it when cereal gets stale. I am not bored by stale cereal; I am not bored by death. I wonder about the people who crashed, whose lives were decided in an instant.

"You know what I read?" Nell asks.

She talks in spurts, and we have been silent for a while, listening to country music on the radio. Now and then Nell sings along to the songs she likes.

"What?" I ask.

The desert has turned into fields here. With water, the Central Valley is the best agricultural land in the world. Water is gold here. Even rows in the irrigated fields slide by us in hypnotic rhythm. The tires still sing. I push water and desert, like bugs and tumbleweeds and singing tires, out of my mind.

"Nell?"

"It was in the newspaper a week or so ago. It happened in some big city. I dunno, New York or Chicago or something."

Nell cannot remember, does not care about the differences and beauty in cities, in the same way that city people do not see the beauty or the differences in land.

"It was in a park. I think they said it used to be a nice park but then druggies and prostitutes and homeless people took it over."

She says this in a scornful voice. We have problems here in the Valley, but this is not one of the biggest ones.

"One day some people found this cooler under some bushes—a cooler like you pack a picnic in, you know. And there were beers on top of a package that was all wrapped up in plastic, like you would wrap up a great big sandwich, baloney and cheese and lettuce and . . ."

Her voice trails off. I look at her. Her face is expressionless, but she is fidgeting in her seat, snapping her fingers incessantly, nervously.

"So this guy unwrapped it. Only it wasn't a sandwich. It was a little girl. She'd been dead for a while and the cops said that no one had even reported her missing. And, Kat, the guy who found her?"

She is looking at me, I know, and I nod.

"He drank the beers. Before he reported it to the police." Tears slide down Nell's face. "It bothers me, you see."

I look at Nell. The tears there; the face without expression. We are about the same height and dressed similarly, though she has more of a tough country look about her. She is wearing jeans and scuffed western boots—not the kind you see line dancing on TV—and a white tank that shows off strong, tan, muscled arms. Her hair is blond and pulled back into a no-pretension ponytail. No makeup. She is pretty, with tan skin showing sun damage. Her features are even, her smile ready. I guess that she is in her forties.

I am wearing jeans too, and Reeboks and a long-sleeved T-shirt that is pushed up over my elbows. Curly brown hair and green eyes. I am thirty-three, and I smile a lot, too. We could be cousins or neighbors, though I look more city than she does. I *am* more city. I am white wine as well as beer.

For a while Nell cries and I drive.

"Tell me about the crime," I ask, because I need to say something and because this is why we are here. This is why she came to Sacramento and asked me to come to Bakersfield.

"Nothing much. You know, I told you already."

"Tell me again," I persist.

"I was little; five or six, I think; I don't remember that I was in school. Something scared me bad. Real bad. My pa was there and others who worked on the ranch."

"Men?"

"Yes. I remember loud, angry voices and shouting. I had been holding my pa's hand, but then, when I got scared, I stood behind him. I was holding on to his legs and peeking through them. I used to play peek-a-boo with him like that. I'd look through and call, 'Pa, where am I?' and he'd bend over and look me in the eye and holler, 'There y'are,' and pull me through and swing me high. He was a big man, a good man. He—"

She is in safe territory now and drifting.

"Something besides the voices frightened you?" I pull her back.

She turns away from me slightly, leaning an elbow out the open window, letting the wind rush hit her face and flip her ponytail. Reluctant.

"I—I remember something metal. Bright and flashing. Flashing and dirt and—"

"And?"

"I ran. We were at the edge of one of the fields. I ran back to the house. Ma had done a wash that day. I remember that Pa's overalls and faded-out shirts and a dress of Ma's were hanging on the line. There were sheets too; they came to the ground, almost. I hid behind them. I felt safe there. I remember holding them in my hands, peeping around them.

"The sheets were damp, so Ma must have just hung 'em out. It's so hot in August, by the time you hang out the last one, the first is ready to come down, just about."

Laundry is safe too. And weather.

"What did you see?" I ask gently. "A five-year-old is old enough to understand and remember a lot of what she sees."

"I don't know." Her voice is confused, maybe sad. "I don't, and it's plumb driving me crazy. It comes back to me all the time but just those pictures, those little bits. Like a puzzle with all the important pieces gone."

On the radio, a woman cries over a honky-tonk hero in neon lights. In real life there is more honky-tonk and neon than there are heroes. No kidding. And honky-tonk and neon is often more attractive than real life. Too bad.

"You were frightened," I say. "What else did you feel?"

"I don't know."

"Try to remember. Were you sad, maybe, or—"

"Sad?" Her voice tightens. "Not sad, exactly. My ma beat me that night. What over? What over?" she croons to herself, then speaks in a low voice, saying, "'Nell, you're a bad girl. Look at them white sheets, they're stained and now I got to wash 'em again.' Ma said that, and then she beat me."

"Dirt doesn't stain."

"No, no, it sure don't." Her voice wanders. She looks at her hands. "It was blood. I had blood on my hands. Ma beat me, and she kept hollering, 'You're a bad girl. Now you forgit about this, hear? You forgit about it!'

"Well, and I guess I did. For a long time. I don't remember much now, but Lord, it bothers me. Blood?" She looks at me. "Where'd that come from?"

"Did you slaughter animals?"

"Not there, not in the fields."

"Could you have been hurt?"

"Not bad. I would have remembered. I remembered the whuppin', didn't I?"

"Perhaps someone else was hurt?"

"I don't know, I just don't know."

We pass a sign that says LOS ANGELES 185, and on the radio a woman sings about how someone hurt her bad in a real good way. I don't hear enough of the song for it to make sense. Or I hear too much.

"Look, Kat . . ."

"Yes?"

"We're gonna have to put you up at a motel." She pronounces it *mo*tel.

"All right."

"I wish I could take you to my home, but I can't. My husband, he'd go nuts on that one. No way I can come on home and say, 'Howdy, this here's Kat Colorado, she's a private investigator, and she's gonna help me figure out a crime I don't remember and don't know nothin' about but I'm sure as shootin' happened.' No way. He'd just go through the roof on that one. He don't believe in raking up the past."

"Okay."

"Too bad, huh? I mean, it sounds just like TV." She laughs. "Like *Magnum, P.I.*"

Minus the .357 and the Hawaiian shirt, I think.

The song on the radio tells us the answer is in sad songs, good whiskey, and easy lovin'. I wonder what the question is. I don't agree with the singer, maybe not with Nell. Maybe with her husband. Like him, I'm not sure raking up the past is such a good idea.

"You know how it is in tule fog, Kat?"

I nod. I know.

"Maybe you're up early 'cause you want to be somewhere, only the fog is so thick you can't see anything, not what's in front of you or alongside the road. Time and distance don't seem right, and nothing is familiar. It's like driving into endless white that never clears. You follow the white line on the road because that's all you can see and you think: What in tarnation am I doing here?—only the damn fog is going to be there for months, and you've got to live. You've got to do.

"You don't see cars until you're on 'em, and then the headlights make two fuzzy circles of light in all that whiteness and disappear before you can tell anything. In town maybe the lights on a gas station will jump out as you pass and then a flash of neon, maybe, red and yellow, and it's a café, so you say to yourself: Hey, I reckon I could do with a cup of coffee and a doughnut. Just to get out of the fog you say that. And maybe you have two cups of coffee. Just to stay out of the fog you do that. You know?"

I know. Memories of winter days and Valley fog stretch between us. Many's the time I've driven fifty miles to get into the foothills, to get out of the fog and into sunshine, to see the sky.

"That poor little girl wrapped up like a baloney sandwich is never going to get out of the fog. She'll never have a gravestone with her name on it. Never have anyone to remember her or mourn over her. I've got two little girls, Kat. Their names are Maylene and Ellie."

It is almost a non sequitur. Almost.

"The past, it comes over me sometimes like tule fog. Sometimes it takes me over, makes me feel like I'm disappearing, makes me all cold and shivery. You? You're the neon lights at the café—red, yellow, and hope. Coffee and doughnuts."

This is a tall order, I think, and I hope I can fill it.

"You want, you could stay with my aunt May. Maylene is named for her. She'll understand these things."

These things? The past. The fog.

"I'd like that," I say.

"She was Pa's sister. She's the only one left now, with Ma gone and Pa . . ." Her voice falters. "Well, he's gone too, in a way, gone in his mind, gone into the fog."

After that we drive in silence for a long time. I look at the blue sky and feel the spring sun, warm now, not heavy and relentless, thick and oppressive as caramel the way it will be soon.

At the junction of I-5 and 58, we head east on 58 into Bakersfield. Bakersfield is mostly oil and cotton, although there are other crops. We drive through cotton fields and orchards and past oil pumps kerchunking relentlessly like huge demented workaholic grasshoppers, then past trailer parks and fast food and small businesses and into an older part of town.

Aunt May's house is a one-story, probably two-bedroom wooden house trimly painted in cream and rust. Huge trees in the yard shade it. The cement walkway is cracked but swept. Nell rings the doorbell twice and, when there is no answer, lets us in with her key. The house is cool and furnished neatly with worn but well-cared-for overstuffed furniture. The walls are covered with religious pictures and tracts.

DO UNTO OTHERS, stern gilt letters admonish me. I follow Nell to the back bedroom. A single bed with an iron frame and a well-washed chenille spread, a straight-back chair, a simple dresser, and a mirror.

Here an embroidered tract informs me that GOD HELPS THOSE WHO HELP THEMSELVES. It's faster if you do it on your own, if you just count on yourself, I think. I put my overnight bag on the chair and join Nell in the kitchen, where she is filling tall glasses with iced tea. We sit at the Formica table and drink it.

"Did you ever ask your mother?"

"No." She shakes her head. "She died before the memories, before the nightmares came."

"Your father?"

"I've tried, but it's so rare that he recognizes me, even. The fog hardly ever clears out of his head now. Last time I went to see him, he wouldn't talk to me. I don't think he knew who I was. He wouldn't even let me hold his hand." Her voice is sad.

"The men who were there that day, who were they?"

"I don't know."

"Let's go out to the ranch, look around, talk to people. Is it still in your family?"

"No. And we can, but I don't think it will do any good. I tried. It's all new folks. They don't know my pa, they mostly never heard tell of our family. A few *maybe* recognized the name, but that was it, that was all. Kat, it was forty years ago."

"How about your father's friends or family friends who are still in the area?" *Who are still alive?* is the unspoken question.

"I think they're all gone. Or dead."

Nothing, I've found, is ever all anything. I let it go.

"Aunt May?"

"She wouldn't know anything, not about the ranch."

"You asked?"

"Yes. Many times. She has two answers for everything, and she gave me both of them. 'Let sleeping dogs be' and 'God will take care of it.'"

Perhaps that kind of thinking was why, in forty years, Nell heard nothing about the incident that troubles her now. I look at my watch. Three-thirty. "Let's go to the library."

"Library?" Nell wrinkles her nose at me.

"Newspapers. Very informative."

"Oh, *no*." She dismisses the idea. "I'm sure there wouldn't be anything *there*."

"Okay." I fold my hands and look around at the religious tracts in the kitchen. GOD IS THE ANSWER, says one. "Let's sit here and wait for divine guidance. Maybe writing on the wall?"

"I'm sorry." Nell's voice is contrite. "We'll go to the library, then. I just don't see how it could help, that's all."

"Nell, you believe there was a crime almost forty years ago. We have no details, no clues. Except in memory, the crime scene is long gone. But it may not be just in your memory; it may be in other people's as well. We're looking for a mention of a possible incident, of local issues and conflicts, of names of other growers who might have known your family, of names linked with your family in the social pages. I'm assuming that, like in many small papers, much of the 'news' was social news."

"Okay, I get it."

"Good. Let's go."

First we narrowed it down to the three summers when she had been four, five, and six. With two of us working on it, it wasn't so bad. And the librarian was a help.

"Here!" Nell said.

"Local Growers Meet," the caption read. The picture showed eight men in work clothes standing in front of a public building I didn't recognize. All were named. One of the men was Nell's father, Jack Harding. Nell's mother, Rose, was mentioned in numerous social items. She had been active in quilting bees, school bake sales and events, church meetings and drives.

The same names came up over and over, the men in a farming or political context. Jack wasn't mentioned every time but frequently. The same names were linked again and again too.

What wasn't reported was also interesting. No sudden

deaths—accidental or otherwise—on a ranch. No major accidents of any kind. No bloody incidents of note, with the exception of barroom brawls.

We made copies of everything relevant and left.

Nell squinted into the late-afternoon sun, rubbed her eyes, and sighed. "We didn't learn much, did we?" She kicked a crumpled Dr Pepper can, sent it flying into the street, then pounded a palm tree that stood in silent, majestic guard over the Bronco.

I smiled. "We did, actually."

"We did? What?"

"We know where to go now."

"We do? Where?" She climbed into the Bronco and slammed the door a little too hard.

"Nell, did anything strike you?" I pulled into sparse traffic.

"I don't know. Life sure seemed simpler, friendlier. People knew each other and helped each other out. It damn sure wasn't so built up hereabouts."

A pickup hit its horn and whipped in front of me. A bumper sticker on the tailgate read IF YOU LOVE SOMETHING, SET IT FREE. IF IT RETURNS, IT'S YOURS. IF IT DOESN'T, HUNT IT DOWN AND KILL IT.

"Kat, I look at those papers, the photos and stories, and I wish life was still like that. Simple. Uncomplicated."

Almost. She was forgetting the blood on her hands. Blood is complicated.

"Do you have any family records, photos, memoirs, financial records, any anything from that period?"

"Not really. There's a couple a boxes of stuff up in the attic. I saved it when Pa went into the Home and I cleaned out the house. I don't think there was anything like that though."

"And the newspapers and magazines your father showed you, did you save them?"

"Uh huh."

"Good. We need to go through them."

"Okay. Drop me off at home. Later on—"

"We have something else to do first."

"Yeah. Eat. I'm starved. I could eat a horse. I could eat a *boot*."

"Something else."

She groaned.

She groaned again when I told her, but she got into it. First lists. Any name that had been mentioned in any connection, however remote, with her father or mother. Then phone numbers. I started with the least common names. Then calls. Nell did that.

"Me? Why me? I can't do it; *you* do it."

"I would if you weren't here, but you are. You'll get more out of people than I will. You're a local; I'm an outsider."

She thought it over. "What do I say?" Reluctance made her voice heavy and thick.

"Say you're Jack Harding's daughter and you're looking for someone who remembers him."

"And if they ask why?"

"Say you're trying to put together a family history, and you want personal recollections."

She said all that many times. Call number twenty-three was pay dirt. George Gilburt. Still on the phone, Nell started jumping up and down. *Yes yes yes,* she mouthed to me in soundless words, and then she thank-you'd someone almost to death and hung up.

"Well, goddamn, god*damn*." She bounced around. "He said, yes, ma'am, he was George Gilburt, but he wasn't the man I wanted, his pa more'n likely was. He said he remembers his pa talking about Jack. They used to go fishing 'n' all."

"Is he still in Bakersfield?"

"Yes." More bouncing. "I've got his number." She waved a slip of paper under my nose and reached for the phone.

So it was an anticlimax when no one answered even though Nell let the phone ring twenty or so times. "In case he's doing chores or something," she said, and let it ring another five or ten.

"Let's get the boxes out of your attic and grab something to eat."

"No." Her face clouded up. "I got to feed Bill and the kids. You drop me by home, and I'll be back soon as I can. I'll bring the boxes and a pizza. What do you like?"

"Everything but anchovies."

She made a face at the mention of anchovies. "No problem. It'll be eight, probably, before I'm back."

By eight-fifteen, everything is spread out on the kitchen table in front of us. Pepperoni pizza, old newspapers and magazines, family snapshots and records. The records are not personal—two land deeds, an insurance policy cashed in long ago, bills of sale for farm machinery, that sort of thing.

"Will you look at this?" Nell speaks with her mouth full of pizza as she points toward a snapshot with a greasy finger. "Look at Ma, she's so young and pretty."

I push the documents and papers away, and we spread out the photos. I study them as Nell explains. "Here's Pa and my brothers and the old horse we all rode. This here was the new barn and this the old one." The new one is beautiful, twice the size of the old, which is beautiful in its way too—paint peeling, worn buckled boards, and a rusted metal roof.

"Look at our tractor. Lord, but Pa was proud of that." There are pictures of newly plowed and planted and harvested fields; of a Packard, almost new and gleaming; of a dusty yard filled with old cars and machinery; of Nell's mother with a chicken on her shoulder and a smile on her face; of fields and field hands and a fishing hole at the River, which is how we refer to the Kern River hereabouts.

"What's this?" I point to a photo half hidden by the others. It is a small wooden cross tied or nailed lopsidedly together and stuck in bare dirt not far from the base of an ancient Valley oak. The tree stands in stark relief against a background of cloudless sky and endless field bleached almost white in the summer sun.

"I don't know. I don't remember. Maybe one of the boys' dogs died. Nothing important."

I turn it over. On the back, in ink now faded to watery blue, is written:

> *Forgive us O Lord*
> *Manuel*

"Did you have a dog named Manuel?"

"No. Or not that I remember anyway."

"Whose writing is this?"

"Ma's. Kat, look at this." Nell pushes a snap toward me. A man with dark hair, even white teeth, and brown skin smiles at the camera. He has a hat on, and it is pushed back. "I think he was there. That day. I just seem to remember."

"What was his name?"

"Jesus. Pa called him Jesse. He never could get used to the Mexican way of naming a man same as the Lord."

"He worked for your family?"

"Yes."

"All year round?"

"I—I don't think so. Mostly it was seasonal. The Mexicans stayed while there was work, then moved on."

"Was he one of the loud and angry voices?"

"I don't know. I remember he smiled a lot. He was nice, and he had a wife and baby."

"Did you speak to him?"

"No. He didn't speak much English."

"Your father spoke Spanish?"

"Some, yes. Enough."

"Did—"

"That's all I remember. *God*, Kat, it's so frustrating."

"Do your brothers remember anything?"

"No. I asked them a million times. They were older, and they must've been working someplace else on the ranch. There was always more work than there was hands to do it."

Nell flips through an old *Life* magazine, then stops and shivers. I look too. It is a Depression-era photograph of a man walking behind horses that pull a disk plow.

"You'd think that a farm girl would've gotten used to the machinery, wouldn't you? But I never did, I never have."

The sun in the photograph hits the farmer's hat and the horses' backs and glints off the roll of shining circular blades on the disk plow.

"Except for cars, I guess I just don't like machinery." She laughs. "Shoot, I don't own a blender. Even that makes me nervous." She pushes the photos and magazines away and rests her head in her hands. I listen to the mindless babble of the TV show Aunt May is watching in the front room. Nell stands, kicking her chair back. "I'm getting a beer. Want one?"

"Sure."

"I'm calling George again too." She's been trying with no success every half hour or so. This time someone answers and she stutters in surprise.

"Tomorrow," she says to me as she hangs up.

"What time?"

"He said anytime after sunrise. A farmer's habits die hard."

Sunrise. I groan.

She laughs. "Eight o'clock. Sharp. I'll pick you up."

The man who sat across from us at the beat-up pine table was tall once, was stooped now. His shoulders were wide, his arms knotted with the muscles that years of hard and unrelenting work give a person. The morning sun splashed in through the dusty uncurtained kitchen window and spilled across us, across the lines and furrows of his heavily tanned face. He was smiling.

"I remember you, Jack's girl, a little-bitty thing just as cute as a button. You used to tag along behind your pa. That's what we called you, remember? Tagalong."

Nell laughed. "That's right; I'd forgotten that. When did it stop?"

He looked at her evenly. "Don't recollect. What can I do for you?"

"I'm trying to remember something, Mr. Gilburt."

"Reckon you can call me George."

"George." She nodded at him and then stared at the hands she had clenched tightly on the table. "It's something that's giving me nightmares. It was a summer day, and I recall that I was with Pa, just a little kid then. There were a lot of men there and loud angry voices and shouting. Something was flashing in the sun. There was blood and a box, maybe, and—and I don't know. I can't remember the next part. Afterward Ma whupped me."

George's face was closed over and immobile, the way a man gets farming, the way a man gets staring the future in the face and never knowing what one day or the next will bring.

"I can't help you there. I never heard tell of nothin' like that. I'm sorry, Nell." He moved his hand as if to dismiss us. His eyes met neither mine nor Nell's.

"Can you think of someone who might know, who might help?" Her voice was desperate.

"Sorry." The hand dismissed us again. He was looking out the window in the direction of newly plowed and seeded fields. We sat in silence. His eyes flickered over us, then went far away once again. "Sorry," he said. "Pray to God, child, that He may lift this burden from your shoulders."

Nell stood to leave.

"I think you were there."

My voice was hard. I had not spoken so far except to say hello. But I wanted answers now; I am far too impatient to wait for God to sort it out.

"There was trouble going on, and you were Jack Harding's friend. You would have been there, you would have stood by him."

This was not a guess. I thought of the newspaper accounts I had read. Of the photos: open spaces with neat houses and straight irrigation rows. Of the farmers who didn't smile into the camera but stood proudly, often next to farm equipment, some of it—like the caterpillar tractor, the Fresno scrapper, and the Stockton gangplow—invented right here in the Valley. That was part of it. One side.

The other side was darker. In 1939 a sign at a Bakersfield movie theater directed "Niggers and Okies upstairs." Today, in the Valley, you can hear a siphon hose used for stealing gas referred to as an "Okie credit card," or the statement that a machine is so simple it is "Mexican-proof."

Then and now, California agriculture was built on the backs of cheap immigration labor. There was anger and hatred. There were haves and have-nots. Those years, the years we had flipped through in the library, were the years just before Delano became a battleground, before Cesar Chavez and the United Farm Workers and the grape strikes. Those were the years before it was out in the open, but it was there. I had seen ample proof of it in a newspaper that was the daily record of a time, a town, and a people.

"They were difficult times, weren't they, George? Workers were demanding better wages and working conditions; growers were fighting those demands. There was a lot of anger. There were disputes."

Nell sat down again. We both stared at George, who finally met my eyes.

"Nothin' happened. *Nothin'*. It was so long ago. Why you want to be diggin' it all up? Won't do nobody no good."

"Tell us," Nell said.

"No."

Stubborn old man, I thought.

"Almost everyone's dead. Won't do nobody no good. Leave it to God. Leave it be." His eyes were hooded over, dark.

Nell started crying.

George ignored her. I spoke.

"I think there was an altercation between Nell's pa and his workers. Not just angry words. More. Violence. Whole families used to work side by side in the fields, men and women, children as young as five. Somehow a child got involved, was hurt or killed."

Blood. Something bright and shiny and flashing. . . .

"Perhaps it was a child that Nell, the little tagalong, knew. There was machinery involved."

I guess I just don't like machinery. . . .

"The child was killed, or was hurt and died soon after."

It was blood. I had blood on my hands. . . .

"Was his name Manuel?"

Forgive us O Lord. . . .

"The child was buried in a field, not returned to his family, not buried properly."

That poor little girl wrapped up like a baloney sandwich. . . . She'll never have anyone to remember her. . . . It bothers me.

There was silence all around us. Nell was no longer crying. The silence was broken first by the roar of a small plane that sounded like a crop duster, then by a kamikaze fly that alternately buzzed and smashed against the window screen.

George spoke into the silence, his voice slow and heavy. "It was August. One hunerd and fifteen degrees, and tempers ran as hot as the days. It was an accident. I don't know a man what would kill a child. Not me. Not Jack. It couldn't come out, though. Tempers ran high, and it wasn't just the heat. It was the differences between grower and worker. You was right.

"There's always accidents around machinery. Many's the man who's lost an arm or a finger to a machine. But a child? That was different. Maybe they wouldn've believed it an accident. Too much would have been made of it."

The fly smashed and buzzed, buzzed and smashed.

"Jack and me was the only white men there. We ran that bunch off."

"Guns?" I asked.

He nodded. "Guns. We kept that little child's corpse so they wouldn't have nothin' on us, and we ran 'em off. Without the baby, there was nothin' they could do, most of 'em illegal, most of 'em only speaking Spanish, and not one of 'em with a thought to go to the police.

"We buried that child, like you said, out in a field and

under a tree. We wasn't bad men. It was an accident. Rose, Nell's ma, knew. It bothered her some, it did, and she put up a cross. I didn't know that the little tagalong here saw. I'm sorry about that."

"Take me to the grave." The tagalong who had grown up into Nell spoke.

"I don't remember."

I couldn't tell by George's voice if he did or if he didn't, but it was the same, I knew.

"And if I remembered, I wouldn't tell you. I ain't disturbing those pore little bones no more. It's in God's hands now."

The morning is still cool when we leave. There is a breeze. Birds sing. A butterfly, orange and yellow and black, flies by, but Nell doesn't notice.

"There's no way of knowing where that tree is, Kat. Forty years? There's no way of knowing if it's still standing." She sucks in a breath.

"No. Nell, the child wasn't forgotten. Rose put a cross on the grave."

"Not like the little girl wrapped in plastic and left in a picnic cooler with cans of beer."

"No." Not like her at all.

"Kat?"

Nell is asking me something, but I do not understand the question. I answer anyway. "The altercations, the injustices? They are not a thing of the past," I say. I remember the song now, the one about Bakersfield, about a guy looking for something he couldn't find anywhere else. "The answer is here."

"I could do something, you mean, something to make things better?"

"Yes." I look at her steadily. Yes. That is what I mean.

On the radio, there is static that sounds like gunfire, then silence, then a listener asks the DJ to please, *please* play "Drop Kick Me Jesus Through the Goalposts of Life."

Nell and I laugh.

"I was wrong," I say.

She smiles at me in acknowledgment. "Hey—" Her voice is husky. "The blood is gone. The fog too."

We are in sunshine, surrounded by fields that once were desert.

THE RIVER MOUTH

LIA MATERA

Lia Matera's witty novels of law and lawyers have won her a zealous following among readers and critics alike.

In most of Matera's work there's an appealing hint of melancholy, as if her characters never quite want to accept what they've become, or never quite quit dreaming of what they'd hoped to be.

In this story, Matera shows us that she knows the outdoors just as well as she knows courtrooms and boardrooms.

▼▼▼▼▼

TO REACH THE MOUTH of the Klamath River, you head west off 101 just south of the Oregon border. You hike through an old Yurok meeting ground, an overgrown glade with signs asking you to respect native spirits and stay out of the cooking pits and the split-log amphitheater. The trail ends at a sand cliff. From there you can watch the Klamath rage into the sea, battering the tide. Waves break in every direction, foam blowing off like rising ghosts. Sea lions by the dozens bob in the swells, feeding on eels flushed out of the river.

My boyfriend and I made our way down to the wet-clay beach. The sky was every shade of gray, and the Pacific looked like mercury. We were alone except for five Yurok in rubber boots and checkered flannel, fishing in the surf. We watched them flick stiff whips of sharpened wire mounted on pick handles. When the tips lashed out of the waves, they had eels impaled on them. With a rodeo windup, they flipped the speared fish over their shoulders into pockets they'd dug in the sand. We passed shallow pits seething with creatures that looked like short, mean-faced snakes.

We continued for maybe a quarter mile beyond the river mouth. We climbed some small, sharp rocks to get to a tall, flat one midway between the shore and the cliff. From there we could see the fishermen but not have our conversation carry down to them.

Our topic of the day (we go to the beach to hash things out) was if we wanted to get married. Because it was a big, intimidating topic, we'd driven almost four hundred miles to find the right beach. We'd had to spend the night in a tacky motel, but this was the perfect spot, no question.

Patrick uncorked the champagne—we had two bottles; it was likely to be a long talk. I set out the canned salmon and crackers on paper plates on the old blue blanket. I kicked off my shoes so I could cross my legs. I watched Pat pour, wondering where we'd end up on the marriage thing.

When he handed me the paper cup of bubbles, I tapped it against his. "To marriage or not."

"To I do or I don't," he agreed.

The air smelled like cold beach, like wet sky and slick rocks and storms coming. At home, the beach stinks like fish and shored seaweed buzzing with little flies. If there are sunbathers on blankets, you can smell their beer and coconut oil.

"So, Pat?" I looked him over, trying to imagine being married to him. He was a freckly, baby-faced Scot with strange hair and hardly any meat on him. Whereas I was a black-haired mutt who tended to blimp out in the winter and get it back under control in the summer. But the diets were getting harder, and I knew fat women couldn't be choosers. I was thinking it was time to lock in. And worrying that was an unworthy motive. "Maybe we're fine the way we are now."

Right away he frowned.

"I just mean it's okay with me the way it is."

"Because you were married to Mr. Perfect and how could I ever take his place?"

"Hearty-har." Mr. Perfect meaning my ex-husband had plenty of money and good clothes. Pat had neither right now. He'd just got laid off, and there were a thousand other software engineers answering every ad he did.

"I guess *he* wasn't an 'in-your-face child,'" Pat added.

Aha. Here we had last night's fight.

"With Mr. Perfect you didn't even have arguments. *He* knew when to stop."

Me and Pat fight on long drives. I say things. I don't necessarily mean them. It was too soon to call the caterer, I guess.

I held out my paper cup for more. "All I meant was he had more experience dealing with—"

"Oh, it goes without saying!" He poured refills so fast they bubbled over. "I'm a mere infant! About as cleanly as a teenager and as advanced in my political analysis as a college freshman."

"What is this, a retrospective of old fights? Okay, so it takes some adjustment living with a person. I've said things in crabby moments. On the drive up—"

"Crabby moments? You? No, you're an *artist*." You could have wrung the scorn out of the word and still had it drip sarcasm. "Reality's just more *complicated* for you."

I felt my eyes narrow. "I hate that, Patrick."

"Oh, she's calling me Patrick."

Usually I got formal when I got mad. "I'm not in the best mood when I write. If you could just learn to leave me alone then." Like I said in the car.

His pale brows pinched as he flaked salmon onto crackers. I made a show of shading my eyes and watching a Yurok woman walk toward us. When she got to the bottom of our rock, she called up, "Got a glass for me?"

Usually we were antisocial, which is why we did our drinking at the beach instead of in bars. But the conversation wasn't going the greatest. A diversion, a few minutes to chill—why not?

"Sure," I said.

Pat hit me with the angry-bull look, face lowered, brows down, nostrils flared. As she clattered up the rocks, he muttered, "I thought we came here to be alone."

"Hi there," she said, reaching the top. She was slim, maybe forty, with long brown hair and a semi-flat nose and darkish skin just light enough to show some freckles. She had a great smile but bad teeth. She wore a black hat almost like a cowboy's but not as western. She sat on a wet part of the rock to spare our blanket whatever funk was on her jeans (as if we cared).

"Picnic, huh? Great spot."

I answered, "Yeah," because Pat was sitting in pissy silence.

She drank some champagne. "Not many people know about this beach. You expecting other folks?"

"No. We're pretty far from home."

"This is off the beaten path, all right." She glanced over her shoulder, waving at her friends.

"We had to hike through Yurok land to get here," I admitted. "Almost elven, and that wonderful little amphitheater." I felt embarrassed, didn't know how to assure her we hadn't been disrespectful. I'd had to relieve myself behind a bush, but we didn't do war cries or anything insensitive. "I hope it isn't private property. I hope this beach isn't private."

"Nah. That'd be a crime against nature, wouldn't it?" She grinned. "There's a trailer park up the other way. That *is* private property. But as long as you go out the way you came in, no problem."

"Thanks, that's good to know. We heard about this beach on our last trip north, but we didn't have a chance to check it out. We didn't expect all the seals or anything."

"Best time of year; eels come upriver to spawn in the ocean. Swim twenty-five hundred miles, some of them," she explained. "Its's a holy spot for the Yurok, the river mouth." A break in the clouds angled light under her hat brim, showing leathery lines around her eyes. "This place is about mouths, really. In the river, the eel is the king mouth. He hides, he waits, he strikes fast. But time comes when he's got to heed that urge. And he swims right into the jaws of the sea lion. Yup." She motioned behind her. "Here and now, this is the eel's judgment day."

Pat was giving me crabby little get-rid-of-her looks. I ignored him. Okay, we had a lot to talk about. But what are the odds of a real-McCoy Yurok explaining the significance of a beach?

She lay on her side on the blanket, holding out her paper cup for a refill and popping some salmon into her mouth. "Salmon means renewal," she said. "Carrying on the life cycle, all that. You should try the salmon jerky from the rancheria."

Pat hesitated before refilling her cup. I let him fill mine too.

"King mouth of the river, that's the eel," she repeated.

"Of course, the Eel River's named after him. But it's the Klamath that's his castle. They'll stay alive out of water longer than any other fish I know. You see them flash that ugly gray-green in the surf, and thwack, you get them on your whipstick and flip them onto the pile. You do that awhile, you know, and get maybe fifteen, and when you go back to put them in your bucket, maybe eight of the little monsters have managed to jump out of the pit and crawl along the sand. You see how far some of them got and you have to think they stayed alive a good half hour out of the water. Now how's that possible?"

I lay on my side too, sipping champagne, listening, watching the gorgeous spectacle behind her in the distance: seals bobbing and diving, the river crashing into the sea, waves colliding like hands clapping. Her Yurok buddies weren't fishing anymore; they were talking. One gestured toward our rock. I kind of hoped they'd join us. Except Pat would really get cranky then.

Maybe I did go too far on the drive up. But I wished he'd let it go.

"So it's not much of a surprise, huh?" the woman continued. "That they're king of the river. They're mean and tough, they got teeth like nails. If they were bigger, man, sharks wouldn't stand a chance, never mind seals." She squinted at me, sipping. "Because the cussed things can hide right in the open. Their silt-barf color, they can sit right in front of a rock, forget behind it. They can look like part of the scenery. And you swim by feeling safe and cautious, whoever you are—maybe some fancy fish swum upriver—and munch! You're eel food. But the river ends somewhere, you know what I mean? Every river has its mouth. There's always that bigger mouth out there waiting for you to wash in, no matter how sly and bad you are at home. You heed those urges and leave your territory, and you're dinner."

Pat was tapping the bottom of my foot with his. Tapping, tapping urgently like I should do something.

That's when I made up my mind: Forget marriage. He was too young. Didn't want to hear this Yurok woman

talk and was tapping on me like, Make her go away,
Mom. I had kids, two of them, and they were grown now
and out of the house. And not much later, their dad went
too (though I didn't miss him and I did miss the kids, at
least sometimes). And I didn't need someone fifteen years
younger than me always putting the responsibility on me.
I paid most of the bills, got the food together (didn't cook,
but knew my delis), picked up around the house, told Pat
what he should read, because engineers don't know squat
about literature or history; and every time someone
needed getting rid of or something social had to be handled or even just a business letter had to be written, it was
tap-tap-tap, oh, Maggie, could you please . . . ?

I reached behind me and shoved Pat's foot away. If he
wanted to be antisocial, he could think of a way to make
the woman leave himself. We had plenty of time to talk,
just the two of us. I didn't want her to go yet.

"Got any more?" the Yurok asked.

I pulled the second bottle out of our beat-up backpack
and opened it, trying not to look at Pat, knowing he'd
have that hermity scowl now big-time.

"You picnic like this pretty often?" she asked.

"Yeah, we always keep stuff in the trunk—wine,
canned salmon, crackers. Gives us the option." That was
the other side of it: Pat was fun, and he let me have control. If I said let's go, he said okay. That means everything
if you spent twenty years with a stick-in-the-mud.

"You come here a lot?" she asked.

"No. This was a special trip."

"It was supposed to be," Pat fussed.

I hastily added, "Our beaches down around Santa
Cruz and Monterey are nice, but we've been to them a
thousand times."

"Mmm." She let me refill her cup. I had more too. Pat
didn't seem to be drinking.

"Now, the sea lion is a strange one," she said.
"There's little it won't eat, and not much it won't do to
survive, but it has no guile. It swims along, do-de-do, and
has a bite whenever it can. It doesn't hide or trick. It's

lazy. If it can find a place to gorge, it'll do that and forget about hunting. It doesn't seem to have the hunting instinct. It just wants to eat and swim and jolly around. Mate. Be playful." She broke another piece of salmon off, holding it in fingers with silt and sand under the nails. "Whereas an eel is always lurking, even when it's just eaten. It never just cavorts. It's always thinking ahead, like a miser worrying how to get more."

"Until it leaves home and washes into the sea lion's mouth." I concluded the thought for her.

"What the eel needs"—she sat up—"is a way to say, Hell no. Here it is, the smarter, stealthier creature. And what does nature do but use its own instinct against it. Favor some fat, lazy thing that's not even a fish, it's a mammal that lives in the water, that doesn't really belong and yet has food poured down its gullet just for being in the right place." She pointed at the sea lion heads bobbing in the waves. "Look at them. This is their welfare cafeteria. They do nothing but open their mouths."

Pat put in, "You could say you're like the seals. You're out there with those steel-pronged things, spearing eels."

I wanted to hit him. It seemed a rude thing to say.

"The Yurok are like the eels." She removed her hat. Her dark hair, flattened on top, began to blow in the wind coming off the water. "The Yurok were king because the Yurok knew how to blend in. The Yurok thought always of food for tomorrow because Yurok nightmares were full of yesterday's starvation. The Yurok were part of the dark bottom of history's river, silent and ready. And they got swept out into the bigger mouths that waited without deserving."

She leaped to her feet. She looked majestic, her hair blowing against a background of gray-white clouds, her arms and chin raised to the heavens. "This is where the ancient river meets the thing that is so much bigger, the thing the eel can't bear to understand because the knowledge is too bitter."

Behind me, Pat whispered, "This is weird. Look at her friends."

On the beach, the Yurok men raised their arms too. They stood just like the woman, maybe imitating her to tease her, maybe just coincidence.

"Where the ancient river meets the thing that is much bigger, and the eel can't understand because the knowledge is too bitter," she repeated to the sky.

Pat was poking me now, hardly bothering to whisper. "I don't like this! She's acting crazy!"

I smacked him with an absentminded hand behind my back, like a horse swatting off a fly. Maybe this was too much for a software engineer—why had I ever thought I could marry someone as unlyrical as that?—but it was a writer's dream. It was real-deal Yurok lore. If she quit because of him, I'd push Pat's unimaginative damn butt right off the rock.

She shook her head from side to side, hair whipping her cheeks. "At the mouth of the river, you learn the truth: Follow your obsession, and the current carries you into a hundred waiting mouths. But if you lie quiet"—she bent forward so I could see her bright dark eyes—"and think passionately of trapping your prey, if your hunger is a great gnawing within you, immobilizing you until the moment when you become a rocket of appetite to consume what swims near—"

"What do they want?" Pat's shadow fell across the rock. I turned to see that he was standing now, staring down the beach at the Yurok men.

They'd taken several paces toward us. They seemed to be watching the woman.

She was on a roll, didn't even notice. "Then you don't ride the river into the idle mouth, the appetite without intelligence, the hunger that happens without knowing itself."

Pat's anoraked arm reached over me and plucked the paper cup from her hand. "You better leave now."

"What is your problem, Patrick?" I jumped to my feet. Big damn kid, Jesus Christ. Scared by legends, by champagne talk on a beach! "Mellow the hell out."

My words wiped the martial look off his face. A

marveling betrayal replaced it. "You think you're so smart, Maggie, you think you know everything! But you're really just a sheltered little housewife."

I was too angry to speak. I maybe hadn't earned much over the years, but I was a *writer*.

His lips compressed, his eyes squinted, his whole freckled Scot's face crimped with wronged frustration. "But I guess the Mature One has seen more than a child like myself. I guess it takes an Artist to really know life."

"Oh, for Christ sake!" I spoke the words with both arms and my torso. "Are you such a white-bread baby you can't hear a little bit of Yurok metaphor without freaking out?"

He turned, began to clamber down the rock. He was muttering. I caught the words "princess" and "know everything," as well as some serious profanity.

I turned to find the Yurok woman sitting on the blanket, drinking sedately, her posture unabashedly terrible. I remained standing for a few minutes, watching Patrick jerk along the beach, fists buried in his pockets.

"He doesn't want my friends to join us," she concluded correctly. From the look of it, he was marching straight over to tell them so.

The men stood waiting. A hundred yards behind them, desperate eels wriggled from their sand pits like the rays of a sun.

I had a vision of roasting eels with the Yuroks, learning their legends as the waves crashed beside us. What a child Pat was. Just because we'd fought a bit in the car.

"I know why he thinks I'm crazy," the woman said.

I sat with a sigh, pulling another paper cup out of the old backpack and filling it. I handed it to her, feeling like shit. So what if the men wanted to join us for a while? Patrick and I had the rest of the afternoon to fight. Maybe the rest of our lives.

"We came out here to decide if we should get married," I told her. I could feel tears sting my eyes. "But the trouble is, he's still so young. He's only seven years older than my oldest daughter. He doesn't have his career together—he just got laid off. He's been moping around all month getting in my way. He's an engineer—I met him when I was researching a science fiction story. All he knows about politics and literature is what I've made him learn." I wiped the tears. "He's grown a lot in the last year, since we've been together, but it's not like being with an equal. I mean, we have a great time unless we start talking about something in particular, and then I have to put up with all these half-baked, college-student kind of ideas. I have to give him articles to read and tell him how to look at things—I mean, yes, he's smart, obviously, and a quick learner. But fifteen years, you know."

She nibbled a bit more salmon. "Probably he saw the van on the road coming down."

"What van?"

"Our group."

"The Yurok?"

She wrinkled her nose. "No. They're up in Hoopa on the reservation, what's left of them. They're practically extinct."

"We assumed you were Yurok. You're all so dark. You know how to do that whip-spear thing."

"Yeah, we're all dark-haired." She rolled her eyes. "But jeez, there's only five of us. You're dark-haired. You're not Yurok." Her expression brightened. "But the whipstick, that's Yurok, you're right. Our leader"—she pointed to the not-Yuroks on the beach, I wasn't sure which one—"made them. We're having an out-of-culture experience, you could say."

Patrick had reached the group now, was standing with his shoulders up around his ears and his hands still buried in his pockets.

"How did you all get so good at it?"

"Good at it?" She laughed. "The surf's absolutely crawling with eels. If we were good at it, we'd have hundreds of them."

"What's the group?"

Patrick's hands were out of his pockets now. He held them out in front of him as he began backing away from the four men.

"You didn't see the van, really?"

"Maybe Pat did. I was reading the map." I rose to my knees, watching him. Patrick was still backing away, picking up speed. Up here, showing fear of a ranting woman, he'd seemed ridiculous. Down on the beach, with four long-haired men advancing toward him, his fear arguably had some basis. What had they said to him?

"The van scares people." She nodded. "The slogans we painted on it."

"Who are you?" I asked her, eyes still locked on Patrick.

"I was going to say before your fiancé huffed out: What about the sea lions? They get fat with no effort, just feasting on the self-enslaved, black-souled little eels. Do they get away with it?"

The sky was beginning to darken. The sea was pencil-lead gray now, with a bright silver band along the horizon. Patrick was running toward us across the beach.

Two of the men started after him.

I tried to rise to my feet, but the woman clamped her hand around my ankle.

"No," she said. "The sea lions aren't happy very long. They're just one more fat morsel in the food chain. Offshore there are sharks, plenty of them, the mightiest food processors of all. This is their favorite spot for sea lion sushi."

"What are they doing? What do your friends want?" My voice was as shrill as the wind whistling between the rocks.

"The Yurok were the eels, kings of the river, stealthy and quick and hungry. But the obsessions of history washed them into the jaws of white men, who played and gorged in the surf." She nodded. "The ancient river meets the thing that is much bigger, the thing the eel can't bear to understand because the knowledge is too bitter."

She'd said that more than once, almost the same way. Maybe that's what scared Pat: her words were like a litany, an incantation, some kind of cultish chant. And the men below had mirrored her gestures.

I knocked her hand off my ankle and started backward off the rock. All she'd done was talk about predation. She'd learned we were alone and not expecting company, and she'd signaled to the men on the beach. Now they were chasing Patrick.

Afraid to realize what it meant, too rattled to put my shoes back on, I stepped into a slick crevice. I slid, losing my balance. I fell, racketing over the brutal jags and edges of the smaller rocks we'd used as a stairway. I could hear Patrick scream my name. I felt a lightning burn of pain in my ribs, hip, knee. I could feel the hot spread of blood under my shirt.

I tried to catch my breath, to stand up. The woman was picking her way carefully down to where I lay.

"There's another kind of hunter, Maggie." I could hear the grin in her voice. "Not the eel who waits and strikes. Not the seal who finds plenty and feeds. But the shark." She stopped, silhouette poised on the rock stair. "Who thinks of nothing but finding food, who doesn't just hide like the eel or wait like the sea lion but who quests and searches voraciously, looking for another—"

Patrick screamed, but not my name this time.

"Looking for a straggler." Again she raised her arms and her chin to the heavens, letting her dark hair fly around her. Patrick was right: She did look crazy.

She jumped down. Patrick screamed again. We screamed together, finally in agreement.

I heard a sudden blast and knew it must be gunfire. I watched the woman land in a straddling crouch, her hair in wild tendrils like eels wriggling from their pits.

Oh, Patrick. Let me turn back the clock and say I'm sorry.

I looked up at the woman, thinking: Too late, too late. I rode the river right into your jaws.

Another shot. Did it hit Pat?

A voice from the sand cliff boomed, "Get away!"

The woman looked up and laughed. She raised her arms again, throwing back her head.

A third blast sent her scrambling off the small rocks,

kicking up footprints in the sand as she ran away. She waved her arms as if to say good-bye.

I sat painfully forward—I'd cracked a rib, broken some skin, I could feel it. Nevertheless, I twisted to look up the face of the cliff.

In the blowing grass above me, a stocky man with long black hair fired a rifle into the air.

A real Yurok, Pat and I learned later.

NO BETTER
THAN HER FATHER

LINDA GRANT

Linda Grant's novels about San Francisco
private eye Catherine Sayler are especially
notable for the realism they bring
to the form.

This doesn't mean that Catherine knows the
secret private-eye handshake. Rather
it means that she's a fully realized human
being, reacting in a believable fashion
to some of the more troubling aspects
of our society.

In the following story, Grant gives us a new
character and a new environment, both of
which you'll remember for a long time.

THE MOUNTAINS SWAM behind the white heat of the plains, shimmering as if reflected in water. From out on the prairie, they were bleached of color, dark forms that rose like islands from the heat mist at their base.

AJ Thomas took a drink from the water bottle she always carried on the seat beside her in the pickup. The water was warm and tasted stale. She sloshed some of it down between her breasts and enjoyed the sensation of the wind blowing over it. About an hour and forty-five minutes more, she estimated. A little over an hour to Walsenburg, then thirty minutes on to the ranch. She'd be there well before sundown.

She doubted that the surplus airplane parts in the back of the pickup were worth what her dad had paid for them or the time it had taken to drive to Kansas for them. But she'd been glad to make the trip anyway. She enjoyed being out on the eastern plains—pointing the pickup down the long, straight road, finding some good kicker music on the radio, and just taking off.

Most people hated this part of southern Colorado, the miles of rocky arid soil studded with tough stunted brush. As a kid she'd hated it too. But now, coming back after many years, she appreciated its sparse, stark beauty.

In the dry air, distances stretched and the sky seemed to go forever. The clouds were as much a part of the landscape as the twisted piñon trees beneath them. They billowed up into towers hundreds of feet tall or spread into soft, ever-shifting shapes that sailed over the land like giant ships.

On the rise ahead she spotted jackrabbit ears. It was the fifth or sixth rabbit she'd seen this trip. The plains taught that—the ability to see clearly at a distance. To spot the tiny bit of color or motion in an otherwise uniform landscape. Desert people had that same skill. They'd identify an approaching camel before city folk had even spotted the dust. Her skill had won her a certain amount of respect among her Bedouin guides and irritated more than one city-bred Arab colleague who'd been chided because the foreign woman could see better than he did.

Sweat ran down between her shoulders. It was hot out here. Not nearly as hot as the Saudi desert or the Danakil in Ethiopia, but hot nevertheless. "You could be in Somalia," she reminded herself, "ducking bullets and interviewing people who didn't want to talk to you."

Then again, she could have been in Prague, talking with young American entrepreneurs who were hoping the fall of the iron curtain would give them a chance to play J. P. Morgan. Or in rural Turkey, checking out changes in the bazaar. That was what she loved about being a correspondent: you could be anywhere next week or next month. There was always something new to learn, someplace new to visit.

And now, when she was finally established, when she could pitch an idea and have someone take it seriously enough to pay up front, she was looking at giving it all up. Damn. This place might be home, but for AJ, home was a place you came back to visit, not one where you stayed.

The sight of her dad at the airport had forced the recognition that she had some hard choices to make. She'd been shocked by his appearance. He seemed to have shrunk; his clothes hung loosely on his six-foot-three frame, and his flesh seemed a size too big for the bones under it. She knew he'd been sick. But she was still unprepared for the change.

He had plenty of hair, but it was coarser now and shot through with gray. "Less than yours," he'd said, running his hand over her head and laughing hoarsely. She could hear the years of Camels in his voice. A dry, raspy edge.

He'd asked her to drive home. Claimed it tired him.

She thought sadly of the years she'd had to beg him to let her drive. He'd fallen asleep on the way. In the failing light, she'd sneaked sidelong glances at the old man who'd taken over her father's body.

He still kept horses, but she hadn't seen him ride. And he insisted on continuing what he called "his business." She'd always had trouble with forms that asked for father's occupation. Things appeared at the ranch, sat around for a while, then they disappeared. Or usually they disappeared. The Sherman tank down by the stream had been there for as long as she could remember.

He said he was an auction hound or a war surplus dealer, and that covered about eighty percent of it. But the other twenty percent had cost him two years in prison. And it was that twenty percent that worried AJ now. When you dance on the edge of the law, you need good balance. She didn't want to see him lose his footing and spend his last years in a jail cell.

It worried her that he'd let a cut become infected and get all the way to blood poisoning. He should have been more careful. The reaction to the drugs that had made him so sick was probably unrelated to his age, but it was a reminder of his vulnerability. He had to be in his seventies, though she'd never known for sure exactly how old he was. His age, like everything else about Eulin Thomas, was subject to change when it suited his purpose.

Eulin Thomas peered into the case that should have contained World War II rifles and sucked air through his teeth. Damn. Whatever those things were, they were not rifles and they sure as hell didn't go back to World War II. They looked high-tech, nasty, and new. Nothing you'd find at a surplus auction, which was where he'd bid on lot 106, one case of World War II rifles.

The number stenciled on the case was 108, which explained something but not enough. It explained why they weren't what he'd ordered, not why high-powered modern ordnance was being sold.

Eulin had been hanging out at auctions for over fifty

years. He knew more about what the U.S. government put on the block than most military men. And he was damn sure that the stuff in this box did not belong in an auction.

He was more than a little tempted to keep the stuff and see what he could get for it. The damn army'd take at least a couple of years to figure out the mistake, if they ever did, and he considered it a citizen's duty to take advantage of military inefficiency. But it broke one of his cardinal rules. No arms deals. Eulin Thomas had no desire to deal with the kind of folks who bought and sold weapons.

Eulin took his hat off and wiped his forehead with the bandanna he carried in his back pocket. The damn barn was like an oven in summer and a freezer in winter. And dusty. Made your nose itch. He'd tried to seal the cracks, but standing here in early afternoon, he was surrounded by laser beams of sunshine that testified to the futility of that effort.

He looked around fondly at the piles of what anyone else might have described as junk. Junk it was, but it was all junk that was worth something, sometimes a lot, to somebody. The trick was finding the right buyer.

This was a hell of a time for a shipment of high-tech weapons to land on his doorstep. AJ was already fussing about how dangerous it was for him to live alone on the ranch. If she wasn't careful she'd talk herself into moving back home. Daughters. One day she was fifteen and wouldn't listen to a thing he said, seemed like the next she was fifty and wanted to become his mother. He dearly loved his daughter, but he did not want her looking over his shoulder all the time.

He gazed back down at the crate and its deadly contents. The first step was to figure out what he had and how he'd gotten it. That was easy enough. A call to Ernest Sims would take care of that.

Ernest was a sergeant at the army supply center outside Denver. He'd been in charge of the auction, and the scrawl at the bottom of the bill of lading on lot 108 was his. Eulin had dealt with him many times over the years, and while he wouldn't call the portly black sergeant a friend, they'd done a couple of deals together. Ernest would give him a straight answer.

Eulin found Sims's number and punched it in. But the voice at the other end wasn't Sims. It was some prissy officer. No point in talking to him.

It took a bit longer to find Sims's home number. The phone was answered by a woman. When he asked for Sims, he could hear her take a breath, and he got a bad feeling for the second time that day.

"Ernest died last night," she said.

Eulin stammered his condolences. "I saw him just last week; he looked fine," he said. "I just can't believe he's gone. Was it his heart?"

"No." There was a pause. "No, he was shot to death. A robbery. They came right in the house, tore it apart, beat him up and shot him." The voice was bitter; not the grieving widow, he guessed, but a relative. "He didn't have anything worth stealing," she went on. "The police think maybe that's why they killed him. Why they were so vicious. They were probably high on crack."

"I'm so sorry, ma'am," he said. "He was a fine man."

"Too good to die like this," she said.

Eulin put the phone down and sucked on the soft flesh of his right cheek. Oh, Ernie, he thought, what'd you get yourself into? And why the hell did you bring me along?

The dark-blue Buick Skylark pulled into the Best Western motel outside Walsenburg late in the afternoon, and three men got out. One wore a nice-looking suit and had cinnamon-colored skin. The lines in his face were cut deep, as if they'd been carved, and his hair was pure white at the right temple. The other two were younger— late twenties, early thirties—and wore jeans and western-style shirts, brand-new from the look of them.

"You fellas heading north or south?" the desk clerk asked.

One said, "South," and the other, "Denver." The

older guy looked pained. "They don't teach geography much in school anymore," he said, and hustled the other guys out of the office.

They didn't stop to check the room, just took off into town. The road ran uphill through a cut in a low bluff, then turned into Main Street as it curved down into town. Walsenburg itself looked like a hundred other small western towns—squat, aging buildings, bleached by the sun, lined up like yellowing dentures along the principal street. Dirty windows and empty storefronts testified that the town was slowly shrinking, dying.

The crew in the Skylark drove up and down Main a couple of times, then parked. The older man went into the Wagon Wheel Bar. One of the younger guys, a weasel-faced kid in a red plaid shirt, walked into the drugstore, and the other, a good-looking blond wholesome enough to sell toothpaste, headed for the Pine Cone Coffee Shop.

After the bright sun, the inside of the Wagon Wheel was too dark for the stranger to see much beyond the neon signs that decorated the wall behind the bar and a small lamp at the far end. The room was empty except for a tall, rangy guy with shaggy salt-and-pepper hair, who sat next to the lamp, reading a paperback book. He got up and came down the bar. "What can I get you?" he asked.

"Scotch," the customer said. "Black Label." He leaned against the bar and looked around. Drank his Scotch slowly.

After a couple of minutes he cleared his throat. "My cousin has a friend in this region," he said. His voice was accented, but the bartender couldn't place it. "A man by the name of Eulin Thomas. Do you know of him?"

The bartender nodded. "Yep."

"My cousin asked me to stop and say hello. Do you know where he lives?"

"Yep." The bartender pulled a pen from his pocket and sketched a map on the back of a cocktail napkin. He did it quickly, like he'd done it before.

The stranger made several attempts to start a conversation but met with no success. He finished his Scotch and left.

In the Pine Cone Coffee Shop, the all-American was having more luck. He'd taken a seat at the counter and ordered pie and iced tea from a woman with tightly curled white hair that was so thin you could see her scalp.

"I hear there's a fella down here who deals in war surplus," he said when she brought the pie. "Funny name, U-something."

She nodded, and her mouth pulled tight so the little lines around her lips deepened. "Eulin Thomas," she said.

"That's it. That's the name. He still buy and sell stuff?"

She nodded, lips pursed. "Far as I know, he does," she said. "But you don't want to be involved with his type, son. He's not an honest man. He spent a couple of years at Leavenworth, the federal prison."

The kid looked concerned. "Really? I didn't know that. What'd he do?"

"Stole some things from the government," she said. "The man's no good. And . . ." She paused for effect. "He's a bit crazy." She touched her temple.

By the time he'd finished his pie, the all-American had learned a good deal about Eulin Thomas and his daughter, Andrea Jo.

The subject of the three men's interest was at that moment struggling to move a large wooden crate from the back of his jeep into what remained of the Delcarbon Mine. He'd brought his buddy, Jack, to help with the heavy lifting, but even with the two of them and a hand dolly to move the crate, it was hard going.

Delcarbon didn't look like much from the road—a couple of old buildings made of rotting wood, some rusting iron, and a red-black slag heap. That was all that was left of what had once been a reasonably successful coal mine. Southeastern Colorado was coal country, and Eulin had often thought it was a cruel god who'd given this land that was already short on water such a meager mineral endowment.

Didn't seem fair that the Rockies, already blessed with great beauty, better weather, and plenty of water, had also gotten the silver and gold. That, at least, was worth enough to justify the backbreaking work to get the earth to give it up. But coal, dirty and dangerous to mine and profitable only so long as you could virtually enslave the poor souls who mined it—that was as much a curse as a blessing.

The three-story tipple that had once been used to load coal onto railcars had been covered with corrugated iron, but much of that had been carried away, reducing the building to a skeleton. The mine entrance was up the hill behind it, and Eulin had driven the jeep as close to it as he could. The ground was too rough for the dolly, so he and his friend had to carry the crate to the iron door at the entrance to the old mine.

There was a large padlock on the door and a sign warning of dire consequences to anyone trespassing, but Eulin had a key to the lock and a deal with the man who owned the land. For a small sum, Charles Graham allowed Eulin to store certain items that he didn't want lying around the ranch. The crate sure as hell qualified as something Eulin preferred to keep at a distance.

He'd brought hard hats, and lights to put on them, so he and Jack could see their way for the twenty or so feet they had to go before the tunnel jogged right into the blind passage where Eulin stored his "goods."

"You sure this is safe?" Jack asked.

"Course it's safe. I wouldn't be goin' in if it wasn't safe," Eulin said.

"There must be a bunch of vertical shafts around here. Stumble into one of those, and they'd never find you."

"The only vertical shaft you have to worry about around here is the air shaft. That's about forty feet down the hill." He pointed in the direction of a pile of rubble that had once been a wooden shed. "Stay away from there, and you'll be fine. Now come on."

His friend followed him in, but Eulin could tell he was nervous.

On the drive back, Jack asked, "AJ home to stay?"

"Lord, I hope not," Eulin said. "I love that girl, but she's got her life and I got mine. Last thing I want is her fussin' over me."

Jack nodded. "I know what you mean. My daughter Beth's always trying to get me to give up smoking, move into town, eat better. You'd think she was the parent and I was the kid."

Eulin nodded. That was his fear. That AJ'd take it into her head to move home so she could take care of him. All just because he hadn't paid attention to that damn cut. Sure, he'd been sick, lost some weight, sometimes forgot stuff, but that didn't mean he was getting old, not the way AJ thought.

And then there was the damn crate. The last thing he needed right now was her getting the idea that his business could be dangerous.

AJ didn't need the green sign on the highway to tell her she was approaching Walsenburg. She'd watched the Spanish Peaks first appear as twin bumps on the horizon and slowly grow larger, until they dominated the landscape. They seemed to rise straight out of the plains, separate from the mountains behind them. It was no wonder the native people had called them *Huajatolla*—"Breasts of the Earth."

Gray clouds were collecting around the top of the west peak. It'd be raining up there soon, but above Walsenburg the sky was a deep blue, marred only by the hazy white lines of several jet trails.

As she pulled off the highway, she thought how good a cold beer would taste. There'd be beer in the fridge at the ranch, but the tension there made it hard for her to relax. She found herself watching her father for signs of frailty, gauging how much longer he could live alone out on the ranch. And he, in turn, watched her, growing edgy and irritable under her scrutiny.

The thought of it made the cool darkness of the Wagon Wheel appealing. She took the turnoff and headed for town, realizing as she did that she was also looking forward to seeing Paul Donati behind the bar.

AJ'd been home several days, and the town was beginning to look familiar again. But she couldn't drive down Main without noticing how it had changed—aged, shrunk, grown careless about its appearance, like her father. There wasn't a lot on the street anymore. The movie theater where she'd watched Saturday matinees had closed twenty years ago, followed by two of the three car dealerships. The Pine Cone Coffee Shop was still there, tended by Mrs. Guilcrist, town busybody and moral arbiter. And so was the Wagon Wheel, only now the old guy behind the bar was Paul, her cousin's best friend and the object of many of her lustful teenage fantasies.

Paul Donati smiled when he saw AJ come through the door. She was tall for a woman, five nine, he guessed, long-limbed and rangy like her dad. Not a woman you'd describe as beautiful, but with a generosity and liveliness to her face that was appealing. Some women grew brittle or too soft with age; she moved with the same casual confidence he remembered from high school.

The tough facade she'd used to protect herself as a teenager had mellowed, but she still had the air of a woman who made her own rules. It probably came from growing up on the wrong side of the tracks in a small town that never let you forget.

He remembered her as a skinny thirteen-year-old who seemed overnight to sprout the most amazing set of breasts the horny males in town had seen. One day she was Jimmy's tag-along cousin; the next she was as good as anything in *Playboy*. It must have been hard on her; he realized that now. At the time, all he'd thought about was not getting an erection when she was around.

They'd been doing a subtle dance since the day she got back and stopped in for a beer. Sensing the attraction, deciding what, if anything, they wanted to do about it. But this afternoon he had other things on his mind.

"Yo," she said.

"Yo yourself," he replied, and got her a draft. "Your daddy doing any deals?" he asked as he set the mug down.

She shook her head. "Not that I know of. He still orders stuff, like he always has, but I don't know that he has any buyers. I've got a bunch of airplane parts out in the pickup. Why?"

"There was a guy in here, maybe an hour ago. Arab, I think. He was asking where Eulin lived. It seemed strange. When your daddy's got a customer, they know where to find him. I called, but no one's home. Would you tell him someone was asking?"

"They ask for him specifically? By name?"

"Yeah. Then he tried to get me talking."

AJ laughed. "I know how hard *that* is," she said. Paul just shrugged, the way he always did.

"I don't know what's going on with Daddy," AJ said. "The doctor says he's fine now and he'll put on weight in time, but he's not the same. I'm afraid he's losing it."

"Eulin? Not that I see," Paul said. "He's still sharper than any of us townies. He's got lots of folks convinced he's a tad crazy, but you know that's just the fox fooling the hens."

AJ shook her head. "I wish that were true, but even he admits that he doesn't always think so clearly. And he forgets stuff."

"Hell, I forget stuff," Paul said. "I bet even you forget stuff sometimes."

"Look," AJ said strongly. "It's not just a matter of him being a bit forgetful. We're talking about a man who's charitably described as eccentric and more frequently as being downright nuts, and who keeps explosives in his barn."

Paul frowned.

"I've seen the stuff," AJ continued. "He has a whole shelf of land mines, a bunch of detonators, God knows what else." She stopped herself. Paul's cousin was a deputy sheriff. She hoped she hadn't already said too much.

"I see why you're worried," Paul said.

About the time AJ pulled off the highway, Eulin arrived back at the ranch. He sent Jack off and headed for the kitchen to get a beer.

No matter how you looked at it, the crate meant trouble. If someone had killed Ernie for what was inside, they'd be looking for it, and sooner or later they'd end up on his doorstep. Then there'd be two clear options, as Eulin saw it, neither of them acceptable. He could refuse to give them what they wanted, in which case they'd probably beat the crap out of him and kill him. Or he could give them the case, and they'd probably kill him to shut him up.

If the idea of calling the police occurred to Eulin, it passed through his mind so quickly that it never registered. Two years in the federal pen was more contact with the authorities than a man needed in one lifetime. Eulin knew how the police regarded ex-cons in general and him in particular. They'd most likely lock him up and give the crate to the killers.

Eulin heard a vehicle pull up and could tell from the sound that it wasn't the pickup. He peered out the kitchen window and saw three men get out of a dark-blue car. Even in another situation, he'd have known they were trouble.

Clint Eastwood would have taken down his shotgun and blown them away, but Eulin wasn't even sure where the shotgun was. So he used what he'd always used, his wits.

He tugged his shirt out of his pants, pulled off his belt, and gave the jeans a good yank so they'd ride low down on his hips and bag at the bottom. Then he ran his hands through his hair to get it going in six directions and pushed the door open.

He dragged his right foot just a bit as he approached the men. "Howdy," he said. "You fellas looking for something?"

"We're looking for Mr. Thomas, Eulin Thomas," the older of the men said. He sounded foreign.

"Hey, tha's me," Eulin said. He thumped his chest and gave them a big, stupid grin. "You bring me something?"

The men exchanged looks. "Mr. Thomas, we came about a box that was delivered to you by the Denver Army Supply Center. It would have come yesterday or today."

Eulin looked confused. He scratched his head. "Don't remember no box," he said. "Say, I like that shirt, young fella," he said, pointing at the red plaid western shirt worn by a young guy whose features looked pinched into his face. "I had a shirt like that once. My daddy give it to me, I think. Back when I was in high school."

"Mr. Thomas, did you receive a large crate yesterday?" the older man asked, in a tone of carefully controlled patience.

"Yesterday." Eulin paused and furrowed his brow as if trying to concentrate. "Yesterday I had oatmeal for breakfast. The day before I had scrambled eggs. No, maybe the oatmeal was today and the eggs was yesterday. Yeah, I think that was it. The eggs was yesterday. It's important to remember that, 'cause you can't eat too many eggs when you get to be my age. You gotta keep track so you don't get forgetful and eat 'em too often."

Eulin could have laughed out loud at the look on the faces of the three men. This was terrific, he thought. He'd acted a bit crazy around town for years, but this was much better. He worked his lower lip forward and back the way old Amos Martin did.

The young guys were looking at the older guy to tell them what to do. The older guy was studying Eulin. "The day you had the eggs, Mr. Thomas—did a crate come that day?" the guy asked. "A big crate?"

Eulin kept working his lips. He frowned and kicked his boot in the dust. "I don't remember," he said. He looked down as if he was embarrassed. "Sometimes I don't remember so good."

"Mr. Thomas—"

Eulin interrupted. "I got a tank, down by the river. You want to see it?"

The men didn't move. "And there's lots of neat stuff in the barn. If there was a crate, tha's where it'd be."

The foreign guy smiled. "We'd love to see your barn," he said.

It took almost an hour, and Eulin was tiring of his senility act by the time the three men were finally convinced that the crate was not in the barn or anywhere nearby. They finally climbed back into their car and drove off.

Eulin didn't fool himself that this was the last he'd see of them. They wouldn't give up easily. If AJ hadn't been there, he might have tried to con them, but with her around, he couldn't risk it. The safest thing was just to clear out and lie low for a while.

When she got back, about a half hour later, she found him sitting on the porch, smoking a cigarette. He met her at the truck to examine his latest prizes, and after they'd unloaded the parts, AJ told him that Paul said someone was asking for him.

Eulin was good, good enough not to react. But AJ had spent her first twenty years with him and the next thirty watching other devious people, and she didn't miss a thing. She couldn't have said exactly what it was in his face that tipped her off, but she knew something was up.

"Okay, Dad," she said. "What's going on?"

Eulin had an awful moment when he thought that maybe he was losing it. For the first time he could remember, he couldn't come up with an easy lie. "It's no big deal," he said. "But I've seen those guys, and I don't like the look of them. I was thinking that maybe we should take a vacation, till they leave town."

"What's so serious that we need to leave town?" AJ asked.

"Nothing," Eulin said. "But I'm getting too old to deal with guys like that. They're looking to take advantage of an old man, and . . . it's just not worth the effort. Besides, you're not home for long. It'd be nice to have some vacation together."

AJ watched him and tried to figure out what was real and what was scam. Damn the man, you never knew where you stood. "You can't just up and leave," she said. "Who's going to look after the stock? A ranch doesn't run itself."

"This one can," Eulin said. "Cattle belong to the Dunbars. I just lease them the land. I can board the horses with them. Cats'll take care of themselves. What do you think of going to Mesa Verde? I haven't been there in over twenty years. I'd like to see it again. We could leave tomorrow morning."

"I arranged to meet Paul after closing tonight," AJ said.

"You could still do that. You could pack your stuff before you go. Take the Pinto; I might need the pickup."

AJ decided to go into town around nine. The Wagon Wheel wouldn't close till midnight, but she needed to talk to Paul as soon as possible. Needed to get his sense of the men who'd asked after her dad and of Eulin himself—whether he was fading or faking.

A quarter moon hung just over the eastern horizon, and the blue-black sky was filling with stars. She paused to take in the vastness of it, to listen to the loud buzz of night insects whose names she no longer remembered and to savor the air, still warm on her skin.

She was only a hundred yards from the ranch when she spotted headlights in her mirror. They couldn't have turned in from another road because there wasn't one, so that meant they'd been waiting for someone to leave the ranch.

Her heart kicked up a notch, and she pushed the accelerator down hard. She knew the road; that gave her an advantage. But she was driving the Pinto, too small and too slow to outrun anything more powerful for long.

The lights were so close they blinded her if she looked in the mirror. Her foot was on the floor, and still the car behind was gaining. The lights swept out; they were coming alongside, probably trying to force her off the road.

There was a left curve in a few miles. By then, the other car would be on her left. If she could time it just right and brake in time, she'd stop and it would sail off the road. If not, they'd both miss the curve.

But they never reached the curve. The other car was a pickup and faster than she'd realized. Too quickly it was beside her. The driver swung it hard into the front fender of the Pinto, and she had to fight to keep control as the car bounced off the road.

The Pinto snapped a fence post, hurtled on a bit farther, then slammed to a stop when it hit something solid. AJ was thrown against the wheel, and the shock of it stunned her just enough to slow her reactions. Before she could jump out and run, the door beside her was yanked open. Someone grabbed her arm and pulled her out.

There were two of them and not enough light to see much more than that they were young, big, and male. A beam of light struck her in the eyes, and she raised her hand against the brightness.

"You're Eulin Thomas's daughter," one of the men said. A nasal voice with a hint of someplace southern in it.

"Yes," she said. The light stayed in her eyes, forcing her to squint against it.

"Your father has something that belongs to someone else. That someone else wants it back," the voice said.

"I don't know anything about it," AJ said, wishing that were not the truth.

"Well, someone sure as hell does. We traced that crate to your father's ranch. Now he says he can't remember it. We want that crate."

AJ did some fast thinking. "He might have got it and not remember," she said. "He's an old man. His mind's not good. He forgets things."

"Where would he put something if it wasn't in that barn of his?"

"I don't know," she said. "Sometimes he hides stuff."

"I don't know if it's you or him that's trying to pull something funny, but we want that crate." She could hear anger in the voice. "And if someone doesn't hand it over soon, one of you is going to get hurt real bad."

"Look, I honest to God do not know what you are talking about," she said, "but I will do everything I can to get your crate."

"You got till noon tomorrow, then we'll be back to the ranch to pick up the crate. And don't even think about calling the cops. You bring the law into this, and we'll kill you both. You got that?"

"I got it," she said.

"Good."

The light snapped off, and they walked back to the truck. AJ leaned against the Pinto. Her body was shaking so hard she had trouble standing, and she shivered as the wind hit her sweat-soaked shirt.

The Pinto wouldn't start, so she had to walk back to the ranch. It was far enough for her to get through her fear to anger.

The light was on in the kitchen. She could see Eulin sitting at the table. "I want to know what's going on here before you get us killed," she said as she slammed the kitchen door.

Eulin jumped up. "What happened?" he demanded.

"Two guys in a pickup ran me off the road and told me that if you don't give them some crate, they'll kill us both. Now, what the hell is going on?"

"Oh, shit," Eulin said.

"Dad!"

It was not in Eulin's nature to tell the truth if there was any way out of it, but AJ wasn't going to give him time to come up with a reasonable lie, so he told her about the crate, Ernie's death, and his trip to the Delcarbon mine.

"Why the hell didn't you just give them the damn crate?" she asked.

"Then they'd have killed us to keep us quiet. They've already killed Ernie."

AJ got a Coors from the fridge and sat down at the

table. "So we can't give it to them and we can't keep it and we can't call the cops."

Eulin nodded grimly.

"You have any idea what's in that crate?" AJ asked.

"Can't be sure, but I'd guess they're some sort of missiles, probably those hand-held things that can knock down a plane."

"So we could be dealing with foreign terrorists, local arms dealers, or international criminals," AJ said.

That sent Eulin for another beer. "I think you should get out of here," he said.

"And leave you to deal with them? No way. Too bad you don't know how to use those missiles. We could at least give them one hell of a surprise."

"Whoever sent them would just send a new bunch. There's never a shortage of their type." Eulin turned his beer bottle in his hands, studying it. "What we need to do is destroy those missiles without making it seem to be our fault."

"That's a goal, not a plan," AJ said.

"Well, I got these mines out in the barn . . . ," Eulin began.

"Oh, no." AJ stopped him. "Not those mines. How old are those things anyway?"

Eulin shrugged. "I don't know, exactly."

"Great, you've got explosives out there that could kill you, and you don't know what kind of shape they're in."

"Well now, we're not talking cream or butter here. These things don't spoil, you know."

"But they do, in their own way. They become less stable over time. I interviewed guys who were disarming the mines in Kuwait. Even after only a year, lots of those mines are real unstable. I think we should just give the guys the crate. We don't know who they are. Once they've got it, there's no reason for them to kill us."

"Yeah, you're probably right. That's what we'll do," Eulin said.

AJ's heart sank. He'd given in much too easily.

◆ ◆ ◆

She wasn't surprised when, twenty minutes later, he announced that he was going for a ride. And she wasn't surprised when he stopped by the storage barn before he went to the stock barn to saddle the bay gelding and head out into the night.

Once he was gone, she made her own trip to the storage barn. She found what she expected. Back where Eulin kept the explosives, there was an empty space on the shelf.

It was nearly midnight when Eulin got back. He seemed surprised to find her sitting on the porch.

"You waiting up for me?" he asked gruffly.

"Nah. I just couldn't sleep. Enjoy your ride?"

"Yeah," he said, and sat down in the chair beside her.

They sat quietly for a while. Finally, Eulin spoke. "You like your work?"

"Yeah, I do," she said. "I like it a lot."

"Seems kind of dangerous sometimes."

"It looks that way from the outside, but I don't do the real dangerous stuff," she said. "I stay away from wars and riots." It was mostly true.

"They give you a bad time 'cause you're a woman?" he asked.

"Not so much anymore." They'd talked about all this many times. AJ wondered whether Eulin had forgotten or whether he was leading someplace.

"You'll be fifty soon. Isn't that old for that kind of work?"

"Nah," she said. "Sometimes it even helps. The gray hair's a big advantage."

"Really?"

"Yeah. It's like a cloak of invisibility. I've always tended to attract attention. That's less a problem now."

Eulin knew what she meant. There'd been boys hanging around her since she was thirteen. "Lots of women would have welcomed that," Eulin said.

"Maybe," she said. "It always annoyed me. I felt kind of like a freak."

"A beautiful body isn't freakish," he said.

"Yeah, but it can create problems. Anyway, I notice guys don't pay so much attention to the front range when there's snow on the peak."

Eulin laughed in spite of himself. He doubted that men had stopped looking. His daughter was still a very attractive woman. He'd have liked to tell her that but didn't think it quite proper. "Well, I'm glad getting old's good for something," he said. "I was afraid maybe they wouldn't take you seriously anymore. That happens, you know."

AJ felt a lump in her throat. She waited to see where things were going.

"Folks around here can't understand why I didn't discourage you from doing that kind of work. What with the travel and the danger and all. 'How can you let her do that?' they say to me." He paused, let the moment stretch. "I just tell them that you got to let a person have her life. Even if there is some risk in it. People who can't take a risk, they're as good as dead inside."

AJ didn't respond. Eulin sounded as sharp and sane as anyone she knew. But he'd spent his lifetime fooling people. That ability might last much longer than his judgment. She'd know at noon just how sharp he really was. If he failed the test, they wouldn't be around to worry about whether or not he was capable of living alone.

Once Eulin had gone inside, AJ headed for the barn. She picked up the saddlebags she'd left there and saddled the bay. "You're getting your exercise tonight, aren't you, old man?" she said as she swung up onto his back.

She found the ancient jeep that Eulin kept parked near the county road that ran along the west side of the ranch. She put her hand on the hood. It was still warm. She tied the bay to a fence post and set the saddlebags in the back of the jeep. The key was under the passenger seat, and the jeep started easily. She pulled onto the county road and headed for Walsenburg.

It was half an hour past closing time when AJ got to

the Wagon Wheel, and Paul was beginning to think she'd stood him up. She surprised him by coming to the back door. The look on her face canceled his hopes of a romantic evening.

"Something wrong?" he asked.

AJ'd spent the last two hours debating whether or not to risk telling the truth. If Paul didn't go along with her plan, he'd get them all killed; and in AJ's experience it was a whole lot easier to con a man into doing what you wanted than it was to convince him to take you seriously.

She didn't know Paul well enough anymore to trust him, but she knew that the bartender was one of the few people in town who'd never fallen for Eulin's eccentric act. With him, the truth might be safer than a con.

"I need your help," she said. "And I'm not exaggerating when I say it's a matter of life and death."

Paul listened to the whole story. Then he listened some more as she told him her plan.

"It's risky," he said.

"You think we can get your cousin to go along with it?" she asked.

Paul smiled. "You just might," he said. "Don's had a crush on you since eighth grade."

AJ remembered Don. He'd had a crush on her body. At fifteen he'd have done anything she asked, but he was fifty now, and she doubted that his hormones still ran his brain.

It was a good sign that he responded to Paul's late-night call by coming right over. And when his first reaction was to check out her tits, AJ knew that part of the plan would work.

She told him how she thought Eulin was trying to convince some foreigners that he'd discovered a vein of gold at Delcarbon. "He hasn't broken the law yet," she said. "If we could just scare him a bit now, maybe he'd straighten out. It'd have to be completely unofficial. And I wouldn't want you to do anything that might get you in trouble with the sheriff."

Don looked a little uncomfortable when she got to the part about using the police car.

"I'd understand if you didn't want to help me," she assured him. "If you were afraid to take the risk."

"Oh, it's not that," he said quickly.

It didn't take much more to get him to buy into the plan.

The sky was lightening on the eastern horizon when AJ finally got home. It had taken her a lot longer than she'd figured at Delcarbon. As a kid, she'd spent hours playing out there and had known the area better than any adult, but memory dims in forty years, and nothing's the same in the dark.

It was a long morning. She cooked a big breakfast, partly to keep herself busy and partly because she figured they needed all the comfort they could get. But she couldn't taste a thing.

Afterward Eulin took a tiny, toylike gun from his pocket and handed it to her. "Anything could happen out there. You know how to use this?"

"I know," she said. "But I'd like more than two shots if I've got to use a gun with so little stopping power. You got a .25-caliber Beretta or Browning?"

Eulin looked surprised. "Yeah, I got a Browning. You're right, it'd be better. You can hide it in your boot."

"I don't carry a gun in my boot," she said. "I have a better place."

"Have to be a place they wouldn't look," Eulin said.

"Men rarely think to check between a woman's breasts," AJ replied. "All I'll need is a long Ace bandage and a loose shirt."

Eulin realized then that there was a lot he didn't know about his daughter. He shook his head, but he couldn't suppress a smile when he brought her the gun.

"I know you're planning something," AJ said finally. "Might work better if you let me in on it."

"Just keep your eyes open and take care of yourself," he said.

The blue car arrived right at noon, as promised. AJ went out to meet the men as they got out. One was dark-skinned and short; the other two were younger and larger, about the size of the men who'd driven her off the road last night. She wondered where they'd gotten the pickup, figured they'd stolen it.

"We're in luck," she said as she reached them. "He's having one of his good days. I got him to tell me where the crate is. I'll take you there."

Before they could answer, Eulin came out the kitchen door. "Howdy," he said, grinning again. "Want me to show you where that crate is?"

"I'll take them, Dad," she said.

"You'll both come," the older man said. "You ride with us," he said to AJ, then turned to the young guy who looked like a rodent. "And you take the old guy in his pickup."

Before they got in the cars, the rodent and his clean-cut buddy searched them. They found the derringer in Eulin's boot, but they never got close to the Browning AJ had strapped under her breasts.

On the way to Delcarbon, AJ said, "He's having a good day, but you best not push him. If he gets nervous, he'll lose it."

The older man grunted. "You just get us that crate, so no one needs to get nervous."

As they passed the road to the Pearsons' place, AJ checked her watch and surreptitiously pushed the timer. Twenty minutes. She hoped to hell she had the timing right.

When they got to Delcarbon, Eulin hopped out of the pickup as soon as it stopped. "I'll take you to the crate," he said.

"Your daughter can take us," the older man said.

"Ha," Eulin said. "Only a fool goes in a mine with a woman. It's bad luck. 'Sides, she don't know her way around in there. Like as not, you'd all fall down a shaft."

AJ was pretty sure what he was up to, and her stomach

went hollow at the realization. "I know my way," she said to the older man. "You think you're safer with a crazy old man who can't remember where he put his boots? He gets nervous, you'll end up lost in there."

They were at the iron gate to the mine now. Behind the bars, the rough rock walls were gray in the dim light. A few feet farther, all was blackness. The rodent looked nervous, but the older man was unflappable. He considered. "Take the daughter," he said to the younger guys. "I'll keep the old man out here. Who's got the key?"

"I ain't givin' you no key 'less you let me go in with you," Eulin said petulantly. AJ stole a look at her watch. A delay of more than a couple of minutes could be fatal.

"Fine," said the older man. "You can come too. Now open that door or I'll shoot your daughter."

Eulin started to fuss some more about letting a woman in the mine, but one of the guys pulled out a gun and pointed it at AJ, so he opened the door and led the way to the side tunnel.

It took both of the musclemen to carry the crate. Eulin and AJ were ordered to lead the way with the flashlights. In the dark, she couldn't check her watch.

As they emerged into the bright sunlight, AJ was temporarily blinded. By the time her eyes adjusted so she could read her watch, it read 00, and she thought she could hear the siren. It took the men a few seconds longer.

They froze, still holding the crate between them, and listened. Unaccustomed to the way sound travels on the plains, they couldn't gauge how far away it was. They lowered the crate to the ground and strained to tell whether it was coming closer.

As it became apparent that the siren was growing louder, the rodent's face twisted in fury. "I told you no cops," he said as he pulled his gun.

"Shit," AJ yelled. "You think we want to be out here with whatever you've got in that crate? What is it? Drugs? Damn you, they'll bust us all. We've got to get rid of that stuff."

"Back in the mine," Eulin cried.

"No. They'll find it," AJ said. The siren was still fairly far off, but to the three men, it probably sounded like it was just beyond the hill. They looked confused.

"I don't want to go to jail," AJ shouted. "We've got to get rid of that thing. Quick, there's an air shaft about twenty feet that way." She pointed to the right. "Dump it down there. You can haul it out later."

Eulin started to object, then stopped. The siren was getting louder. "Dump it," he shouted. "Down the shaft. It's the only place they won't find it."

The older man hesitated, then said to the younger men, "Do it."

The men got the heavy crate to the shaft with surprising speed. They set it on the edge and pushed.

"Be careful," AJ said as they shoved it over. "Those old shafts aren't very stable."

Her last word was drowned out by an enormous boom. The two men were thrown backward, and dirt and rock flew twenty feet in the air and rained down on all of them as the shaft closed in on itself.

"Holy shit," the man next to AJ said.

The explosion left them all a bit deaf and disoriented, and the police car had pulled up beside the other two vehicles before they realized it.

Don jumped out, leaving the flashers on, and ran up toward them, with Paul a few steps behind. "Eulin, what in the hell . . . ?" he yelled.

Eulin stared at the pile of rubble that had been the air shaft. "I was just showing these fellas the mine," he said. "Tossed a rock down the air shaft, and *boom*."

"Those old shafts can be real unstable," Paul said before Don could think too hard about how a rock could cause such a big explosion. "What're you doing out here?"

"Well, like I said . . . ," Eulin started.

"You trying to fool these men into believing there's gold or something else in this old coal mine, Eulin?" Don asked sternly. Before Eulin could answer, he continued:

"Because you could get into a lot of trouble doing something like that. I'd have to arrest you. You wouldn't want to spend your last years in a jail cell, would you?"

"No, sir, I wouldn't," Eulin said. "I wouldn't cheat these city fellas. I told them it was coal, and not very good coal, didn't I?" Eulin said, a whine rising in his voice. He turned to the older man. "Tell him I didn't say a word about gold, did I?"

Don turned to the man in the suit. "I have to warn you, sir, that this man has a criminal record." He indicated Eulin. "And he has no legitimate claim to this property. It's owned by someone else."

"I wouldn't . . . ," Eulin whined.

"Thank you very much, Deputy," the older man said. "I appreciate your warning."

Don threatened Eulin a couple more times, warned the outsiders again, and gave AJ a big smile, then he returned to the patrol car. AJ had hoped the three men would be in a hurry to put some distance between themselves and the sheriff's deputy, but they made no move to leave.

As the patrol car pulled away, Eulin turned back to the pile of rubble. "I hope you ain't gonna ask me to dig that stuff up," he said. "That shaft was at least fifty feet deep, maybe a hundred. Oh, shit. I just hate to lose stuff. That was a nice crate, too."

"He's losing it," AJ said to the older man. "You mind if I get him home before he starts raving like a wild man?"

The older man was studying her. He might believe her or he might not, but he knew that a sheriff's deputy had seen him with AJ and Eulin. AJ watched him weigh the urge to kill them against the possible consequences of the investigation that would follow their disappearance.

"Get out of here," he said.

"Did I have eggs this morning?" Eulin asked as AJ led him toward the pickup. "I didn't, did I?"

When they were out of sight of the mine, AJ let out a whoop. "We did it. We made it out alive."

Eulin was watching his daughter with new respect. "What'd you put down that old shaft anyway?"

"Just a bunch of stuff from the storage barn and a couple of land mines to set it off," AJ said. "I didn't mean to make such a big blast. I was afraid some of the stuff might not work."

"I told you that stuff don't spoil," Eulin said. "Damn good work for an amateur."

"But I wasn't the only one with a plan," AJ said. "You put something in with the missiles, didn't you? That's why there was such a big explosion."

Eulin didn't answer.

"You were going to go in there with those guys and blow up the tunnel, weren't you?"

"Only if I couldn't get them to go in alone," he said. "It wasn't a bad plan. I'd have been ahead of them on the way out and I could have started acting crazy and run ahead of them. When I hit the entrance I was going to detonate the bomb. With luck I'd have been blown clear. You'd have had time to get out your gun."

"How?" AJ asked. It sounded like a good plan, but she had to be sure. "How were you going to detonate it?"

Eulin pulled a rumpled pack of Camels from his shirt pocket. "The detonator's in here. Cute little thing."

AJ smiled broadly and felt something inside relax. "I like my plan better," she said.

"Yeah, but you had to use the cops," Eulin said. "Mine wasn't bad for a crazy old coot who's barely fit to live alone."

She wanted to hug him but wouldn't have even if she hadn't been driving. Instead she just punched his shoulder. "Not bad at all," she said.

▲▲▲▲▲▲▲

DUST DEVIL

REX BURNS

Rex Burns has spent many years as a college professor and nearly the same number developing a series of excellent novels about Detective Gabriel Wager of the Denver Police Department. Burns has also written about ex-secret-service-agent and industrial-espionage-expert Devlin Kirk. He now introduces his latest character, "Snake" Garrick, whom we'll see in future stories.

Burns has said that he tries to do two things with his work: "Create life and make the reader ask, 'What happens next?'"

In this very modern western story, involving the fate of a girl and a horse, Burns achieves both his stated goals.

GARRICK STUDIED the girl's face while the older woman did all the talking. She was in her mid-teens at best, and despite the tautness at her mouth, and eyes red from crying, she was a cute kid who promised to grow into a good-looking woman: black hair straight down to her shoulders, a nose not quite long enough for the width of her mouth, eyes as blue as the mid-September sky filling the office window. She sat silent while her aunt Louise made it clear that their whole visit was probably a waste of time and promised to be a waste of money. "I thought private detectives were supposed to be big and tough. You don't look no wider than a fence post. Not much taller, either."

Mrs. Louise MacIntyre's face was long of jaw and nose both, and might charitably be described as "strong." Garrick figured she wouldn't object to that; she apparently thought of herself as a strong woman—strong voice, strong hands, and words that matched.

"I make up for it by being quick, sneaky, and mean, ma'am." Garrick didn't add that some of his fellow P.I.'s called him "Snake" in admiration of those virtues. "Why do you need to hire a private detective?"

"I don't—it's my niece. Her idea, not mine. As far as I'm concerned, a horse you can't ride is better off gone, and if Kristie wasn't as stubborn as a blind mule, she'd agree with me."

In the silence, Garrick heard the chatter of a windowpane behind him. It spoke of the traffic on Canyon Boulevard, Boulder's busy east-west street, two houses away from the cottage that served as office and home. It was a noise that, more and more, he was growing inured

to, but he hadn't learned to like it; it reminded him of the
cost of Colorado's growth, not only in small cities like
Boulder but all across the state. And though that growth
had brought his agency more business, because more people meant more crooks, he had long ago decided that life
wasn't measured by the bottom line, and didn't know
why his town had to be.

"He showed us the bill of sale when he came for her,"
said Mrs. McIntyre. "That was enough for me. Should be
for you too, Kristie."

"But Uncle Hank never would have sold her—especially not without telling me! She was . . . " The girl's lips
clamped against another surge of tears, and she tried to
explain to Garrick. "He told me he was training her for
me! She was going to be a present from him—from Uncle
Hank!"

"She" was Dust Devil, a four-year-old mare that,
according to the sister of the man killed in an auto accident, couldn't be ridden, was too spoiled to work, and
had no claim to the feed her brother wasted on her. "Dog
food on the hoof! That's all she's good for."

"She learned to pull the gig," said Kristie. "She really
likes that. She's a sweet horse if you treat her well—and
Walter and Uncle Hank were starting to saddle-train
her!"

"Well, maybe they were. But Elson has that bill of
sale, Kristie."

Mrs. MacIntyre's brother had adopted the girl when
her parents had died in the crash of a small airplane, one
of those common accidents in the twisting winds of the
Front Range. Now he was gone too, so the horse meant a
lot to Kristie. "Who's Walter?"

"The hand," said Mrs. MacIntyre. "Walter Williams."
A sharp wag of her head. "Talks more than he works,
but ranch help's hard to find."

The new owner had come two days ago, claiming that
Hank Patterson sold the mare for fifteen hundred dollars
the day before he was killed in an automobile accident.
Since then, Kristie had been crying so much about that

horse being a gift from her uncle that Mrs. MacIntyre couldn't stand one more minute of it and called Ferris Elson to explain about buying back the mare, but he wouldn't hear of it. A deal's a deal, he said, and that mare was his. Period. Hang up. Now, that got under Mrs. MacIntyre's skin—that man's tone of voice and the nasty way he talked to her—so she called her lawyer. He advised her to hire a private detective first. "He said you were pretty good and wouldn't cost nearly as much as he'd have to charge to look into it himself."

Garrick nodded and added the lawyer's name to his gift list. Most lawyers would have taken the case, charged their full fee, and turned the legwork over to a P.I. for a small percentage. But now and then, just enough to keep your hopes up, you ran across an honest one. Still, even that kind liked to be remembered at Christmas. "Why did he think the sale should be looked into?"

"Because we never saw nothing of that fifteen hundred dollars!" Mrs. MacIntyre figured what Garrick was going to ask next. "I'm the ranch bookkeeper, among a lot of other things around that place. My brother would've told me about that money. Every penny gets logged in and counted up. Have to, given the IRS and running on a shoestring like we do."

"Was the payment in check or cash?"

"If I knew that, then I'd know where it was, wouldn't I? You sure you're a detective?"

Garrick ran a hand across the bone of his lean jaw to hide his grin. "Sometimes I wonder, at least before my first cup of coffee. Did your brother need money?"

"Ain't often we don't need money. And Hank could get rid of it a lot quicker than we got it, too!" She added, looking at something in her memory, "Fool. Reckless fool!" The words sounded less like a curse than a benediction.

"Might he have had any debts he wouldn't tell you about?"

Mrs. MacIntyre's frown mixed thought and doubt. "Can't imagine it. Anything at all to do with money, he turned over to me. Good with his hands, but he couldn't stand paperwork—hated it!"

"Uncle Hank never lied. Not to Aunt Louise, not to me, not to anyone! Never!"

Garrick nodded as if he believed the girl. But he avoided those eyes, whose blue turned hot and angry and dared anyone to doubt her uncle's virtue. "Still," he reminded her, "Mr. Elson showed you a bill of sale."

Mrs. MacIntyre thumped a sun-browned hand on Garrick's desk: broad across the palm, short fingernails, and no polish. A trace of grime over the forefinger marked where a rope or rein often rested. "If that man did pay fifteen hundred dollars for that horse," she said, "I never saw a penny of it. You think you can find out what happened to it?"

It was a good question and one that lent more conviction to the niece's story than her blue eyes and innocent face. Those were nice, but what you usually looked for was where the dollars were. "Suppose I do find the money, Miss Walters?"

The girl looked down and was silent for a long moment. "You won't," she said. "I know you won't!"

Aunt Louise sniffed; she wasn't all that sure the money hadn't been paid, but, as her glance said when they were leaving, she wasn't so sure Garrick could find it, either.

The ranch where Kristie and her aunt lived was a good three hours' drive across the prairies northeast of Boulder. Garrick had drawn a few more details out of Mrs. MacIntyre, before explaining very carefully what his fees were and that he could not guarantee the results. Mrs. MacIntyre wanted to know why not, for that much money, but he told her all he could do was try to determine the truth. Kristie Walters had a pretty good idea what the truth was, so she wasn't worried; and her aunt had enough money to get him started proving it, which sent Garrick on his way early the next morning. His first stop had been the Centennial Bank and Trust in Fort Morgan, where, armed with authorization from Mrs. MacIntyre, he had asked questions about her joint account with Henry Patterson. Besides a welcoming smile followed by a concerned frown and an expression of regret at Mr. Patterson's unfortunate accident, the letter had been good for a printout of the transactions for the past six months. No deposit of $1,500 was listed prior to the man's death ten days ago, though there was one larger amount that might include the price of the horse.

"Can you tell me the source of these funds?" Garrick pointed to a deposit of $5,700.

The assistant manager, a slender man in his late twenties, who wore pointy-toed boots of gray snakeskin, studied the printout, then turned to his computer and rattled its keys. "It came in on August 25, an interinstitutional transfer from Citizens Trust up in Sterling. I'm afraid that's all the information I have on it."

"A single payment?"

"Yes, sir. Here's their transaction number, in case you want to talk to them." He jotted figures on a slip of paper.

"Did Mr. Patterson apply for any loans in the last six months?" The balance in his account showed $14,021.18; it wasn't much cash, but Garrick knew that a lot of small ranchers had more acres than they did dollars. Grazing fees, hay sales, leased land for farming— these kept a small landowner going between cattle sales, and to judge by the empty acres he had passed driving up from Denver, a lot of ranchers hadn't scraped up enough to survive.

Another computer probe into the records. "Not with us, Mr. Garrick."

The last withdrawal was for $75.83, on a check that cleared eight days ago, two days after his death.

"Can you tell me who the payee is on this final entry?"

The young man shook his head. "Only the check number. We no longer keep the canceled checks once they've been processed."

"Does a Mr. or Mrs. Elson have an account here?"

Rattle. "No one by that name." His manner grew slightly stiff: Garrick was reaching beyond the area authorized by Mrs. MacIntyre and sanctioned by respect for the dead. "Is there anything else I can do for you, Mr. Garrick?"

There was, but it was obvious the assistant manager wouldn't like him to ask. Garrick thanked the man and headed north on State 52 into Weld County.

Twenty-five miles of blacktop cut straight across a prairie whose waist-high grass, tawny with the end of summer, looked like the vast rough pelt of some animal. The patched road climbed over one gentle swell after another, almost an exact mile apart, and glided down toward the next horizontal line of pale-brown expanse and hard blue sky. Here and there a hawk made a hovering black dot against the blue, and flashes of dull yellow at the roadside marked meadowlarks fleeing the car's tires. Garrick knew there were other animals in this seeming emptiness that stretched from the North Pole to the Gulf of Mexico—deer, antelope, snakes, coyotes, badgers, even an occasional bear that followed a creek down from the wall of snowy peaks making up the Laramie Range and the Medicine Bows, which glittered sixty more miles to the west.

The map half-folded on the seat beside him marked both the H Over P ranch and the Rocking E, where Elson lived. They were beyond the end of the state highway, where even county roads were sparse. A corner of the Pawnee National Grassland separated the ranches by about twenty miles. If the wind had blown any harder, both ranches might have tumbled across the state line into Nebraska or Wyoming. This vast flatness wasn't the tourist image of Colorado; the mountains were only a ragged whiteness topped by a thin streak of clouds at the edge of the sky. But Garrick could understand why people wanted to stay: the horizon could still swing the whole way around, unbroken by a house or telephone pole or windmill. If it weren't for the streak of highway bobbing up and down over the ridges ahead, a man could know what this earth was like before Colorado was a state, or even before the Spanish had landed. Clean—that

was the feeling and the view: pristine hillsides and shallow valleys of brown, thigh-high grass, and even the hot
blue sky seemed scoured by the wind. Except for that
microwave relay tower making a spidery column on the
northeast horizon. And now a distant cluster of trees that
erupted dark in the heat-silvered distance and looked
unnatural and were unnatural—planted to shelter some
farmhouse from the wind and the sun and maybe to close
out a little of the world's empty rim—if they were the
kind of people who stayed less out of love than by accident, or inertia, or madness.

His odometer gave him the mileage, a small wooden
sign stenciled VV told him where a county road met the
pavement. The crossing was marked by faint traces of old
mud and a scattering of gravel. Behind him, as Garrick
sped along the unpaved bumps, a haze of yellow dust
angled with the wind across the roadside ditch, the
barbed-wire fence, the sun-dried grass.

The Rocking E was off a dirt section road that cut
across the graveled county road. Cottonwood trees
marked the ranch house, tucked in a small draw where
water could collect; and Garrick, bouncing along the
two-rut track in second gear, studied the scattered buildings as he tilted down toward the shady grove. The barn
stood by itself, long eaves sweeping away from a high
peak to provide braced overhangs where hay and equipment were piled. A concrete silo that looked unused stood
beside it, yellow-brown with dust like the other buildings.
Sheds and smaller structures were behind the stone house,
which was two-story and square and had deep porches
along its south and east sides. Beyond the barn, weathered rail fencing corralled two or three horses, which
lifted their heads to stare toward the sound of Garrick's
car. One of them was probably Dust Devil herself. He
turned off the motor and sat in the tick of cooling metal
to let the house know he had arrived. Up close, the buildings looked run-down, which didn't surprise Garrick; the
brief credit check he'd run on Elson from his office had
shown increasing problems with payments over the last

five years. But the trashy look of the place—tools left out
to rust, a snarl of fence wire dumped where people had to
walk around it, sun-warped boards scattered about—said
less about the checkbook and more about a bankruptcy
of spirit. Leisurely, he stepped into the dusty heat of the
sun and slammed the car door loud. A dog, sleepy and
head-down, plodded toward him from beneath a well-
used GMC pickup truck. Garrick held out his fist for the
dog's inspection, then clumped up the warped board
steps to rattle a rusty screen door with his knuckles.

Quick heels thumped inside, and a moment later a
short, square figure hovered behind the screen. "Help
you?"

"Mrs. Elson?" When the woman nodded, Garrick held
up a business card and introduced himself. "I understand
Mr. Patterson sold your husband a horse. I wonder if I
could ask him a few questions about that transaction."

"Ferris isn't here just now. He'll be back this evening."
Her voice was taut, and she sounded as if she'd run a
long way to answer the door. "You want to come back
then."

"Maybe you can save me a trip—I'm asking for Mr.
Patterson's sister. You heard he was killed in an auto
accident recently?" When the woman finally nodded,
Garrick added, "She's trying to settle the estate, so any
help you can give us would be appreciated." From somewhere behind the house came the crow of a rooster, defiant but almost lost in the wind and space that made up
the shallow draw sheltering the ranch house. "Did Mr.
Patterson pay by check or cash, Mrs. Elson?"

"I . . . I'm not sure."

"Mrs. MacIntyre can't find any record of the money.
She hired me to look into it." He smiled. "You understand—the estate of the deceased is subject to scrutiny for
tax purposes."

The shape of the woman's head made Garrick think of
a triangle: broad forehead with a face that narrowed
quickly down to a pointed chin; a small, cramped mouth.
The lines around that mouth did not come from smiling.

Her tightly curled gray hair still had some black in it. Eyes like flakes of black glass tried to read Garrick's face without saying anything in return. "Cash. Ferris paid him cash."

"I see." Garrick nodded and looked off to where the dog was lifting a leg against one of his car's tires. "But like I say, Mrs. MacIntyre hasn't been able to find any trace of the money." The dog finished and sniffed. "You do have a bill of sale—something to show that the horse is yours?"

"Yes . . . yes, we do!"

"It's just a formality, but may I see it?"

Mrs. Elson thought about it and then let the screen door close. A few moments later the tread came back. "Here."

It was a standard sale form, pink in color, with the blanks filled in. The paper was creased from careful folding, and Garrick read it over. "This is a carbon copy. Don't you have the original?"

"This is all we got. It's all Mr. Patterson gave us. You tell his sister how sorry we are and all, but we paid cash! My husband, he paid cash for that horse, and it's ours!"

Garrick nodded again. "Thank you for your trouble, Mrs. Elson."

The H Over P Ranch, like the Elson place, was tucked in a shallow draw for shelter from the wind. But it opened enough to the west to show a distant jagged whiteness about a finger width high above the rim of prairie. Garrick figured that whoever placed the ranch thought the view was worth suffering the winter wind that would slice in from that direction. A row of tough-looking chrysanthemums, stunted and water-starved, lined the red-stone flags that led to the porch, whose shade lifted the midday heat from Garrick's shoulders.

Kristie was in school; Mrs. MacIntyre was surprised to see him. "Thought you'd be looking for that money."

"Just what I'm doing." He asked her about the $5,700 deposit and the check for $75.83.

"The check's for the electricity bill, and a high one too. That other money's from water rights. We lease some shares of our water to Mueller Farms."

She explained some of the other entries on the printout and, draining her coffee cup, told Garrick that so far he hadn't told her one thing she didn't already know.

"Yes, ma'am. But *I* hadn't found it out yet. I wonder if I can talk to your hand—Walter Williams."

"Probably out in the barn, waiting me to call lunch. Give a yell."

Garrick found him on the shady side of the barn, the grating rasp of a file noisy against an ax blade. He introduced himself, then asked, "I wondered what you could tell me about Mr. Patterson and the horse he sold to Elson."

If Williams had a chin, it would be hard to find under the scraggly black beard whose short, curly hairs looked like they belonged on some other part of his body. But his nose was right out there, bending first one way, then the other, witness to accidents or fights. His eyes were a pale blue, like some Garrick had seen on huskies, but they blinked a lot more than a dog's and didn't settle on anything for very long.

"Sold it—that's what Elson says."

Garrick nodded. "Fifteen hundred's a little high for a four-year-old, isn't it? Especially one that can't be ridden?"

Williams shrugged, scratching at something under the arm of his blue denim shirt. "She maybe could be broke for a saddle horse. Hank was starting to, anyway. For Kristie."

"Could you break her?"

"Don't know. But Hank was good with horses. Real gentle; took his time."

Mrs. MacIntyre said the man talked more than he worked, but maybe that was just around friends or animals. "So why did he sell her?"

"Maybe Elson offered more than before. He wanted that horse bad."

"Why's that, Mr. Williams?"

"Gut-touchy. That's a natural for rodeo, especially big as she is. Can't stand to feel nothing under her belly. Cinch strap rubbing under her belly drives her plumb crazy. Bucks like a son of a bitch."

"Rough stock? You mean that horse could be rough stock in a rodeo?"

"That's what Elson wanted her for. Kept after Hank, saying it would be a damn shame to ruin a promising bucking horse by saddle training it."

"How'd Elson know about her?"

Williams looked embarrassed and spat a little glob of white into the dirt. "I told him. Had a couple too many beers at Clark's over in Rockport and talked about the damn horse."

Garrick thought about that for a few seconds. "How much money could she bring in?"

"Fifteen, twenty thousand a season. Maybe more. Before expenses, of course."

"Was Mr. Patterson in need of money? Is that why he sold her?"

The man wagged his head. "Not that bad—besides, he was training her for Kristie. She's his brother's daughter. Her and Lou's all the family Hank had." He spit again and studied the dirt and added, "Drunk, maybe."

"Did he drink a lot?"

"Not a lot, no, but when he did cut loose he could stay right up with the best of them." A snort of appreciation. "Outdrank me a few times. That can take some doing."

"Is that how he died? Drunk driving?"

"It's what I figure. Didn't hear nothing about that, though. Just that he ran off the road and broke his neck. Rolled his truck. They found him next morning."

"Where had he been?"

Another shrug. "Left here before suppertime. Said he'd be back later."

"He didn't say where he was going?"

"Never did. He'd say, 'See you in a bit,' and take off. Missed supper that night, and that got Lou pretty hot."

He added, "She feels pretty bad about what she called him."

"Did it happen often?"

"Not like it used to. Fifteen, twenty years ago, before his brother got killed and Kristie come, he was out most every night, pole-vaulting around." The black beard opened in a grin that showed a tangle of narrow teeth so crooked that Garrick wasn't certain if any were missing. "Lot of ladies thought they was going to marry this ranch, but none of them never did."

Garrick watched a chicken walk from behind the barn, head lunging with each cautious step. "Did Mr. Patterson see Elson often? Correspond with him?"

"No. Telephone, mostly. Might've seen him in town once in a while."

"Do you know Elson well?"

"Well enough to know I don't want to know him any better."

"Why's that?"

"Stingier'n boardinghouse soup. I worked for him one year and by God ended up owing more than I made."

"Does he need money?"

"Ain't a place round here don't need money. People even go for six months without a bottle of whiskey because their goddamn cows need medicine. Makes me glad I never got the bug to have my own ranch." He shrugged. "But I reckon Elson's about gnawed down to the bone. What I hear, anyway."

It was Garrick's turn to nod. "Do you think Mr. Patterson drove over to Elson's the evening he was killed?"

Williams's blue eyes touched on Garrick's face and then glided off to stare toward the distant wink of snowy mountain tips. "Might of. Elson was always calling him about that horse. And he sold it to him, didn't he?"

"Did Mr. Patterson's accident happen on a state highway or county road?"

"County road. Over by the chalk bluffs. And what he was doing over yonder, I couldn't guess. It's a hell of a long way from Elson's place."

It was no secret why Elson wanted Dust Devil, but guessing how he claimed her led Garrick back down the highway to Greeley and the Weld County Sheriff's Office. The records clerk, in no hurry, looked up the case number and filled out the receipt for fees paid; Garrick found a quiet corner in the hallway to read over the accident report and then to call Mrs. MacIntyre with a couple more questions. Then he put in a request with the SO dispatcher to meet the investigating officer. The message came back that the officer would be at the Antelope Café in Pierce.

Twenty miles back up U.S. 85, Garrick logged in his distance on the account sheet and found a window table at the small café. Half a cup of coffee later, a high-riding Chevrolet Blazer marked with the sheriff's logo and a set of bubble lights pulled into the gravel parking lot. The officer, about as thin as Garrick but half again as tall, ducked under the doorframe and waved a hand at the woman who was waitress and cashier. "'Lo, Rennie. How about a cup and a sinker."

"Coming up, Wayne."

Garrick—the only customer among the half-dozen Formica tables with their catsup, napkin holders, and mustard jars centered rigidly on the checkered oilcloths—rose to shake hands. The officer lifted off his Stetson. "You're Mr. Garrick? Wayne Richards." Like so many police officers, this one had blue eyes, and they looked down at the shorter man with that coolness most lawmen felt for private investigators. "You wanted to talk about that vehicle accident? Hank Patterson?"

"Thanks for meeting me. I would like to ask a few questions."

The waitress brought Richards's coffee and doughnut; he placed his radio on the table, where its occasional traffic made a crackling sound. Methodically, he emptied the plastic thimble of cream and dumped three packages of sugar into the tan liquid. "Drink too much coffee," he explained. "This way it don't hurt my stomach."

Having tasted the stuff in his own cup, Garrick could understand the caution. "I read your report. You didn't note whether alcohol was involved."

"Sure as hell couldn't run a breath test."

"No open containers? No smell of alcohol?"

"No evidence at all to say there was or wasn't alcohol involved." Richards added, "The coroner might've run a blood test on him, but I doubt it."

Garrick knew that most counties in Colorado had undertakers or pharmacists for coroners; only the major areas had M.D.'s and ran tests routinely. "Did you make a list of the deceased's personal effects?"

Richards's sand-colored eyebrows lifted, and the distance of official politeness was replaced by mild interest. "What are you looking for?"

"A couple of things." Garrick stared down at his coffee and decided there was no easy way to say it. "One is money. He might have been carrying fifteen hundred dollars."

The staring blue eyes blinked twice. "I put his wallet and watch and everything he had in his pockets in the envelope, Mr. Garrick. If there was fifteen hundred dollars in that wallet, it's still there." There was no anger in his voice, nor defensiveness; it was absolutely neutral. He dipped his doughnut in the coffee and shoved half of it into his mouth. "It was logged in to the property clerk when I made my report."

"I said he 'might' have had it on him, Officer Richards. The other thing I'm looking for is his car registration."

"If that was in his wallet, it's still there too. The only thing I looked for was identification." He finished the other half.

Garrick nodded. A lot of people carried a copy of their car registration in their wallet. He did himself. But not Patterson. "Mrs. MacIntyre found one in her brother's personal effects. I'm talking about the one that's supposed to be kept with the car at all times. Do you happen to remember if it was there?"

"I didn't really look for it." Richards stared off at the corner of the café's paneled walls, where the glass eyes of an antelope head stared back. "I don't remember seeing it." His eyes narrowed with suspicion. "Just what is it you're really after?"

"Only testing a theory. The Colorado registration slip has to be signed on the back." Garrick pulled his out of his wallet and unfolded it on the table. "For the insurance affirmation—the vehicle owner has to swear he's insured and sign and date the statement." He pointed to his own name at the bottom of the small rectangle of paper.

The sheriff's officer knew all that. "What's that got to do with anything?"

Garrick told him what he had thought about. Richards sat for a long moment, studying it over. "So why might he put the registration slip back in the car?"

"Wouldn't somebody eventually notice if it was missing? The police? The insurance adjuster?"

"Yeah. Probably wouldn't put it together the way you do, but it could raise a question." Richards studied the sludge in the bottom of his cup. "It did bother me some, him breaking his neck in a piddly-assed rollover like that." He stood and tossed a dollar on the table. "Let's go over to Hollings' Salvage. That's where the vehicle's at."

The Salvage yard was four acres of twisted, dented, and mashed vehicles glittering in the late-afternoon sun. Bart—whose last name wasn't stitched on his overalls pocket—led them to the Patterson truck, his oil-stiffened pant legs making a noise like canvas as he walked. "It's down this row. Ain't done nothing to it—insurance adjuster ain't come to see it yet. Prob'ly trade it for the cost of the tow."

To Garrick's eyes, the pickup didn't look totally wrecked. It had rolled—the roof was dented in and the rider's side showed where the car's weight bent the door. But the windshield wasn't cracked and the wheels seemed firmly in place. The headlights and grille showed no damage at all. Richards had noted a "No" beside the accident report's printed question "Was victim wearing seat belt?" But he had not given an estimated speed. "How fast do you think he was driving?"

"Officially, I don't know. Unofficially, I guess pretty damn slow."

"He wasn't driving all that fast, that's for sure." Bart kicked one of the tires. "Didn't even pull the ball joints loose."

If necessary, a highway patrolman could estimate the speed from the damage, testimony that would stand up in court. Garrick didn't say anything, but Richards squeaked a bit of air through his two front teeth. "Better not salvage anything from it until I tell you, Bart." He ignored the mechanic's questioning glance and reached through the driver's window to flip the visor down. "You take the registration yet?"

"Naw. Like I told you, I ain't touched nothing."

Garrick went to the rider's side, reaching in through the window. Drivers who didn't have a registration holder on the visor or steering column often tossed the slip into the glove compartment. He pushed through a tangle of small tools—screwdriver, pliers—and a few papers to find the folder with the owner's manual and maintenance book. A folded square was slipped behind a small plastic window. "Here it is."

By the time Garrick and Richards reached the Rocking E, the shadow of the western rise of the land had almost filled the small wash, and the cooling air had that peppery smell mountain willow gets in the early autumn. It was a near-fragrance that Garrick usually associated with twilight and peace.

Richards had looked carefully at the registration slip with Garrick and then telephoned the sheriff from the salvage yard to talk about exhuming Patterson's body. Now he knocked on the ranch house door, a tall, thin man whose narrow shoulders sagged a bit more than they had that afternoon. Elson, broad torso almost filling the doorway, looked at Richards, then at Garrick, and back at the sheriff's officer. "Heyo, Wayne."

The Stetson nodded hello. "Got to see that bill of sale for Patterson's mare, Ferris."

The heavyset man's eyes came back to Garrick with a gleam of anger. "This the nosy son of a bitch been saying I didn't pay for her?"

"Kind of. I just need to see that bill of sale."

"Goddamn it, I bought that mare! Paid for that mare!"

"That's fine, Ferris. Just show me the paper, is all."

"Goddamn nosy bastard!" The man wheeled away from the door.

They listened to his tread in the waiting house, to a drawer yank open and slam shut, to muffled voices tangled in short sentences. Then two sets of returning steps. The pink sheet Elson had was a carbon copy of the sale, and the signature, too, was a copy. If Garrick had figured right, it was a copy of the signature on the vehicle registration that Richards had carefully tucked away in his shirt pocket and that bore a dent where a pencil had ridden over the inked name of Hank Patterson.

"Here. Read it and then get the hell off my ranch!" Glimpsed behind the man's thick shoulder, Mrs. Elson's face was a pale mask.

Garrick held the pink sheet flat. Richards pulled out the slip of paper and compared signatures. One was an exact trace. The officer spoke to the wide-eyed face half hidden behind her husband. "You followed Ferris out to the chalk bluffs, didn't you, Ruth? So he'd have a ride back."

The staring eyes shifted to her husband's white fingers, holding to the doorframe of their home.

A WOMAN'S PLACE

D. R. MEREDITH

Carolyn G. Hart has described D. R.
Meredith's detective John Lloyd Branson
as "the West Texas equivalent of
Lord Peter Wimsey."

While Elizabeth Walker, Meredith's pro-
tagonist in this story, may not remind you
of Wimsey, she shares some of his bemuse-
ment. In the course of this tale about
small-town gossip and small-town enmity,
a character notes that "if folks didn't want
to be talked about, then they better stay
indoors behind lowered
window shades. Otherwise they
were fair game." Wimsey would
understand.

SECRETS IN HIGHWATER, TEXAS, had a twenty-four-hour life expectancy if measured from ten o'clock one morning to ten o'clock the following morning. That was the hour when certain of the ranchers and farmers and what few businessmen there were in a town of four hundred fifty-five people gathered at Buddy's Café on the south end of Main Street, just before its junction with State Highway 54. Buddy's had started life as a filling station back in the late teens, after the land syndicate sold off the three-million-acre XIT ranch to whoever could beg, borrow, or steal enough cash to start their own spread on the western edge of the Texas Panhandle. With the influx of small ranchers, it looked like Highwater might grow from an XIT division headquarters into a major ranching community. After all, it was the county seat of Bonham County, with a fancy new three-story courthouse and a fine hotel that covered a whole city block. There was talk of paving all the streets and building more cattle pens down by the depot.

Highwater bustled, and Buddy's grandpa built a filling station with two pumps and a mechanic's shed to service all the Fords rolling off the assembly lines into the hands of Highwater's prosperous new ranchers. Everyone said Buddy's grandpa got in on the ground floor of a major new industry and would be a rich man before he could blink twice.

That was then, and this was now.

The hotel burned down in 1928, some said with a little help from its owner, who took his insurance money and moved to Fort Worth. It was never rebuilt, since the cattle buyers and traders stopped coming to Highwater when the XIT passed into legend. The county finally claimed the property for back taxes, cleared the burned timbers and filled in the foundation at public expense, and put a For Sale sign on the empty lot. The sign rotted away about the time the hitching rails around the courthouse were torn down, in 1956.

The streets never were paved except for Main Street, Amarillo became the major shipping point for cattle, and the bank never reopened after Roosevelt declared a bank holiday. Highwater had voted Republican ever since.

Buddy's grandpa never got rich and finally went out of business when the government rationed gasoline during World War II. Buddy opened a café in the old building in 1970, there being no restaurant in Highwater. The XIT Bar down the street sold peanuts and barbecue beef sandwiches, but a man couldn't take his wife and kids into a bar for Sunday lunch. In fact, a man didn't take a respectable woman into the XIT at all except for the dances on the last Friday night of every month, which were generally a strain on Highwater men because cussing wasn't allowed in the presence of ladies and only beer was sold. The rest of the month, women bought their alcoholic beverages at Highwater Grocery or Denny's Liquor Store and drank at home if they wanted something stronger than coffee or iced tea, and left the men to spit and cuss and let their hair down with their own kind.

Not that women didn't patronize the XIT between dances, but they didn't do it often and they were always accompanied by their husbands or boyfriends, who generally acted sheepish and embarrassed. There was an unwritten law in Highwater that superseded the Civil Rights Act forbidding sexual discrimination: a bar wasn't a woman's place. At least, not a respectable woman, and Highwater denied having any other kind, occasional evidence to the contrary.

Women weren't invited to join the ten o'clock coffee hour at Buddy's Café either, but exceptions were made at Buddy's discretion or when a woman bulled her way in and grabbed a seat at the round table by the café's front window, where the men drank strong black coffee and argued over Washington's latest agriculture policy. Elizabeth Walker was one of Buddy's exceptions; she doubted that she would ever have forced her way in. Not that Elizabeth lacked grit—she figured she had as much grit as the next woman or man—or felt inferior to men; but she didn't see any sense in making an issue of it. After all, men wouldn't exactly be welcomed at the First Baptist Church's Women's Missionary Circle. There were times when men didn't enjoy a woman's company, and certainly there were times when women didn't want a man underfoot. Elizabeth didn't see anything wrong with men and women having their own place, so long as men understood that a woman's place was likely to change from time to time and not get their dander up when it did.

For the most part, the men at Buddy's accepted Elizabeth into their circle and carried on with their talk as they always had. Sooner or later the conversation turned from national politics to local affairs, specifically their neighbors' behavior. Buddy Whitney, as owner of the café and generally the discussion leader of the morning coffee hour, always told Elizabeth that if folks didn't want to be talked about, then they better stay indoors behind lowered window shades. Otherwise they were fair game.

Elizabeth knew there was nothing malicious in the talk. Folks studied their neighbors in the same way they studied the weather or the latest bulletin from the Department of Agriculture. A man never knew when a storm would dump an inch of hail on his ripening wheat crop, or the government would freeze beef prices, or a neighbor's misbehavior would bring disaster on himself or others. A charitable person might describe the gossip as defensive in nature. Buddy Whitney certainly did.

"You see, Elizabeth," said Buddy earnestly as he refilled her coffee cup, "Highwater is like one of them fancy sweaters my wife knits. Every piece of yarn is knitted right against the next one. If a man was to yank one thread, why, the whole sweater might just unravel. Folks have to guard against anybody yanking too hard. The town's too small and we depend on each other too much to allow any one individual to get too rambunctious."

The leathery-faced men in their faded Levi's and denim work shirts seated around the table nodded their heads in agreement. While not a one of them hesitated to express an opinion on any given subject on any given day, Elizabeth knew that Buddy most often voiced the collective opinion. Metaphorically speaking, Buddy Whitney was the horse's mouth in Highwater.

Encouraged by the unspoken support of his audience, Buddy continued. "Take the time last spring when David Campbell, the county treasurer, was buying lottery tickets like there was a fire sale on them. You understand I ain't against a man gambling. I reckon that's his business and none of mine unless"—Buddy paused, glancing slowly around the circle of men and Elizabeth—"unless he's gambling with money from the public trough. Then his business *is* my business. He's fixing to yank that piece of yarn, don't you see."

Elizabeth nodded. She did see; in fact, she would bet her last dollar that she saw the danger before the men of Highwater did. But then her sex gave her an advantage men lacked. She knew exactly when David Campbell's wife, Mary Lou, canceled her weekly appointment at Sue's Beauty Shoppe and when she started buying cheap hamburger instead of ground round. To an observant and intelligent woman, and Elizabeth considered herself both, such economics meant money was tight. From hair to hamburger to lottery tickets to the county treasury was a pattern any woman could follow. She didn't mention such female reasoning to her coffee companions, though. Men tended not to grasp the finer points of feminine logic.

Buddy smiled at Elizabeth, pleased that his protégée understood. "If we hadn't gossiped about David Campbell, pooled our information, so to speak, why, we might not have reined him in until the county treasury was emptier than the schoolhouse in July. Once the gambling fever takes hold of a man, there's no telling where he'll stop. As it was, the sheriff had a word with David just to let him know he best mend his ways or find another job, and that was the end of it. He straightened right up, and ain't nobody seen him buy a lottery ticket since."

Elizabeth smiled and sipped her coffee. Buddy and the other men at the ten o'clock coffee hour had the best of intentions. They were educating her in the way things were done in Highwater. The fact that she had lived there all of her forty-three years didn't escape their notice so much as they disregarded it. Until her election as justice of the peace, Elizabeth had been an ordinary woman who concerned herself with a woman's pursuits: home, family, church. Even her assuming the management of a sizable ranch when her husband died two years ago didn't change her status. Nothing in a western male's philosophy said a woman couldn't manage a ranch as well as a man—so long as she didn't try to wrestle a twelve-hundred-pound steer into the branding chute without a man's help, or drop into the XIT Bar for a cold beer after her cattle were loaded into trucks for the trip to the livestock auction in Amarillo.

Her election changed Highwater's perception.

She was no longer an ordinary woman; she was the first female elected official in the town's history. She was a womb in a man's world, and the men of Highwater wanted to be certain she knew the rules of that world. In Elizabeth's case, that meant if she saw a dangling piece of yarn, don't yank it. Call the sheriff instead. Let a man handle it.

Elizabeth doubted that the men sitting around her knew that in certain instances her power was greater than the sheriff's, else they wouldn't be slurping their coffee with such bovine complacency. But attitudes changed slowly in Highwater, and Elizabeth saw no purpose in needlessly ruffling male feathers. Time enough for that if there was ever a murder. Then she would yank every piece of yarn she saw if that's what it took, and furthermore, Sheriff Jim Hayworth couldn't lift a finger to stop her.

Elizabeth took a last drink of coffee and pushed her cup away. She figured her education class was over for the day, and besides, she had work to do. The county commissioners had saddled her with responsibility for the employees' life insurance program. She was supposed to find out whether people wanted to increase, decrease, or continue their present coverage, which meant talking to everyone who worked for the county, from road crews to Earl, the county clerk.

The commissioners probably thought it was a good job for a woman—or that she was a good woman for the job. It all depended on how you looked at it, and she admitted she wasn't looking at it in the most positive light.

Elizabeth had picked up her old leather purse and pushed her chair back, when D. B. DeBord cleared his throat and everyone, including her, gave him their full attention. At eighty, D. B. was one of Highwater's oldest ranchers and had been a county commissioner for at least forty-five of his years. His mind wandered a bit but never about anything important, so everybody always listened to the old man's opinions. Age had its privileges in Highwater, and besides, folks all agreed that D. B. must have learned something in that eighty years worth passing along to the next generation.

"I was visiting with the county clerk yesterday, and Earl told me that David Campbell filed for reelection already. The primary ain't till next year, so I figure he wants a good head start on outrunning the rumors about his gambling."

Elizabeth watched as the men silently mulled over D. B.'s gossip. "I ain't heard him make a formal announcement yet," said Buddy finally.

"He don't have to. He told Earl, and Earl passes along everything he knows like he's being paid for it," said another rancher at the table.

Buddy nodded at the truth of that statement. "Of course, that's not to say we're going to reelect him again. It might not do to put temptation in his way for another four years. I suspect Campbell had better plan on working full time on his truck farm after the next election."

"He ain't no luckier at farming than he is at gambling," said D. B. "He plowed up forty acres of good grazing land to plant pinto beans, then let the crop burn up in the field because he didn't drill but one irrigation well, and it was too shallow. I warned him ahead of time, but he told me the well was just to supplement the 'natural rainfall the Lord would provide.' Well, I told him that the Lord didn't provide this county with enough natural rainfall between June and September to wet down the dust, much less water a crop, but he didn't listen to me. Now, I believe in putting my faith in the Lord too, but the Lord expects a man not to take advantage. Campbell's just plain impractical. If he had any sense, he'd plant a vegetable garden he could water with a garden hose and run a couple of head of cattle, so he could at least feed his young'uns instead of waiting for the Lord to provide."

"How many kids has he got now?" asked Buddy. "They're all towheads and all boys and pretty much look alike except for size, so I can't keep track."

"He has five boys," said Elizabeth, wondering how David Campbell would support his family if he lost the election.

"Well, I guess he knows how to do something right," murmured another rancher, then blushed when he caught Elizabeth looking at him. Sex wasn't a suitable topic for conversation when a lady was present.

Elizabeth took it as a cue to leave. "If you boys will excuse me, I have to run. You taxpayers don't pay me to lallygag over coffee till noon. Buddy, figure up my ticket."

There was a scraping of chairs on the linoleum floor as the men stood when she did. None of them were planning to leave just yet, but they got up anyway. A man didn't sit on his backside while a lady stood, any more than he wore his hat at the table. It was a sign of respect left over from when ladies on the frontier were scarcer than hen's teeth.

"You feel like you got your feet wet yet, Elizabeth?" asked Buddy as he rang up her bill on the old cash register his granddaddy bought new in 1923. Like most of Highwater and Bonham County, Buddy believed in the ranching motto "If it ain't broke, don't fix it."

"I haven't run across anything I can't handle yet. If I do, I'll just look it up in my copy of the *Texas Code of Criminal Procedure*. Don't worry, Buddy, the office is in good hands," said Elizabeth, depositing a quarter in the jar Buddy kept next to the cash register for charitable donations for folks down on their luck.

"I never thought it wasn't, Elizabeth. That's why we all voted for you. It just takes a little getting used to, is all, having a woman justice of the peace. It don't seem natural treating you like a man."

"It isn't natural. I'm not a man; I'm a woman, and that's just as good." She slipped on her fleece-lined coat and walked out the door, figuring her remark would give the men something to talk about besides David Campbell's virility.

Elizabeth took a deep breath of the cold February air and turned her collar up. There was still snow on the ground from the last blizzard, and the wind was blowing straight out of the north at a good enough clip to freeze any skin a body might foolishly expose. Like anybody else who lived on the high plains of the Texas Panhandle and ranched for a living, Elizabeth had suffered her share of frostbite. Much as it seemed like laziness to drive her pickup the short block to the courthouse instead of walking, she would do it anyway. She didn't need the exercise, since she got enough of that working cattle with just her son to help her, and she didn't need the frostbite, either.

She climbed the stairs to her second-floor office in the courthouse and unlocked the door. Like many counties in the Panhandle at the turn of the century, Bonham County built a three-story courthouse worthy of its coming prosperity. The building had marble floors, mahogany paneling, brass doorknobs and hinges, molded twelve-foot ceilings, and a gigantic crystal chandelier in the foyer that Jim Hayworth said any first-class whorehouse would be glad to buy anytime the county wanted to sell. The Great Depression arrived in the place of prosperity, and the courthouse fell into a decline, which subsequent decades of dwindling tax revenues failed to halt. The floor was chipped, the paneling cracked, the brass unpolished, the high ceilings made the rooms impossible to heat, the crystal chandelier hadn't worked since 1972, when mice chewed through the wiring, and Elizabeth's was the only occupied office on the entire second floor. Jim Hayworth called the courthouse a monument to failed dreams. Elizabeth called it a reminder not to count your chickens before they hatched.

Her budget didn't run to a secretary, so Elizabeth scooped her mail off the floor where Highwater's one postman always left it when her door was locked and dumped it in the wastebasket. She didn't need to read the circulars from Austin detailing the latest idiocies of the Texas legislature. She heard all about it every morning down at Buddy's.

She picked up her file of county insurance papers. The job had to be done, and she might as well get on it, especially since she hadn't exactly been overwhelmed with official justice-of-the-peace business and had plenty of time. Besides, it gave her an excuse to go up to the sheriff's office on the third floor. Everybody in Highwater knew she and Jim Hayworth were keeping company, but Elizabeth believed that they ought to keep their relationship professional during business hours. No hanky-panky on county time. What they did when the working day was over was nobody's business but their own, which was probably the same thing as saying that Highwater knew every time Jim came to her place for supper and stayed for breakfast, and had agreed such goings-on were private. There were two kinds of secrets in Highwater: those that everybody knew and talked about, and those that everybody knew but didn't mention in idle conversation. David Campbell's gambling was in the first category, and she and Jim were in the second. The difference was that Campbell could hurt Highwater, and she and Jim weren't hurting anybody but themselves. The town didn't care if they went to hell in a handbasket for fornication as long as they didn't take Highwater down with them.

Elizabeth walked into the Bonham County Sheriff's Department's luxurious quarters—luxurious as far as size went: a fourteen-cell jail, a giant squad room furnished with four desks and the dispatcher's station, and Jim's private office, which had its own bathroom. Otherwise the sheriff's department suffered from the same neglect as the rest of the courthouse, except that Jim polished the brass doorknobs and hinges once a month.

"Elizabeth, come in and shut the door," said Jim, rising to his feet and coming around his desk. "Tell me what lesson the members of Highwater's ad hoc government taught you today."

Elizabeth closed the door and sat down in one of the sturdy oak chairs in front of his desk. "How did you know Buddy was holding class for me?"

Jim Hayworth grinned, the skin crinkling up around his eyes more than it used to. He was pushing fifty if not already there, but other than the lines around his eyes, a little gray in his hair, and a certain slackness about the jaw, he didn't look it. His body was still lean, and if the hair on his chest and around his privates was grizzled, Elizabeth figured she was the only one who knew it. Or maybe not. Jim had been a widower for ten years, so there must have been a woman or two in that time, but he never mentioned it and she wasn't about to ask. Sleeping with a man didn't give a woman the right to know all his secrets any more than it gave him a right to know hers. They both were old enough to know that digging up the past was likely to cause trouble in the present. Let the dead bury the dead was good advice, and it went for the past too.

"How did I know?" asked Jim, repeating her question. "Because I know Highwater, and I know that the men in town figure they better teach you the ropes instead of letting you learn on your own. You're as independent as a hog on ice, Elizabeth, and they don't want you falling through."

"Because I'm a woman?"

Jim rubbed his chin and gazed at her thoughtfully. "Partly, I guess," he admitted, "but mostly because you're new to county government, and they don't want you upsetting the applecart, so don't go thinking too hard that your being a woman has all that much to do with it. After all, they voted for you—except for D. B. I think he argued that the county didn't need a justice of the peace and that we ought to let the office stay vacant."

"That figures," said Elizabeth. "He was the one on the county commissioner's court who pushed everybody else into agreeing that I should take care of this insurance business. I guess he wanted to make sure I had something to do to earn my salary—such as it is."

"D. B.'s an old man, Elizabeth, and guess he still thinks a woman's place isn't in the courthouse. He likes you well enough, and he'll come around in time, but a man his age is set in his ways. It takes a while to shift him. Now let me see my insurance papers. I figure to up my coverage."

Elizabeth opened her file and found Jim's policy. "You've already got a hundred thousand. At your age, the premiums for increasing your coverage would take a big chunk out of your salary."

"It's not like I need that salary to live on, Elizabeth. I've got money coming in from the ranch, but I just want to know that my two boys will have some ready cash when I die. After seeing what a mess you found yourself in when Walt died because you didn't have ready money to pay inheritance taxes, I did some hard thinking. I don't want my boys to have to lease out most of the ranch for cash to pay the IRS like you did. A big life insurance policy can make life easier for your heirs, and sometimes it can save them from poverty. Being too poor can make a man desperate, and you never know what a desperate man might do."

"He might even run for justice of the peace, like I did," said Elizabeth bitterly.

Jim reached out and caught her hands. "You sorry I talked you into running for the job, Elizabeth?"

She squeezed his hands and stood up. "No, I'm not. At least now I can buy beans until I finish paying off the IRS."

"Everybody admires your spunk. You didn't lay down and give up when you hit a hard patch after Walt died. You sold what cattle you had to, leased out what land you had to, and hung on. I don't know any man who could do any better."

"I don't, either, Jim, and that's the point. I don't need charity, and I'm afraid that's what D. B. and maybe even Buddy think my holding this job is. There aren't any secrets in Highwater, and everyone knew you were worried about your best friend's widow keeping her head above water. You carry a lot of weight in this county, maybe more than anybody, and you wanted me to have this job. That's the reason I didn't have an opponent."

"Damn it, Elizabeth, I didn't have anything to do with it. You didn't have an opponent because the salary is so bad no man will run."

"It never stopped men from running before."

Jim threw up his hands. "All right, maybe my support did influence a few people, but you know Highwater. The folks around here would starve to death before they'd let someone tell them when to eat. If they hadn't wanted you, they wouldn't have voted for you. And how come you're on such a tear about it this morning? Is it because of this insurance business?"

Elizabeth considered denying it, but she didn't make a practice of lying. "I reckon so. Earl in the county clerk's office always did it before, and the only reason he's not doing it now is because the commissioners think that since I'm a charity case, I might as well do all these piddling jobs nobody else wants. Well, I'll do it just to show I don't shirk from responsibility, but I'm serving notice here and now that Highwater elected me to be justice of the peace whether they meant to or not, and that's just what I'm going to be. They'll get their money's worth out of me, but it'll be for the job I was elected to."

"Why are you jumping on me, Elizabeth? I'm on your side."

"Because I know Highwater as well as you do, and I know that when somebody has a problem, they come to you. Buddy Whitney as much as told me to do the same thing. That was this morning's civics lesson."

Jim laughed. "And I bet that didn't set well with you."

"No, it didn't, now that I think about it."

"You know what you're doing, Elizabeth? You're staking out your claim and telling me not to jump it. Well, I won't. Anytime a man comes to me when he ought to be talking to you, I'll shoo him downstairs to your office. Will that suit you?"

She smiled. "I reckon it will. Now sign that payroll deduction slip for your insurance, and I'll be on my way."

Jim signed and handed her the form. "You're a formidable woman, Elizabeth. I wonder if the voters know they've got a bull by the tail instead of a mama cow."

Elizabeth tucked Jim's slip back in her file and started for the door. "I've never trusted mama cows very far. They look so sweet-natured right up to the time they gore you." Jim's laughter followed her all the way downstairs.

She hesitated at the second-floor landing. She hated to admit it, but sometimes the second floor spooked her, especially when the wind blew and rattled the ill-fitting windows in all the locked and empty rooms. Though Elizabeth didn't consider herself a superstitious woman, there were times when the courthouse felt haunted. But maybe that was fitting. With all the boarded-up buildings along Main Street, Highwater looked a lot like a ghost town.

She squared her shoulders and walked down the hall

to her office, trying to ignore the empty echo of her own footsteps.

Elizabeth was eating a roast beef sandwich at her desk when Butch Jones stuck his head inside her door.

"Elizabeth, if you got a minute, I need to visit with you."

Butch Jones owned Highwater Grocery, on the opposite end of Main Street from Buddy's Café, and everything about him was long and thin: his face, his nose, his legs and arms, hands and feet, even his hair, which curled over his collar between seasonal visits to the barbershop.

"Come in, Butch. I was just having a working lunch and reading my correspondence." Butch looked at her uncluttered desk, and Elizabeth remembered tossing her mail in the wastebasket. She flushed and continued. "But I just finished, so I've got a few minutes to talk." Or a few hours or days or a complete term of office, if folks didn't stop treating her like a charity case.

Butch scratched his head and seemed to have trouble finding words. Elizabeth didn't much care for the ones he finally found. "I went to the sheriff, since I figured he could handle this without hurting a man's pride, but Jim said I was to talk to you. But I don't know. Doesn't seem like the kind of thing you ought to be doing, you being a woman and all. Men sometimes don't take to women dressing them down."

"Then I reckon they'll have to get used to it, won't they, Butch?" asked Elizabeth through gritted teeth. "I am the justice of the peace despite being a woman, so why don't you tell what the problem is."

"Well, since Jim said he can't legally do nothing without your signing some kind of a paper, I guess I'll have to tell you. It's about David Campbell's bill. It's over three hundred dollars, and he keeps putting me off when I ask him about it. That's a lot of money for me to carry on my books, Elizabeth, and most of it is for meat. He don't run no cows on that place of his, so he's got to buy beef across the counter instead of slaughtering his own."

Elizabeth nodded. Almost everyone in Highwater owned cattle and ate their own beef, which Butch cut up for a few cents a pound and stored in his meat locker. What little meat Highwater Grocery sold over the counter Butch bought from local ranchers, and he paid market price for it in cash. Like every other small businessman in Highwater, and there wasn't any other kind, he couldn't afford to let his credit customers run up a big bill or he couldn't pay his own. Like jobs, ready money was scarce in Highwater, and you kept your eye on the bottom line or you went bankrupt.

"I don't want to cut off his credit 'cause he's got all them kids to feed, but I got kids of my own, Elizabeth, and I ain't going to let them go without just because David Campbell ain't got the sense God gave a goose and throws good money after bad. First it was them lottery tickets, then it was pinto beans. Pinto beans, for God's sake! He didn't have a buyer for them even if he'd managed to make a crop. He makes a good salary from the county if he'd just budget it right, but he just keeps saying the Lord will provide. Somebody needs to hit him between the eyes with a fence post to get his attention. He ain't a stupid man, but he sure is dumb about some things."

Elizabeth cleared her throat. She felt sorry for Mary Lou Campbell and her boys, but Butch was in the right. David Campbell needed to be jerked up short. Maybe she could protect Mary Lou and straighten out David at the same time.

"Butch, I'll tell you what let's do. You sign a petition, and I'll take it out to the Campbells' and talk to David. I have to talk to him anyway about his county life insurance policy."

Butch frowned. "Ain't the sheriff supposed to serve the papers on him? That's what Jim told me anyhow."

Elizabeth gritted her teeth again. "If I file the petition, then yes, the sheriff will have to serve a citation, but if I go out there and tell David that I'll hold off filing it if he will agree to pay you so much a month, then maybe we can settle this thing without my having to convene a court and grant you a judgment."

"What do you mean by convene a court? You ain't a judge, Elizabeth."

She took a deep breath. "Yes, I am. I'm the magistrate of what we call small-claims court, and I can grant judgments for any amount of money up to twenty-five hundred dollars. I can also levy fines for all kinds of things."

"Lordy, I didn't know that. When old man Hays was the JP, he just let the sheriff handle things. I bet folks never expected they'd get a judge when they elected you."

"Well, they got one, so I guess they can lump it until next election. So what do you want to do, Butch? You want me to talk to David, or you want me to file the petition and let the sheriff serve a citation?"

"Maybe I ought to sign it and you let the sheriff talk to David before you file it."

"I don't need the sheriff to do my job for me! Now, what's your decision? My way, or do we go to court?"

Butch scratched his chin, then the back of his neck, while he thought. Elizabeth waited. Nobody in Highwater jumped to a decision until they looked at it from all angles, a throwback to the Old West, when a man was expected to keep his word once he gave it.

"I guess we'll try it your way first, Elizabeth," Butch finally said. "But I still think the sheriff—" He stopped and gulped when Elizabeth glared at him and shoved a form across the desk.

"Fill that out and sign it, Butch, and I'll take it from there."

Butch Jones did as she told him, but she noticed a dazed look on his face when he left her office. She watched from her window as he staggered out of the courthouse and crossed the street to the XIT Bar. She figured he needed to down a two-ounce treatment for shock before he went back to work. He might even down a couple of treatments. Elizabeth grinned as she ran downstairs and out to her pickup. Nobody could claim she wasn't doing her share toward helping the economy. If Butch

Jones was any indication, the XIT Bar was in for a land-office business over the next few months, or however long it took for Highwater to realize that a woman had just made a place for herself in county government.

Elizabeth turned left by the vacant lot where the hotel once stood. There was always talk about turning the lot into a park, but nothing ever came of it, and Elizabeth doubted that anything ever would. To put in grass and trees and swings and a merry-go-round would be finally to bury Highwater's dream that what was could be again. There was nothing wrong with that, she supposed. Towns struggling to survive needed dreams—even foolish ones.

Men needed dreams too, but David Campbell's pinto bean fields more likely symbolized a nightmare. Never had Elizabeth seen a more dismal sight than the forty-acre wound in the flat prairie that was David Campbell's dream. The cowboys in the waning days of the big Panhandle ranches used to say that the best side was already up when they watched the early farmers' attempts to plow the prairie. In Elizabeth's opinion the cowboys were right. This flat, arid land was cow country, and nothing would ever change her mind.

Elizabeth parked in front of the Campbell place, a weathered frame house that had once been the home of a small rancher who had gone belly-up during the Depression and moved to California, where rumor said he didn't have much better luck.

Elizabeth knocked on the screen door and waited. She dreaded what was to come. At least Highwater merchants had ridden out the bad times following her husband's death, trusting her to pay when she could and not to take advantage of their generosity. They did not trust David Campbell, and she had to tell him so.

Mary Lou Campbell opened the door carrying the youngest of her five children, a two-year-old whose name Elizabeth couldn't remember except that it began with an S, as did the names of the other four. "Elizabeth! What are you doing out here? Did you need to talk to David?

He was feeling under the weather and didn't go to work today."

She held open the door, and Elizabeth stepped into the living room. Like most old ranch houses in the county, this one had no halls and all the rooms opened off one another. It wasn't all that bad, except that a person might have to walk through several bedrooms to reach his own. It wasn't a floor plan that afforded a lot of privacy, although that hadn't seemed to slow up the Campbells' fruitfulness. Their five boys were what folks in Highwater called stair steps, meaning each one was only minimally older than the next. In fact, the two-year-old represented the longest time that Elizabeth could remember Mary Lou not being pregnant.

David Campbell pushed himself out of a recliner when Elizabeth walked in. "Elizabeth! I never expected to see you out here. Did the county commissioners send you out to see how I was?"

David Campbell had what a novelist might have described as an "open countenance," which Elizabeth took to mean a guileless and innocent look. Curly blond hair, bright blue eyes, and a chubby round face fostered that impression. The women in town said all he needed to look like an angel was a white choir robe and wings. Elizabeth thought he looked more like a spoiled cherub.

"Why should the commissioners send me, David?"

He didn't lose his guileless look, but he flushed. "I've missed a few days of work. My back's gone out on me."

Elizabeth figured his back would feel a lot better if he didn't spend so much time sitting on the end of it. Probably stiffened up from lack of exercise. "I don't keep track of sick leave, David, but I do need to talk to you and Mary Lou. Maybe we could go in the dining room and sit down? You might not want the youngsters listening." She nodded her head toward the floor in front of the television set, where the four older Campbell offspring lay sprawled together like a litter of puppies.

David ran his hand through his curls and managed to look confused. "Well, yes, if you think so, Elizabeth, but

I don't see why Mary Lou is concerned. She has nothing to do with the treasurer's office."

Elizabeth led the way to the dining room and sat down at a long table covered with oilcloth. "This has to do with your personal business, David, and Mary Lou will be held responsible right along with you. Butch Jones signed a petition against you for not paying your bill at Highwater Grocery." She saw Mary Lou turn pale and close her eyes. "I haven't filed it yet because I wanted to talk to you first, see if I could help you work out a payment plan to Butch."

"I don't see why he's on his high horse," said David. Now the cherub was pouting, and Elizabeth felt tempted to slap him.

"David, you haven't paid anything on your bill for three months. He's cutting off your credit."

"He can't do that!"

"He can and he has," said Elizabeth.

"David, what are we going to do?" asked Mary Lou. Elizabeth noticed she looked ill.

"David, if you could pay five dollars a week, and maybe I could help Mary Lou find a job in Highwater. I heard the school is looking for a teacher's aide. It would just be until the end of the semester, but the money would catch you up. Mary Lou, your mama could watch the boys, couldn't she?" Elizabeth looked toward the younger woman, but Mary Lou was staring at David, a hopeless expression in her eyes.

David shook his head. "Mary Lou couldn't possibly take a job. My place is to provide for my family, and hers is to care for the children—"

"Well, you're doing a damn poor job as provider, David!" Elizabeth interrupted. "So Mary Lou just might have to fill in for a while."

David straightened his shoulders. "Besides, Mary Lou is expecting."

"My God!" exclaimed Elizabeth.

"So just tell Butch that I'll do what I can when I can, but I can't promise anything this month. Now, when I win reelection next year, I expect the commissioners will vote me a small raise, and I'll take care of all my overdue bills."

Elizabeth stood up and leaned over the table to glare at him. "David, you won't *be* reelected. Highwater is suspicious after that business with the lottery. The men at Buddy's have already decided not to vote for you, and that means you're as good as out."

Mary Lou grabbed her husband's arm. "David, you have to do something! Apologize to the commissioners, talk to Butch Jones, do something! I won't be able to feed my kids."

He patted her arm, but Elizabeth noticed his face was beet red. "Settle down, Mary Lou. The Lord will provide."

Elizabeth rose, kicking over her chair. She had to get out before she murdered David Campbell where he sat. "I'll send the sheriff out to serve the papers, David—and, Mary Lou, I'm sorry."

She ran out of the house and drove off, cursing David Campbell for half the three miles back to Highwater. That's when she remembered she had forgotten to have him sign his payroll deduction slip for life insurance. She made a U-turn and drove back to the old frame house, still cursing.

She hammered on the door and waited, then hammered again. "I know you're in there, David. Open the door!"

But it was Mary Lou who opened it. "He won't talk to you." The younger woman's voice sounded flat, like all the life and emotion had leaked out.

"That's makes two of us, because I don't want to talk to him, either. Just give him this slip to sign."

"What's it about?"

"His county life insurance policy. It's time to increase or decrease coverage."

"How much does he have now?"

Elizabeth checked the form. "The minimum—ten thousand. I don't imagine he wants any more, because he can't afford the higher premiums to be deducted from his salary."

Mary Lou took the slip and looked at it. Finally, she raised her head. "Better let me take the policy too. He'll want to see it."

Elizabeth passed her the policy, with a schedule of premiums attached, then leaned against the side of the house and waited. Usually she loved being outdoors, even when the wind was chilly and the ground covered with melting snow, but not today. Not when she could see the snow turning dirty brown where it melted over David Campbell's field, and not when she stood on the porch of an old frame house not much better than a shanty, and both were owned by a man who didn't keep his word and had no pride. In Highwater, there were no greater sins.

The door opened, and Mary Lou stepped outside. Her skin looked bloodless in the bright sunlight, and her eyes were sunken. Elizabeth realized with a start that Mary Lou looked like the women in Depression-era photographs of caravans of Okies on their way to California: hopeless, old before their time, yet drawing strength to go on from a source so deep inside that maybe even they didn't know where it came from. They were strong, those women. They persevered. Maybe Mary Lou would too.

"Here's your form, Elizabeth. He signed it."

Elizabeth glanced at it, then gasped. "Good Lord, he's increased his coverage to one hundred thousand dollars!"

Mary Lou wrapped her arms around herself. "It's what he wants to do. No point in talking to him. He won't listen. There's no changing him, either. He really believes that dreams come true and that everything will turn out okay just because he says it will. I know it won't, but I can't convince him."

"Mary Lou, he can't support you and the kids on what the county pays him now. When these premiums come out of his paycheck, you won't be able to keep body and soul together."

"He says the Lord will provide."

"He's crazier than a loco steer too," snapped Elizabeth.

"Maybe you better think about moving into Highwater and staying with your mama."

Mary Lou looked across the yard toward David's field. "Mama lives on Social Security. She can't help me."

Elizabeth started to say something else but stopped herself. She couldn't help Mary Lou until Mary Lou was ready to help herself. Silently, she walked back to her pickup and drove to the courthouse, where she filed Butch's petition and issued a citation.

When she handed the citation to Jim, he looked at it and sighed. "I reckon David wouldn't listen."

"How did you know I talked to him?"

"I saw you drive off and figured that's where you went. You did the right thing, Elizabeth. In a county this small, it's better to try to work things out than to follow the letter of the law. That's what I always do."

"Maybe you should have talked to him," said Elizabeth. "Maybe Butch was right. Maybe he'd take a dressing-down from you better than from a woman."

Jim cocked an eyebrow. "Butch said that? Well, I disagree. Men don't like other men criticizing them. It hurts their pride. But men are used to women nagging them to change their ways, starting with when their mamas tried to teach them right from wrong. They may buck like a wild mustang, but eventually a woman can break most men to the saddle."

Elizabeth shook her head. "Not this man. He wouldn't listen to me and he wouldn't listen to Mary Lou. And she's expecting again, Jim! What are they going to do? What's *she* going to do?"

Jim's face took on a stern expression. "If I were her, I'd make David sleep in the damn barn until he got himself fixed."

"What are we going to do about those kids, Jim?"

He hugged her. "Don't you worry about those kids. Highwater won't let youngsters go hungry just because their daddy's a no-account. I expect a side of beef and sacks of flour and sugar will show up on their front porch often enough to stave off starvation, and God almighty, Elizabeth, the man's not destitute. He makes enough to keep his family if he'll stop throwing away his money on foolishness."

"He upped his county life insurance to a hundred thousand dollars."

Jim let go of Elizabeth and stepped back, his face beginning to turn red. "That's damn foolishness if I ever heard it! Barring any accidents, he'll live long enough to see his kids grown, and that's what insurance is for, to provide for your family if you die before your time. Besides, he's going to lose the next election anyway and his county policy along with it, so why in the hell pay those premiums in the meantime? He needs to use the money to clean up his debts, so he'll at least start with a clean slate when he has to start looking for a new line of work."

Elizabeth sank down in a chair in front of Jim's desk. "I never counted on this kind of business when I ran for this office."

Jim knelt down by her chair and put his arm around her shoulders. "If you can hang in there, Elizabeth, it won't get any worse than this."

She wanted to believe him, but if life had taught her anything, it was that no matter how bad a fix a woman found herself in, it could always get worse and generally did.

She didn't sleep easy for the next two weeks, and when the phone rang near dawn of a cold, blustery day in late February, Elizabeth realized that she'd been expecting Jim's call. David Campbell's bad luck had finally run out.

Elizabeth drove up to the Campbells' place and parked next to Jim's patrol car. There was one other sheriff's department car parked in front of the barn, and a considerable number of pickups belonging to auxiliary deputies. Jim had only four deputies and a dispatcher, so he called in volunteers from Highwater when he felt he needed them. Generally they directed traffic if there was a wreck, or searched for lost children who wandered too far from home on some of the largest ranches and couldn't find their way back. When a place might have thousands of acres, it took a while for youngsters to learn their way around, especially when the land was mostly flat and one acre could look pretty much like another.

But this wasn't a wreck and it wasn't a search party, and Elizabeth figured all those volunteers were good for was to get in her way.

The first one to try was D. B. DeBord, who stepped out of the barn to meet her. "I don't know why Jim called you, Elizabeth. You could order an autopsy without bothering to come out here. That's the way old man Hays handled it."

Elizabeth circled around D.B. "Old man Hays was senile the last four years he was in office and not much better the first thirty. Now stay out of my way, D.B., and don't tell me my business. I have to look at the body, order an autopsy, and hold an informal inquest to determine cause of death."

She pushed through the men crowded in the barn's doorway. "You men get out of here. Go sit in your pickups until I tell you different."

Buddy caught her arm. "Now, Elizabeth, don't get all het up. I know this is the first dead body you'll have to look at as justice of the peace and you're probably a mite upset, but we're auxiliary deputies. You can't just run us out like we were ordinary civilians."

"The hell I can't, and furthermore, I can fine you if you disobey my order. This is a crime scene, and it belongs to me until I say different, and I don't want you men stomping all over evidence in your size-twelve boots and tracking in material that's unrelated to the scene."

Buddy swallowed several times. Elizabeth wasn't sure if he was more shocked by her cussing in front of him or her giving him orders. "Sheriff," he finally managed to say. "Sheriff, I think Elizabeth is a little confused about who's in charge here."

Jim walked over. His face looked washed out and somber. "Out, Buddy, and the rest of you men too.

According to the law, Elizabeth's in charge here, and what she says goes."

"I never heard of no such thing," grumbled Buddy.

"You have now," said Jim, pulling Buddy out of Elizabeth's way. "Now get, and do it fast. You know yourself that Elizabeth's always short of patience when she's in the right and some man doesn't know any better than to argue with her."

There was more grumbling, but Elizabeth didn't pay any attention. She was too busy holding down her nausea and keeping all expression from her face. If she threw up or looked too shocked and horrified, it would be the same thing as admitting she couldn't handle the job. She had no intention of admitting any such thing, even if she had doubts herself.

She walked around David Campbell's body, studying the ground, but the dirt was packed hard as concrete and revealed nothing that she could see. Finally, she knelt down by what was left of the Bonham County treasurer. Several twenty-foot lengths of eight-inch aluminum irrigation pipe lay crisscrossed over his body, while others were scattered around the floor, along with two shorter lengths of six feet or so. Aluminum irrigation pipe wasn't as heavy as steel gauge, but it wasn't light, either. Anyone who thought different had only to look at David Campbell's body.

"You taken pictures yet?" she asked Jim.

He nodded. "Three rolls using a flash, since there's just the three lightbulbs strung the whole of the barn."

"Then help me shift this pipe off him."

Jim motioned to his chief deputy, Larry Coburn, a young man Elizabeth had never liked for his superior ways and fancy clothes, and the two carefully lifted off the pipe and laid it aside.

"I don't see why she needs to look at him, Sheriff. He's dead. It was an accident. And I don't want any autopsy, either."

A figure in a ragged coat thrown over a faded chenille bathrobe stepped out of the gloom of one of the barn's corners.

"Mary Lou!" exclaimed Elizabeth. "You shouldn't be out here. Larry, take her in the house."

"I'm not going in the house. I want to know what you're planning to do to David."

"I have to determine the cause and manner of death, Mary Lou," said Elizabeth as calmly as she could. "I investigate the circumstances, like I'm doing now, then order an autopsy. The two together, my investigation and the autopsy, help me determine if a suspicious death is a homicide, accident, suicide, or a result of natural causes."

"David wouldn't commit suicide," said Mary Lou Campbell, stepping closer to her husband's body. "It's plain as day that it was an accident. See, David's still got the end of the rope in his hand. He was trying to lower that irrigation pipe from the hayloft when it got away from him."

Elizabeth looked up at the loft. David Campbell had tied each end of the stack of pipe with a length of rope to keep it from rolling off the edge of the loft. One loop of rope dangled half over the edge of the loft. The other length of rope was loosely clutched in his hand.

"What was he doing checking irrigation pipe this time of year, Mary Lou?"

The young woman glanced at her dead husband's mutilated features and shivered. Her eyes looked as though she had visited hell and carried some of it back with her. "He got it into his head to plant some more pinto beans this spring, only this time he was going to dig the irrigation well a little deeper so we wouldn't run out of water like last year. He came out to the barn to check the pipe he had on hand, to see if he needed to order more. I went along, arguing that it was foolishness to be worrying about pipe right then, to wait until morning, but he didn't listen. He never listened, never heard anybody's voice but his own, and he heard that often enough. Some nights he even talked in his sleep until I'd kick him and he'd roll over and be quiet."

She stopped and gazed at her husband again, then looked up at Elizabeth. "Know how I knew for sure he was dead and not just hurt real bad? When I sat by him for ten minutes and he didn't talk."

"So you were arguing with David, and then what happened?" asked Elizabeth.

"I went back to the house and sent the older boys to bed, then straightened up the place some, made myself a mug of hot chocolate, and went on to bed. I was tired and had the shakes."

"What time was that, Mary Lou?"

"About nine-thirty or a little after."

"Did you hear anything from the barn?" asked Elizabeth.

Mary Lou bit her lip and finally shook her head. "I wouldn't have thought much about it if I had. You expect pipe to make noise when you're messing with it. Anyhow, I woke up about five-thirty and needed to go to the bathroom. You know how it is when you're expecting, Elizabeth, always having to answer a call of nature."

"Yes, I remember," said Elizabeth, nodding as she studied Mary Lou's ravaged face and the swelling belly that was so much more visible this morning in the too tight bathrobe than it had been two weeks before. Pregnancy made women kin, no matter how different they might be, and was the one experience they couldn't lie about to one another. She wished she had let Jim question Mary Lou, but she supposed it wouldn't make any difference in the long run.

Elizabeth heard Mary Lou's voice continue. "David wasn't in bed, so I came back out to the barn, then I called the sheriff. Then I waited, sitting over there on that old bench. I just waited."

"Thank you, Mary Lou," said Elizabeth. She considered herself a hard woman in a lot of ways, but she wasn't hard enough to look at that poor young woman without crying, and she couldn't let herself do that. Not now. Maybe next week. In the meanwhile, she had given her word to Highwater to perform her duties as best she could, and Elizabeth Walker didn't go back on her word.

She leaned over to study David Campbell's face. His

skull was crushed in several different places, but she suspected the fatal blow was the one that had caved in the bridge of his nose and ruptured both his eyes. She examined the corpse's mangled knuckles and turned one hand over, shuddering at the feel of his cold flesh. His palms were dirty but not bruised. She ran her fingers over the top of David's skull, swallowing back bile as she did so. Finally, she rose and wiped her hands on her Levi's, then walked outside into air that didn't smell of dust and death, motioning Jim to follow her.

"Even David Campbell's not fool enough to stand under a stack of pipe he's about to lower," Elizabeth said quietly.

"Then you're thinking it's not an accident, Elizabeth?" asked Jim. When she shook her head, he continued: "Maybe the autopsy will prove you wrong."

"David doesn't have any bruises on his palms, Jim, just the tops of his hands. I'm real new at this, but I've been doing a lot of reading since my election, and I've learned that a person always throws his hands out to defend himself, so he'll have defensive cuts on his palms if somebody's coming at him with a knife. It seems to me the same thing would apply if a man was about to be hit with a stack of heavy pipe. He'd throw his hands up to stop it. And another thing, David wasn't hit on top of the head by any pipe, just on the face. It's like he laid down and pulled that rope and let the pipe fall on him. I don't think the autopsy's going to prove anything different, once the pathologist knows the circumstances. And then there's the insurance."

"Insurance company will be all over this case like flies on a cow patty. They'll try their damnedest to prove it's suicide."

Elizabeth nodded. "I imagine they will. If I was in their shoes, I wouldn't want to pay out a hundred thousand dollars, either."

"Mary Lou will end up with no husband, no money, and five kids with another one on the way."

"If you've got an opinion, Jim, spit it out."

"It's your call, Elizabeth," said Jim, with a savage note in his voice that Elizabeth had never heard before. She realized suddenly that he knew the same as she did what happened, but she doubted if his conclusion rested on the same evidence hers did.

She heard a door slam and, looking toward the house, saw the five little Campbell boys standing on the front porch, the oldest holding the youngest. D. B. DeBord and Buddy climbed out of their pickup and hurried toward the house. She heard Buddy promising the children doughnuts and felt a lump rising in her throat. Doughnuts instead of a daddy. Swallowing, she walked back into the barn.

She heard Jim following her but knew he wouldn't interfere. As he said, it was her call.

Mary Lou was sitting on the old wooden bench again at the far side of the barn. Waiting. Larry Coburn stood at one end of the bench. Watching.

Elizabeth sat down beside Mary Lou. She saw Jim take Larry Coburn's arm and move him away until the two men stood at some distance. Jim didn't know what she was about to say, but he knew instinctively the way the best men always did that this was women's business. In the end it all came to this, two women talking together about a woman's place.

"Mary Lou, it looks to me like it could have been suicide. I think that's what the insurance company will say, and I don't think the autopsy will prove anything one way or another except that David didn't die a natural death."

"David didn't commit suicide," Mary Lou said stubbornly, pulling the ragged old coat more tightly about her.

"If the death's ruled a suicide, then the insurance company won't have to pay benefits."

Mary Lou stared at her for the longest time. "It was an accident," she said weakly in a voice without hope.

"I checked over all the county insurance applications before I sent them in. I noticed your boys listed on the policy as beneficiaries in case you can't collect for some reason."

Mary Lou nodded. "I made David list them."

"Mary Lou, you said you had a mug of hot chocolate when you went to bed at nine-thirty and you woke up at five-thirty to go to the bathroom, and that's when you saw that David hadn't come to bed."

Mary Lou frowned. "That's what happened."

"I've had two boys myself, Mary Lou. The younger one is eighteen, but I still remember what it's like to be pregnant. If I drank anything right before I went to bed, I was up to go to the bathroom. In fact, I never remember sleeping more than three hours at one time without having to get up when I was showing as much as you."

Mary Lou huddled inside her coat. To Elizabeth's eyes she seemed to have shrunk in the last few minutes, but then that's how most people looked when hope was gone. "I don't remember."

Elizabeth took a deep breath and expelled it slowly. "David didn't die of natural causes, and his injuries are all wrong for an accident. That leaves suicide and homicide. Neither you nor the boys can collect the insurance if it's suicide, but the boys still can if you confess to murder."

"It was an accident," repeated Mary Lou in what had become a litany.

"I hope it was, Mary Lou. I'd hate to think that you were so weak as to kill a man over money. I like to think that if it hadn't happened you would have had gumption enough to take your boys and go home to your mama and get a job. But once you killed David, you got to thinking about that insurance and how it would help your boys, and when you said you straightened up around the place, you meant you came back to the barn to try to make murder look like an accident. But you didn't know how. You also said you went to bed with the shakes. I believe you. I'd have the shakes, too, if I'd just killed my husband and had to cover it up. I think you waited until five-thirty to call the sheriff because it took you that long to get hold of yourself. Also, you were afraid to go out to the barn any sooner because you were afraid David might still be alive, and he'd wake up and start talking. I don't know what you would have done if that had happened; gone crazy, maybe."

If Mary Lou had been stone, Elizabeth didn't think she could have been more still. She took another deep breath and continued. "Two wrongs don't make a right, and killing David and trying to defraud the insurance company are both wrong. But sometimes a right can cancel out a wrong, or at least go partway toward making up for it. You killed your boys' daddy, but if they collect on the insurance, at least they'll have something from him, even if it's only money. I suppose lots of folks would say that's a callous way of looking at it, but I've noticed it's always the folks who aren't hard up who look down their noses at people like us. It's real easy to criticize when you know where your next meal is coming from. Survival is the strongest instinct men have, but women are born with a stronger one: protecting their children."

"My boys will hate me," Mary Lou burst out.

Elizabeth nodded. "I suspect they might, but it's a woman's place to care for her children. Nobody ever promised they'd love us for it."

"What will happen to them"—she placed her hands over her belly—"and to the one I'm carrying?"

"I reckon Jim and I can talk to the welfare people and to the judge and get your mama custody. She'll have money to raise them, and we'll have to trust that Highwater and the Lord will provide the rest."

Mary Lou burst out laughing, grabbing her belly and rocking back and forth on the bench. Jim started forward, but Elizabeth motioned him back. This was no time to distract the young woman, no time to tell her what men so often did, that everything would be all right. It wouldn't, and Mary Lou had to face up to it.

Mary Lou's laughter trailed off, and she looked up, tears running down her face. Elizabeth would bet it was the first tears she had shed tonight. They wouldn't be the last.

"That's why I killed him. We were arguing over that damn pipe, and I told him we didn't have the money to be buying any more, and he said the Lord will provide. That's when I picked up one of those short pieces of pipe that were leaning against the wall, and I swung it as hard as I could right at his face. I was aiming for his mouth, because I just couldn't stand to hear any more of his talk, but I missed and hit him across the eyes. He went down like a ton of bricks, and I ran in the house. I was real calm, even felt better than I had in a long time, like I'd gotten rid of my anger. I put the boys to bed and then got to thinking I better see about David. I went back to the barn, and he was still laying right where he fell. And you know, I got mad all over again. Here he was doing nothing, like he always did, and leaving me to get the boys to bed. I walked over to him and gave him a nudge with my foot, but he didn't move. That's when I knew he was gone—that and he wasn't talking. You know what I did then? I stood right there and told him if he hadn't been too lazy to put that short pipe up the loft with the longer pieces, he wouldn't be dead. And it's the truth!"

She stopped and wiped her eyes on the hem of her nightgown before she spoke again. "Then I climbed up in the loft and I jerked off the rope on one end of that stack of pipe and gave the stack a shove. I told David, 'Here's your damn pipe, and I hope you choke on it!' It wasn't until I saw that pipe go bouncing around on his body that I realized what I'd done and started shaking. But I still don't remember it making any noise, so I didn't lie to you about that. I sat down on the edge of the loft and wondered what in the world I was going to do. All I could think of was that I couldn't go to jail and leave my boys. That's when I thought maybe everybody would think it was an accident. I didn't know about the injuries being wrong. I buried that piece of pipe I killed him with in the pinto bean field. I thought that was fitting. Then I went to the house and laid in bed all night, worrying about what was going to happen to all of us, and then I thought about the insurance. I swear that was the first time I thought about the money. And you're right, Elizabeth, I wouldn't kill a man for money. If he'd just listened to me. I told him that pinto bean field would be the ruin of us, and it was."

Elizabeth gathered the young woman into her arms then and rocked her while she cried, then turned her over to Jim and walked outside. The sun had risen and the wind was picking up, blowing hard from the north. She figured there would be snow before evening and by this time tomorrow David Campbell's field would be covered up again. Jim would dig up that pipe before the snow started, but she didn't need to stay around for that. She had done her job, determined the cause of death, and Jim could do his. She didn't think she'd have coffee at Buddy's this morning, either. She figured the town needed a few days to mull over the lesson she'd just taught them: There was a woman in the courthouse, and nothing in Highwater would ever be the same.

POSTAGE DUE

SUSAN DUNLAP

Susan Dunlap has written three different suspense series, all set in California, all filled with the beauty and noise and despair and joy of the place.

Dunlap consciously makes her state a living character in her books: "I believe where people live has a strong influence on how they think, live, react, and who and how they choose to kill."

The Berkeley of this story can be summed up by a sign that appears in one of its scenes: no vexation with liquification.

BERKELEY IS NOT like other towns.

We are proud of that. Other towns are proud of that.

The citizens of Berkeley pride themselves on being on the cutting edge. Historically, their communal sharp teeth have bitten into segregation (the first major city to voluntarily integrate its schools), verbal restraint (the Free Speech Movement, the mother of all protests), viewing restraint (the Tree Ordinance, intended to resolve conflicts between citizens who have trees and their neighbors who *used* to have views), and lack of restraint (the Nudity Ordinance: no rash uncoverings—or, depending on their locations, uncovering rashes). Berkeleyans thrive on controversy. All issues, all institutions, have potential for the Berkeley bite. Over the years it has pleased Berkeleyans to chew lovingly and long on the failings of their city, their state, their nation . . . and their post office.

Perhaps, if the Berkeley postmaster hadn't been on leave, and if the temporary postmaster, John Malvern, had not insisted on making one—and only one—change in the operation of Berkeley's post offices . . . perhaps things would have worked out differently.

Malvern did it quite innocently, he told me later. It just seemed a commonsense move. He was sitting at dinner in the house he had rented in the city of Pleasant Hill, an inch to the right of Berkeley on the map, considerably more than an inch in life (the Pleasant Hill post office is not catercornered from a park formerly named for a Dutch anarchist group), and complained to his wife that he had seen a Berkeley postal customer spill her caffè latte on the post office floor. "Why do you let them bring drinks into the post office?" the wife had asked. "Stores don't allow food and drink."

And so John Malvern had posted NO FOOD OR DRINK notices on the post office doors.

In Berkeley, you don't make bureaucratic decisions without consulting the citizens you've decided for—or against. And you certainly don't separate a Berkeleyan from his latte. But John Malvern didn't realize that. Not then, anyway.

The "situation" began normally enough, at 4:54 A.M. the morning after the NO FOOD OR DRINK signs went up.

"Control? This is Adam 38," the patrol officer said into his radio mike.

"Go ahead, Adam 38."

"I've got a citizen's report of a possible 207 in the main post office."

"Did the reporting party see the possible kidnap victim?"

"RP says she saw a man dragging something that could have been a person inside the post office."

"Did she describe the victim?"

"Negative."

"The responsible?"

"WM, short dark hair, average height, thin, no hat, dark jacket. No descript for the pants."

"Did the RP see a weapon?"

"She thinks so, but she can't be sure. I'm going to do an exterior check."

"Copy, Adam 38. With Adam 31 to cover."

"Adam 31 here. Copy."

"Ten-four."

The wind, thick with the damp of the Pacific Ocean and San Francisco Bay, whistled down the open arcade of the Beaux Arts main post office, strumming off the rough edges of the stucco, humming over the terra-cotta, whipping through the eleven arched bays of the portico. *Sunny* California it was not, not in January. And not at five in the morning.

By the time Adam 38 pulled his patrol car into the 10 Minutes at All Times zone in front of the post office, three other patrol cars had notified Control they were in the area and were heading to the scene. Adam 38 eased out of his car, noting to himself that 5:00 A.M. was about the only time to find a parking spot here, ten minutes or otherwise.

The building was a rectangle, the long side facing him. Cement steps ran the length of the portico. He was almost to them when he spotted the barricade inside the glass door and the sign outside it:

NO VEXATION WITHOUT LIQUIFICATION

Pasted to it was an empty paper cup from Peet's Coffee and Tea. Beside that, in small letters, was written: "I've got a hostage."

The police dispatcher flipped through her private numbers directory, one of the many volumes Control kept for emergency contacts. She dialed the postmaster's home number, listened to the phone ring three times before the answering machine picked up and announced that the supervisor would be gone for ten weeks, consulting in the third world. "Maybe he'll pick up some tips," Control muttered, then dialed the number to which the message referred her: John Malvern's, the acting postmaster.

"An intruder in the main post office?" Malvern said sleepily. "Can't you handle that? You're the police! I've got a big day coming up."

"We thought you'd want to know," Control said, with the exquisite politeness of one whose calls are recorded and can be subpoenaed into court. "There is a strong likelihood of a hostage situation. We'll need keys and a layout of the building for the tac team."

Malvern sighed mightily. "Very well. Let's see, I have to shower and dress and get something to eat and warm up the car."

"This is an emergency, Mr. Malvern."

"Emergencies are for the ill-prepared." He sighed irritably. "Very well, I will be in Berkeley in forty minutes."

Control hadn't called me yet, but at five-thirty I was awake. Awake and freezing. It was freezing in bed, and freezing outside. Freezing is something we don't get much of in Berkeley. Here, it has snowed once in the last quarter century—and then the snow didn't stick. But when the wind blows in off the Pacific, batting the fronds of palm trees, creaking the eucalypts, any warmth generated during the day departs, leaving 120,000 people in ill-insulated dwellings and grumpy moods. No mood was grumpier than mine; no house draftier than the shambling brown shingle where Howard and I lived. Inside here it might have been a few degrees above 32, heated by the intensity of my complaint when the furnace belched its last.

"Look at it like camping," Howard had said.

I recalled why people don't camp in the middle of the winter. We had spent one Christmas in Yosemite, where we came to realize that the ultimate gift would have been a motel room. Now I nudged Howard with the icy lump at the far end of my leg.

"Gerumph?" He turned over, pulling all three blankets and the comforter with him. I followed, trying to press as much of myself against him as possible. But he might have been comfortable enough to sleep. Warm he wasn't. And I was still shaking. I could have gone downstairs and turned on the oven. I could have gone farther—to a motel. But after hours of waking from dreams of ice plants, ice hockey, Iceland, and icebergs, I wanted more than mere warmth. I wanted recompense. Well, revenge. I poked both berglike feet in the small of Howard's back and pulled away the blankets.

It was a petty thing to do. I know this because the Powers That Be punished me. At quarter to six, my beeper went off.

I scrambled out of the cold bed and prepared to race

to the station to find out why they needed the primary
negotiator of the hostage negotiation team.

Howard glanced up at me and went back to sleep.

Sun doesn't rise in California; the fog merely thins and
the dark fades. And when—and if—the sun appears, it's
full blown, like Athena from the head of Zeus. A sort of
Olympian Excedrin Moment.

The sky was still charcoal gray as I wedged my old
Volkswagen bug between two pickups and ran the
remaining block and a half to the station, up the curving
stairs, and into the main meeting room, where the
hostage negotiation team was gathering. If a motel room
could have passed for a gift from heaven, this scene
would have been an anteroom in hell. The tac team guys
in their black duds and half-combed hair looked downright satanic, and we in the negotiating segment of the
team, still waiting for the first burst of caffeine to hit,
could have been mistaken for the newly dead. By the
door stood Inspector Doyle, the team field commander,
who looked like he'd just passed over after a long,
painful, and debilitating illness. But Doyle always looked
like that. The tables were pushed together in the middle
of the room, forming a twelve-foot square covered with
charts, papers, clipboards, coffee cups, and enough
doughnuts to supply every office meeting in the Bay Area.
There were sugars, glazeds, maples, crullers, old-fashioneds,
chocolate old-fashioneds. But not one jelly.

I like all doughnuts; they form the crux of my diet. But
a luscious, gooey jelly is to an ordinary doughnut as a
dinner at Chez Panisse is to one at Chez San Quentin.

Still too sleep-dazed to hide my disappointment, I
groaned.

Before I could speak, Inspector Doyle handed me a
napkin-wrapped mound with a telltale red glob at the
end.

I saluted him with the jelly doughnut. And he, whose
finicky stomach had balked at sugar for the last year,
held up his well-lightened coffee in return. I took a big,

luscious—and careful—bite: with jelly doughnuts, the heedless eater courts disaster. "Thanks. This is high-level thoughtful, particularly for six-fifteen in the morning."

"Just good management practice on my part. You're going to need every bit of sugar you can muster today."

"So," I said, with a new level of awareness, "what've we got?"

"Probable hostage taker holed up in the post office. Don't know how many hostages. Don't know who he is or what he wants."

I nodded.

"We've notified the feds; they'll be here in an hour or so."

"Eager to tell us how to run our operations," I put in.

Diplomatically, Doyle didn't comment. But he had seen enough of his orders overruled, enough credit snatched, enough ill will left for him to deal with from previous joint endeavors over the years, to be even less pleased than I was about the prospect of the feds striding in. "In the meantime," he said, "I've closed off the streets around the PO."

"And the high school?" The high school complex was directly across Milvia Street, though the actual classrooms were at the far end of it.

"Heling," Doyle called. "Get ahold of the principal. Tell her to close the school."

"Right."

I swallowed another bite of the doughnut. "So it looks like I'm going to start negotiating with zip."

"Not quite. There's the note."

"Note?"

"Note, Berkeley style." He pointed to the two-by-three-foot sheet of oak tag.

NO VEXATION WITHOUT LIQUIFICATION
I've got a hostage.

I shook my head. "If I'm on target about this, I'm going to need a dozen jellies to get me through."

He nodded.

"Looks like the handiwork of Willard Wright."

Willard Wright had been a Berkeley fixture when I was still a high school student in New Jersey. By some he was called an activist, by others a pain in the ass. Wright was aptly named; he'd had made it his lifework to see that things were done right. No confrontation, from the Free Speech protests of the sixties to the People's Park demonstrations of the seventies, eighties, and nineties, escaped the watchful eye, pen, mouth, and legal connections of Willard Wright. No business was too well-operated to evade advice from Willard. No public transport was too fast, too safe, too graciously run to avoid his public letters of remonstrance. Rarely did the local newspaper hit the street without a missive from WW. "The Keystone Kops Strike Again" was his favorite opener.

But it wasn't just us Willard chewed up. His taste was catholic. He could see every side—and find fault with them all. When the city and merchants proposed a plan to revitalize the shopping strip of Telegraph Avenue, Willard was first to grumble about the umbrellas proposed for the blocked-off street (potential sails in the sunset, he'd called them), the street people who might take up residence under them, and the beat officers who would spend every windy sunset and a good bit of the taxpayers' money guarding and chasing those umbrellas.

Willard was nothing if not evenhanded. He whined about everyone, and he irritated everyone. He had once complained that the patrol car I was driving was dirty. And worst of all, from the viewpoint of us, his subjects, there was almost always a word of truth in his screed.

He would have been dismissed as a pest, had he not also been the founder and tireless supporter of the Berkeley City Fair, an annual June event that benefited many of the city charities. The fair had garnered him the support of influential political forces in the city and, frankly, made him all the harder to deal with about everything else.

Power and the certainty of rightfulness are an appalling combination.

Willard was a man who prided himself on spotting inefficiency. Settling his gaze on the Berkeley Post Office, he must have felt like the first gold rusher at Sutter's Creek. Gold as far as the eye could see.

"Inspector." Heling handed him a sheet of paper.

Doyle read it and stood, his head rotating very slowly back and forth. "Christ, Smith, the man's a genius." As operations commander, Inspector Doyle had never completed a hostage negotiation situation without a full Wrightian review—or roast—in the local paper.

"Willard, you mean?" I asked.

"Oh, yeah."

"More of a genius than just to choose the post office?"

"Oh, yeah. Sitting in the post office is like drinking cold coffee. Barricading himself in the main post office is lukewarm. But this, Smith, this is hot from the stove." He didn't wait for any words of encouragement. "Seems we already had a call for security at the main post office for ten this morning. Seems the acting postmaster has scheduled a news conference then. He's going to announce this city's implementation of the new Postal Service logo on all the trucks and envelopes and whatever. The seven-million-dollar change of logo."

"If I know Willard Wright, that won't be all the postmaster will be discussing."

"If he gets to speak at all."

"How is the postmaster taking all this?"

"He's not. He hasn't arrived."

"Shouldn't he have been here half an hour ago?"

"Smith," Inspector Doyle said, returning to shaking his head, "this is the post office we're dealing with."

The sky had lightened to a battleship gray; it hung thick and close, the way a battleship must appear to a mackerel. The line of cars slowing at the detour was ten long now as Berkeleyans headed toward Oakland or San

Francisco for jobs that started at eight. Men in watch caps and layers of gray-brown unwashed coats gathered up their blankets and rags from the blue-tiled walls in Provo Park and looked suspiciously at the van Doyle had sent to drive them to one of the churches that provided a hot breakfast.

"Better breakfast than we got," one of the patrol officers grumbled.

"We're not doing it for nutritional enhancement," I said. Doyle's goal was to clear the area. But as I reached the corner across from the post office, I could see that was a losing effort. Half of Berkeley is addicted to police scanners. Nothing we do is a secret. Already a crowd pressed at the barricades. I hated to think how big that crowd would grow once the sun came out. Down here, near restaurants, bus stops, the rapid transit station, and parking lots, it was a gawker's paradise. By the time of the 10:00 A.M. press conference, there wouldn't be room in front of the post office for reporters or camera operators or—at this rate—the postmaster himself. The lure of free publicity would draw every protester in town. If I couldn't get Willard Wright out of the post office quick, we'd have a circus here.

I stepped over the yellow tape, walked into the operations van across the street from the post office, and called Doyle. "Has the postmaster arrived yet?"

"Nope," he said, and hung up.

I looked over at the big building. Willard Wright had been known to complain about public waste of electricity, but that issue wasn't on his mind now. Lights shone from both floors, flowing out between the pillars through the arches, and the decorative grating beneath them. The light was so bright I could see the sculptured medallion at the left end of the portico.

For a moment I stood gathering in my concentration, seeing afresh the pillars and cornices, the ornamental tiles beneath the red tile roof. I raced up here two or three times a week to toss in a letter, wait in line to mail a package; I never stopped to note what a lovely building it was.

"He's in the postmaster's office in the corner, Smith," the guy in the van said as he handed me the phone. I took it outside, where I could see the postmaster's windows. The wind was still icy, but at least it kept the crowd too chilled to make much noise. I dialed the postmaster's number.

Willard picked up on the third ring. He didn't sound breathless, as if he'd run for it; it was more like he was doing other things, and answering a call from the police negotiator was not a pressing need.

"Willard, this is Detective Smith. We have to make arrangements to get you out of there safely."

"You're the primary negotiator, huh?" Of course he would know our lingo.

"Right. It's you and me. So, Willard, who else is in there with you?" Intentionally I said "with," rather than "subjugated," "threatened," "endangered," "under your power." "How many of you are there?"

He laughed. "Is that a metaphysical question?"

"This is serious." I really do hate playing the straight woman. "How many people are inside the post office?"

"Not as many as there'd be in line at the window when it opened." He laughed again. "Not that that limits it much, does it? Could be twenty of us in here, all waiting for one clerk to sell us stamps because the other windows are closed."

I couldn't argue with that. Who could? The lines in post offices in Berkeley were so long that one branch had put couches in the waiting room! And once people got accustomed to them, the postal authorities removed them. I tried another tack. "The best way for you to come out—"

"I'm not coming out."

"Then send out your hostages, and we can start talking."

"My hostage? Can't do that, either."

So—no more than one hostage. It's standard operating procedure for a hostage taker to inflate his numbers, unheard of for him to minimize them. You don't commit a high-profile crime like this and then opt for modesty.

With an unknown perp, I'd have still been skeptical, but Willard Wright wasn't likely to be fuzzy about the number of his hostages. "So, Willard, who is your hostage?"

"Want to know about my hostage, huh? Not just any old hostage: one the citizens of Berkeley would really miss."

"Would," not "will." A good sign. "Let me speak to him."

Willard laughed. "Not so fast. Let's see a little good faith first."

Who was he holding in there? A night janitor already in the post office when he broke in? Did the post office *have* a night janitor? The postmaster could tell me, *if* he ever got here.

Another perp I would have pressed, but with Willard, as much of a pro in adversarial situations as I was, that would be a waste of time and a foolhardy expenditure of what personal credit I had with him. "So what can we do for you, Willard?"

"First clear off the cops and open the street."

I laughed. "Willard, be serious. I can't let civilians wander up to drop their letters in the box. You could have an M-16 in there."

He made a sound somewhere between a snort of laughter and a grunt of disgust. "I'm insulted that you'd think that. Surely you know my reputation better than that. I wouldn't harm the people in the street. It's them I'm protecting."

"Protecting from who?"

"From *whom*."

Shees!

"They'll be thanking me."

"Who . . . *me?*"

"Anyone who's waited for a letter to make its way through the Berkeley Post Office."

"Willard is going to get a lot of sympathy. The post office is not people's most esteemed institution," I said to Inspector Doyle, in the understatement of the day.

"Yeah, Smith. My mother in New York writes to my brother in Marin County and me. Sends the letters on the same day. By the time I'm opening mine, he's already got an answer back to New York. Don't think I don't hear about that. 'Don't understand about Jimmy,' she says. 'He can run an entire police investigation, but he can't answer one letter from his mother. Now, my son Tony, in San Rafael . . .' "

"So, sir, you're willing to clear the street? We can tell him we'll keep the side entrance to the YMCA open. Then use the gym for surveillance."

I expected Inspector Doyle to sound abashed about his uncharacteristic outburst, but he didn't. "Tell you, Smith, if the post office wasn't such a marvelous old building, I'd be tempted to wait Willard out. We'd just seal off the building. Customers would never know the difference. They'd just assume the lines were a little slower than normal."

"Willard, Jill Smith here. I've got the street cleared—my part of the bargain. Yours was to let me speak to your hos—your companion in there."

"Go ahead."

"This is Detective Smith. Give me your name." I could hear breathing on Willard's end of the phone line. I smiled.

No one spoke.

I stopped smiling. "Hello?" I said to the hostage.

No reply.

"Willard! We made a bargain. A fair, just bargain. Surely you of all people will do the right thing."

"And I have. I said I'd let you speak to the hostage. Neither one of us mentioned an answer."

"Don't play semantic games."

"Smith, I am doing what I agreed to. It's you who wants to change the rules because *you* weren't paying attention."

I could have slammed him headfirst in the mailbox—happily. It was, I reminded myself, not an unusual feeling in hostage negotiating, and a distinctly normal one in dealings with Willard Wright. He had, in fact, been the recipient of several 240s (assault) and one 217 (240 with intent to murder), and by the end of the investigation into them I had asked the DA if there was a legal category of justifiable assault.

"In the meantime, I'll make you another deal, Smith. Pay close enough attention now. I'll swap you two for two. You with me?"

I had to swallow before I could be sure my voice wouldn't betray me. It was going to take more than a jelly doughnut to get me through this. "Go ahead."

"I'll give you the identity of the hostage, and I'll tell you what my weaponry is."

"In return for?"

"The postmaster. Give him to me."

"Willard, you're an intelligent man. You know we can't give you a hostage." The idea of letting the postmaster handle this situation had a lot of appeal. *If* the postmaster ever showed up.

"Regulations, huh? Just like the post office."

"Common sense. This is Berkeley. We've got moral, ethical, and political disputes all over town. If we delivered people to settle scores, we wouldn't have a police department, we'd be running a taxi service."

"Touché! Much as I hate to inconvenience you . . . get him down here." He hung up.

The command center moved from the station to the YMCA lobby across the street from the post office and right behind the communications van. I walked in and found myself facing Inspector Doyle and, next to him, a man whose expensive suit was creased at both elbows, whose expensive shirt was open at the collar, leaving his silk tie hanging limp and to one side. His pale skin shone with sweat, clumps of his well-cut and sprayed hair stuck up in unseemly directions, and he clutched a half-crumpled map.

"Get lost, did you, Mr. Malvern?" Inspector Doyle asked with a straight face. "We thought you would take

680 to 80, get off at University Avenue, and be right here."

"You didn't tell me about *980!* I thought I was going to spend the rest of my life lost in Oakland." He glared from Doyle to his map and back.

I looked at Doyle and he at me. Neither of us said a word. Doyle, I knew, was thinking about the circuitous path of those letters from his mother.

"The criminal hung up on *her.*" Malvern glared from me to Inspector Doyle. "I demand you treat this case as a priority. Show him you're serious," he said, wagging a finger at Doyle. "*You* do the negotiating."

Inspector Doyle waited a beat. "When you deliver mail from New York on time, Mr. Malvern, then you can run the police department."

Malvern turned as red as the jelly in my doughnut had been. "Well, I demand to see everything that goes on in these negotiations."

"There's a perfect vantage point right here in the Y, Mr. Malvern," I said, smiling at his pudgy form with the full pleasantness of insincerity. "You can keep an eye on the post office from the fitness center. Willard can see in the window there, so you'll have to pass as one of the center members. All you have to do is climb on an Exercycle and make sure you keep the pedals going."

As Malvern clambered aboard his stationary cycle, Inspector Doyle and I exchanged knowing looks. "Maybe," I said, grinning, "we should hold off till the feds get here and watch them battle it out between Malvern and Willard." But as soon as I said it, I knew that was the last thing I wanted. The feds would no more understand Berkeley than Malvern did. And, I realized, despite his many, many extremely irritating qualities, I didn't want to see Willard Wright become the focus of a federal attack brought on by misunderstanding, the feds' intransigence, or Willard's infuriatingly quixotic behavior. I didn't want to see Willard dead.

I dialed Willard and let the phone ring. No answer. I

switched lines and dialed the main number. No answer. Then I dialed the philatelic office and let that ring. By the time I got to the sixth line and called back the postmaster's number, six phones were ringing in the post office. I might want to save Willard, but he sure wasn't opening up a way for me to do it.

He picked up on the twelfth ring. "You're making me mad."

"Likewise, Willard. Do you want to showboat, or do you want to deal realistically? You let me see and talk to the person with you, and tell me your weaponry in return for . . . ?" I held my breath, wondering what Willard would come up with next. The Postal Service underwriting his beloved City Fair? Malvern giving him keys to all the postal trucks in town? A million dollars in postcard stamps?

"A scone and a caffè latte—a doppio alto low-fat latte."

"Chocolate or cinnamon?" I asked.

If Willard caught my sarcasm, he chose to ignore it. "Chocolate. From Peet's, of course."

"Of course." No situation was too extreme to deny a true Berkeleyan his cherished brew.

"And the scone—a *blueberry corn* scone from the Walnut Square Bakery."

"Peet's isn't open yet. We'll have to get the owner up."

"It's worth it."

"He'll be pleased to hear that," I said, the sarcasm all too apparent. "Now have the person with you answer my questions."

"When I get the latte."

I took a breath. "Willard. You're on federal property. The FBI is on its way. They're not going to waste time with you and your breakfast preferences. You better deal with me while you've got the chance."

"How do I know I'll get the scone and the latte?"

"You've got my word, *if* you cooperate about your companion." God, it was hard not to use the term "hostage."

"Okay, okay. You want the hostage, you're looking at it."

"He's holding . . . the post office . . . hostage?" John
Malvern's expensive jacket was off; his new shirt was
sodden with Exercycle-induced sweat; and his face was
the color of a Christmas stamp. Clearly, it had been many
years since John Malvern had walked a postal route. "If
that building blows—the main post office—replacing all
the records and documentation will be a nightmare."

"And people will lose their mail," I said.

"Yeah. That too." Glancing through the glass doors
toward the post office, he added, "And the stamps, thousands of dollars of stamps. They'll go up in the explosion.
It'd be an accounting disaster!"

"Willard will negotiate."

"I'm the postmaster; I can't bargain with a criminal."
He shot a glance at the counter before leaning a soggily
clad arm on it. "He's bluffing."

"Don't count on it."

"If I give in to one of you Berkeley crazies, I might as
well run the post office for free."

The area around the post office was blocked off. Busy
any time of day with Berkeleyans coming to the library,
the YMCA, the post office, Armstrong College, or the
Déjà Vu metaphysical store, the block—where finding
even a ten-minute parking spot was like discovering a
green curb of gold—was now startling in its emptiness.
Once the sun cut through the fog, the main post office
would shine the golden yellow of the California mis-
sions. But now all that was visible from the street was
the post-dawn muted light pouring out through the
postal wall of mullioned windows—and opposite it,
inside the YMCA, facing the window, four patrol officers pedaling briskly and one postmaster puffing like he
had the Everest route.

In the distance I could hear brakes screeching as rush
hour drivers, no doubt clutching travel mugs of French
roast they hoped would wake them up before they got to
work, checked out the scene. I could see a TV crew at the

barricade. And just behind the barricade, half a dozen students walking into the high school!

From the communications van I called Doyle, a few yards away inside the Y, and reported that.

"Yeah, Smith," he said. "They couldn't cancel school. Too late, they said. No way to get the word out. Be more dangerous to have kids get here and then turn them loose in the street. So they'll just close the campus and keep the kids inside the buildings or the courtyard all day."

"Weren't they considering closing the campus full time anyway? Wasn't that already a hot issue at the high school?"

Doyle paused. I could picture him shrugging his loose sloped shoulders. "Not our problem."

"Words a cop loves to hear." I clicked off and turned my attention back across the street to Willard Wright. This time he picked up on the second ring.

"Here's your scone and your latte, Willard."

"What took so long? Did you have them mailed here?"

"Willard!"

"Okay, okay. Put the box in front of the right side door—the departure door."

"You want me to walk over in front of the windows when I don't know what kind of weapon you have? You think I'm crazy?"

"We have a bargain. You promised food."

"You promised a name and weaponry. I'm not taking the chance of being blown sky-high."

"Smith, I told you the street wasn't in danger. Can't you trust me?"

"You want the food, you tell me what you've got in there."

He hesitated so long I thought he'd wandered off. Finally, he said, "Okay. I've got bombs. Not big enough to endanger the street, but hefty enough to turn this building into rubble."

Bombs. Small, numerous bombs. Would Willard blow

the building down around him? I doubted it. But then
yesterday I wouldn't have said Willard would barricade
himself inside the post office. When the feds got here,
they wouldn't view Willard as a local eccentric who
might have a homemade explosive or two that could con-
ceivably go off if things got very extreme. To them he'd
be a lunatic bomber with a sizable rap sheet.

I gave the sack of food to one of the tac team guys and
watched as he got an extender tray and maneuvered the
box in front of the post office door.

As soon as the box hit the mat, the door opened auto-
matically, and what looked like a shepherd's crook
scooped it inside.

My phone rang. It was Willard. "Now bring me the
postmaster."

"No! Willard, the FBI is going to be here any minute.
You deal with *me* now. Or you deal with them. That's
your choice. The FBI is not tolerant of bombers, Willard."

For a moment there was silence from his end of the
line. Then chewing. The man was eating his breakfast!
"Willard, you've gone to an enormous amount of trouble
to put yourself in jeopardy. You could end up dead!
Now, what is your real gripe?"

"I should be in Acapulco."

"I'll second that."

"And you know why I'm not in Acapulco?"

"No."

"Because of the inefficiency of the Berkeley Post
Office, that's why! Because the notice of the first prize
that I won, an all-expense-paid week in sunny Acapulco,
had to be acknowledged by the end of the year. The
notice, Smith, didn't hit my mailbox till the third of
January! Now some guy from Willow Spring, North
Carolina, is sunning his butt on the beach in Mexico."

"Willard—"

"And how did the post office offer to recompense me,
you're asking?"

"Well—"

"The postmaster told me there was nothing he could

do. But if it made me feel better—he actually said that: *if it made me feel better*—I could write a letter!"

I restrained comment.

"He can't be bothered to make the post office more efficient. He can't make sure they have books of stamps to sell. Or that letters are delivered on time. But forbid coffee in the postal lobbies—that he can do!"

I started to speak, but Willard was not to be denied.

"No food or drink in the post office! I've been in lines so long I've phoned out for pizza. It got there before I got to the window!"

"Willard, just what is it you want?"

"I want the postmaster to take responsibility."

"You want the postmaster to allow coffee?"

"I want my week in Acapulco."

I was just thinking things couldn't get worse when I spotted a beige car speeding through the barricade and screeching to a halt. Two brown-suited men leaped out and ran into the YMCA. Feds.

I looked down the street to the barricades. The television vans from more stations than I had realized existed crowded behind them. Print reporters, photographers, hung over the wooden horses. The sky was a pale gray now, the wind almost still. It was going to be a good day, a perfect day for hanging out in the park, watching the show at the post office. Already the crowd had seduced workbound drivers out of their cars, morning cyclists off their bikes, and joggers to jog in place, and enticed hundreds of high school students out to see government in action. A man who could have been Neptune carrying a loaf of French bread harangued the crowd from a park bench. A trio of shivering nudists was handing out flyers. Once the sun came out and news of the standoff hit the airwaves, all three rings of the circus would be going.

I grabbed Malvern, pulled him into the communications van, and called Willard. "Willard, the FBI's here. This is your absolute last chance. I've got John Malvern

from the post office. Now let's negotiate." I switched on
the phone speaker so Malvern could hear.

"I want Malvern to take responsibility. He can pay for
my week in Mexico."

I glanced at Malvern.

He looked like Willard had suggested a return to the
penny postcard. "I can't do that. The United States Postal
Service doesn't send criminals on vacation!"

"Only packages, eh, Malvern?" Willard called. "And
the bulk mail—you must send that to Club Antarctica
before you get it to Berkeley!"

Malvern glared at the mike. "Listen, you—"

"Gentlemen, be reasonable!"

"Sure, Jill," Willard insisted. "That's what *they* always
say. 'Don't rest your packages on the post office display
cases!' they say. Why not, huh? So we can develop muscles holding our boxes for half an hour?"

Malvern scowled.

"I'll tell you why—so we can see those enamel pins
and sweatshirts and T-shirts with the pictures of stamps
on them—the ones no one ever buys."

For the first time, Malvern looked abashed.

An enormous noise went up outside, so loud it stung
my ears and defied naming. The van shook. Malvern hit
the floor. I braced myself, then moved to the window and
looked out.

In the street between the Y and the post office, nothing
had changed.

Then sirens wailed, loudspeakers barked, and the
source of the noise—a crowd that by now must have
comprised every high school student in the city—gave
roar and began chanting: "No closed campus! No closed
campus!"

"Was it a bomb?" Malvern, still down on the van
floor, asked.

"Flash-and-sound device? A stun canister? Some illegal
fireworks left over from last July Fourth, maybe." To
Willard, still on the phone, I said, "I'll get back to you." I
hung up and turned to Malvern. "The longer this goes

on, the worse it will get. By the hour of your press conference, we'll have every demonstrator in town here, all
vying for airtime. The press will be eating it up. Between
the demonstrators, the crazies, and Willard and the threat
of blowing up the post office, there'll be a circus that will
have the Ringlings drooling out here. And you, Mr.
Malvern, will be the chief clown."

Malvern paled.

"But," I went on, "if we work fast, we can pull off a
deal here that will benefit everyone."

He looked about as trusting as if I'd asked to send my
letter postage due.

"Have a few of those T-shirts and sweatshirts left, do
you? Enough to dress the poor of Berkeley? Offer them to
Willard in lieu of his week in Mexico. There's no way he
can turn that down, not and maintain his counterculture
credentials. He'll look good; you'll look good."

"No. The United States Postal Service does not
barter."

"Just what are you going to do with tons of rejected
sweats? The Postal Service should be pleased to be rid of
them."

"That's an internal decision."

I could have smothered Malvern with his own excess
sweatshirts. Or crammed one down his throat. I felt like
. . . like Willard. "Willard Wright is about to make an
internal decision." I took a breath. "Look, Mr. Malvern,
I know accommodation is not the way of the Postal
Service. You could, after all, make do with your old logo
and use the seven million dollars to put more staff at the
stamp windows—"

"No, we cou—"

"But this time you don't have a choice. You're not a
monopoly here. Willard Wright can take your offer or he
can turn it down. And if he turns it down, he may not
blow up the post office, but you can be sure this situation
will blow sky-high. Willard Wright will be a hero not only
in Berkeley but nationwide. Willard Wright imitators will
turn up in post offices from Portland to Pensacola. And

Mr. Malvern, you will be responsible. Unless you find a way out right now."

It was another five minutes before I was able to say, "Willard, I've got you a deal. Worth a whole lot more than a week in Central America. Warm sweatshirts for every needy person in town."

Willard Wright, the adversarial pro, was stunned. Gamely, he tried a save: "If the post office wants to support the poor, why don't they take the money they're spending on the Olympics and give it to the homeless? Or direct some of that new logo money locally to something like the Council for Economic Fairness. They could underwrite their booth in the City Fair next summer." His voice trailed off. He knew I had him. He had won: a moral victory but no week in Acapulco. It was only a moment before he said, "Okay, but I want to talk to the head of the Council for Economic Fairness. Get him down here."

The good news was that the chief councillor was easy to find. He was already in the crowd behind the barricades. The bad news was he strode into the van, picked up the phone to Willard, and said, "Hell, no! Don't you be stigmatizing the poor with those sweatshirts! Poor got enough problems without pasting the post office on their chests!" With that, he strode back out behind the lines.

"Don't blame them," Willard said with obvious glee. "No sensible American would advertise the post office! Serves them right for wasting money on a fool idea like that—and then wanting to raise rates."

I didn't look at Malvern. I was sure he'd mutter something about different sources of revenue.

Inspector Doyle walked in, followed by the two feds. Before they could take over, I said, "I think we've got a deal."

Malvern stared.

I put my hand over the mike before Willard could

shriek. "Mr. Malvern, the Postal Service supports good causes like the Olympics, right?"

"Of course," he said, pushing himself up. "We pride ourselves on that kind of commitment."

"And you would be glad to represent the Postal Service at a booth in this summer's City Fair?"

Malvern glanced at the feds; the feds glanced at their watches, crossed their arms, and glared expectantly at Malvern. Hesitantly, Malvern said, "I would be happy to do something suitable for one of my rank. Not some crazy Berkeley thing; some traditional charitable endeavor."

I let my hand ease off the mike. "A booth like the Lions Club does?"

Malvern had qualms, I could tell. But there was nothing tangible for him to hook them to. "Well, yes, that would be suitable."

"And you'll announce that at this morning's press conference?"

"I see no need to rush—"

"I'm sure *you* don't," Willard muttered, for once too softly for Malvern to hear.

Muffling the receiver, I said to Malvern, "You won't have to announce it as a compromise. It can just be a goodwill gesture from the post office."

"Very well. As long as this guy Wright won't have anything to do with that booth."

"That okay with you, Willard?"

"What choice do I have?"

The press conference went off beautifully. Malvern made his public commitment to the fair. The city was happy, the postal officials were happy.

Willard went to jail, of course. But jail was not unfamiliar territory. For him, an old lefty, stripes were stripes of honor.

And while he's had to wait six months for a report on John Malvern in a City Fair booth like the one the Lions Club traditionally hosts, those months have been warmed with anticipation.

Eager to put the whole unpleasant morning with Willard behind him, John Malvern didn't worry about the fair. He didn't bother to contact the Lions. And so it wasn't until he arrived at the fair booth this July day that he had his first inkling of the traditional Lions dunking booth.

There's a lot John Malvern doesn't know about Berkeley. One thing is that some days in July can be as cold as January. But he has come to realize that—as he's been sitting on the platform waiting for each ball to hit the mark, ring the bell, and drop him into the tank of chilly water.

There are a lot of Berkeleyans willing—anxious—to contribute to this charity. The line of them John Malvern sees is as long as in any of his post offices.

And since the agreement is that he must stay till the line is gone, he'll have the same opportunity to learn patience that the post office provides the rest of us.

THE BEAST IN THE WOODS

ED GORMAN

*Rural America plays a major role in both
the detective novels and the western novels
of Ed Gorman.*

*In the last decade and a half, violence in
rural America has soared, one of the reasons being the collapse of the family farm
and the despair felt by so many farmers
driven from the land.*

*Here, Gorman looks at the effects of all
this turmoil on the human victims.*

▲▲▲▲▲▲▲▲▲

▼▼▼▼▼

BY THE TIME I get to the barn, there's already a quarter moon in the September sky, and the barn owl who always sits in the old elm along the creek, he's already hooting into the Iowa darkness.

For the first twenty minutes, I rake out the stalls and scatter hay around the floor. Dairy cows take a lot of work. After that I spread sawdust to eat up some of the dampness and the odors.

Not that I'm paying a whole hell of a lot of attention. All I can think of really is his old army .45. Ordinarily it hangs from a dusty holster on a peg in the spare room upstairs, where he moved after Mom died two years ago of the heart disease that's run in her family for years. Dad says he moved in there because whenever he was in their room, lying in their bed, he'd start to cry, and he's a proud man and doesn't think tears are proper. Also, when he was drunk one night, he told me that a few times when he was in her room, he talked to her ghost and that scared him. So now he keeps their bedroom door shut and sleeps in the room down the hall.

I wonder where he is now. I wonder what he's doing.

Three hours ago, he left, saying he'd be back for dinner, but he wasn't.

And then when I went in to wash up and heat up some spaghetti, I passed by the spare room and noticed that his .45 was gone from its holster.

When I'm finished with the sawdust, I go outside and stand in the Indian-summer dusk, all rolling Iowa hills and bright early stars and the clean, fast smell of the nearby creek, and the distant smoky smells of autumn in the piney hills to the east.

All the outbuildings stand in silhouette now against the dusk, the corn wagon parked by the silo reminding me of tomorrow's chores.

There's only one reason he'd take that goddamned gun of his to town. I'm sure glad Mom isn't here. She tended to get real emotional about things. She would've had a real hard time with the past year: Dad's loan going bad at the bank when the flood wiped us out, and the bank being forced to give Dad until three weeks ago to settle up his account or lose the farm. They gave him a little extra time, but this morning he got a phone call telling him that the bank'd have to file papers to get the farm back and auction it off. ("It isn't the same anymore, Verne," I heard the banker Ken Ohlers tell him on the porch one afternoon. "We don't own the friggin' bank now—the boys in Minneapolis do, big goddamned banking conglomerate, and frankly they could give a shit about a bunch of Iowa farmers, you know, whether the farmers go out of business or not. They just don't make enough on this kind of farm loan to hassle with it.")

Later he went into town with his gun.

To the north now I see plumes of road dust, inside of which is a gray car that I recognize immediately.

As I expect, he turns right into our long gravel drive and shoots right up to the edge of the outbuildings. He has one of those long whip antennas on the back of his car, Sheriff Mike Rhodes does, giving his car a very official and menacing look.

He jumps out of the car almost before the motor stops running. In his left hand is a shotgun. He's a beefy man of Dad's age, fifty or so. In fact, they served in 'Nam together and were the first two 'Nam vets to be allowed in the local VFW, some of the other vets, from WWII and Korea, feeling that Vietnam wasn't an actual war. Fifty thousand fucking Americans die there, and it isn't actually a war, as my Dad used to say all the time.

One more thing about Sheriff Mike. He's my godfather.

"Bobby, is your dad around here?" he says, coming at me like he's going to hit me or something.

"He went into town. How come you got the shotgun, Mike?"

But he doesn't answer my question. He just gets closer. He smells of sweat and aftershave. And he scares me. The same way my dad scares me sometimes when I sense how mad he is and how terrible it's going to be when he lets go of it.

"Bobby, I need to know where your dad is."

"He ain't here. Honest, Mike."

He takes my arm. His fingers hurt me. "Bobby, you listen to me." He is still catching his breath, big man in khaki uniform, wide sweat rings under his arms. "Bobby, you got to think. Think like a normal person. You understand me?"

Sometimes people talk to me like that. They remember when I fell off the tractor when I was seven and how I was never the same. That's what my mom always said. That poor Bobby, he was never the same. In school I didn't read so good, and sometimes people would tell me stuff but I couldn't understand them no matter how hard I tried. And that's when I'd always start crying. I guess I must have cried a lot before I quit school in the tenth grade because the kids, they called me "Buckets" and they always made fun of the way I cried.

"I'll listen good, Mike. I promise."

"You know Ken Ohlers down to the bank?"

"Uh-huh."

"Your dad killed him about an hour ago. Shot him with that forty-five of his he used in Song Be that time."

"Oh, shit, Mike, I wish you wouldn't've said that."

"I'm sorry, Bobby. I had to tell you."

"It makes me scared. You're gonna hurt my dad now, aren't you?"

"I don't want to, Bobby. That's why I need your help. You see him, you got to convince him to give himself up. There's just you now, Bobby, your ma bein' dead and all. You're the only one he'll listen to."

"I'm scared, Mike. I'm real scared."

And I start crying. Don't want to. But can't stop.

And Mike, he just looks kind of embarrassed for me, the way folks do when I start crying like this.

And then he comes up and slides his arm around me and gives me a little hug. Dad, he'll never do that, not even when I cry. Says it doesn't look right, two grown men hugging each other that way.

He digs in his pocket and takes out his handkerchief. Smells of mint. Mike always carries mints in his right khaki pocket.

"You want a mint, Mike?"

"You bet."

I blow my nose in his handkerchief and try to hand it back to him but he nods for me to keep it and then he digs a mint out and drops it into the palm of my hand.

"You remember what I told you, Bobby?"

"Uh-huh."

"You tell your dad to give himself up."

"Uh-huh."

"'Cause the mayor, he won't mess around. He never liked your dad anyway."

"They gonna get the dogs out after him the way they did that time with that black guy?"

"Dogs're already out."

"And the helicopter?"

"Already out too."

"Scares me, that helicopter."

"Don't like it much myself. Hate ridin' in the friggin' thing." He wipes sweat from his face. "He shows up around here, you give him that message, all right?"

"I will, Mike. I promise."

I'm scared I'm going to start crying again.

He looks at me a long time and then gives me another quick hug. "I'm sorry this happened, Bobby."

"I'll bet he's scared too. I'm gonna say a prayer for him. Hail Mary. Just like Mom taught me."

"I'll check back later, Bobby."

Then he's trotting back to the big gray car that smells of road dust and oil and gasoline and heat. Inside, he kind of gives me a little wave, and then he whips the car around so he can go back out headfirst, and then he's lost again inside heavy rolling dust that's silver now in the moonlight.

I go in the house. Upstairs, I go into their bedroom. Mom always kept a framed picture of Blessed Mother on her nightstand. She always said that Blessed Mother listens to boys like me—you know, boys that don't seem just like other boys. I try not to cry as I pray. Hail Mary full of. Sometimes I get confused. Mom wrote it down for me a lot of times, but I have a habit of losing things. Hail Mary full of grace. This time it goes all right. Or mostly all right. And when I'm done praying I light this little votive candle the priest gave her one time he came out here. The match smells of sulfur. The candle smells of wax. Red glow plays across the picture of the Blessed Mother. Hail Mary full of grace. I say a whole nother one. In case she didn't hear it or something.

Then I'm outside, pretty sure where I'll find Dad. There's a line shack up in the hills. Dad and his brother used to play up there. His brother died in 'Nam. Poor goddamned bastard, Dad always says whenever he gets drunk. Poor goddamned bastard. Uncle Win and Mom are buried up to Harrison Cemetery, and couple times a month in the warm season, Dad goes up there and puts flowers on their graves. In the winter months he just stands graveside and stares down at their grave markers, leaning over and brushing away the snow so that their names can be read real clear. He even went up there one night when it was ten below and nobody found him till dawn and Doc Hardy said it was a miracle him being exposed like that—should've died for Christ's sake (how old Doc Hardy always talks) and probably would have if he hadn't been so drunk.

And now I'm running through the long prairie grasses, and it feels good. The grasses are up to my waist, and it's like running through water, the way the grasses slap at you and tickle you. My mom always read me books about the Iowa Indians and about nature stuff. I liked the names of the flowers especially and always made her read

them to me over and over again, sort of like singing a
song. Rattlesnake master and goldenrod and gay-feather
and black-eyed Susan and silverleaf scurfy pea and rag-
wort and shooting star. Some nights I lie in my bed when
I can't sleep and just say those names over and over and
over again and imagine Mom reading them to me the way
she used to and making me learn new words too, three
"five-dollar words" (as she always called them) each and
every week.

A couple times I fall down. I try not to cry. But the
second time I fall down I cut my knee on the edge of a
rock and I can't help but cry. But then I'm running along
the moonsilver creek, ducking below the weeping willows
and jumping over a lost little mud frog, and then I'm
starting up into the red cedar glade where the cabin lies.

Halfway there I have to stop and pee. Dad always says
be proud I don't pee my pants no more. And I am proud.
But sometimes I can barely hold it. Like now. And I have
to go. The pee is hot and rattles the fallen red leaves. I
should wash my hands the way Mom always said but I
can't so I run on.

Behind me once, I think I hear something and I stop.
I'm scared now, the way I am when monster movies come
on TV. You shouldn't watch that crap, Dad always says,
snapping off the set when he sees that I'm getting scared.
The forest is vast. Dark. Slither and crawl and creep, the
things in the forest, possum and snake and wolf. And
maybe monsters, the way there are in forests on TV. The
Indians always believed there were beasts in the woods.

I start running again. Need to find Dad. Warn him.

Now I think of the things Mom read me about the
Indians who used to live here. I like to pretend I'm an
Indian. I wish I could wear buffalo masks the way they
did when they danced around their campfires. Or the
claws of a grizzly bear as a necklace, signifying that I am
the bravest brave of all. Or paint stripes of blood on my
arm, each stripe meaning a different battle. They had to
come get me sometimes, Mom and Dad, at suppertime,
scared I'd wandered off, but I was always up at the old

line shack playing Indian, talking to the prairie sky the way the Indians always did, and watching for the silver wolves to stand in the long grasses and sing and cry and nuzzle their young as the silver moon rose in the pure Iowa night.

I see the shape of the little cabin through the cedars now. It sits all falling down in the middle of a small clearing. No lights; no sound but an owl and the soft soughing of the long grasses; and the smell of rotted wood still wet from the rain last week.

I know he's in there. I sense it.

I crouch down, the way an Indian would, and reach the clearing. And then I start running fast for the cabin.

I am halfway across the clearing when I hear a voice say, "You go back home, Bobby. Right now."

Dad. Inside the cabin.

I am chill with sweat. And shaking. "Mike, he came out to the house, Dad, and said—"

"I know what he said."

"He says you killed Mr. Ohlers."

"I had to, son. He didn't have no right to take our farm back. He said he was our friend, but he wasn't no friend at all."

I don't say anything just then; there's just the soft, soft soughing of the wind, like the breathing of some invisible giant, sleeping.

"Mike, he says he's afraid you'll get killed."

"I don't want to go to prison, Bobby."

"I wish I could see you."

He's in the window, in darkness. He's like Mom now. I can talk to him, but I can't see him. It's like death.

"I want to see you, Dad."

"You just go on back, Bobby. You understand me? You just go on back to the farm and wait there."

And then I hear something again, and when I turn I see Mike coming out into the clearing.

He looks all sloppy, his shirt untucked and his graying hair all mussed. He carries his shotgun, cocked in his arm now.

"I figured you'd lead me to him, Bobby."

"He won't let me see him, Mike."

He nods and then says to the cabin, "I want to come in and talk to you."

"Just stay out there, Mike."

"You don't need to make this any worse than it already is. I'm supposed to be your friend."

"Yeah, just the way Ohlers was my friend."

"He didn't have nothing to do with taking your farm back. It was those bastards in Minneapolis."

"That's what he liked to say, anyway."

"I'm coming in."

"I'll shoot you if you try."

"Then you'll just have to shoot me, you son of a bitch."

One thing about Mike, he makes up his mind, there's no stopping him. No, sir.

I say, "Can I go with you?"

He shakes his head. "You just stay here."

"He's my dad."

"Bobby, goddamn it, I got enough on my mind right now, all right? You just stay right here."

"Yes, sir."

"I'm sorry I swore at you like that."

"Yes, sir."

"I won't be long."

From the cabin, my dad shouts, "You just stay out there, Mike. You hear me?"

But Mike walks toward the cabin.

My dad fires.

The shot is loud and flat in the soughing prairie silence.

"Next time I'll hit you."

"You'll just have to hit me, then."

This time the bullet comes a lot closer. This time it echoes off the hills.

But Mike doesn't slow down.

He walks right up to the one-room cabin and kicks in the front door and then goes inside.

I walk back to the edge of the clearing and look at trees. Mom always used to read me the names of trees too, white oak and shagbark hickory and basswood and pin oak and green ash and silver maple and honey locusts and big-tooth aspens. Say them over and over and they're like a song too.

I need to pee again.

I go into the woods.

I wish I could wash my hands. It always makes me feel bad not to do what Mom says, even when she's gone.

In the clearing again, I hear them yelling at each other inside the cabin, and I get scared. And they're starting to fight. They slam up against the walls, and the whole cabin shakes. I want to run down there, but I'm too scared. I don't want to see Dad hurt Mike or Mike hurt Dad. This shouldn't ought to be like this.

And then the shot.

Just one.

And it's louder and the echo is longer and then there is this terrible silence and you can't even hear the wind now.

And then the cabin door opens up and Dad comes out.

He walks to the center of the clearing, his .45 dangling from his right hand. "You get back to the farm, you hear me, Bobby?"

But I can't help myself. I go up to him. And I put my arms around him. And the funny thing is, this time he doesn't push me away or tell me grown men shouldn't hug each other. He holds me real tight and I can feel how rawboned he is, all sharp shoulders and bony elbows and gaunted ribs.

He holds me tight too, just as tight as I hold him, and says, "I messed it all up, Bobby. I messed it all up."

And then he starts choking and crying, the way he did at Mom's funeral, and I hold him and let him cry the way Mom used to hold me and let me cry.

And then he's done.

And standing in the clearing. And staring up at the moon the way Mom told me Indians used to. She said they believed they could read things in the moon, portents for what would happen to them in the future.

Then he looks at me, and he speaks very, very softly, and he says, "You get on back now, Bobby. And you call Mr. Sayre, the lawyer. He'll know what to do."

"Is Uncle Mike dead?"

"Yes, he is, Bobby."

"How come you shot him, Dad?"

"I'm not sure why, Bobby. I'm not sure why at all. I just wish I hadn't."

I wanted to say something, but I was afraid I would start crying again.

And Dad was already looking back toward the cabin.

"You go on back to the farm now, Bobby, and you call Mr. Sayre."

I reach out gently for his .45, but he pulls it back. "Maybe I should take that from you, Dad."

"You just go on, Bobby."

"I'm scared, Dad, you havin' that forty-five and all."

"You just go on. You just hurry and call Mr. Sayre."

"I'm scared, Dad."

"I know you are, Bobby. And I'm scared too." He nods to the woods and says, very final now, "Git, boy. Git and git fast. You understand?"

"Yessir."

"You run till you get to the farm, and then you call Mr. Sayre. You understand?"

"Yessir."

And that is all.

He turns away from me, his face lost in moonshadow, and he goes on back to the cabin.

I know better than to argue or disobey.

I start walking slowly toward the woods again, and by the time I reach the front stand of trees, the shot rings out just as I thought it would, and I try to imagine what it must look like, their two bodies there inside the cabin, blood and flies and stink the way it is when any kind of animal is dead like that, and then I get scared, real scared, and I start crying.

I want my dad to hold me again the way he did just a few minutes ago, the way my mom used to hold me anytime I asked her. I want somebody to hold me, and hold me tight, and hold me for a long, long time, because the night is coming full now, and there is a beast in these woods, just the way the Indians always said, a beast in the dark, dark woods.

BLOWOUT IN LITTLE MAN FLATS

STUART M. KAMINSKY

*Stuart M. Kaminsky is the author of three
very different (and very good) mystery
series.*

*First came the breezy Hollywood tales
staring Toby Peters, great good fun for
everybody and, in the case of* Down for
the Count, *a serious look at the sad life of
Joe Louis.*

*Next came the Inspector Porfiry
Rostnikov books, about the life and times
of a modern policeman in the chilly environs of Moscow. And now there are the
Leiberman novels, trenchant looks at the
life and times of modern Chicago.*

And here is something else entirely.

▲▲▲▲▲▲▲▲

▼▼▼▼▼

THE LAST MURDER in Little Man Flats was back in, let me
see, 1963, before Kennedy was shot by who knows who
or why," Sheriff George Fingerhurt told his prime suspect. "Want some tea? Do you good in this heat."

"No . . . thanks."

"Suit yourself."

Fingerhurt sat back drinking his herbal peppermint tea
from the Rhett Butler cup his daughter had brought him
from Atlanta. George Fingerhurt liked Rhett Butler and
herbal tea. Rhett was cool, never mind the temperature—
like today, pushing a hundred in the shade.

"Got a theory about tea, got it from my grandfather
Ocean Fingerhurt who was half Apache. Grandpa Ocean
said hot tea cooled you off. Since Grandpa Ocean had got
lost and wound up in Little Man Flats, New Mexico,
back in 1930, when he thought he was in southern
California, he was hardly a man to trust, at least not
about directions. He was better about tea. Sure you don't
want to change your mind?"

"Okay," said the suspect. "I'll have some tea."

"Get dry out here," said the sheriff, pouring a cup of
dark-green tea into a Scarlett O'Hara cup and handing it
to the truckdriver, whose name, as he had told the sheriff,
was Tector (Teck) Gorch. "Careful—hot."

"Obliged," said Teck.

They drank for about a minute, and Teck looked out
the window.

"Quite a crowd," the sheriff said.

"Umm," Teck grunted.

There were eight people outside the one-story adobe
town hall and sheriff's office. One of them was Ollie

Twilly, from the feed store, wide-brimmed Stetson shading his eyes as he leaned back against the front fender of his '88 Ford pickup. Ollie had reason to be there. His brother Stan was one of the three people who had been killed, probably by the trucker sitting across from George drinking herbal tea.

The trucker was, George figured, maybe thirty-five, forty. One of those solid mailbox types. Curly hair cut a little long, could use a shave, but considering what had happened, made sense he hadn't considered the social graces. Teck the trucker was wearing slightly washed-out blood-specked jeans and a bloody T-shirt with the words I'M HAVING A BAD DAY written across the front in black. Amen to that sentiment, George thought.

"Last murder, back when I was a boy," George explained after a careful sip. "Indian named Double Eagle out of Gallup on a motorcycle went ravin' down 66 and plowed into Andrew Carpenter. Jury figured it was on purpose. Not much point to it. Andrew was near ninety. Am I getting too folksy for you? I haven't had much practice with murder cases. Haven't had any, really."

Teck shrugged and tried to think. The tea was making him feel a little cooler, but the sheriff was making him nervous. Fingerhurt was wearing matching khaki trousers and short-sleeved shirt. His black hair was freshly cut, combed straight back, and he looked a hell of a lot like the crying Indian in the TV commercials about polluting the rivers.

A sweat-stained khaki cowboy hat sat on the empty desk.

"Hey," said Fingerhurt, pointing out the window. "Crowd's growing. Those two are Mr. and Mrs. Barcheck, what passes for society in Little Man Flats. Own a lot of the town, including the Navajo Fill-up."

Teck looked out the window for the first time.

"Nice-lookin' woman," the sheriff said. "Not enough meat for me, but we're not in Santa Fe, so one's voyeuristic choices are limited. You wanna just tell your story? State police'll be here in a half hour, maybe less, to pick you up. Won't have a good report on what it looks like up there till Red comes in."

Teck held his cup in two hands, feeling warm moisture seep into his palms.

"Red's my deputy, one you saw out at the Fill-up."

"His hair isn't red," said Teck.

"Never was. His father had red hair, was called Red. Deputy was Little Red. When his daddy died, deputy was just plain Red."

"Interesting," said Teck.

It was the sheriff's turn to shrug.

"Say, listen, information like that counts for lore in Little Man Flats."

He looked out the window and observed,

"Crowd's getting bigger. I'd say twenty out there, coming to take a look at you. Four, five more people, and practically the whole town'll have turned out. State troopers are gonna be here soon, asking if I found anything. You want to tell your story? I'll take notes."

"I'm arrested? I need a lawyer?"

"You're here for questioning in the murder of Miss Rose Bryant Fernandez, Mr. Stanley Twilly, and a man who had a wallet in his back pocket strongly suggesting he was Lincoln Smart. You know the man?"

"Trucker, like me," said Teck. "Knew him to say hello. Where's my rig?"

"Safe, gathering dust out at the Fill-up, where you parked it. Wanna tell me what happened out there?"

"Someone cut your population almost in half," said Teck without a smile.

Sheriff Fingerhurt shook his head. He put down his Rhett Butler cup and folded his hands, looking unblinking at the trucker.

"Educated?"

"A little too much," said Teck. "Almost finished college. Almost a lot of things."

"Feeling a little sorry for yourself?"

"Considering, I think I've got a right."

"Maybe so. Story?"

Teck sat back, looked out the window at the gathered crowd, focused on a little boy about nine, who was looking directly back at him and covering his eyes to shade out the sun.

"Came thundering in a little before four in the morning," Teck began, nodding his agreement to the sheriff, who had pulled a tape recorder out of a desk drawer. Fingerhurt pushed the button and sat back.

"Came thundering in before four in the morning," Teck repeated. "Wanted to make Gallup, usually do. Never stopped at the Navajo Fill-up overnight before. One bad tire out of sixteen didn't stop me. I'd have even tried outlasting the knock in the diesel, even with nothing but desert for fifty more miles. Rain and backache did me in. Learned enough in eleven years in the high cab to know that when the back says stop, you stop, or you will have one hell of a tomorrow."

Sheriff Fingerhurt nodded and shook his head.

"Grit and sand on my neck, air conditioner gone lazy, shirt sticking to my chest, back, and deep down into my behind," Teck continued. "I was a sorry mess by one in the A.M. I never stopped in your town before last night except for diesel. I don't know the two locals who got killed, and I barely knew Linc."

"Lincoln Smart, the other driver?" asked the sheriff.

"There was only one rig in the opening beyond the pumps, Linc's big silver-and-blue, bigger than mine. I own my truck out there, and I've got a load of furniture from a factory just outside of Baines, Arkansas. Taking it to a pair of stores in Bakersfield."

"Where you from, Teck?"

"Tupelo. Tupelo, Mississippi."

"Elvis's town?"

"Yeah."

"You ever see the King himself?"

"He was long gone when I was growing up."

Sheriff Fingerhurt sat back, shaking his head.

"Well," Teck went on, "I—"

"Married?" asked the sheriff.

"Divorced. One kid. A boy, about seven or eight."

"You don't know?"

"Seven. His birthday's February 11. I just forget the year. Haven't seen him for three years. My ex-wife won't let me."

"Sorry," said Fingerhurt.

"I got bigger things to worry about today," Teck said, putting down his now empty cup.

"Yeah," said the sheriff.

"Got out of my rig, with my rain poncho over my head, duffel in my hand, locked up, and went inside the café. Woman behind the counter was reading a paperback."

"Remember what it was?"

"Make a difference?"

"Who knows?" said Fingerhurt.

"Woman behind the counter looked up at me like I was a surprise she could have done without," Teck went on. "People tend not to be overjoyed when I walk in, but this woman—"

"Rosie Fernandez," Fingurhurt supplied.

"I guess," Teck said with a shrug, looking out the window.

The small crowd had grown. There were more men now, and they were talking, arguing.

"You ever have a lynching in this town?" Teck said, his eyes meeting those of Ollie Twilly, whose Stetson was now tilted back on his head. Ollie either had a very high forehead or he was bald. Bald or balding, he was clearly in one hell of a bad mood.

"Not a white man," said the sheriff. "Last Indian was shot in 1928 by a mob for drunk talk to a white woman."

"Your grandfather picked one hell of a town to settle in," Teck said.

"He was lost."

"We keep this up, I won't get my story told before the troopers get here," Teck said.

"Go on. Rose Fernandez was behind the counter, reading a paperback."

"Dean Koontz. It was Dean Koontz."

"Read one by him," said Fingerhurt. "People turned into machines in a small town. Scared shit out of me."

"I asked her for a room and something to eat," Teck went on. "I wasn't particular as long as it wasn't trout. I'm allergic."

"We don't have much call for trout in New Mexico," the sheriff said.

Outside the window, the crowd was getting louder, and there was, the sheriff noted, a very bad sign even a white man could read. The children were being sent off, as if there might be something the adults didn't want them to see.

"I think they're working themselves up to come here and lynch me," said Teck, following the sheriff's line of vision.

"Closest yucca that'll hold your weight is two miles out of town," said the sheriff, reaching for his hat. "Shoot you is what I'm thinking."

"Like the Indian in 1928?"

"Something like that," George Fingerhurt agreed. "But we'll stop 'em."

"We?"

"Me and Red. He's pulling up."

About twenty-five yards beyond the window where the crowd had gathered, a dust-covered pickup pulled in and a man in jeans, a khaki shirt, and a hat climbed out.

People flocked around him as he strode forward, shaking his head.

"He found something," the sheriff said.

"How can you tell? Your Indian blood?"

"Got the look. Known Red for almost forty years. You know things like that about people you know."

The door behind Teck flew open, and voices from outside came in, full of fear and anger. Red closed the door and stepped in. He was thinner and, considering the mood of the mob, less formidable than Teck would have liked. Red looked at the sheriff and then at Teck.

"Wanna talk in the other room, George?"

"What'd you find?" asked the sheriff.

"You sure you—"

"You found what, Red?"

"Troopers came with a truck. All over the place. Told me I could go. They'd be here quick. Said we shoulda held Gorch at the murder site. Found this under Rosie's body. Said you should have a look at it."

Red stepped to the sheriff's desk, avoiding Teck's eyes, pulled a crumpled paper bag out of his jeans pocket, and handed it to George Fingerhurt. The sheriff held the bag open behind the desk, looked into it and then out the window and then at Red.

"Damn," said Fingerhurt.

"Damn right, damn," said Red.

"Sheriff . . . ," Teck tried, but the door behind him opened with a jolt. He turned and found himself facing Ollie Twilly, both Barchecks, and a variety of others, mostly with the look and matching intellect of bewildered cattle. Twilly was carrying a shotgun.

"We want him," said Ollie, pointing his shotgun barrel at Teck, who jumped up and stood with his back to the wall behind the still seated sheriff.

"You all want him? You too, Mrs. Barcheck?" Fingerhurt asked.

"Yes," she said.

She was, indeed, a fine-looking woman, freckled brown with yellow hair tied back, could have been any age from thirty to fifty, Teck thought, and wondered how he could do such thinking with a shotgun cocked and aimed in the general area of his gut.

"And what'll you do with him?" asked the sheriff.

"Take him out. Shoot him," said Twilly. "Shoot him through the brains like the dog he is."

The shotgun came up toward Teck Gorch's face, and Ollie Twilly continued with, "You shot my brother like a dog, and I'm—"

"How'd you know Stan was shot, Mr. Twilly?" the sheriff asked, as two of the more oxlike men stepped toward Teck.

"Red told us," said Andrew Barcheck, who was decidedly a slouching Saint Bernard to his wife's well-groomed poodle.

The sheriff closed his eyes and shook his head before he looked up at Red, whose left cheek twitched.

"George, you and Red go out for a shake at Veronica's," said Ollie Twilly. "When you come back—"

"No, Mr. Twilly," said the sheriff.

"We'll have your goddamn job, George," Twilly said through gritted teeth.

"You couldn't live on my salary, Mr. Twilly. You take him. You shoot him. Red and I arrest you for murder," said the sheriff. "Is it worth going to jail for, Mr. Twilly?"

"Yes."

The two bovine men were now about three feet in front of Teck, who had sucked in his stomach, feeling more than a little sick.

"Rest of you feel the same way?" the sheriff asked. "You got murder looking at you, conspiracy, impeding a lawman in the dispatching of his duty. Hell, folks, you're looking at a lot of bleak years in the state house."

"No jury will convict us. Not after what he did."

"Act your age, Ollie," Mrs. Barcheck said. "There isn't a jury that wouldn't convict us."

"Then by shit and a wild pig," shouted Twilly, "I don't give a crap. I'll shoot him right here."

The two bulls in front of Teck jumped out of the line of fire.

"Man was telling his side when you came in," said the sheriff. "Think you can hold off till he finishes? Give him that?"

"Let him speak, Ollie," Mr. Barcheck said.

Someone behind the front line let out a groan and an "Oh, shit."

"Miguel, that you?" the sheriff called.

A heavy, hard-breathing dark man with bad skin worked his way forward through the crowd.

"Let him say," Miguel said.

"No," said Twilly, the gun now firmly against the chest of Miguel.

"My sister got killed last night too," Miguel Fernandez said. "We can listen. Who knows what Leon Harvey Oswald would have said if the Jew guy hadn't shot him?"

"Lee. Oswald's name was Lee," Mrs. Barcheck corrected.

"And the man who shot him was Jack Ruby."

"This isn't goddamn Trivial Pursuit," screamed Twilly. "Can't you see Fingerhurt's stalling till the state police get here?"

"I'll look out the window," said Miguel. "We see them coming, and you can shoot."

Defeated for the moment, Ollie Twilly let the shotgun point toward the floor.

"Finish your story, Tector," the sheriff said.

Teck, back to the wall, looked at the faces of anger, hate, and confusion around the room.

"I don't think I . . . ," Teck began, and then said, "I walked in, soaking wet, told the woman I needed a room for the night and a mechanic in the morning. She said . . . "

Teck's eyes met Miguel's and then went to the sheriff.

"I don't . . . "

"Tector," said the sheriff, "I don't see a hell of a lot of choice here, do you?"

"She said all she had was eggs any way I wanted 'em, and if I wanted company in bed for a couple of hours, she could handle that too, for a reasonable fee."

Teck's eyes were watching Miguel Fernandez. Fernandez betrayed nothing but heavy breathing.

"I said I'd think on it," Teck went on.

"A fine-looking woman, Rosie," said the sheriff. "Some meat on her bones. Nothing to hold back here, Teck. Rosie was the town—begging your pardon, Mrs. Barcheck—lady of the afternoon and evening."

"She was a whore, yes," said Miguel, "but she was a good person. Anybody in this room say anything else?"

No one in the room had anything else to say relating

to Rosie Fernandez's behavior, so the sheriff nodded at Teck, who went on.

"She said she'd make me two over-easy sandwiches with mayo and onions and figured from the onion order that I wasn't interested in company. I said I wanted to change into something dry, and she told me to go up the stairs off in the corner and go into room three, where I could shower and get decent and dry."

"What else?" the sheriff said.

"Jukebox in the corner near the window was playing Patsy Cline," Teck said hopefully.

"She was reading Dean Koontz and listening to Patsy Cline," the sheriff said.

"Stairs were dark. I started up. This guy passed me coming down."

"Guy?" asked Fingerhurt. "What'd he look like?"

"Don't know. Wasn't really looking. About my height, weight. Maybe."

"Met himself coming and going," said Twilly. "We heard enough here yet?"

"Wait," Teck said. "He had a big silver belt buckle."

"Every man in this room and a few of the women are wearing big silver belt buckles," the sheriff said. "Even me and Red."

"I'm telling you what I remember," Teck pleaded. "I'm telling the truth."

"Okay, Sha-hair-a-zadie," said Ollie Twilly. "Keep going."

"Not much more to tell. I went to room three, got my clean jeans, socks, and the shirt I'm wearing out of my bag, took a quick shower, got dressed, and headed back down. Patsy Cline was still singing, eggs were burning bad, and Miss Fernandez was laying there in the middle of the room, dead and bloody. I tried to help her, but she was—"

"And you were covered in her blood," the sheriff said.

"Yes."

"And then?"

"I called for help. No one answered. The rain was

harder. It was pushing dawn. I ran back up the stairs and knocked at doors and yelled. No answer. One of the doors was open. Linc Smart was naked, bloody, and dead. I kept opening doors. One was an office. Bald man was laying across the desk, dead."

"That was my brother. That was Stan," cried Ollie. "You lying son of a bitch and a half."

"No," said Teck, holding up his hands to ward off the anticipated shotgun blast. "No lie. I found the phone, called the operator, told her that someone had murdered who knows how many people at the Navajo Fill-up. And that was it."

The sheriff eyes met Teck's and then moved for an instant to the running tape recorder before returning to Teck's face.

"Question, Mr. Gorch," the sheriff said. "You didn't hear gunshots when you drove up to the Fill-up and walked in?"

"No. It was raining hard. Whoever it was must have shot Linc and the other guy before I got to the door."

"How many times were they shot, Red?" the sheriff asked.

"The trucker three times, Mr. Stanley Twilly twice. Then Miss Rosie twice."

"Why," the sheriff asked, "did Miss Rosie sit there reading a Dean Koontz and offer you eggs and companionship if she just heard five shots?"

"Yes," said Miguel, turning angrily toward Teck.

"I don't know," said Teck.

"And why didn't you hear Rosie getting shot?" the sheriff went on.

"I was in the shower. It was raining hard. I don't know."

"This is the stupidest damn story," Ollie said. "Everybody step back. Fairy tale's over."

The shotgun came up toward Teck again.

"Why would I kill those people?" Teck said.

"You thought Rose was alone," said Ollie. "You went for her behind the counter. She fought you, threatened to call the sheriff. You shot her. Then you panicked and went to look for any witnesses who might have seen you. You shot that truckdriver and my brother."

"And then I called the police?" Teck cried.

"Maybe you were trying to be tricky," Miguel Fernandez said. "Maybe you just got damned confused, decided you couldn't get away, tire tracks, whatever. So you made up your story."

"No," cried Teck. "Sheriff."

"What'd he do with the gun?" Sheriff Fingerhurt asked.

"Threw it away, maybe buried it couple hundred yards off in the desert," said Barcheck. "What's the difference?"

"Troopers are coming down the street," said Miguel softly, turning his eyes to Teck's frightened face.

"That does it," said Ollie. "Everybody stand back. We in this together?"

The two bulls who had approached Teck grunted something. The rest of the crowd was shuffling, silent now that the troopers were a minute or two away.

"I've got one thing I can't figure," said the sheriff. "If his story is true, why didn't Rose call me and Red, or go upstairs to see what was happening? Why did she sit there reading a book?"

"He made up a dumb story," said Miguel.

"Miguel," said the sheriff, "how long I know you?"

"Your whole life."

"What if Rose did hear the shots? What if Rose knew Stan and the trucker were dead when Gorch came in looking for a warm room and meal? What if he surprised her, she picked up a book, looked as if she didn't want company, and then, to keep him from getting suspicious, offered to bed down with him for the night, not forgetting to say it wasn't free. Gorch goes upstairs. Killer comes down. Rose tells him about Gorch. Killer gets the idea of blaming everything on the dumb trucker. Sorry, Tector."

"No offense," said Teck.

"Why would anyone want to kill my brother?" Ollie said.

"Property, money's my guess," said Sheriff Fingerhurt. "Killer probably considered burying Stan and the dead trucker and having Rose say Stan just got fed up, grabbed some cash, and took off for northern California."

The troopers' car door opened and then slammed shut a beat later. All eyes turned to the window. Two troopers were walking toward the Little Man Flats municipal building, where most of the adult population was gathered in the sheriff's office.

"That's crazy," shouted Ollie.

The sheriff lifted his right hand and displayed a crinkled brown paper bag.

"Red found this on the floor under Rose's body," he said, pulling a bright silver buckle out of the bag and holding it up for the congregation to see. The silver was hammered into the shape of a buffalo, with huge horns in relief.

"So," said Miguel, "everybody around here has a belt buckle like that, something like that. It could be this guy's, this truckdriver's."

"Right," said the sheriff, "but he's got a buckle on his belt, and he had time to look for it if Rose pulled it off in a struggle with him. But the killer, the killer heard the shower go off, made a decision not to kill the trucker, and ran without finding the buckle. Hell, maybe he didn't even notice till he got home or too far to turn back."

The door behind the crowd opened, and a deep voice said, "What the hell is going on in here?"

"I'm not interested in who has a buffalo-head silver buckle," said Fingerhurt, ignoring the troopers who were muscling their way forward through the gathering. "I'm interested in who *doesn't* have one anymore. With the cooperation of the troopers who have just arrived, I'm going to ask a few of you who I know have buffalo buckles to go back to their houses with me and show me the buckle. Miguel, Dan Sullivan, Mr. Barcheck, and you, Ollie."

The troopers were in front now, near twins, well built, unwrinkled uniforms, hats flat on their heads and brims perfectly parallel to the ground.

"What's going on, George?" the older of the two said.

The sheriff held up a finger to show that he needed only a minute more.

"All right with me," said Barcheck.

"Me too," said Miguel.

"I'm wearing mine," said Danny Sullivan, stepping forward to show the buckle in question.

"Mr. Twilly?" Sheriff Fingerhurt asked.

"Lost," he said defiantly. "I looked for it a few days ago. Someone stole it."

"You wore it yesterday, Oliver," Mrs. Barcheck said.

"Hey, that's right," said Danny Sullivan. "You sat next to me at Veronica's for lunch. You were wearing the buckle. You had the meat loaf with chilies, and I had . . . who the hell cares what I had?"

"Is there a punch line here, George?" the older trooper said, doing a magnificent job of hiding his complete confusion.

"I think Mr. Twilly here has some questions to answer," the sheriff said.

The shotgun was coming up again, but before Twilly could level it at anyone, Teck Gorch pushed himself from the wall with a rebel yell and threw himself at the armed man. The shotgun barrel was still coming up toward Teck's face when Miguel Fernandez punched Twilly in the gut. Twilly went down with Teck on top of him, and the shotgun spun around in the air like the bone at the beginning of *2001*.

Three people made it out the door. Some went for the floor. Barcheck pushed his wife against the wall. The troopers and Red dived behind the desk, where Sheriff George Fingerhurt sat shaking his head.

The gun hit the ceiling, dropped quickly to the floor with a clatter-clack, and didn't discharge.

It took Red about twenty seconds to clear everyone but the troopers, the sheriff, Teck, and Ollie out of the room.

It took Ollie Twilly two minutes and some resuscita-
tion from the younger trooper to revive enough to deny
everything, from his affair with Rose to the murder of his
brother. He even managed to deny a variety of crimes,
including felonies of which no one had yet accused him.

Within four minutes, the troopers were being led by
Red, with Ollie in tow, for a tour of Ollie's home and
office.

"Can I go now?" Teck asked when he was alone with
the sheriff again.

"Nope," said Fingerhurt. "You're our key witness."

"But . . . "

"Up to the troopers now," the sheriff said. "They can
let you go when they take you off my hands, but who
knows. Maybe they'll get a statement and let you deliver
your furniture to Bakersfield."

"Okay, if I go back to my rig and pick up some clean
clothes?"

"Sure," said the sheriff. "I'll give you a lift."

George Fingerhurt backed his wheelchair from behind
the desk and carefully maneuvered it through the space
between it and the window. From that point, it was out
the door, down the ramp, and another day starting.

SMALL TOWN MURDER

Harold Adams

Harold Adams's novels about the Midwest
during Depression years are among the
finest examples of modern mystery fiction,
books ripe with pith and pity, humor and
great crushing sorrow.

All of that is on display here, in this brief
but powerful tale rich with incident and
resonant characterization.

Adams is a genuine American
treasure, and you should seek out his
books at once.

You'll be glad you did.

▼▼▼▼▼

AT SEVENTY-FIVE, Hank was still bright-eyed and bushy-haired. He drove his Cadillac with skill and a certain flair, always traveling at precisely five miles per hour above the posted limits. It was as though he had personal cruise control.

"Look at all that green," he gloated as we wheeled along State Highway 212. "Sixty years ago, all you'd see would be sunburned crops and bare-assed pastures. It was so bad the millions of grasshoppers couldn't get enough to eat and were down to gnawing on fence posts. The only thing they didn't chew on was barbed wire and concrete, and you can bet they'd tried them."

"How come there were so many hoppers?"

"All their natural enemies were dried out. Birds came around in the spring, took one look, and headed back south. You never saw ducks in those days. Nothing but mangy-looking mud hens, flopping around in dried-up sloughs. Even if you found a lake, you had to walk a half mile of beach to find water. It was pitiful. Now look. Old lakes are running over, and there are new ones I never saw before. There's even water in the ditches, all clear and lovely."

"You'll have mosquitoes. And from what I've seen, the corn is never going to be knee-high by the Fourth of July. It's about drowned out."

"Could be, but I'll tell you something. Nobody around here is bitching about too much rain. It'd have to be two feet deep across the state before there'd be a peep—at least by old-timers who lived through the drought. They'll worry but keep their mouths shut."

After a few minutes of silence, I asked if he had any theories about why murder was so rare in rural areas.

"It's because all these people have one common enemy: the weather. It makes them close. Besides, they live far enough apart that they don't bug each other too much. Sure, they squabble and gossip and mind each other's business, but most everything anybody does is common knowledge. Makes it about impossible to hide a murder, or commit one casually, like in the cities, where most of the people you see are strangers."

All I knew about the murder we were going to investigate was what an old friend of Hank's told him when he called a few days after the killing. According to Hank, some character named Barney, who still lived in Corden, had this wild-assed notion that the nephew of Carl Wilcox ought to come and solve the crime, since it had the town all torn up and the local cop wasn't getting anywhere with it.

Besides solving murders, Hank's uncle Carl had made quite a reputation in the thirties for a number of things, like practical joker, ex-convict, hobo, occasional cop, and, like me, part-time private eye.

According to Barney, a man named Kirkwood, a lawyer and a landowner, had been shot on one of his own farms, late last Sunday afternoon.

As we covered the last few miles, Hank told me that sixty years ago Corden had two hardwares, a Woolworth's five-and-dime, two butcher shops and drugstores and bakeries. The finest movie theater in South Dakota during the early thirties was Corden's. They had a dance hall on Main, two grain elevators, two banks, and even a blacksmith shop. The theater, the dance hall, and one grain elevator were gone now. There was only one grocery, one drug and hardware store. Butcher shops and bakeries were history, along with the railroad line, right down to the tracks. The old depot had been moved just west of the commercial district and now served as a history museum devoted to Corden's past.

"Folks here have to look back," Hank said. "There's no future in Corden. Young folks leave."

Before going to the Widow Wolsey's boardinghouse,

we stopped at City Hall to meet the chief of police, Al Abernathy. He was of medium height, stocky, brown-haired, and firm-jawed, with pale-blue eyes and laugh wrinkles, though he was notably sober now.

When telling Abernathy about me, Hank shrewdly omitted any mention of my messing with murders in the past. As far as the cop was concerned, I was strictly a guy who wrote magazine articles and was in Corden to gather material about life in the Dakotas after the great drought and the Depression.

"There's nothing simple about this murder," the chief told us. "Kirkwood was killed behind a farmhouse he owned south of town, about two miles from here. Shot through the left ear with a long rifle, twenty-two caliber. The shooter was either luckier than hell or damned good. Kirkland died like now."

"Where do you think the shot came from?" I asked.

"Most likely the windbreak woods to the north."

"Couldn't it have been from the house?"

"I don't think so, not from the way the body lay. But we can't be positive."

"Any suspects?" asked Hank.

Abernathy looked pained. "Well, naturally there's the wife, Hildegard . . . or the former wife. They've been divorced a little over a year. The trouble with that is, there's no real simple reason they broke up. I mean, he wasn't tomcatting around, she never claimed he abused her, and there were no big hassles anybody knows about. I think she just got bored and wanted to go back to her high school boyfriend, who she's been seeing ever since the bust-up."

"No money problems?"

"Well, I guess he wasn't too great about paying alimony on schedule, but shooting him wouldn't exactly fix that. Since the divorce was her idea, it's not likely she'd stand to inherit anything when he checked out."

"Did he have a practice in town?" I asked.

"Actually, he hadn't practiced much since a rich aunt died and left him money and property—including that farm where he died. He liked to travel a lot. That was one of Hildegard's beefs. She claimed he was always gone. Since everybody knew they bored each other stiff, that should have suited her fine, but she had to have some kind of reason to ask for the divorce, and that was one of them. Neglect, she called it."

He told us a little more about Hildegard, and I got the impression he disliked her. He conceded she wasn't bad-looking, but he did it grudgingly, as though resenting the fact.

"There's another possibility, but pretty unlikely. That's Tim Tanner. Tim's got this wild daughter, Verne, who's pregnant, and for some reason she claims it's Kirkwood's fault. You can hardly think of a less likely combination. She insists Kirkwood knocked her up, and Tim had been making noises about forcing Kirkwood to marry her. He's just about nutty enough to have made the try, but again, shooting Kirkwood wouldn't exactly make her kid legit, so what'd be the point? Tim's probably a certifiable idiot, but I can't imagine even him taking a shot at Kirkwood with a twenty-two to scare him to the altar. To make it interesting, Verne claims her daddy was with her at the time of the shooting. And Hildegard and her boyfriend, Chris Banks, claim they were together that afternoon."

"Back when Kirkwood was practicing law, did he make any enemies among clients, or maybe beat somebody out of a bundle?"

The chief shook his head. "Nothing promising there. He never did anything I've been able to dig up that would produce a motive for spit."

"Did Kirkwood have any close friends?" asked Hank.

"Yeah. Closest were Jud Perkins, our banker, and Nat Hughes, who owns the gas station west of town. They'd all known each other since high school days."

Hank said the gas station reference reminded him he needed a refill, and after wishing the chief luck, we bowed out and headed west.

Nat Hughes was sitting at a cluttered desk inside the

station, and after exchanging names and explaining my line, Hank invited him to join us for coffee. Nat called in a helper to take over, and we drove down to the town's only remaining restaurant.

"Woody's going to be missed," said Nat, as he stirred sugar into his coffee. "I'll admit he could be a nut in some ways, but he was always good for a laugh and a story."

"What was the trouble between him and his wife?" I asked.

"Oh, hell, just about everything. They were two of a kind in all the ways that can wreck a marriage. She didn't like cooking or housekeeping, he wouldn't shovel a walk or carry out the garbage. They both grew up spoiled, as only children, and I'm pretty sure they were both cherry before they had each other. Once they tried it, they figured that's all you need between a pair."

"What about the business with Verne Tanner?"

"Unbelievable. Why Verne tagged him as the father is beyond me or anybody else. I mean, for God's sake, she'd been laid by about every young buck in town. She was the last girl he'd mess with, even if he was the kind, but he just wasn't. I figure she told her old man it was him because he had more money than anybody else around who wasn't married. She imagined they could clip him for a share."

"Does anybody in town believe her?"

"In Corden, you can find a few people who'll believe any story, no matter who tells it."

I asked what made Jud Perkins and him Kirkwood's best friends.

"Well, he did business with both of us, but mostly it's because we went to the same grade and high schools, even played on the same basketball team. With a common background like that, and living in a town like this, you're either friends or enemies. There's not much between."

After leaving Nat at his gas station, Hank and I went around to the bank and were admitted to Jud Perkins's office. He seemed genuinely disturbed by Kirkwood's death and spoke of him with warmth. No, he couldn't believe Woody could have been the one who impregnated Verne Tanner, and he thought it inconceivable that Hildegard could have killed him. Not only was there no believable motive, but she simply wasn't the sort of woman who'd locate a weapon, sneak around a farm woods, and potshot her ex-husband. It was too ridiculous to mention.

"What about her boyfriend, Chris Banks?"

"What would he kill him for? Woody wasn't trying to get Hildy back. No, this has to have been a freak accident. A boy wandering in the woods with his rifle, shooting at squirrels or crows."

"Did the Kirkwoods have any children?" I asked.

"Oh, yes. Jonah. He's seventeen, starting college this fall at Minnesota. Did very well in high school. In debate but never active in athletics. Very short—almost a midget. It made things tough for him in school. Got teased a lot and looked down on by girls. That's awfully tough on a kid in high school."

"You have any children?"

"No, we've never been so blessed."

"How about Nat?"

"He's got a boy in college at Brookings, and a girl who's thirteen. Think she's in high school now. A bright kid. No beauty but not bad-looking." After a brief pause, he said, almost apologetically, "She's kind of pushy for her age."

Hank and I returned to the restaurant for dinner and talked things over. Neither of us bought the accidental-death theory. While we were having dessert, Chief Abernathy came into the restaurant, looked around, and joined us. He asked what we'd learned, and Hank gave him a rundown and then asked if he'd been working on the accidental-shooting notion any.

"Yeah. But it's dicey in a town like this to start asking who's got a twenty-two, when they all know that was what killed Kirkwood. The county sheriff has checked neighboring farms to see if anybody's noticed kids wandering their fields with rifles. Came up with zilch. If any of them have been hunting, they've kept well away from houses and fields where farmers are working. A couple farmers admit they've got twenty-twos, and one even admits his kids have used theirs for potting gophers and woodchucks—but not lately."

Hank asked how Kirkwood got along with neighboring farmers.

"Most of them never met him. One, to the south of his place, talked with him once about a dispute over property lines, but that was worked out easy and there were no grounds for trouble."

He leaned back in his chair and scowled. "As you might guess, Mr. Wilcox, my being a Californian and only in town a little over a year makes me a total outsider. That's an advantage sometimes, but not when I'm trying to pick up inside gossip from the natives. They tell each other everything, true and false, but they're damned careful about spilling any beans around me."

We decided to go over to the Widow Wolsey's place, deposit our suitcases, and meet the landlady, who Hank knew only through his telephone call from Minneapolis.

Mrs. Wolsey was a tall, bony woman with tangled hair, not quite all gray yet, and a sharp chin under a wide, shrunken-lipped mouth. She was happy to discuss the town's favorite topic and mostly confirmed what we'd already heard about Kirkwood, Verne Tanner, her wild father, and "that stuck-up" Hildy.

"What's Jud Perkins's wife like?" I asked.

"Adel? Oh, she's something else. A year younger than her friends. Norma Sue is Nat's wife, you know. Chubby and nice, a great laugher. Adel, Jud's wife, is a foxy dresser and rather fancies herself. It's a wonder she doesn't bankrupt her husband, with the clothes she buys and the way she keeps her house in silver and china, furnishings and whatnot. Goes to the Cities near once a month, shopping."

"She got any kids?"

"Heavens, no; wouldn't be caught dead in maternity clothes."

"And the Kirkwoods?"

"Well, you wouldn't think, considering how they got on, that they'd have had any, but they did. A boy named Jonah. They say he's bright, but you'd never guess it to see him. Always looks mad. Didn't get along with kids in school. I suppose it's tough, being the runt of the class."

"I hear the Hugheses have two children."

"That's right. They've got a son in college. And Marit. She's thirteen, going on twenty-one, if you know what I mean. Very precocious, and stuck on—of all people—Jonah. Which doesn't go over that big with either of the parents involved, but they've never had the gumption to squelch it, although I hear Woody tried to."

The following day was Sunday, and Hank persuaded me to attend services at the Congregational church. He said it would give us a chance to see the natives together.

It was a bright, warm morning, and the turnout must have been gratifying to the minister. Hank kept identifying citizens he knew, mostly advanced in years, and pointed out the Perkinses, the Hugheses, Hildegard Kirkwood and her boyfriend, Chris Banks. I learned that the Tanners occasionally attended services at the Lutheran church, a block north.

After the services ended, Nat Hughes came over to speak with us and brought his wife, Norma Sue, who was a comfortably dressed, somewhat spreading blonde with lovely pink cheeks and sparkling teeth. She wanted to know if it was true I'd once had a TV news show in the Twin Cities. I pleaded guilty and said I'd lived an honest life once I got out of that.

Hughes wore a shabby gray suit, a blue shirt with the collar a size too large, and a dark striped tie, wide enough to double as a bib. I caught a glimpse of Jud Perkins moving off toward the exit at the end of services with a slim brunette, who no doubt was his wife, Adel. She looked a good ten years younger than Norma Sue, and her trim white dress made the most of her finely tapered waist and slim hips. Her deep-brown hair looked almost black.

Norma Sue invited us to join her and Nat for dinner at

the restaurant. We agreed and strolled under shading elms along the side street to Main, where the sun had a clear shot and burned down on our Sunday best. Inside the café it seemed cool at first, and we got a table near the east wall. Norma Sue launched into a monologue covering the sermon we'd heard, recent weather, and the virtues of our waitress, who, I began to suspect, must be related.

Hank finally caught her taking a breath and asked where her daughter was.

"Oh, she's home, reading the Sunday paper. I think she reads every word—news, editorials, comics, and even the ads. She's really the limit about newspapers."

"Does the Kirkwood boy ever come to church?"

"Yes, but I didn't see him this morning. I suppose he's too upset about his father's death to think about leaving the house."

"Were they close?"

"Oh, sure. Woody insisted on it, you know. He centered all his family love on Jonah after the divorce."

"Who was Jonah living with?"

"He went back and forth. I don't think that was a very good idea, but it was a compromise Woody and Hildy worked out."

"Would you mind," I asked, "if I talked with your daughter a little? I'm trying to get a feel for Corden's people, and it would help, I think, to get some slant on what the younger generation feels about its hometown and the future."

Nat looked somewhat pained, but Norma Sue was delighted by the notion and, after coffee, escorted us back to their house. She explained, as we walked, that Marit wasn't too fond of family dinners, so when they went out to eat after church, the girl stayed home and fixed her own meal.

"Nothing fancy, of course; she does hamburgers and scrambled eggs or just gets a frozen pizza at the grocery. Marit is very self-sufficient."

"All too much," muttered her father.

When we got to the house, Marit was nowhere around. That bothered Nat, but Norma Sue said it was not in the least unusual. She'd probably gone for a walk. She did it often.

We said goodbye to the couple and headed back toward town. Hank said he thought he'd recognize the girl if he saw her: he'd examined a picture of her in the living room. We didn't find her in any of the places we checked along the street or even in the park nearby. So Hank found a public phone and called the Kirkwood house. He got Hildegard and talked her into letting us make a visit.

Hildegard was a solidly built woman, barely five feet tall, with a broad face, a square chin, and smooth, faintly freckled cheeks. She took us through the small vestibule, left of a staircase, and into a large living room through an open arch to the right. We sat on a blue couch behind a glass-topped coffee table, and she settled into an over-stuffed chair across the room. I don't remember ever receiving a more calculating examination by man, woman, or child. My first interview with television execs, four years back, was relatively informal and friendly compared with this.

Hank overdid his job of trying to impress her with my background as a news reporter and TV anchor, but before long it seemed to work. She actually gave hints of being interested in me rather than in any threat I might offer. It helped, of course, that he omitted mentioning anything about the semi-private-eye work I'd done a few times in the past couple of years. All we were after, Hank assured her, was a story about the ways South Dakota had changed since he had grown up in this town.

She said the biggest changes were in the weather and the drop in population all through the county. It was about a quarter of what it had been three generations back. "Farmers," she said, "are becoming about as rare as buffalo. And the moment kids get out of high school they're off to college if they can make it, and that's the last we see of them."

"Where do you think your boy will go?"

"Lord, I've no idea. I don't think he knows, either, but it will be far from South Dakota, you can depend on that."

"Where is Jonah now?" I interjected.

"He's probably over at his father's house. He's been spending a lot of time alone there."

"Who do you think killed your husband?" Hank asked.

If he expected to shock her, he was disappointed. She just gazed at him thoughtfully.

"That's been on my mind, of course. Believe it or not, I keep coming around to Jud Perkins. That's wild, isn't it? Imagine a stuffy banker shooting a man on a farm with a little boy's rifle. But I can't get away from the notion."

"Why him?" I asked.

She gave me a bitter smile. "Have you seen his wife?"

"Just a glimpse."

"I call her the virgin harlot. Flirts with every man she sees. Not by words or even deeds, but what she wears, the way she smiles, the talent for making any damned fool man feel he's interesting and maybe even brilliant. She's the only woman that ever brought lustful thoughts into my ex-husband. And the beautiful irony is, she never let him have so much as a feel. Strictly a teaser. She never got to him until we divorced, but somehow that changed things, at least for Woody. He had aspirations, you could say. And he wasn't clever or subtle, so it was plain, and that was more than Jud could tolerate."

"Does Jonah have any close friends?" Hank asked suddenly.

"I suppose he must have, but I'm afraid I don't know any names. He isn't a confiding boy."

"Are you bothered by his involvement with Marit?"

"Well, please, let's not call it that. They like each other. She's a very precocious girl, and Jonah, being so small, hasn't felt comfortable with girls his own age, so it's natural enough for him to find her appealing. I'm sure it's all innocent, but of course Woody didn't see it that way. He insisted it was unhealthy. He couldn't believe, with the difference in their ages, it could be anything but a physical attraction. He was actually an awful prude. There's something about men of his type that makes them always suspicious and distrusting. I suppose because of his own weaknesses."

"You think he was unfaithful?"

"I'm sure he was, in his mind. But I doubt he ever had the gall to act on it."

"What chance would he have had to get Adel alone?" asked Hank.

"Well, Jud goes to the Cities at least once a month, sometimes even to Chicago. As long as a week. It would give Jud time enough to wonder what might be going on back home."

"How could Adel and Mr. Kirkwood have gotten together without people knowing?"

"Well, everybody figures love will find a way, right? Especially when the parties live across the alley from each other and there are always telephones to arrange things by."

And, I thought, there were all those trips Adel made to go shopping, and Kirkwood's travels.

Hank told Hildegard that we really appreciated her cooperation and could we impose on her a bit more and borrow her telephone? He wanted to call Adel and arrange for us to make a visit. The idea seemed to tickle Hildegard, and she gave him the number and waved him to the phone.

As we left her house, she warned us to be careful.

The Perkins home was painted dark brown and stood back on a lot that sloped steeply upward. It gave the place a castlelike remoteness. Adel appeared promptly when Hank hit the doorbell on the enclosed-porch door. She opened it, smiling, and stepped back.

She was slightly taller than I'd thought on seeing her at the church, but every bit as smartly dressed and trim. She led us through a large vestibule and into a broad sunken living room with a deep maroon carpet, where she waved us into easy chairs that faced a large TV set and stereo equipment, dominating the far wall.

She told us, as she sat down and demurely crossed her ankles, that she had heard much about both of us. Her eyes were deep brown, with unnaturally long lashes, and her mouth was full-lipped, also unnaturally. She had the smile of a professional politician.

Hank explained that we'd been talking to several Corden citizens, and she interrupted, gently, to ask who. He ran over a few, and when he mentioned Hildegard, she smiled, settled back a little more in her easy chair, and asked if that hadn't been a particularly interesting interview. Hank tried to wave it off, and she laughed.

"I suppose she told you I was involved with Woody?"

"I got the impression she suspected he was in love with you but that you were too clever to let anything serious happen."

"How sweet. The fact is, she was regularly unfaithful to Woody, well before they divorced, and she's always wanted people to think he was a philanderer, when in fact he was simply indifferent. You know what she's honestly jealous about? The fact that her son thinks more of me than he does of his mother. And she's furious because she thinks I encouraged the romance between Jonah and Marit Hughes. The only time Woody talked to me alone was when he tried to make me use my influence to convince Jonah that it was foolish, even dangerous, for him to get involved with a girl only thirteen years old. He tried to make Jonah think he had to be sick to even think about a girl that much younger."

"How long have they been close?"

"They've been fond of each other just about all their lives. Because he's so small and Marit is far smarter than any of her classmates, they've both felt they're outcasts. Being close neighbors and both highly imaginative and exceptionally sensitive, they were drawn together."

"How far did Kirkwood go in trying to split them up?"

"I'm not sure. I haven't really talked with Jonah since about a week before his father was murdered. Maybe it was less."

"Did he visit with you before that?"

"Occasionally. For several years before the divorce, we three couples were rather close, mostly because the fellows had been school pals. We did nearly everything together, and the children were exposed to each other regularly, especially during summers, when we picnicked and even went camping once together. Jonah and Marit always got along beautifully, such dear friends. And since I have no children of my own, I used to give them little snack parties on my porch. I taught them to play chess. It just seemed likely they'd both enjoy that and be good at it, and they were, and are. They would play here, but when Woody got unpleasant about that, they just went somewhere else. Marit said she didn't want me getting into trouble with their parents because of Jonah and her. She's a thoughtful child."

"Where *do* they go?"

"Well, you can be sure they haven't advertised it. I suspect they just hop on their bikes and ride out in the country somewhere. Probably by a lake or slough."

When we left the Perkins house I suggested a talk with Verne Tanner.

"Why?" asked Hank. "You want to get laid?"

"Not that bad. But I'm curious about her, and how come she tagged Kirkwood as her lover. Nothing we've heard makes it figure."

Surprisingly, she didn't live with her father but occupied the upper half of a small duplex on the north side of town. It turned out she was a clerk in the grocery store—or had been until she got fired after putting the finger on Kirkwood.

I'm afraid both Hank and I expected to find a slutty woman, probably well along in pregnancy, overweight and sloppy. Instead she looked like a high school kid, was slim as a colt and about as long-legged, with light-brown hair cut short to frame a slender face with a nose just a

shade too long and a mouth almost too wide. She said
she didn't have a lot of time, she was going to baby-sit in
an hour.

Hank grinned at her and said she didn't look old
enough to baby-sit.

"I'm much older than I look."

"You ever baby-sit for the Kirkwoods?" I asked.

"What made you think that?"

"A hunch."

"You've got good ones. Yeah, I did. For two years.
Long ago."

"Like the kid?"

"Sure."

"How about his dad?"

"At the time he was just Jonah's old man. I didn't
think anything of him, except he was stingy."

"When did he get close to you?"

"Let's sit down," she said, and led us into the living
room. It was very small, and I guessed the couch was a
sofa bed. Hank and I sat on it, and she stayed on her feet,
watching us. Her stomach showed only a hint of swelling.

"I suppose you're going to think I'm weird, but with
Woody dead, it doesn't make any difference now. He got
close to me way back when I was their baby-sitter. He
drove me home one night, and he was the first guy I ever
did it with. It wasn't rape; I liked it. What I hated was,
he'd never look me in the face again after that. Like I was
filthy. And when he started giving poor Jonah a lot of
shit about Marit Hughes, I decided to lay it on him after I
was stupid enough to get pregnant early this spring. I figured he was just lucky I didn't get pregnant when he did
me, and it wouldn't hurt him to pay some expenses."

"You own a twenty-two?"

She grinned. "No. Never owned or shot one in my life."

"Does Marit visit you now and then?" I asked.

"Another hunch, huh?"

"Yeah."

She moved over to a chair and sat down. "Yes. She visits me. What's it to you?"

"We've been trying to get the picture of what things were like that led up to Kirkwood's murder. There are some who figure it was your father, others suspect Jud Perkins. Some even like Hildegard for it, but we can't buy that."

"Well, it sure as hell wasn't Dad. We were together that afternoon, and nobody can prove different."

"I guess you know Kirkwood was pretty violently against any hanky-panky between his son and Marit, right?"

"She mentioned it once."

"How long ago?"

"I don't remember. Why?"

"You know where Marit and Jonah were when Kirkwood got it?"

She looked at me for several seconds.

"Marit was here, with Dad and me."

"Where was Jonah?"

"Home, I guess. At his father's place. He was like grounded, Marit said."

"Any idea why Kirkwood was out at the farm that afternoon?"

"He was thinking of moving out there. I understand he liked the house and thought it would be nice to live outside of town."

"Who told you that?"

"Marit. She got it from Jonah."

"How did he feel about that?"

"He hated it."

She told us that Kirkwood had absolutely forbidden Jonah to see or even talk on the telephone with Marit. While ranting at Jonah, Kirkwood had always referred to Marit as an oversexed little bitch. He'd made arrangements for him to attend the University of Minnesota in the fall and ordered him to spend the remainder of the summer on the farm

We talked a little more, thanked Verne, left the duplex, and discussed it all as we walked toward downtown.

"How about we go over to Kirkwood's house in town and see if we can corral Jonah."

"What's your plan?"

I told him. He didn't like it but said he'd go along.

When Hank and I introduced ourselves, Jonah nodded in recognition. He was small and slight, though not as short as I'd expected, and he looked rather haunted.

"Okay. First, we want you to know we're not against you, or trying to trick you into anything. It happens we've learned some things about your father's death and want to talk about it. You willing?"

He looked at Hank, then back at me, finally shrugged and asked us in. When we were seated in the sparely furnished living room, I began.

"From what we've learned, you had understandable reasons for killing your father—"

"I've got an alibi."

"Yes. One offered by your girlfriend, Marit, who loves you and would do anything to protect you. Including giving false testimony."

"You can't prove that."

"I won't try. But Chief Abernathy will. And keep in mind, Jonah, this is a very small town. You couldn't have left this house in daylight and come back in daylight and not had someone see you. A witness will show up, probably several. And if only one comes forth, and is at all convincing, not only will you get convicted, but Marit will go to jail and have her life ruined. You want that to happen?"

"It won't."

"You hope it won't. Frankly, we hope it won't, either. But are you willing to take the chance of ruining her life along with yours? Think of the odds. On top of that, if you confess, a good lawyer can probably make a case that you were practically driven into killing by your father's cruelty in all this. And because of your age, chances are good that you'll get a relatively short sentence and very likely early parole. Marit's young; she'll survive this and maybe even wait for you. The easier you make this case, the more willing authorities will be to give you whatever breaks they can."

Gradually he lost confidence, and finally he stood up.

"I want to talk with Marit. Alone."

We walked to the Hughes home, and he went inside to talk with Marit. We waited on the porch. It wouldn't have surprised me if they'd ducked out the back door and run. Maybe I even wished they would.

In half an hour, he came out and said he was ready to go talk with the police chief. He was going to confess.

As we drove back toward Minneapolis the following day, Hank was silent for a good while, but finally he began talking of the case.

"I think the most ironic thing is the fact that Kirkwood taught his kid to shoot. Made an expert of him with that damned gun."

Later he muttered about the stupidity of adults who forgot the intensity of first love and the madness brought on by elders trying to rule their children's lives.

"I'll tell you one thing," he said at last. "If Uncle Carl had handled this case, it would've been different. He'd have figured out a way to get the boy off. The next time somebody asks me to poke my nose into other people's business, I'll damn well handle it myself."

Hank hasn't invited me on any more trips.

BINGO

JOHN LUTZ

The smash-hit film Single White Female
was based on one of John Lutz's recent
novels and demonstrated that Lutz is at
home in virtually every type of crime
fiction, from the classic puzzle to the gritty
private-eye tales he writes about
Alo Nudger.

Like J. A. Jance elsewhere in this collection, Lutz here takes a sardonic look at an
aspect of the Great American Retirement
Plan.

As he notes: "If life's declining years were
golden, that gold could melt fast
in the searing Arizona sun."

▼▼▼▼▼

IT WASN'T AS IF Harry Archambault needed the money. Not that he and Gretta couldn't use it, as might anyone living in the sprawling retirement community of Sun Colony a few miles west of Phoenix. Retirement wasn't at all what most people imagined or wished for. If life's declining years were golden, that gold could melt fast in the searing Arizona sun.

Sun Colony comprised over nine hundred homes that seemed to have been created with a combination of half a dozen cookie cutters. That was the way developers built them nowadays; cost containment through duplication. All of the homes were single story, with decorative fireplaces, pale-shingled roofs to reflect the sun, two-car garages, and no basements. Each had been sold with a small Phoenix palm tree in the front yard; now many of those squat, indigenous trees were huge, some of them hacked and trimmed of low branches but left bushy on top so they resembled mutant, oversized pineapples. Individual houses were landscaped with saguaro cacti and citrus trees and were painted their own faded pastel colors, yet in Harry's eyes they were the same, wood and aluminum clones with only the slightest variation.

There was very little actual grass in Sun Colony; the neat, well-kept homes had yards made up of different-colored gravel, mostly reds and greens, the various hues separated by curving plastic or stone dividers laid low to the ground by skilled Mexican laborers. There were no children in Sun Colony, and no noise of any sort. It was illegal to park cars on the street. Trash was deposited in lidded underground containers in front of each house and collected three times a week. Though there were sidewalks, there was nowhere interesting to be reached on foot. There were only the neat rows of houses and the symmetrical, multicolored yards and the pale, sun-washed concrete. And beyond all that, like an extension of it, stretched the strange, stark beauty of the desert. It was like the landscape of the moon.

That was why Harry decided to break the law; he was tired of living on the moon.

"I don't see why you keep doing that," Gretta said. She seemed content since they'd moved to Sun Colony two years ago. She was in a book discussion club, did group aqua-aerobics in the community clubhouse swimming pool several times a week, and had just signed up for weaving classes. Most of these activities she did with her friend Wilma, a widow five years younger than Gretta, who lived in the next block. "We have too many cans of tuna now."

"This is Arizona," Harry said, "miles from the ocean. You can never have enough tuna."

He glanced over at his wife of forty years. She had evolved into a pleasant-featured but bland gray-haired woman who at times seemed like someone's grandmother rather than his wife. Did other seventy-year-old men think like that about their wives?

Of course Gretta *was* someone's grandmother— Harry's grandkids'. Gretta and Harry were grandparents five times over. But their children—and *their* children— were more than a thousand miles away. Ben, the nearest of Harry and Gretta's offspring, lived in Rockport, Illinois, with his wife and two sons. The daughter, Vera, lived with her husband and three children in Morristown, Tennessee. The other boy, Freddy, was single and worked in what he described as "various creative enterprises" in New York City.

Harry shrugged off these musings and concentrated on setting up the printing calculator so the tape looked like a genuine receipt for the purchase of two cans of Fish Ahoy chunk white tuna. If the labels of two cans with proof of purchase were mailed to Fish Ahoy headquarters in

Maine, the company would return a free can of tuna plus two dollars. At Norton's supermarket, a twelve-ounce can of Fish Ahoy tuna sold for $1.59 including tax. Which meant Harry could buy two cans of tuna, send in their labels, receive a free can with a check for two dollars, purchase a third can of tuna, send in its label with the free can's label (and a Harry-generated receipt falsely signifying the purchase of two cans), and so on, each time making a profit of forty-one cents. Gretta didn't seem to understand this.

"You're a driven, wacky old man," she told him, "sitting there counterfeiting grocery store receipts so you can swindle a company out of free cans of tuna. Shameful!"

"It isn't the tuna," he said in exasperation. "It's the profit."

"You're not an entrepreneur, Harry, you're a retiree."

"So I should sit in the sun and die?"

"No, you should play boccie ball or go to aquatic exercises with me or play bingo at the recreation hall Saturday nights."

"Sitting in the sun and dying sounds better."

She glared at him with cold blue eyes behind thick prescription lenses. "Did you ever stop and think what your time is worth? Figure that in your calculations and you're probably hundreds of dollars in the hole."

"That's why I'm doing this," Harry said glumly, "because of what my time is worth."

Gretta, preferring not to think or talk in the abstract, began to read a glossy magazine about weaving. Harry noticed a free-offer coupon on the back cover and decided he'd examine the magazine later.

A week later Freddy, on his way home from Las Vegas, drove up in a rental car for a short visit. He suggested that there were people who might be looking for him in Vegas and in New York, so it was a rare opportunity to spend quality time with his folks.

Freddy was the son most like Harry, only with a certain additional ability to overcome moral inhibitions.

Harry looked at his son's permed and styled hair and obviously expensive suit and speculated that Freddy was doing very well in New York.

The third evening of his visit, Freddy sauntered outside and sat down next to Harry on the vinyl-padded glider on the patio, facing a lemon tree.

"Quiet out here," he observed.

"Always is," Harry said. "Like the grave."

"Hot too."

"But it's a dry heat."

"So's an oven. You and Mom ever drive out to Vegas or Laughlin and gamble?"

"No. Too expensive, your mother says, and no gambler wins in the long run. Your mother can quote the odds to back up that statement."

Freddy gazed for a while at the lemon tree, along with Harry, then grinned. "Something supposed to happen in that tree, Pop?"

"Something does happen. Lemons get larger, riper, then they drop on the ground and I have to pick them up or they rot."

"Why don't you pick them from the tree before they drop and eat them?"

"Don't like lemons. Useless, bitter fruit from useless trees."

"Mom's worried about you. She told me about your sales receipt–coupon scam. That very profitable?"

"Not really," Harry said. "It's just something to do so I feel useful."

"Kind of clever, though," Freddy said.

"Enough so that it works. Paid for that beer you're drinking."

Freddy sipped beer and continued contemplating the lemon tree with his father.

"Your mother worries too much," Harry said.

"Yep," Freddy agreed. He sighed loudly, stretched, then stood up. "You ever think about planting a different kind of tree, Pop?"

"All the time," Harry said.

The day before he left for New York, Freddy ushered
Harry into the den. "Bought you a little gift," he said,
"for putting me up here when I needed a place to go."

Harry stared dumbfounded at what was on the table
near the window. "A copy machine," he said.

"The latest Mitziguchi-Nagasaki model. Copies anything, in shades of gray or in vivid color."

"I don't know a thing about copiers."

"You will, though," Freddy said. "I know you."

"Copiers got something to do with your business in
New York, Freddy?"

"Sorta."

Harry felt like questioning Freddy about New York,
about why he'd needed a place to stay and who might be
looking for him, but he knew when not to pry. "Not that
I don't appreciate your generosity," he said, "but I've got
no use for a copier."

"You won't feel that way for long," Freddy said. "It
comes with instructions, and it's not as hard to operate as
you might imagine. Have fun with it."

He walked into the kitchen and told his mother goodbye, then went out to the garage to get in the rental car
and drive it to the airport to catch his flight to New York.

"You be careful in that city," Gretta called, as he was
backing the car down the driveway. "I mean, with the
crime and all."

"There's crime here in Sun Colony too, Mom," Freddy
said, and winked at Harry.

Harry and Gretta stood on the porch and watched
their son's car until it was out of sight, a glimmering fragment of their past retreating into memory like all the rest
of their lives.

"He must mean muggers," Harry said, and turned to
go back in the house.

Freddy was right. Within a few days Harry could work
the copy machine without a problem. Within a week he
felt he had it mastered.

"I wish you'd get tired of that thing," Gretta told him. "Seems there's at least two of every piece of paper in the house."

Which got Harry thinking. Just fooling around, mind you, he bought some very thin paper and ran copies of a twenty-dollar bill. Astoundingly accurate and precise as they were, he knew they would hardly fool anyone. Besides, counterfeiting was against the law.

But he soon found that coupons were different. It was relatively easy to find copy paper the approximate thickness and glossiness of magazine pages and run off very impressive duplicates of coupons.

The next day—just as a kind of test—Harry copied half a dozen two-for-one coupons for a brand-name athlete's foot spray. He spent the afternoon and part of the evening going to drugstores and supermarkets and passing the bogus coupons. Not one store clerk gave the slightest indication that the coupons might be copies.

"What did all that gain you?" Gretta asked after breakfast the next morning. "Now we've got a dozen aerosol cans of fungus spray we don't need."

"Half of them were free," Harry pointed out. "And don't forget the money we saved on magazines."

"And don't you forget that neither of us has athlete's foot."

Gretta's trouble, as Harry had long known, was that she lacked imagination.

Soon Harry was duplicating scores of coupons. Half off this, a free one of that, a dollar refund with this and proof of purchase. Then he learned to alter dates and figures on genuine sales receipts and run copies of them to send in with his phony coupons. By the end of the month, Harry was turning a tidy profit.

Harry never thought of what he was doing as counterfeiting; it was more like simple and harmless duplicating. He even referred to his duplicates as doppelgängers, a German word meaning "double . . . a shadow self." All he was doing was creating doppelgänger cereal coupons. So what if an old man, a doppelgänger shadow of his old self, made a few dollars in his spare time? Where was the harm?

He did most of his work while Gretta and the widow Wilma played bingo Wednesday and Saturday evenings at the Sun Colony recreation hall.

"I know what you're up to while I'm away," Gretta told him one Sunday morning several weeks later.

"What I'm up to?" Harry said guiltily.

"You're going to bring the FBI down on us, Harry!"

"The FBI doesn't care about an old retired codger like me with a hobby."

"Your hobby's illegal, Harry!"

"You copy rental videos," he pointed out. "That's illegal too."

She sniffed irritably and showed him the twenty-dollar bill she'd won the night before at bingo.

Two days later, Billy, the checkout clerk at the supermarket, paused as he was bagging tuna and said, "Fella was around here asking questions, Mr. Archambault."

"Questions?" Harry said. "Like what aisle's the cereal in?"

Billy smiled. He was too old to be thought of as a boy, really, probably in his mid twenties, but his frail build, blond hair, and poor complexion made him seem like a teenager. "Like he was asking if anybody knew Mr. Archambault, and directions out to your house."

"Anybody tell him?"

"Sure. You ain't got nothing to hide, do you, Mr. Archambault?"

Harry shook his head no, watching Billy begin stuffing a second plastic bag with tuna. "Fella say who he was with?"

"With?"

"You know . . . an insurance company, the Internal Revenue Service, that kind of thing."

"Nope. Barry, the store manager, said the guy was probably a relative of yours, needing directions to pay you a visit. I didn't see him that way, though."

"Oh? Why not?"

"He was a big fella dressed all wrong for Arizona—had dark clothes and wore a tie. Spoke with a slight accent I couldn't quite place. But more than that, he didn't seem, well, friendly. Seemed more . . ."

"Official?"

"Sort of. But with a meanness about him."

Harry's heart began slamming against his ribs. "Like a cop?"

"No, nothing like a cop."

The manager's voice came over the store's speaker system: "Billy, help out on register one."

"He seen us talking," Billy said with a smile. "Barry don't like conversations with the customers on company time."

Harry gathered up his bulging plastic sacks. "Thanks for the information, Billy. If the man turns up, I'll let you know who he is."

"Do that, Mr. Archambault." Billy scurried around the counter and started toward an end register. Then he turned, wiping his hands on his white apron. "One other thing, Mr. Archambault. I figured the guy wasn't a relative because he didn't know your name. Called you Fred."

Freddy, who wrote that his business in New York was doing well, sent Harry a small notebook computer, again with thanks for providing safe haven between Las Vegas and New York. "I'm sure you'll think of something to use it for," Freddy's accompanying note read. "It's in the genes."

Harry wasn't quite sure what his son meant by that. It was as if Freddy knew something about him and was toying with him, providing opportunities and opening doors to see if Harry would step through. Harry had always been scrupulously honest and in fact a bit of a prig, in Freddy's view. Freddy had said so more than once. Now it seemed the amoral Freddy was deriving some sort of pleasure from exploring his father's capacity for corruption. And oddly enough, Harry didn't mind. He'd always been closer to Freddy than to the other kids, and now he felt that only Freddy understood how stultifying life was here in Sun Colony. It was as if Freddy wanted to rescue dear old dad from the tragic and seemingly inevitable trajectory of his remaining years on the moon. Maybe in repayment for all those Cub Scout meetings and horrendous PTA spaghetti dinners.

Harry considered writing or calling Freddy to tell him about the man who'd inquired about him at the supermarket, then decided it wasn't necessary. Freddy had known people were searching for him, and he'd already left, so what was the point?

But he did call Freddy after the man appeared at the front door. It had to be the same man, large, dressed in dark clothing, even a tightly knotted tie that made his thick neck bulge.

"Had a helluva time finding this place," the man said. His features were thickened, as if he'd had an unsuccessful boxing career. The smile he attempted only made him uglier. "All the houses look alike."

"They do at that," Harry said.

"I'm looking for a Fred Archambault," the man said, in what Harry knew right away was a New York accent.

"I'm Harry Archambault."

"Yeah, I knew you wasn't him. You know him?"

Harry thought about his answer. Freddy's rental car had been parked out of sight in the garage during his visit, and as far as Harry knew, no one had seen him. One of the advantages of living on the moon. "I've got a son named Fred," Harry said, "but he lives in New York and I haven't set eyes on him in over a year."

"Long way between here and New York," the man said, staring hard at Harry.

"I guess it is," Harry said. "I never made the trip."

"Fred ever made it? To pay you a visit, I mean."

"Let's see . . . Last time he was out here was three Christmases ago."

The big man wiped his forehead with the back of his wrist. "Sure is hot out here."

"But it's a dry heat."

"Mind if I step in outa the sun?"

"Guess not." Harry moved back and let him enter. He felt small next to the man, and old. And slightly sickened by the overpowering scent of stale sweat and cheap deodorant.

With his ugly smile spread wide on his face, the man idly began walking about, gazing through doors and down halls. "Nice place," he commented.

Harry thanked him, glad Gretta was at weaving class.

"Mind if I use the bathroom?" the man asked.

Harry told him where it was.

He listened while the toilet flushed. While the man roamed around the back of the house, making sure all the rooms were unoccupied.

After a few minutes the man returned to the living room, his hands lingering near his belt buckle as if he'd just zipped up his fly. "Thanks," he said.

"I doubt my son's the Fred Archambault you're looking for," Harry told him. "Archambault's a more common name than you might think."

"I suppose you're right." The big man lumbered toward the door.

"Want me to give him your name if he calls? Just in case?" Harry asked.

"Naw, you just be a good senior citizen and don't mention I was here." The smile dropped away from his face, as if it had been too much of a strain for him to hold it there. He nodded goodbye to Harry and walked out the door.

Harry heard a car start and went to the window in time to see the man drive away in a dark-blue Chrysler, probably a rental. He stood watching the car until it was out of sight, feeling angry, not liking that "senior citizen" remark.

After a while, he went to the phone and called Freddy to tell him about the man's visit.

The computer was more difficult than the copier, but Harry soon caught on to it and became quite proficient.

About that time, Freddy called from New York and said not to worry about the man who'd visited Harry, that everything had been taken care of and Freddy was sending Harry some new software to go with the computer. Out of gratitude. Freddy had rarely shown gratitude in the past.

Strangely enough, Harry felt a kind of gratitude toward Freddy. He realized that he'd enjoyed the visit from the big man, uneasy though it had made him at the time. It was as if something from the outside world had made it through space to the moon, as if for a change something real had happened in Sun Colony.

A month later Harry surprised Gretta by saying, "I think I'll tag along when you go to play bingo tonight."

"Stay out of my way, then," Gretta said, when she'd lowered her eyebrows. "The other girls and I take our bingo seriously."

"Wilma gonna be there?"

"No, she hasn't been going lately. Got in an argument with Marge about how much pineapple juice was in the punch. Marge punched her. Just stay out of our way."

Harry took her at her word and sat in a corner by himself, near where sweaters, shawls, and light jackets were hung, listening to the bingo caller sing out the numbers, playing with quiet intensity.

Sun Colony buzzed for weeks about the string of winning bingo cards Harry had played. It was a run of luck worth a write-up in the Sun Colony Bugle under the heading LUCKY SUN COLONY RESIDENT WINS $1000's AT BINGO.

Harry knew it hadn't exactly been luck. He'd worked out a program on his little computer that enabled him to create an index system for the bingo cards he'd duplicated and kept next to him while he held the computer in his lap. When the computer showed a string of numbers corresponding to a winning card in Harry's file, he quickly and unobtrusively eased the appropriate card up onto the table, covered the necessary numbers with bingo chips, and raised his hand to signify that he'd won.

Easy money. Harry had heard about it all his life, and now here it was, when he was too old to really enjoy it.

Between coupon money and his bingo winnings, Harry had over five thousand dollars: $5,021.26, to be exact. Gretta pointed this out to him when she discovered the money in a coffee can in the garage.

The dollar amount seemed to assuage her guilt, so that she stopped harping at him to quit occupying himself with his high-tech toys. Harry had reached her price.

"What we're going to do with the money," she told him, "is to buy up to a bigger house right here in Sun Colony."

"We don't need a bigger house," Harry pointed out.

"I suppose," Gretta said, frowning, "that you'd rather buy a second house exactly like this one. You've developed a fixation on duplication that's a real irritation."

"That rhymes," Harry said, "like a rap song."

"You're too old for rap music."

"Not as old as you think. Not too old to live."

"You're as old as you *are*, Harry, even though you've developed a foolish streak of vanity and begun to dye your hair."

"You noticed?"

"I found the bottle in the trash. What are you going to do about it?"

"Keep dying it, I suppose."

"I mean the larger house. What are you going to do with the money?"

"I'm going to drive to Las Vegas and gamble," Harry said.

She appeared startled, then she smiled. "My, my, you are full of surprises." She rose from where she was sitting on the sofa and began to stalk about the room. Her feet in her practical rubber-soled shoes made no sound on the thick carpet. "It's time you came to your senses, Harry. You've had fun and made money with your electronic toys, but there's a limit. You're going to stop now with your doppelgänger nonsense and—"

But it was Gretta who'd stopped. Her pacing had

taken her near a window, and she'd glanced out at the front yard and driveway. Her voice was, for the first time, frightened.

"Harry, who is that woman sitting in our car?"

Harry and Wilma loved Vegas. The system was simple there. You gave a casino cashier money and the cashier gave you chips. Later, if you were lucky, you gave the cashier chips in exchange for more money than you started out with.

Harry didn't see why luck had to have anything to do with it.

ENGINES

BILL PRONZINI

Long an acknowledged master of the
humanistic crime story, Bill Pronzini has
distinguished himself as both a novelist
and a short story writer.

Here, in this tense and surprising story set
in the grim splendor of Death Valley,
Pronzini reminds us that the suspense tale
travels very well—in this case giving us a
glimpse of a world that is almost science
fictional.

Pronzini's novels include Shackles and the
noir classic Masques.

WHEN GEENA MOVED OUT and filed for divorce, the first two things I did were to put the house up for sale and to quit Unidyne, a job I'd hated from the beginning. Then I loaded the Jeep and drove straight to Death Valley.

I told no one where I was going. Not that there was anybody to tell, really; we had no close friends, or at least I didn't, and my folks were both dead. Geena could have guessed, of course. She knew me that well, though not nearly well enough to understand my motives.

I did not go to Death Valley because something in my life had died.

I went there to start living again.

October is one of the Valley's best months. All months in the Monument are good, as far as I'm concerned, even July and August, when the midday temperatures sometimes exceed 120 degrees Fahrenheit and Death Valley justifies its Paiute Indian name, *Tomesha*—ground afire. If a sere desert climate holds no terrors for you, if you respect it and accept it on its terms, survival is not a problem and the attractions far outweigh the drawbacks. Still, I'm partial to October, the early part of the month. The beginning of the tourist season is still a month away, temperatures seldom reach 100 degrees, and the constantly changing light show created by sun and wind and clouds is at its most spectacular. You can stay in one place all day, from dawn to dark—Zabriskie Point, say, or the sand dunes near Stovepipe Wells—and with each ten-degree rise and fall of the sun the colors of rock and sand hills change from dark rose to burnished gold, from chocolate brown to purple and indigo and gray-black, with dozens of subtler shades in between.

It had been almost a year since I'd last been to the Valley. Much too long, but it had been a difficult year. I'd been alone on that last visit, as I was alone now; alone the last dozen or so trips, since Geena refused to come with me anymore five years ago. I preferred it that way. The Valley is a place to be shared only with someone who views it in the same perspective, not as endless miles of coarse, dead landscape but as a vast, almost mystical place—a *living* place—of majestic vistas and stark natural beauty.

Deciding where to go first hadn't been easy. It has more than three thousand square miles, second only among national parks to Yellowstone, and all sorts of terrain: the great trough of the valley floor, with its miles of salt pan two hundred feet and more below sea level, its dunes and alluvial fans, its borate deposits and old borax works, its barren fields of gravel and broken rock; and five enclosing mountain ranges full of hidden canyons, petroglyphs, played-out gold and silver mines, ghost towns. I'd spent an entire evening with my topos—topographical maps put out by the U.S. Geological Survey—and finally settled on the Funeral Mountains and the Chloride Cliffs topo. The Funerals form one of the eastern boundaries, and their foothills and crest not only are laden with a variety of canyons but contain the ruins of the Keane Wonder Mill and mine and the gold boomtown of Chloride City.

I left the Jeep north of Scotty's Castle, near Hells Gate, packed in, and stayed for three days and two nights. The first day was a little rough; even though I'm in good shape, it takes a while to refamiliarize yourself with desert mountain terrain after a year away. The second day was easier. I spent that one exploring Echo Canyon and then tramping among the thick-timbered tramways of the Keane, the decaying mill a mile below it which in the 1890s had twenty stamps processing eighteen hundred tons of ore a month. On the third day I went on up to the Funerals' sheer heights and Chloride City, and the climb neither strained nor winded me.

It was a fine three days. I saw no other people except at a long distance. I reestablished kinship with the Valley, as only a person who truly loves it can, and all the tension and restless dissatisfaction built up over the past year slowly bled out of me. I could literally feel my spirit reviving, starting to soar again.

I thought about Geena only once, on the morning of the third day as I stood atop one of the crags looking out toward Needles Eye. There was no wind, and the stillness, the utter absence of sound, was so acute it created an almost painful pressure against the eardrums. Of all the things Geena hated about Death Valley, its silence—"void of silence," an early explorer had termed it—topped the list. It terrified her. On our last trip together, when she'd caught me listening, she'd said, "What are you listening *to*? There's nothing to hear in this godforsaken place. It's as if everything has shut down. Not just here; everywhere. As if all the engines have quit working."

She was right, exactly right: as if all the engines have quit working. And that perception, more than anything else, summed up the differences between us. To her, the good things in life, the essence of life itself, were people, cities, constant scurrying activity. She needed to hear the steady, throbbing engines of civilization in order to feel safe, secure, alive. And I needed none of those things; needed *not* to hear the engines.

I remembered something else she'd said to me once, not so long ago. "You're a dreamer, Scott, an unfocused dreamer. Drifting through life looking for something that might not even exist." Well, maybe there was truth in that too. But if I was looking for something, I had already found part of it right here in Death Valley. And now I could come here as often as I wanted, without restrictions; resigning from Unidyne had seen to that. I couldn't live in the Monument—permanent residence is limited to a small band of Paiutes and Park Service employees—but I could live nearby, in Beatty or Shoshone or one of the other little towns over in the Nevada desert. After the

L.A. house sold, I'd be well fixed. And when the money
finally did run out I could hire out as a guide, do odd
jobs—whatever it took to support myself. Dreamer with a
focus at last.

For a little time, thinking about Geena made me sad.
But the Valley is not a place where I can feel sad for long.
I had loved her very much at first, when we were both
students at UCLA, but over our eleven years together the
love had eroded and seeped away, and now what I felt
mainly was relief. I was free and Geena was free. Endings
don't have to be painful, not if you look at them as begin-
nings instead.

Late that third afternoon I hiked back to where I'd left
the Jeep. No one had bothered it; I had never had any
trouble with thieves or vandals out here. Before I crawled
into my sleeping bag I sifted through the topos again to
pick my next spot. I don't know why I chose the Manly
Peak topo. Maybe because I hadn't been in the southern
Panamints, through Warm Springs Canyon, in better than
three years. Still, it was an odd choice to make. That
region was not one of my favorite parts of the Valley.
Also, a large portion of the area is under private claim,
and the owners of the talc mines along the canyon take a
dim view of trespassing; you have to be extra careful to
keep to public lands when you pack in there.

In the morning, just before dawn, I ate a couple of
nutrition bars for breakfast and then pointed the Jeep
down Highway 178. The sun was out by the time I
reached the Warm Springs Canyon turnoff. The main
road in is unpaved, rutted and talc-covered, and primarily
the domain of eighteen-wheelers passing to and from the
mines. You need at least a four-wheel-drive vehicle to
negotiate it and the even rougher trails that branch off it.
I would not take a passenger car over one inch of that terrain. Neither would anyone else who knows the area or
pays attention to the Park Service brochures, guidebooks,
and posted signs.

That was why I was amazed when I came on the Ford
Taurus.

I had turned off the main canyon road ten miles in, onto the trail into Butte Valley, and when I rounded a turn on the washboard surface there it was, pulled off into the shadow of a limestone shelf. The left rear tire was flat, and a stain that had spread out from underneath told me the oil pan was ruptured. No one was visible inside or anywhere in the immediate vicinity.

I brought the Jeep up behind and went to have a look. The Ford had been there awhile—that was clear. At least two days. The look and feel of the oil stain proved that. I had to be the first to come by since its abandonment, or it wouldn't still be sitting here like this. Not many hikers or offroaders venture out this way in the off-season, the big ore trucks use the main canyon road, and there aren't enough park rangers for daily backcountry patrols.

The Ford's side windows were so dust- and talc-caked that I could barely see through them. I tried the driver's door; it was unlocked. The interior was empty except for two things on the front seat. One was a woman's purse, open, the edge of a wallet poking out. The other was a piece of lined notepaper with writing on it in felt-tip pen, held down by the weight of the purse.

I slid the paper free. Date on top—two days ago—and below that, "To Frank Spicer," followed by several lines of shaky backhand printing. I sensed what it was even before I finished reading the words.

I have no hope left. You and Conners have seen to that. I can't fight you anymore and I can't go on not knowing if Kevin is safe, how you must be poisoning his mind even if you haven't hurt him physically. Someday he'll find out what kind of man you really are. Someday he *will* find out. And I pray to God he makes you pay for what you've done.

I love you, Kevin. God forgive me.

I couldn't quite decipher the scrawled signature. Christine or Christina something—not Spicer. I opened the wallet and fanned through the card section until I found her driver's license. The Ford had California plates, and the license had also been issued in this state. Christina Dunbar. Age 32. San Diego address. The face in the ID photo was slender and fair-haired and unsmiling.

The wallet contained one other photo, of a nice-looking boy eight or nine years old—a candid shot taken at a lake or large river. Kevin? Nothing else in the wallet told me anything. One credit card was all she owned. And twelve dollars in fives and singles.

I returned the wallet to the purse, folded the note in there with it. In my mouth was a dryness that had nothing to do with the day's gathering heat. And in my mind was a feeling of urgency much more intense than the situation called for. If she'd brought along a gun or pills or some other lethal device, she was long dead by now. If she'd wanted the Valley to do the job for her, plenty enough time had elapsed for that too, given the perilous terrain and the proliferation of sidewinders and daytime temperatures in the mid nineties and no water and improper clothing. Yet there was a chance she was still alive. A chance I could keep her that way if I could find her.

I tossed her purse into the Jeep, uncased my 7 x 50 Zeiss binoculars, and climbed up on the hood to scan the surrounding terrain. The valley floor here was flattish, mostly fields of fractured rock slashed by shallow washes. Clumps of low-growing creosote bush and turtleback were the only vegetation. I had a fairly good look over a radius of several hundred yards: no sign of her.

Some distance ahead there was higher ground. I drove too fast on the rough road, had to force myself to slow down. At the top of a rise I stopped again, climbed a jut of limestone to a notch in its crest. From there I had a much wider view, all the way to Striped Butte and the lower reaches of the Panamints.

The odds were against my spotting her, even with the powerful Zeiss glasses. The topography's rumpled irregularity created too many hidden places; she might have wandered miles in any direction. But I did locate her, and in less than ten minutes, and when I did I felt no surprise. It was as if, at some deep level, I'd been certain all along that I would.

She was a quarter of a mile away, to the southwest, at the bottom of a salt-streaked wash. Lying on her side, motionless, knees drawn up to her chest, face and part of her blond head hidden in the crook of one bare arm. It was impossible to tell at this distance if she was alive or dead.

The wash ran down out of the foothills like a long, twisted scar, close to the trail for some distance, then hooking away from it in a gradual snake-track curve. Where she lay was at least four hundred yards from the four-wheel track. I picked out a trail landmark roughly opposite, then scrambled back down to the Jeep.

It took me more than an hour to get to her: drive to the landmark, load my pack with two extra soft-plastic water bottles and the first-aid kit, strap the pack on, and then hike across humps and flats of broken rock as loose and treacherous as talus. Even though the prenoon temperature was still in the eighties, I was sweating heavily—and I'd used up a pint of water to replace the sweat loss—by the time I reached the wash.

She still lay in the same drawn-up position. And she didn't stir at the noises I made, the clatter of dislodged rocks, as I slid down the wash's bank. I went to one knee beside her, groped for a sunburned wrist. Pulse, faint and irregular. I did not realize until then that I had been holding my breath; I let it out thin and hissing between my teeth.

She wore only a thin, short-sleeved shirt, a pair of Levi's, and tattered Reeboks. The exposed areas of her skin were burned raw, coated with salt from dried sweat that was as gritty as fine sand; the top of her scalp was flecked with dried blood from ruptured blisters. I saw no snake or scorpion bites, no limb fractures or swellings. But she was badly dehydrated. At somewhere between 15 percent and 22 percent dehydration, a human being will die, and she was at or near the danger zone.

Gently I took hold of her shoulders, eased her over onto her back. Her limbs twitched; she made a little whimpering sound. She was on the edge of consciousness, more submerged than not. The sun's white glare hurt her eyes even through the tightly closed lids. She turned her head, lifted an arm painfully across the bridge of her nose.

I freed one of the foil-wrapped water bottles, slipped off the attached cap. Her lips were cracked, split deeply in a couple of places; I dribbled water on them, to get her to open them. Then I eased the spout into her mouth and squeezed out a few more drops.

At first she struggled, twisting her head, moaning deep in her throat: the part of her that wanted death rebelling against revival and awareness. But her will to live hadn't completely deserted her, and her thirst was too acute. She swallowed some of the warm liquid, swallowed more when I lifted her head and held it cushioned against my knee. Before long she was sucking greedily at the spout, like an infant at its mother's nipple. Her hands came up and clutched at the bottle; I let her take it away from me, let her drain it. The idea of parceling out water to a dehydration victim is a fallacy. You have to saturate the parched tissues as fast as possible to accelerate the restoration of normal functions.

I opened another bottle, raised her into a sitting position, and then gave it to her. Shelter was the next most important thing. I took the lightweight space blanket from my pack, unfolded it, and shook it out. A space blanket is five by seven feet, coated on one side with a filler of silver insulating material and reflective surface. Near where she lay, behind her to the east, I hand-scraped a sandy area free of rocks. Then I set up the blanket into a lean-to, using takedown tent poles to support the front edge and tying them off with nylon cord to rocks placed at a forty-five-degree angle from the shelter corners. I secured the ground side of the lean-to with more rocks and sand atop the blanket's edge.

Christina Dunbar was sitting slumped forward when I finished, her head cradled in her hands. The second water bottle, as empty as the first, lay beside her. I gripped her shoulders again, and this time she stiffened, fought me weakly as I drew her backward and pressed her down into the lean-to's shade. The struggles stopped when I pillowed her head with the pack. She lay still, half on her side, her eyes still squeezed tight shut. Conscious now but not ready to face either me or the fact that she was still alive.

The first-aid kit contained a tube of Neosporin. I said as I uncapped it, "I've got some burn medicine here. I'm going to rub it on your face and scalp first."

She made a throat sound that might have been a protest. But when I squeezed out some of the ointment and began to smooth it over her blistered skin, she remained passive. Lay there silent and rigid as I ministered to her.

I used the entire tube of Neosporin, most of it on her face and arms. None of the cuts and abrasions she'd suffered was serious; the medicine would disinfect those too. There was nothing I could do for the bruises on her upper arms, along her jaw, and on the left temple. I wondered where she'd got them. Not stumbling around in the desert: they were more than two days old, already fading.

When I was done I opened another quart of water, took a nutrition bar from my pack. Her eyes were open when I looked at her again. Gray-blue, dull with pain and exhaustion, staring fixedly at me without blinking. Hating me a little, I thought.

I said, "Take some more water," and extended the bottle to her.

"No."

"Still thirsty, aren't you?"

"No."

"We both know you are."

"Who're you?" Her voice was as dry and cracked as her lips, but strong enough. "How'd you find me?"

"Scott Davis. I was lucky. So are you."

"Lucky," she said.

"Drink the water, Christina."

"How do you know . . . ? Oh."

"That's right. I read the note."

"Why couldn't you just let me die? Why did you have to come along and find me?"

"Drink."

I held the bottle out close to her face. Her eyes shifted to it; the tip of her tongue flicked out, snakelike, as if she were tasting the water. Then, grimacing, she lifted onto an elbow and took the bottle with an angry, swiping gesture—anger directed at herself, not me, as if for an act of self-betrayal. She drank almost half of it, coughed and then lowered the bottle.

"Go a little slower with the rest of it."

"Leave me alone."

"I can't do that, Christina."

"I want to sleep."

"No, you don't." I unwrapped the nutrition bar. "Eat as much of this as you can get down. Slowly, little bites."

She shook her head, holding her arms stiff and tight against her sides.

"Please," I said.

"I don't want any food."

"Your body needs the nourishment."

"No."

"I'll force-feed you if I have to."

She held out a little longer, but her eyes were on the bar the entire time. When she finally took it, it was with the same gesture of self-loathing. Her first few bites were nibbles, but the honey taste revived her hunger, and she went at the bar the way she had at the water bottle. She almost choked on the first big chunk she tried to swallow. I made her slow down, sip water between each bite.

"How do you feel?" I asked when she was finished.

"Like I'm going to live, damn you."

"Good. We'll stay here for a while, until you're strong enough to walk."

"Walk where?"

"My Jeep, over on the trail. Four hundred yards or so, and the terrain is pretty rough. I don't want to have to carry you, at least not the whole way."

"Then what?"

"You need medical attention. There's an infirmary at Furnace Creek."

"And after that, the psycho ward," she said, but not as if she cared. "Where's the nearest one?"

I let that pass. "If you feel up to talking," I said, "I'm a good listener."

"About what?"

"Why you did this to yourself."

"Tried to kill myself, you mean. Commit suicide."

"All right. Why, Christina?"

"You read my note."

"It's pretty vague. Is Kevin your son?"

She winced when I spoke the name. Turned her head away without answering.

I didn't press it. Instead I shifted around and lay back on my elbows, with my upper body in the lean-to's shade. I was careful not to touch her. It was another windless day, and the near-noon stillness was as complete as it had been the other morning in the Funerals. For a time nothing moved anywhere; then a chuckwalla lizard scurried up the bank of the wash, followed a few seconds later by a horned toad. It looked as though the toad were chasing the lizard, but like so many things in the Valley, that was illusion. Toads and lizards are not enemies.

It was not long before Christina stirred and said, "Is there any more water?" Her tone had changed; there was resignation in it now, as if she had accepted, at least for the time being, the burden of remaining alive.

I sat up, took one of the last two full quarts from my pack. "Make this last until we're ready to leave," I said as I handed it to her. "It's a long walk to the Jeep, and we'll have to share the last bottle."

She nodded, drank less thirstily, and lowered the bottle with it still two-thirds full. That was a good sign. Her body was responding, its movements stronger and giving her less pain.

I let her have another energy bar. She took it without argument, ate it slowly with sips of water. Then she lifted herself into a sitting position, her head not quite touching the slant of the blanket. She was just a few inches over five feet, thin but wiry. The kind of body she had and the fact that she'd taken care of it was a major reason for her survival and swift recovery.

She said, "I guess you might as well know."

"If you want to tell me."

"Kevin's my son. Kevin Andrew Spicer. He'll be ten years old in December."

"Frank Spicer is your ex-husband?"

"Yes, and I hope his soul rots in hell."

"Custody battle?"

"Oh, yes, there was a custody battle. But I won. I had full legal custody of my son."

"Had?"

"Frank kidnapped him."

"You mean literally?"

"Literally."

"When?"

"A year and a half ago," Christina said. "He had visitation rights, every other weekend. He picked Kevin up one Friday afternoon and never brought him back. I haven't seen either of them since."

"The authorities couldn't find them?"

"Nobody could find them. Not the police, not the FBI, not any of the three private detectives I hired. I think they're still somewhere in the southwest—Nevada or Arizona or New Mexico. But I don't know. I don't know."

"How could they vanish so completely?"

"Money. Everything comes down to money."

"Not everything."

"He was a successful commercial artist. And bitter because he felt he was prostituting his great talent. Even after the settlement he had a net worth of more than two hundred thousand dollars."

"He liquidated all his assets before he took Kevin?"

"Every penny."

"He must've wanted the boy very badly."

"He did, but not because he loves him."

"To get back at you?"

"To hurt me. He hates me."

"Why? The custody battle?"

"That, and because I divorced him. He can't stand to lose any of his possessions."

"He sounds unstable."

"Unstable is a polite term for it. Frank Spicer is a paranoid sociopath with delusions of grandeur. That's what a psychiatrist I talked to called him."

"Abusive?"

"Not at first. Not until he started believing I was sleeping with everybody from the mayor to the mailman. I was never unfaithful to him, not once."

"Did he abuse Kevin too?"

"No, thank God. He never touched Kevin. At least . . . not before he took him away from me."

"You think he may have harmed the boy since?"

"He's capable of it. He's capable of anything. There's no doubt of that now."

"Now?"

Headshake. She drank more water.

"Conners," I said. "Who's he?"

She winced again. "The last straw."

I waited, but she didn't go on. She was not ready to talk about Conners yet.

"Christina, why did you come here?"

"I don't know. I was on the main road, and there was a sign—"

"I mean Death Valley itself. All the way from San Diego, nearly four hundred miles."

"I didn't drive here from San Diego."

"Isn't that where you live?"

"Yes, but I was in Las Vegas. I came from there."

"Why were you in Vegas?"

"Fool's errand," she said bitterly.

"Something happened there. What was it?"

She didn't answer. For more than a minute she sat stiffly, squinting in the direction of Striped Butte; the sun, on its

anamorphic conglomeration of ribbons of crinoid limestone, jasper, and mother minerals, was dazzling. Then—

"A man called me a few days ago. He said his name
was Conners and he knew where Frank and Kevin were
living, but he wanted a thousand dollars for the information. In cash, delivered to him in Vegas."

"Did you know him?"

"No."

"But you believed him."

"I wanted to believe him," she said. "He claimed to've
known Frank years ago, to've had business dealings with
him; he mentioned the names of people I knew. And the
last detective I hired . . . he traced Frank and Kevin to a
Vegas suburb six weeks ago. They disappeared again the
day after he found out where they'd been staying."

"Why didn't you send the detective to meet with
Conners?"

"He stopped working for me a month ago, when I
couldn't pay him anymore. All the settlement money was
gone, and I had nothing left to sell. And no friends left to
borrow from."

"Then you couldn't raise the thousand Conners
demanded?"

"No, I couldn't raise it. So I stole it."

I didn't say anything.

"I was desperate," she said. "Desperate and crazy."

"Where did you steal it?"

"From the hardware supply company where I work . . .
worked. My boss is a nice guy. He loaned me money
twice before, he was supportive and sympathetic, but he
just couldn't loan me any more, he said. So I paid him
back by taking a thousand dollars out of the company
account. Easy; I was the office manager. Then I drove to
Vegas and gave it to Conners."

"And it was all just a scam," I said. "He didn't know
where Spicer and Kevin are."

"Oh, he knew, all right. He knew because Frank had
set the whole thing up. That was part of the message
Conners delivered afterward."

"Afterward?"

"After he beat me up and raped me."

"Jesus," I said.

"Frank is tired of being dogged by detectives. Frank says I'd better leave him and Kevin alone from now on. Frank says if I don't, there'll be more of the same, only next time he'll do it himself, and it won't just be rape and a beating—he'll kill me. End of message."

"Did you call the police?"

"What for? Conners isn't his real name, and he doesn't live in Vegas. What could the police have done except maybe arrest me and send me back to San Diego to stand trial for theft? No. No. I stayed in the motel room where it happened until I felt well enough to leave, and then I started driving. By the time the car quit on me I was way out here in the middle of nowhere and I didn't care anymore. I just didn't want to go on living."

"You still feel that way?"

"What do you think?"

I said, "There are a lot of miles between Vegas and Death Valley. And a lot of remote desert. Why did you come this far?"

"I don't know. I just kept driving, that's all."

"Have you ever been to the Valley before?"

"No."

"Was it on your mind? Death Valley, dead place, place to go and die?"

"No. I didn't even know where I was until I saw a sign. What difference does it make?"

"It makes a difference. I think it does."

"Well, I don't. The only thing that matters is that you found me before it was too late."

She picked up the water bottle, sat holding it in brooding silence without drinking. I gave my attention to the Panamints, Manly Peak and the taller, hazy escarpments of Telescope Peak to the north. To some they were silent and brooding—bare monoliths of dark-gray basalt and limestone, like tombstones towering above a vast graveyard. But not to me. I saw them as old and benevolent guardians, comforting in their size and age and austerity. Nurturing. The Paiutes believe that little mountain spirits, *Kai-nu-suvs*, live deep in their rock recesses—kindly spirits, as beautiful as sunset clouds and as pure as fresh snow. When clouds mass above the peaks, the *Kai-nu-suvs* ride deer and bighorn sheep, driving their charges in wild rides among the crags. For such joyous celebrations of life, the Paiutes cherish them.

Time passed. I sat looking and listening. Mostly listening, until I grew aware of heat rays against my hands where they rested flat on my thighs. The sun had reached and passed its zenith, was robbing the shelter of its shade. If we didn't leave soon, I would have to reset the position of the lean-to.

"How do you feel?" I asked Christina. "Strong enough to try walking?"

She was still resigned. "I can try," she said.

"Stay where you are for a couple of minutes, while I get ready. I'll work around you."

I gathered and stowed the empty water bottles, took down the lean-to and stowed the stakes and then strapped on the pack. When I helped Christina to her feet she seemed able to stand all right without leaning on me. I shook out the blanket, draped it over her head and shoulders so that her arms were covered, showed her how to hold it in place under her chin. Then I slipped an arm around her thin body and we set out.

It was a long, slow trek to the Jeep. And a painful one for her, though she didn't complain, didn't speak the entire time. We stayed in the wash most of the way, despite the fact that it added a third as much distance, because the footing was easier for her. I stopped frequently so she could rest; and I let her have almost all the remaining water. Still, by the time we reached the trail her legs were wobbly and most of her new-gained strength was gone. I had to swing her up and carry her the last two hundred yards. But it was not much of a strain. She was like a child in my arms.

I eased her into the passenger seat, took the blanket, and put it and my pack into the rear. There were two quarts of water left back there. I drank from one, two long swallows, before I slid in under the wheel. She had slumped down limply in the other seat, with her head back and her eyes shut. Her breath came and went in ragged little pants.

"Christina?"

"I'm awake," she said.

"Here. More water."

She drank without opening her eyes.

I said, "There are some things I want to say before we go. Something important that needs to be settled."

"What would that be?"

"When we get to Furnace Creek, I'm not going to report you as an attempted suicide. We'll say you made the mistake of driving out here in a passenger car, and when it broke down you tried to walk out and lost your sense of direction. That sort of thing happens a dozen times a year in the Valley. The rangers won't think anything of it."

"Why bother? It doesn't matter if you report me as a psycho case."

"You're not a psycho case. And it does matter. I want to keep on helping you."

"There's nothing you can do for me."

"I can help you find your son."

Her head jerked up; she opened her eyes to stare at me. "What're you talking about?"

"Just what I said. I want to help you find your son and take him back from his father."

"You can't be serious."

"I've never been more serious."

"But why would you . . . ?"

"A lot of reasons. Because you're still alive and I'd like you to stay that way. Because I don't want Frank Spicer to get away with kidnapping Kevin or with having you raped and beaten. Because it's right. Because I can."

She shook her head, trying to shake away disbelief so she could cling to hope again. "The heat must have made you crazy. I told you, I'm a fugitive; I stole money from my boss in San Diego—"

"You also told me he was supportive and sympathetic. Chances are he still is, or will be if he gets his thousand dollars back. I'll call him tonight, explain the situation, offer to send him the money right away if he drops any charges he may have filed. With interest, if he asks for it."

"My God, you'd do that?"

"You can pay me back after we find Kevin. Money's not a problem, Christina. I have more than enough for both of us."

"But Frank . . . you don't know him. He meant what he said about killing me. He'd kill you too."

"He won't harm either of us, I'll see to that. Or Kevin, if I can help it. I'm not afraid of men like Frank Spicer. He may be disturbed, but he's also a coward. Sending Conners proves that."

Another headshake. "How could we hope to find them? The FBI couldn't in a year and a half, the detectives couldn't. . . ."

"They didn't spend all their time looking," I said. "You and I can, as long as it takes. Time's not a problem, either. Before I came out here my wife filed for divorce and I quit my job. That part of my life is over. There's nothing to keep me from spending the rest of it any way I see fit."

"Why *this* way? Why would you do so much for a stranger? What do you expect to get out of it?"

"Nothing from you, Christina. It's as much for myself as it is for you."

"I want to believe you, but I just . . . I don't understand. Are you trying to be some kind of hero?"

"There's nothing heroic about me. My wife once called me an unfocused dreamer, drifting through life looking for something that might not even exist. She was half right. What I've been looking for I've had all along without realizing it—Death Valley, and my relationship to it. I've been coming here ever since I was a kid, more than twenty years, and I've always felt that it's a living place, not a dead one. Now . . . it seems almost sentient to me. As if it were responsible for bringing us together. I could have gone anywhere in three thousand square miles today, and I came to the exact spot you did two days ago; I could easily have missed finding you, but I didn't. The feeling of sentience is illusion, I suppose, but that doesn't make it any less important. If I don't finish saving your life—help you find your son, give you a reason to go on living—then none of what's happened today will mean anything. And my relationship with the Valley will never be the same again. Does that make any sense to you?"

"Maybe," she said slowly. "Maybe it does."

"Will you let me finish what's been started, then? For your son's sake, if not for yours or mine?"

She had no words yet. Her head turned away from me, and at first I thought she was staring out through the windshield. Then some of the hurt smoothed out of her ravaged face, and her expression grew almost rapt, and I knew she wasn't looking at anything. Knew, too, what her answer would be. And that there was a closer bond between us than I'd thought.

She was listening.

What are you listening to? There's nothing to hear in this godforsaken place.

Yes, there was. Geena just hadn't been able to hear it.

It's as if everything has shut down. Not just here; everywhere. As if all the engines have quit working.

No, not all. There was still one engine you could hear if you tried hard enough. The engine I'd been listening to out in the wash, when I'd been making up my mind about Christina and Kevin and Frank Spicer. The engine she was listening to now. One engine clear and steady in the void of silence, the only one that really counts.

Your own.